72   10.24

a

THE BATTLE CRUISER
HINDENBURG

A Novel

Michael Kirk

[signature: Michael Kirk]

authorHOUSE®

AuthorHouse™ UK
1663 Liberty Drive
Bloomington, IN 47403 USA
www.authorhouse.co.uk
Phone: UK TFN: 0800 0148641 (Toll Free inside the UK)
      UK Local: (02) 0369 56322 (+44 20 3695 6322 from outside the UK)

Published by AuthorHouse 11/16/2021

ISBN: 978-1-6655-9350-2 (sc)
ISBN: 978-1-6655-9349-6 (e)

Library of Congress Control Number: 2021919386

This book is printed on acid-free paper.

For Bren

List of Characters

All characters are fictitious, except for those marked(*).

German

Anna - Eckhardt's prospective fiancée.
Alfred - Körner household manservant.
Bergmann, Otto - *Kapitänleutnant*, commander of zeppelin *L14*.
Beyer - Sailor, Eckhardt's mess, SMS *Hindenburg*.
Brandmann, Klaus - *Kapitänleutnant*, pilot and oic seaplane section, SMS *Hindenburg*.
Bräkow - *Kapitänleutnant*, Gunnery Officer, Spotting Top, SMS *Hindenburg*.
Brandt, Erich - *Oberstabsbootsmann*, oic seaplane ground crew, SMS *Hindenburg*.
Bünzlin, Walter - *Kapitän zur See*, Hipper's chief of staff.
Dahl, Hugo - Körner's steward, SMS *Hindenburg*.
Eckhardt, Wilhelm - *Obermatrose*, look-out, SMS *Hindenburg*.
Eckel, Ulrich - *Kapitänleutnant*, captain of the supply ship *Torsten Meyer*.
Faber, Heinrich - *Korvettankapitän*, Chief Engineer, SMS *Hindenburg*.
Falbe, Günther - *Flugmeister*, seaplane observer/gunner/wireless operator, SMS *Hindenburg*.
Fassbinder, Werner - *Oberleutnant zur See*, Spotting Top, SMS *Hindenburg*.
Gärtner, Wolfgang - *Korvettankapitän*, Navigation officer, SMS *Hindenburg*.
Geiger, Karl - *Leutnant zur See*, seaplane pilot, SMS *Hindenburg*.
Grützmacher, Paul - Fitter, seaplane ground crew, SMS *Hindenburg*.
Harberer, Klaus - *Kapitänleutnant*, captain of the supply ship *Erda*.
Hamm, Friedrich - Bünzlin's *Oberleutnant* at Kiao-chau 1897.
Heinrich, Prince - *Großadmiral*, CinC Baltic Fleet, the Kaiser's younger brother. *
Helling, Alfred - *Deckoffizier*, SMS *Hindenburg*.
Helmers, Otto - Sailor, Eckhardt's mess, SMS *Hindenburg*.
Hillmann - *Leutnant zur See*, SMS *Hindenburg*.
Hipper, Franz, Ritter von - *Vizeadmiral*, Commander Scouting Forces, *HochSeeFlotte*. *
Hindenburg, Paul von - *Generalfeldmarschal*, by 1918 head of the German Army High Command. *
Jahncke, Hermann - *Fähnrich zur See*, SMS *Hindenburg*.
Kardorf - Sailor, Eckhardt's mess, SMS *Hindenburg*.
Kehlmann, Rolf - *Oberleutnant zur See*, SMS *Hindenburg*.
Knappe - *Deckoffizier*, SMS *Hindenburg*.
Körner, Hans - Rupprecht and Maria Körner's eldest son.
Körner, Manfred - Rupprecht and Maria Körner's youngest son.

Körner, Rupprecht - *Kapitän zur See*, SMS *Hindenburg*.

Körner, Viktoria - Rupprecht and Maria Körner's daughter.

Körner, Maria - Rupprecht's wife.

Körner, Lothar - Rupprecht's younger brother.

Körner, Rolf - Rupprecht's elder brother.

Kruse, Robert - *Korvettenkapitän*, First Gunnery Officer, SMS *Hindenburg*.

Kühl, Ernst - *Leutnant zur See*, seaplane observer/gunner/wireless operator, SMS *Hindenburg*.

Lang, Werner von - *Korvettenkapitän*, Paymaster, SMS *Hindenburg*.

Lohr, Alfred - *Leutnant zur See*, second-in-command, the supply ship *Erda*.

Ludendorff, Erich - *General*, by 1918 with von Hindenburg on German Army High Command. *

Manekeller, Gustav - *Kapitänleutnant*, Surgeon, SMS *Hindenburg*.

Michelsen, Andreas - *Kommodore*, Commander of the U-boats. *

Müller, Georg von - *Admiral*, Chief of the Naval Cabinet. *

Müller, Richard - Sailor, Eckhardt's mess, SMS *Hindenburg*.

Nerger, Karl - *Fregattenkapitän*, captain of auxiliary cruiser SMS *Wolf*. *

Petersen, Lukas - *Fähnrich zur See*, SMS *Hindenburg*.

Reichelt - *Leutnant zur See*, SMS *Hindenburg*.

Reinhold, *Frau* - lady at Maria Körner's 'Women's Group'.

Scheer, Reinhard - *Vizeadmiral*, CinC *HochSeeFlotte*. *

Schellenberg, Peter - *Fregattenkapitän*, First Officer, second-in-command, SMS *Hindenburg*.

Schirmer, Else - Körner household maidservant.

Schönert, Erich von - *Korvettenkapitän*, Signals Officer, oic intelligence operations, SMS *Hindenburg*.

Schwarz, Johann - Look-out, SMS *Hindenburg*.

Schwenke, Arnauld - Maria Körner's elder brother, Uhlan captain.

Schwenke, Henning - Maria Körner's youngest brother, soldier.

Schwenke, Max - Maria Körner's father.

Spee, Maximilian, Reichsgraf von - *Vizeadmiral*, East Asia Squadron. *

Tirpitz, Alfred von - *Großadmiral*, former Secretary of State of the Imperial Naval Office. *

Weber, Gustav - Look-out, SMS *Hindenburg*.

Wenzel - *Bootsmann*, SMS *Hindenburg*.

Wilhelm II, Kaiser - Emperor of Germany. *

Winter, Ernst - *Leutnant zur See*, navigating staff, SMS *Hindenburg*.

The Allies

Beatty, David - Admiral, CinC Grand Fleet. *

Benham, David G. - Captain, USS *Seattle*.

Backhouse-Smith ('Smitty'), Arthur - Acting Vice-Admiral, First Cruiser Squadron.

Cook, Albert - Rear Admiral, Second Battle Cruiser Squadron.

Cooper, Donald - Telegraphist/hydrophone operator, HM submarine *E28*.

Cox, John - Lieutenant-Commander, Admiral Backhouse-Smith's Flag-Lieutenant, First Cruiser Squadron.

Framlington, Edward George, the Honourable - Lieutenant, HMS *Courageous*.

Goodyear, John - Captain, HMS *Inflexible*.

Harding - Captain, HMS *Chester*.

Inglethorpe, John ('Jack') - Captain, HMS *Leviathan*.

Jackson, Owen - wireless operator/gunner, Felixstowe F.2A flying boat.

Lambert, Ken - engineer/gunner, Felixstowe F.2A flying boat.

Lee, Richard - Commander, USS *Seattle*.

Mackay, Edward - Lieutenant, HM submarine *E28*.

Miller, Frank - Lieutenant (junior grade), USS *Seattle*.

Nicholls - Captain, HMS *Courageous*.

Pennywell, 'Jack' - RAF Second Lieutenant, Sopwith Camel pilot, HMS *Glorious*.

Pike, Charles - Sub-Lieutenant, Surgeon Probationer, HMS *Nereus*.

Rowland, David - Lieutenant, HM submarine *E28*.

Reid, Alasdair - Sopwith Camel pilot, HMS *Glorious*.

Smith, Kenneth - Lieutenant-Commander, captain HM submarine *E28*.

Wainright, Archie - Lieutenant, HMS *Courageous*.

Walton, Robert - RAF Captain, co-pilot, Felixstowe F.2A flying boat.

White - Ensign, USS *Seattle*.

York, Edward ('Ted') - RAF Captain, pilot, Felixstowe F.2A flying boat.

Maps

Western North Atlantic

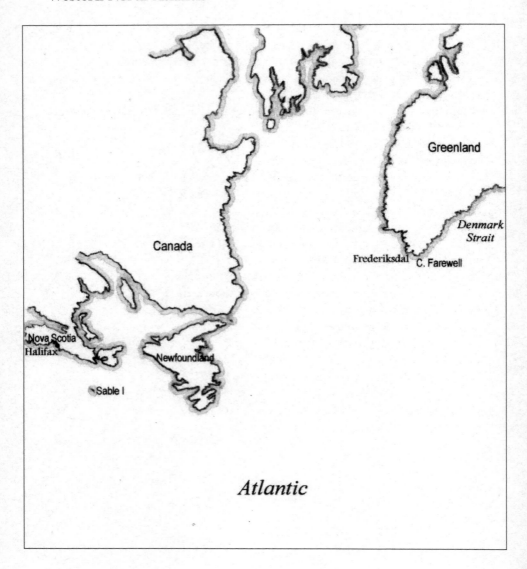

Eastern North Atlantic and North Sea

1

Smoke Sighted
5 May 1918

Would this be the day? Everyone was ready. Everyone was at Battle Stations. Everyone was prepared for what at last seemed a real possibility: engaging the enemy. Some outwardly seemed very confident about the likely outcome. After years of war, he never took anything for granted or underestimated the enemy. He couldn't speak for others, but he felt some apprehension, though was not yet really scared about the possibility of conflict. Any fear would come once fighting was imminent. There were times, in the past, when he had been frightened at an earlier stage. In such moments, if there'd been time, he'd said a silent prayer or turned his thoughts to his loved ones. Now, his training, experience, duties and belief in his ship all focused his mind on the job in hand.

No one would believe a look-out's job could be so tiring. Obviously his neck and arms ached, but even his eyes seemed to ache. The binoculars, lightweight affairs, seemed heavier each time he raised them to his eyes, but Eckhardt scanned the horizon again. Every single time he expected to see something, but funnily enough every time was not surprised to see nothing but sea. In any event, it was still dark. The sun was only just lifting above that far line, blindingly bright if you looked straight at it. He concentrated on his starboard sector, south of the ship, where the new light was scratching the surface of the sea.

Obermatrose—Leading Seaman—Wilhelm Eckhardt was 23 years old, one metre 76 tall, short dark hair, clean shaven, blue eyes. He was from Stolpmünde, in eastern Pommern, on the *Ostsee*—Baltic—coast, the youngest of the four Eckhardt children. He was a quiet-spoken individual, who largely kept to himself and worked hard. Coming from Pommerania, he was proud to be seen as part of the Prussian kingdom, but wasn't outspoken about it. Despite his Prussian status, he expected that his betters probably saw him as mere peasant stock. After finishing school, he'd been a fisherman, working with his father and older brother in their ten-metre fishing boat. However, he felt war was coming and, filled with patriotic beliefs, though very much contrary to his father's wishes, had joined the navy in late 1912. As a fisherman, the navy was an obvious choice. He seemed bound for service in destroyers, like many other fishermen, but, he thought, due to his Baltic and not North Sea origins, he ended up in big ships. He was content with big ship life, though dreamed of the less disciplined existence he'd heard of in smaller ships. Then again, he expected that the Fleet's officers would be the same *bastards*, whatever size ship they were in.

Eckhardt now seemed much older than his age would belie. He had seen much service and some action since leaving his home. He was little more than an immature youth then, no one would say that now. He was single, though like all his comrades was not one to turn down the chance of female companionship and going ashore was in no small part with this aim. Since he'd joined the navy, he'd always figured marriage was not something to contemplate in wartime, but a year ago he'd met a beautiful girl—Anna—and all his high-minded values had been disrupted. He had not proposed marriage to her, but was now thinking that that was a possibility. His thoughts, at times lustful, could easily turn to his new love and in boring moments could easily interfere with his job. She was something to savour. She was then just 18 years old, had a round face, piercing blue eyes, fair hair and smooth pale skin and a very womanly figure. On a rare leave home, he'd met Anna when he reluctantly agreed to attend a family wedding. There had been precious little time to get to know her in that short spell at home. They'd walked along the sea shore, talking about their families, the weather, the sea and even her factory job, but surprisingly little about the war itself, except what they'd do when it was over. When he thought back on those few days, they'd only kissed once, if you could call such slight lip contact a kiss. Unlike women he'd met in port, she'd resisted the further amorous intentions he had, but that had not diminished his interest. He'd written to her and she'd replied, which led to a regular flow of letters between the two of them. He always looked forward to her next letter and would read it repeatedly. Each one seemed to give him a new focus on life, something beyond the war, and made him think of marriage.

He lowered the binoculars from his eyes, removed his right glove and rubbed each eye in turn with the back of his hand. Despite the call to battle, he took a moment to look down from his lofty perch, watching everything unfold as the sunlight crept over it. He was standing in the Spotting Top of one of Germany's most powerful warships—and the best one, as far as he and the crew were concerned. *Seiner Majestät*—His Majesty's—27,000 ton battle cruiser *Hindenburg* was moving slowly, but serenely through the unexpectedly calm sea. However, this was no icy Baltic, nor foggy North Sea, but the Atlantic Ocean.

The ship had slowed, practically to a halt, as the seaplane was lowered on the port side. Eckhardt couldn't see what was happening to the plane from his position, but could see that the ship was now moving forward again, picking up speed. Once the plane was safely on the water, the ship always moved off without delay for fear of lurking submarines. After a few minutes, the plane flew over the ship from astern. He watched it go, as it sped along their intended course.

The ship was increasing speed all the time. By his estimation, she was soon at 12 knots. If there was to be action, no doubt the captain would bring her up to full speed, at least 26 knots. This would be considerably faster than anything they'd done since leaving Germany and in sharp contrast to much of the operation thus far. For most of the time they'd been journeying across the Atlantic, the ship had seldom exceeded 14 knots, her normal cruising speed. He knew that deep in the ship, the stokers would be working much harder than at any stage so far. A major course change to the south-east before dark, now quite some hours ago, had been accompanied by a great increase in speed, but had then been reduced during the night reportedly to enable a dawn contact with the enemy. It was past dawn now; no enemy in sight.

The Spotting Top, a massive three-level affair, was at the convergence of the *Hindenburg*'s tripod mast—the whole structure, tripod mast and Spotting Top, was a rare feature, only found in a few of Germany's big ships. From his high vantage point, Eckhardt took in the whole array of sensations: the sights and sounds of the ship, along with the caress of the wind and the smell of the sea. The sea presented a completely different vista to the land, but could present just as variable a range of surface features, depending on wind and weather. It could easily change in a day from flat calm sea to violent, frightening tempest, from a clear sky with extreme visibility to rain squalls or fog limiting vision to a few tens of metres. For a few days now, they had enjoyed good weather. The previous day was especially good, with almost no clouds, blue skies, light winds and a relatively calm, blue sea. This was not expected and at variance to the rough, usually grey-blue seas and overcast and sometimes stormy clouds they'd encountered along the way.

The sun was now just above the eastern horizon and, as the dawn light progressively illuminated everything, he could see that the ocean still looked calm, though with a gentle swell rolling in from the south. Some distant clouds could be seen away to port, but the rest of the sky remained largely cloudless. He noted a small increase in the northerly wind. Occasionally, it whipped the tips of the few wave crests, spraying white foam along them, producing patches of smooth water in their lee. The swell impacted on the ship's starboard side. As she ploughed on, the ship's slight pitching motion periodically caused her to smash into the swell and, coupled with the bow waves produced at higher speed, threw clouds of spray out and up onto the ship giving everything for'ard a wet sheen.

No one was complaining about the spell of better weather. It also enabled them to utilise their seaplane to the full. The change of course and higher speed had come about the previous day as a result of sightings by the plane. There had been no formal announcement of what was afoot, but officers' comments left everyone in no doubt that they were in pursuit of a convoy. This was the latest and definitely the biggest topic so far on the voyage to capture the crew's attention and had provoked no little debate and speculation.

Although the ship was pitching and rolling slightly with the swell, such movement was magnified for those in the Spotting Top, though no problem for seasoned sailors. From this lofty position, over thirty metres above the sea, the whole fo'c'sle was in view, especially the two front gun turrets—Anton and Bertha—each with their twin, thirty-point-five-centimetre guns jutting out, like fingers pointing the way forward. In common with other German dreadnoughts, both turret roofs were painted black, with Bertha, the superimposed, second turret, also sporting a narrow white circle almost the width of the turret. The two aft turret tops followed the same colour scheme. The circles were for aerial recognition, though Eckhardt wondered if they would serve enemy planes better.

Eckhardt's primary station was in the Spotting Top. At other times he might be on the Bridge or the aft control position. This time in the Spotting Top he was at his usual position covering the starboard quarter. Looking aft, his view was partially obscured by the black smoke pumping out from the ship's twin funnels. Even though several of her boilers were oil-fired, there was still plenty of smoke. Being high above the funnels, he could easily track the smoke's journey, as it was pushed over to starboard by the light wind, before rising and expanding into much bigger, though less dense clouds and then dissipating a few lengths astern. He let his eyes wander down the length of that side of the ship. Through the smoke and beyond the aft funnel and mainmast, he glimpsed the *Hindenburg*'s aftermost turret and her narrowing quarterdeck. At her stern he caught sight of the white water churned up by the propellers and the lighter wake, edged with a thin white line of foam that stretched away behind them, visible in the early light for half a kilometre or more.

Whether looking astern or ahead, the ship's profile was etched in his mind. From his first sight of her, he had accepted that the *Hindenburg*'s long, flush-deck hull, unique to her class of German dreadnoughts, gave a most graceful appearance. Her four big-gun turrets were the evidence of her great power. There was no denying the whole arrangement of hull, turrets, funnels and superstructure was a very balanced layout, though also conveyed both a beautiful and a powerful impression to the eye. He wondered what an enemy ship would make of her, especially in these waters.

Whatever they might encounter, he reckoned the *Hindenburg* must be the most powerful warship this far out into the Atlantic, or at least that was the considered opinion down on the mess decks. This sortie was, however, completely different from any they'd been on before. Up to now the ship had always steamed out with some of her First Scouting Group stable-mates or with the rest of the *HochSeeFlotte*—High Seas Fleet. Normally, they'd be part of a four or five-strong battle cruiser force, supported by cruisers and destroyers, with the battle fleet somewhere behind them. He found he gave little thought to such past events or rather had little time to consider all those scores of ships and their crews now thousands of kilometres astern, except that, as usual, they would most probably be berthed in Wilhelmshaven or waiting beyond in Schillig Roads. On the other hand, his thoughts had often conjured up British dreadnoughts and he wondered whether any were even now pursuing the *Hindenburg* or if, hopefully, they were all slumbering in Scapa Flow. The prospect of meeting American dreadnoughts, especially now they were on this side of the ocean, also attracted some of the crew's interest, enhanced by recent recognition sessions, particularly for the look-outs, on American warship silhouettes.

There had been some real apprehension when they first heard of their mission, with a few grumbling concerns that the intention to attack convoys was really a one-way, suicide trip, designed to give the officer corps a heroic 'death or glory' mission before the war ended. A trouble-maker, if you could call him that, had even been 'dealt with' when he unsuccessfully sought to whip-up such disquiet. The mutinies last year had spread into all ships, but the battle cruisers had been the least affected amongst the big ships. Their morale was always better than in the battleships. That said, boredom and disappointment were telling factors in this war for all Germany's big-ship sailors. There were few gunnery actions, interspersed by long periods of inaction. The sailors knew that the Kaiser was frightened for his Fleet and, especially after the first battle and fearful of the enemy's larger *Grand Fleet*, word had come down to husband the Fleet, keep it safe for the end-of-war peace conference. Such an approach did little for morale and made sailors think they were not doing their bit, in comparison to the army, fighting and dying daily on the Western Front.

Whatever might be said of the exploits of the army or the navy, Eckhardt could not deny to himself that Germany was suffering. Shipboard life was no picnic, but he saw the evidence every time he went ashore, infrequent as those occasions were. The British blockade was biting, especially hurting the ordinary people of Germany, even if their armed forces had not been defeated. Eckhardt harboured his own feelings. He was not overly fearful of the future and never imagined defeat, only victory for the Fatherland, yet he longed for the end of the war and hoped each Christmas, birthday or other anniversary would be the last before peace. Nevertheless, many, like him, saw this mission—formally labelled as Operation *Georg*—as a real chance to strike at the enemy. Some thought the mission could even win the war, though Eckhardt could not see an action by a single ship winning this war. Many of the crew were just content to be doing something other than swinging around their anchor. Like any mission, there was a chance of action, but any apprehension was tempered by the crew's experience and confidence in their ship. The Atlantic was also enormous, so finding the *Hindenburg* would be no easy task. Even if they encountered a whole squadron of British warships, wouldn't their high speed get them out of danger, if their guns didn't smash the enemy? They had successfully got through the British blockade, refuelled from their colliers and were now only three or four hundred kilometres off the coast of America. What could stop them now?

The *Hindenburg* was the latest and most powerful of Germany's *Große Kreuzer*—large cruisers—though most of the crew tended to use the more traditional *Panzerkreuzer*—armoured cruiser—when describing ships of her type. Eckhardt accepted these classifications, though he thought the English designation for such ships of *Schlachtkreuzer*—battle cruiser—seemed the most appropriate. Anyway, whether she was called an armoured cruiser or a battle cruiser, all the crew knew the *Hindenburg* was more of a fast battleship. She was not like other battle cruisers, especially the British ones, with their much thinner armour. Several British battle cruisers had spectacularly exploded during the *Skagerrakschlact**, when hit by a few German shells. Eckhardt had seen one destroyed from his post on the battle cruiser *Moltke*, which was in the thick of the battle. The *Hindenburg* was said to have thirty-centimetre armoured sides, not to mention thick armour elsewhere. The *Lützow*, her sister-ship, had been lost at Skagerrak, but, rumour had it, only after suffering a tremendous battering and being brought almost to a halt by considerable flooding. In the end, when it was determined that she couldn't be saved from the flooding, survivors said she had to be sunk by torpedoes from an escorting destroyer. Their other sister-ship, the *Derfflinger*, had also suffered many hits from big shells, but had got back to base. The *Moltke* had suffered about the least damage of the Scouting Force's big ships, but Eckhardt had been injured when a near miss deluged his position with tons of water and he fell awkwardly, cracking a shinbone. His leg mended slowly and he was on crutches for some months. Recovering, but still able to feel a slight pain when he put his foot down hard, he was sent for shore duty and then some training. That development had led to him becoming a look-out and promotion. When he was allocated to the new battle cruiser *Hindenburg*, he was sanguine about the move. He was a seaman and life afloat used to be eminently preferable to a shore job, but his desire for a quick end to the war plagued his thoughts. However, he was weary of the war. He had weathered all he had seen and avoided injury, until his broken leg had reminded him of his mortality. His leg made him wonder if he would get through unscathed. He was fairly matter of fact about death, giving it little or no thought, other than hoping it would be quick. His leg and the sights of men ashore with a missing arm or leg left him greatly concerned that he would be maimed not killed. Whilst he had some misgivings about what lay ahead for him, if he was to face the enemy, where better but to be back with the battle cruisers? The Scouting Force's big ships were the Fleet's élite group and everyone knew it.

Although the prospect of action was in the wind, Eckhardt was tired and cold and hoped that, if nothing came of the convoy, there would soon be a chance to go below and get warmed up. In the Spotting Top, even in the good weather they were enjoying, it was cold. He steadied himself, once again putting the glasses to his eyes. There was no denying the difference in this enterprise over other sorties,

---

* *Skagerrakschlact* was Germany's Battle of the Skagerrak, which was Britain's Battle of Jutland.

but there was also a different underlying tension, which got to everyone, though morale was still high. There was immense pride in what had been achieved thus far. However, above all, he and the rest of the crew were confident in the ship being able to cope with anything the enemy or the weather could throw at them.

The Spotting Top was fairly crowded with officers and seamen. Most were scanning the horizon, all wanting to be the first to sight the enemy, something that had been a very infrequent experience during this long war. This new day was their fourteenth since leaving Germany and definitely a record for him and the *Hindenburg*, especially when previous sorties into the North Sea had mostly been no more than one or two days and nights.

'Listen up,' said an officer behind him. Eckhardt stiffened. 'Good news! We've just been told that the plane has found the enemy convoy. It's away off the starboard bow.'

At this, Eckhardt, the other look-outs and virtually all those in the Spotting Top immediately brought their binoculars up and scoured the sea ahead and to their right, all no doubt expecting to see the shapes of numerous merchantmen rising over the horizon. As in the rest of this mission, there was nothing out there. Even though the enemy might now be near, Eckhardt wondered if it was really possible to find anything in this ocean. They could only see so far; looking for a needle in a haystack was probably easier. Even in reasonable weather, a ship just thirty kilometres off their beam might pass without either realising the other was there. When he came on watch, he'd been told of the possible convoy and, unnecessarily, of the need to be especially vigilant. If they did find a convoy, he thought, other than some fishing boats they'd encountered, it would be the first ships they'd seen since leaving the Fleet. There was no denying the advantages provided by their seaplane. Everyone had eventually taken the flimsy craft to heart and earnestly hoped it would provide early news of the enemy, be that merchantmen or warships. Those who could always watched its take-offs and landings, many apprehensive that the canvas-covered, wood affair would suffer some calamity or other problem, as it nearly had in previous days. Now it had only just taken off and, it seemed, had immediately sighted their target.

He risked another glance at the southern horizon, slowly shifting from dark to light. Nothing in sight. Searching the horizon was all too often an unrewarding and at times alarming experience, as far off breaking waves could so often give the fleeting illusion of being a ship, and kept a look-out busy and on edge. Added to that, he reckoned the visibility did not seem as good as the previous day, patchy in places, though still quite good. His honed look-out skills suggested it was at least twenty kilometres to the horizon.

He felt the ship swing round to starboard, some half-dozen points. She was obviously on a heading towards the seaplane sighting. His allocated starboard viewpoint had thus changed, from one looking more or less in the right direction to one further aft. After only a few more minutes of fruitless searching, his mind wandered, this time wondering when, rather than if, he'd get back to Anna. A call from another look-out brought him immediately back to earth, all tiredness completely banished.

'Smoke!' shouted seamen Johann Schwarz. 'Smoke,' he repeated, 'fine on the starboard bow!' His words were intended for the senior officer, though electrified everyone.

Tall, inappropriately named, blonde Schwarz began pointing away to the distance, just starboard of the advancing bow. Eckhardt swung round, but could see no trace of smoke. *Kapitänleutnant*—lieutenant-commander—Bräkow, one of the ship's gunnery officers, was quickly at Schwarz's side, binoculars straining in the indicated direction. Everyone else was looking and for a moment there was a silence not normally encountered, even though the Spotting Top was never noisy.

'I see nothing,' said the 32-year-old officer, in his correct Hannoverian accent.

'It was very faint, Sir,' responded Schwarz. 'Just like … like a small vertical line on the horizon. I can't see it now. The visibility is worse.'

Forgetting his allocated piece of the horizon, Eckhardt scanned across the indicated position. He could see nothing. Although visibility was good, it was still limited, though one might see further at some points. It wouldn't be the first time a look-out had made an incorrect sighting; there had been several during this mission.

Without further comment, Bräkow moved to a voice pipe. He lifted the cover and spoke into its funnel opening. 'Smoke sighted, Sir.'

Eckhardt was still looking at the horizon, but took in what he could of *Kapitänleutnant* Bräkow's exchange with his superior, *Korvettenkapitän*—Commander—Kruse, the *Hindenburg*'s *Erster Artillerieoffizier*—First Gunnery Officer. Kruse was located above them, in the uppermost level of the Spotting Top. Eckhardt then heard Bräkow open another voice pipe and, in a louder voice: '*Achtung* Bridge!'

A voice responded, which Eckhardt couldn't hear clearly. Bräkow responded immediately. 'Smoke sighted, green, oh-oh-five. Nothing now in sight. Horizon visibility poor.'

While Bräkow was making his report, still no one else could confirm the sighting. Eckhardt was slightly disappointed not to make the first sighting, but that was soon forgotten as he concentrated on the view ahead. He strained his eyes and pulled his elbows hard to his chest to steady his binoculars, believing that would help to pierce any haziness. He saw a small line on the horizon, a brush stroke from a single hair, a wisp of smoke, Schwarz's smoke. But hardly had the words formed on his lips, when other look-outs reported the same. This must be the convoy, but why, he wondered, was there only one smoke trail. Could it be a single, lone ship, he wondered. No. Other smoke trails were visible. He quickly shouted out his sighting, though only matching the outbursts of others. Several smoke trails must signify the convoy.

There was a new excitement in the Spotting Top, though not something voiced, just felt. At last, the enemy was tantalisingly close. Bräkow again reported through the Bridge voice pipe. After a response, he straightened up. Still looking to the far horizon, he said, 'Well done, Schwarz. Bridge is aware. Everyone keep a look-out, but keep to your sectors,' he continued. 'We don't want to miss something else out there.' Eckhardt swung his glasses to starboard.

Bräkow or one of the junior officers kept giving reports to the Bridge and the first gunnery officer, but apart from that there was no real debate by anyone about the potential impact of the sighting. Eckhardt kept sweeping his binoculars over the starboard horizon, but letting them return to the smoke. He could see at least eight trails; their owners were all below the horizon, perhaps thirty kilometres away.

🏳

The *Hindenburg*'s commanding officer, *Kapitän zur See* Rupprecht Körner, emerged from the Chart Room and headed to the front of the *Kommandbrücke*—Command Bridge. On receipt of the seaplane's signal, he and the navigator, *Korvettenkapitän* Wolfgang Gärtner, had stepped into the Chart Room at the rear of the Bridge to consider its implications. The navigator's earlier calculations had placed the expected dawn position of the convoy as slightly ahead and just to starboard of the battle cruiser. According to the seaplane pilot, the convoy was still ahead and to starboard of the warship, but was almost abeam of them. Körner made no comment on Gärtner's navigation projections; there were any number of reasons for the slight difference in the convoy's expected position. They were no further away from the convoy, just a change in expected bearing. Nothing was lost. Körner had ordered a change in course and an increase in speed to bring the ship into visual contact. He did consider whether to sweep ahead and turn and approach head-on, but, seaplane or not, he did not want to lose touch with his target. In any event, there was little time to debate such matters, he'd been called back to the Bridge.

As he walked the few metres forward, Körner's bearing showed to all that he was clearly the man in charge, but also human, with cap pulled on tight and greatcoat done up in an effort to keep out the cold dawn air. The Command Bridge was largely open to the elements. It was roughly triangular in shape, situated just aft of and overlooking turret Bertha. The forward part of the Bridge was dominated by the almost circular, heavily armoured conning tower. Ahead of the conning tower there was a small roofed-in and windowed section, affording some protection from the elements. The rest was mostly open deck, though chest-high canvas screens fastened to the guardrails provided some shelter from the wind and weather.

Bridge officers and men were busy on various duties, made slightly more animated by the sighting reports, but no more than one would expect in a peace-time exercise. The increased activity slowed for a moment, while officers acknowledged the captain's presence. Körner made his way to the covered section. Inside was *Fregattenkapitän* Peter Schellenberg. The clean-shaven, youthful-looking, though uncompromising Schellenberg was the *Hindenburg*'s *Erster Offizier*—First Officer—and her second-in-command.

'Spotting Top sighted a single smoke plume a few minutes ago, Sir, but now report several. All targets are still beyond the horizon, perhaps as much as thirty kilometres,' said Schellenberg. '*Leutnant* Geiger's convoy, no doubt,' referring to the pilot who had first spotted the convoy the previous day and was now aloft.

'Thank you, *Fregattenkapitän*.' Körner answered, as he raised his binoculars to sweep the horizon ahead. He silently gave Geiger a *well done*. The young pilot of the seaplane had taken off in pre-dawn gloom and quickly discovered the convoy. His wireless message had put it as little more than thirty kilometres away and fired-up an already alert ship. 'Let's get on with this. Please bring her to twenty-five knots.'

'Aye, Sir.'

An officer handed Schellenberg a note.

'Another signal from the plane, Captain,' said Schellenberg. 'He again confirms the convoy's course as south-east and gives a further assessment of its composition: twenty ships, seven columns. He now reports that there are *two* escorts, … possibly cruisers.'

'*Possibly*? It looks like our pilots need to brush up on their warship recognition,' responded Körner.

'Er, yes, Sir.'

'Well, at our speed, we'll know quite soon what we're facing.'

They continued their discussion, particularly as to the escorts' type. Schellenberg hoped the sighting was correct, but Körner knew they had plenty of time to react to whatever the two warships were. Their debate was interrupted by young *Leutnant zur See* Hillmann.

'Sir. Spotting Top now confirms contact to be a convoy, perhaps at least some fifteen vessels. Heading south or south-east. Speed slow.' Clean-shaven, 22-year-old *Leutnant* Hillmann was obviously endeavouring to be calm as he made his report.

'Thank you, *Leutnant*,' responded Körner, equally calmly, though drew some comfort from the fact that the plane and the ship were now looking at the same target.

'Smoke!' shouted an officer.

'Masts!' came from another.

Körner raised his binoculars. Some mast tops were indeed evident, stretching a few degrees across the horizon. Funnel smoke was now clearly seen, black unnatural clouds, which streamed away to the right, dispersing, though darkening the sky. In a few minutes, more masts began to come into view, then smoking funnels and superstructures. They *were* merchant ships. It *was* a convoy. Lowering his binoculars, he noted that the gun barrels of the two turrets below him were elevating and moving, pointing at the merchantmen.

The *Hindenburg* would soon be in action. Körner had been in action several times, but he was conscious that it was going to be a first both for his ship and quite a few of her crew. He wasn't sure why he did it, but he took in the scene around him. Next to him, Schellenberg, binoculars up to his eyes, seemed unmoved by the coming event. Others seemed busy, as expected. If some of the younger officers were apprehensive, they probably had little time to show it, he saw most were just concentrating on their jobs. At this stage all their actions were undoubtedly clockwork repetitions of months and, in many cases, years of training and experience. No one spoke out loud other than in connection with their Battle Station duties—all alert for new orders. Körner imagined that some were wondering, like him, whether the enemy would turn away or scatter or, oblivious to the danger, maintain course. Some were perhaps considering the possible outcomes of the impending clash and what it held for the ship or her sailors. A few might be thinking they would be a casualty or doubting that there could be any risk to them from merchant ships.

Körner gave no consideration to the rights or wrongs of a mighty battle cruiser attacking defenceless merchant ships. If there had ever been such considerations, they were long gone, wiped away by the bloody war. These merchant ships were bringing sustenance to the enemy, it was their duty to stop them. This 'total war' blurred the lines between the fighting men and civilians, combatants and non-combatants. Merchant sailors were in the front-line, as much as any soldier in the trenches or sailor on the deck of a warship, and had been throughout the war.

Leutnant Hillmann again reported to the captain, business-like, though this time looking a little less pleased with himself. 'Sir. Spotting Top reports two enemy warships at the head of the convoy, moving to port. Convoy course, south-east, twelve knots.'

Whether they showed it or not, everyone's attention was again heightened by this announcement. Körner, acknowledging the news, continued to keep calm, his demeanour showing no more alarm than if the sighting of a pleasure yacht was being reported. Through his binoculars he could see no warships, only that the smoke from all the ships seemed to have increased, no doubt as they all sought to increase speed. Körner was naturally interested in the warship escorts, wondering about their type and number, but those issues would soon be resolved.

A voice called out: 'Warship! Starboard, ten degrees!'

All heads turned to it. The top masts of what was obviously a warship were in view, though partially hidden by merchant ships and funnel smoke. The merchantmen themselves were, for now, forgotten, even though the hulls of some were now visible. At their current speed, the two opposing forces would indeed see each other soon enough. *Leutnant* Hillmann reported again to the captain: 'Sir, Spotting Top reports warships are both four-funnelled. The leading one is probably an English cruiser; the second one appears to be American, to judge by her cage mast.'

For a few moments, Körner took in this new situation, thinking this would be very different than shooting at merchant ships, but he certainly had no intention of turning away. He always expected to have to deal with some escort. In the planning for *Georg*, they had expected to find pre-dreadnought battleships escorting convoys across the ocean, being the only available ships likely to pose a threat to an attacking battle cruiser. Two cruisers—to judge by their four funnel description—should still pose no real problem for a battle cruiser. The previous day's debates about the pilot's report of a sole, four-funnelled escort confirmed that the only such ships in the allied navies would most probably be armoured cruisers.

As to the actual identity of the approaching ships, he relied on others for ship recognition expertise, though reckoned he had a fair knowledge of the English fleet. The 1914 *Jane's Fighting Ships* and the latest edition of *Weyer's* pocket-book on the world's navies in his cabin were well-thumbed. He knew that most of the English armoured cruisers had four funnels. He also knew that, despite varying numbers of guns, none of them mounted anything bigger than nine-point-two-inch guns. Körner never thought about how his mind handled the metric and imperial measurements, but he easily managed the systems and comfortably used inches when describing the English ships' armament and centimetres for German ships.

It went without saying that no armoured cruiser of old could match the *Hindenburg*'s guns, armour or speed. The battle cruiser's role may have moved inexorably towards being a ship-of-the-line, but when the first was built—*by the English*—it was conceived as a further development of the armoured cruiser and in so doing made all existing cruisers of that type obsolete. This had been most clearly demonstrated at the Falkland Islands, where two of Germany's finest armoured cruisers had been easily defeated by two English battle cruisers. He called to one of the gunnery officer's team: 'Any identification of the English ship?'

After a couple of minutes, punctuated with a voice pipe exchange, 'Uncertain, Sir, but possibly Drake-class,' came the answer. 'Some were reported to be on the American coast. She may be the *King Alfred* or the *Leviathan*.'

Körner knew that the Drakes only had two main guns. Somewhere in the back of his mind was a memory of some speed record. 'How fast is she?' he asked.

Again a few moments delay, while there were a few words between two gunnery officers.

'*Weyer's* says twenty-four knots, Sir,' said one of the voices behind him. '*Jane's* says the *King Alfred* has achieved twenty-five knots, though that was in nineteen-oh-seven.' After a pause, the voice added, 'I seem to recall the Drakes took part in a high speed crossing of the Atlantic, to test the capability of triple-expansion engines. Sorry, Sir, I can't remember the outcome.'

'Not to worry,' said Körner, 'but if she is still fast, she may use her speed to close and fire torpedoes. Alert look-outs to torpedo tracks.' Then, after a few seconds, he asked, 'Remind me, what American armoured cruisers have four funnels *and* cage masts?' He heard the long pages of *Jane's* flap.

'Only California and Washington classes, Sir,' was the quick response.

For a moment Körner was confused by these class names, but quickly realised he knew them better as the Pennsylvania and Tennessee classes. A debate with his officers on that matter was the last thing he intended now. Whatever their class names, as a gunnery expert, Körner was well aware of these ships' armament characteristics. Both had the typical layout of such pre-dreadnought-era ships: one main gun turret at either end of the ship. While the Californias mounted 8in guns, the Washingtons were armed with 10in guns. The Washingtons were amongst the most powerful armoured cruisers in the world and would undoubtedly have influenced the future development of such ships if not for the advent of the battle cruiser.

If their opponent was an armoured cruiser with 10in guns, it posed a new level of threat, but didn't alter his intentions. Again, he gave no thought to turning away. If he shunned battle now to save damage to his ship, he would waste this opportunity to attack the convoy system. It might be his only chance. A turn away could also damage crew morale and give succour to the enemy. Körner had pondered just such a situation in the many months this operation had been in preparation. What enemy ship or ships he encountered would be key factors in the decision, but he would attack if at all possible. He had been ordered to disrupt the enemy's trade; retreating would not do.

He moved to the voice pipe connecting to Commander Kruse. 'The enemy cruisers are our priority.' He intended his message as purely one of encouragement, especially as he was only reiterating what he and Kruse had already discussed. Enemy warships would be targeted before merchantmen. They had agreed to commence firing beyond the range of the enemy's own guns, but, to avoid wasting shells, not at extreme range. However, the American cruiser's 10in guns had changed all that.

A simple 'Aye, Captain,' came back down the pipe.

It was early morning and now good visibility; there was ample time to dispose of the warships—a victory in itself—and complete the destruction of the convoy. He briefly discussed the situation with Schellenberg. They agreed on the simple tactics to be employed. Schellenberg then left for the aft control station just for'ard of the rear turrets, ensuring a command structure would exist if the Bridge was struck and the captain killed. Before any action, Körner would, or should, go into the armoured conning tower.

Things were happening quickly. The Spotting Top reported the convoy's merchant ships were turning to starboard, away from the approaching battle cruiser, then, almost immediately: 'Enemy cruiser, port side of convoy!' Everyone on the Bridge raised their binoculars. The distance was still great, but they could make out the small shape of a ship emerging from the convoy, making much smoke that indicated her high speed. For those on the Bridge, far lower than those in the Spotting Top, the vessel was still partially hull-down, but its shape showed it was bow-on, coming straight towards the *Hindenburg*. Körner gave an order to bring the ship a point more to port, to ensure all her main guns would bear on the new target, and called for 'Utmost speed!'

As the *Hindenburg* came onto the new course, moving towards her maximum speed, her turrets trained round a little to accommodate the new bearing. The range between the opposing ships was falling quickly, it was now hardly 20,000 metres. Körner gave the 'Open Fire!' As the ship levelled, the starboard gun in each of the *Hindenburg*'s four big turrets almost simultaneously belched a huge white-yellow-orange flame.

2

Most Appropriate Ship
18 December 1917

It was dark outside. The weak electric light provided some illumination, sufficient for a reasonable facial study. His fingers quickly traced lightly around his chin, feeling the slightly soft, but evident stubble, and on up to the right eye, gently pushing, manipulating the skin. There were a couple of crow's feet, lightly streaming from the eyes, small as yet, but noticeable nonetheless. With the face relaxed, several furrows on its forehead presented as faint pencil lines. When the fair, thin eyebrows were raised, the pencil lines reared up like so many sand ripples on a beach. The white scar running back from the cheek bone almost to the centre of the left ear disturbed the facial symmetry. These images all but disappeared at the edges where the small mirror's silver was slowly in retreat. Körner applied the shaving soap and began the day's routine. As the razor cleared away the picture, the hairless face tentatively revealed itself. Although very familiar with his full-frontal visage, Körner could only see today's picture, his memory of the changing facial landscape or how he appeared from other angles was something else. His skin was clean, but even he could see it looked dry and weather-beaten. His hair, combed back, leaving his forehead clear, was short, though not severely cropped at the sides, like on so many officers. His teeth were somewhat yellowed, though most were still present. He was always keen to present himself as smartly as possible, but he had little time for issues like how well his face portrayed his forty-two years.

Körner thanked Dahl for the *ersatz* coffee the steward placed on the table. Dahl, a thin and drawn man, older than his years, went about the breakfast routine. As Körner got ready, Dahl made reverent small talk about the continuing cold weather and the harbour goings-on. Körner made little response. He allowed Dahl, who'd served with him as captain's steward on the *Potsdam*, some licence to speak to him in a way that other members of the crew wouldn't contemplate, though Dahl never really overstepped the boundaries.

'Captain, I managed to get the dirty mark off your greatcoat. You'll certainly need it this morning,' he proferred. 'More snow fell during the night and it's still freezing. I hear someone's already slipped right down the gangway.' With his curt and slang-rich Berlin accent, Dahl fired these and other loosely related insights into the elements, dockyard matters and other shipboard events in rapid succession, seeking approval from Körner's face.

'I'll watch my step,' Körner replied warmly to Dahl's gangway remarks, though they both knew enough about descending a gangway in all weathers not to need such advice.

There were various papers and signals to read, which, on this occasion, Körner was happy for Dahl to intercept from sailors at the cabin door. Körner read these as he breakfasted, scribbling the odd phrase or *yes* or *no* in the margins. At 7am, Schellenberg came to discuss the ship's status in preparation for Körner's meeting with Admiral Hipper. Körner waited till Dahl left, before the two of them began debating the likely issues to come up. The rumour furnace was too easily stoked. They were quite engrossed, when at 7.45, Dahl knocked, poked his head round the door and, as requested, alerted his captain to the time. Schellenberg left and Dahl helped Körner into his greatcoat, sensing the stiffness in the captain's left arm, a legacy of Skagerrak.

Körner, a slim cardboard folder containing notes on the *Hindenburg*'s readiness in hand, left the relative warmth of his Day Cabin and made his way to the *Batterie* deck. Various crewmen and officers stood to one side, saluting him on his way. Emerging into the daylight for'ard of the aft turrets, he silently acknowledged Dahl's observation about the snow and freezing temperature. The sun had now risen into a cloudless sky, its rays brightening colours around the harbour. A light sprinkling of snow covered the ship, like icing sugar on a cake, but was now under slow attack from the lukewarm sun. Where turrets and superstructure had deflected the snow, the deck was damp or icy, elsewhere there were tiny drifts. Crewmen were clearing the snow and making the deck safe. Körner tried hard not to laugh when he saw a sailor slip on some icy patch. This winter was turning out to be another cold one, perhaps colder than last year's, he thought. Only a few days ago the harbour water had had some ice on it. Despite the snowfall, slightly warmer weather of late had dispersed most of it, though ship traffic was keeping the channels open.

In the few steps to the port gangway, he took in the harbour scene. All round were the masts and funnels of other ships in Wilhelmshaven, Germany's principal North Sea naval base. The solid and powerful looking, snow-covered battleships and the even larger battle cruisers presented an instant impression of Germany's commitment to naval might. Some ships looked fresher, newer than others, perhaps just more recently painted, hiding the rapid aging effects of war. Thin smoke trails were rising almost vertically from many funnels. All ships were catching the early morning light and flags were teasing the air, endeavouring with little success to come alive in the light wind. A rusty dredger was moving slowly out of the great port, towards one of the smaller harbour gates leading to the mouth of the *Jade Busen*. It was going out to continue the never-ending work of keeping the harbour and estuary navigable, though he wondered how she'd fare if there was any significant sea ice out there.

Wilhelmshaven appeared busy, wherever he looked. On the quayside, parties of sailors and dockyard personnel were occupying themselves on a myriad of tasks. Körner knew where the *Niobe*, his admiral's headquarters ship, was located, but looked over his shoulder and noted her position some distance away on a far quay and confirming that he had a fair walk to get there by the appointed time. A boat trip would have been easier given the layout of the *Kaiserliche Werft*— Imperial Shipyard—but the prospect of harbour ice dissuaded him and, more than that, he reasoned he would benefit from the walk.

He had been summoned to the *Niobe*, because that was where Admiral Hipper was based when in port. For more than a year, the *Niobe*, an old light cruiser, had served as his flagship when he was in port; at sea, he flew his flag in a battle cruiser. She had been converted to provide superior communication and other facilities that better served his needs as Commander of the Scouting Forces which not only included the battle cruisers, but also comprised responsibilities for reconnaissance and defence of the Bight. The *Hindenburg*, replacing the battle cruiser *Seydlitz*, had been the admiral's new flagship for operations for only a few weeks. With the Fleet's normal activities, this arrangement meant that the admiral was infrequently on board her; at least that had been the case thus far, which suited Körner. Since her commissioning in May, the *Hindenburg* had enjoyed time as a 'private ship', as the English termed it, before becoming a flagship. However, during that time there had been the opportunity for her first action, when she put out from Wilhelmshaven on 17 November to confront the enemy who had attacked light cruisers and minesweepers in the Bight. Alas, with the approach of the Fleet's big ships, the English retired, offering no opportunity for the *Hindenburg* to fire her guns in anger for the first time, though the sortie served as something of a real test for Körner and his crew. A week later she was Admiral Hipper's new flagship.

At the gangway, a Deck Officer, Helling, Körner recalled, and a bosun and other sailors stood at rigid attention. Körner noted with quiet amusement that Helling did not voice any concern about the dangers of the gangway, nonetheless he determined to take a bit more care on each tread. Helling greeted him a cheery, but respectful 'Good morning, Sir', his breath clearly visible, betraying the coldness of the day. With the usual ceremony, Körner left the ship. He descended the gangway, recalling Dahl's comments with every step; to fall on one's backside would be embarrassing for a *Kapitän zur See*.

On the descent to the quayside, Körner saw that ice had formed an almost continuous bridge between the ship and the stone quay, though in an ice free gap, he could see the strangely captivitating inky-black, oil-like water. As he raised his eyes, he saw the battle cruiser *Derfflinger*, the *Hindenburg*'s older sister, hardly thirty metres astern of his ship. Approaching her straight stem bow, he scanned the great ship, mentally comparing the two. She and the *Hindenburg* were the surviving ships of a class of three built to a new design, quite different from their forerunners. Körner's ship was the last to be completed and an improved version of the other two, though a landsman might notice little other than the more splayed legs of the *Derfflinger*'s tripod foremast. There was one important, but hidden difference between the two ships, Körner mused, which he put down simply to *the War*: the *Hindenburg* had taken over four years from laying down to completion, compared to less than three years for the *Derfflinger*. The war was adding to completion times. Other, yet more powerful ships were being built, but Körner had heard that work on most of them had been suspended this year and now doubted if they would join the Fleet before the war was over. So, for now, the *Hindenburg* was arguably the best of the Fleet's battle cruisers and he was quietly proud to be her captain.

His decision to take the longer, more circuitous route around the shipyard, crunching through patches of snow and ice, allowed him to see various ships replenishing or fitting out and he was reminded of the great German fleet that had been produced in such a short time. When he was born in 1875, the newly unified German nation had but a relatively small navy, with some armoured ships and focusing on the protection of overseas trade and defence of German coasts. All that had changed over the last thirty years. The Kaiser's desires for colonies and world status, which Körner suspected were probably fuelled by his envy of Britain's world-wide empire and her truly massive navy, had driven him to seek his own blue-water navy. His majesty's appointment of Admiral von Tirpitz in the last years of the old century as State Secretary of the Navy had seen this aim given a new focus and impetus. Fork-bearded Tirpitz had successfully used all his political skills to overcome traditional objections of those who were content for Germany to be the world's greatest land power and had produced a mighty battle fleet. Körner accepted Tirpitz's view that a desire for a global empire must, sooner or later, put Germany at odds with Britain. To fight Britain meant dealing with the Royal Navy and required a battle fleet that could challenge what Tirpitz labelled the 'greatest naval power'. So, by 1914, what had been a second-rate navy had risen to be the second most powerful in the world. Körner was well versed in the navy's history and his naval career had gone hand-in-hand with and benefited from the rapid development of the *HochSeeFlotte*. He also reckoned that things had not worked out as Tirpitz had envisaged. Germany had never beaten the Royal Navy in the ship numbers game. As Tirpitz introduced successive 'Naval Laws' both to guarantee and expand the size of the battle fleet, the English just seemed to increase their own shipbuilding, always keeping ahead of German shipyard production—and unseating Tirpitz's aim of a fleet which would intimidate the English, even though it was smaller than theirs. However, despite always having fewer dreadnoughts, from the war's events, Körner thought it was clear that German ships were individually better than the English. That said, he reluctantly now feared, but never voiced, that the enemy's superior numbers, doubtless now swelled by American dreadnoughts, would probably make things difficult for the navy. When he passed the *Bauhaven*—building yard—unlike other parts of the shipyard, he noted the limited activity. Only one big ship was on the slipway and he realised it would take years to complete her.

After stepping up his pace, adrenalin surging with each little slip on the wintry surfaces, he boarded the *Niobe* with only a few minutes to spare. He noted the ship's extended ram bow and how it demonstrated the pace of warship design since she was launched in '99. Brought out of reserve at the start of the war, she'd seen some service before assuming her port-flagship role. Now disarmed, she still served a useful purpose, though at 3,000 tons she had limited space in comparison to the *Hindenburg*.

In the small captain's cabin, *Vizeadmiral* Franz Ritter von Hipper welcomed his flag-captain in his usual warm manner. Hipper was a respected and well-liked commander. He was friendly enough, though could lose his temper on occasion. The 54-year-old admiral was largely bald and kept the remainder of his hair very short. His greying, goatee-like beard and moustache complimented the shape of his face. Both he and Körner sported first class Iron Crosses on their chests, but the blue and gold *Pour Le Mérite* at the admiral's neck was something that would capture anyone's attention. Körner saluted, clicking his heels.

'Rupprecht, thank you for coming here,' said Hipper.

Körner smiled, 'Not at all, Sir.' It was nice of the admiral to thank him, but he would meet wherever his admiral said.

Hipper was not alone. Also at the meeting table was *Kapitän zur See* Walter Bünzlin, Hipper's Chief of Staff. Bünzlin rose quickly as Körner entered the small cabin and the two acknowledged one another. Bünzlin, a tall, thin, Westphalian, was about the same age as Körner. He had taken up post shortly before Hipper transferred his flag to the *Hindenburg*. Körner knew little of Bünzlin's war service other than what Bünzlin himself had mentioned. Outside a short period with the *HochSeeFlotte* in 1914, his service since then had been in various shore jobs, including the Admiralty, service in Turkey supporting the German ships *Goeben* and *Breslau*, and then Baltic operations on the staff of *Großadmiral* Prince Heinrich of Prussia, the Kaiser's younger brother. Although Körner did not recall it, Bünzlin said that he and Körner had met briefly many years before, in Kiao-chau, in China in '97, when they were both serving on ships involved in the 'acquisition' of Germany's asiatic colony. They'd both been young officers leading detachments of armed sailors and Bünzlin said he saw Körner, but they never spoke.

Hipper invited Körner to sit on his left, with Bünzlin to his right. Hipper was smoking a cigar, Bünzlin a cigarette. Körner took the offer of a cigarette. His smoking was now largely a social affair, though he would be the first to admit that it depended on the degree of stress he was facing. To some extent, Maria, his wife, had changed his smoking habits. As a non-smoker, she had never been keen on smoking and was disinclined to kiss him if he'd been smoking. The three men engaged in some brief chat about the cold weather, Christmas and the *Hindenburg*, but Hipper, not normally one for small talk unless it was about hunting, his main interest after the navy, got down to business.

'Yesterday, I met with Admiral Scheer,' Hipper announced. 'We discussed the latest U-boat sinkings. They are … *satisfactory*.'

Körner was not aware of the latest U-boat figures. He knew that, since Germany had once again adopted unrestricted submarine warfare back in February, the U-boats quickly notched up large numbers of kills, indeed two or three times previous levels. On the flagship, Hipper had mentioned to him that these very high levels of sinkings had not continued, but were still considered sufficient to bring Britain to her knees. He interpreted this latest announcement to mean they had fallen below the required level, but did not wish to enquire at this stage, figuring Hipper would explain all.

Hipper went on: 'We discussed our options and I mentioned your report on an Atlantic sortie.'

At this, Körner tried to show no special interest, but gave a slight nod of acknowledgement, knowing what Hipper was referring to. During his time on Hipper's staff he had written a report—really an update on earlier work—on use of the battle fleet against merchant shipping, which concluded that a single battle cruiser should be sent into the Atlantic. The aim of such an operation was outwardly to sink enemy merchant ships, though he had suggested that the numbers sunk would be unlikely to be large. Arguably more important, it would probably serve more to disrupt such traffic and force the enemy to send dreadnoughts after the ship. Reducing the Grand Fleet's numbers could then provide opportunities for North Sea operations by the battle fleet. While no one denied there were attendant risks, there seemed to be real material, propaganda and morale-raising possibilities in an Atlantic foray. When written in late 1916, Körner's report was seen as an interesting study, but carried no real weight at the time and no longer concerned him with his move to captain the new *Hindenburg*.

'The Admiral recalled our earlier discussions on it,' said Hipper, adding, with a small smile, 'Indeed, he knew of my first proposals.'

Körner knew Hipper was referring to the original idea for such an operation, which dated back to the first months of the war, one which Hipper had endorsed.

'In view of the situation,' Hipper continued, 'he wants a full plan developed.' Körner gave no response. 'You will be aware,' looking at both men, 'that after Skagerrak, the Admiral saw a successful fleet action as unlikely and, as he had always done, advocated an all-out submarine offensive on Britain's merchant ships, pledging the battle fleet to the support of the U-boats. An Atlantic sortie would be seen as yet further support. The successful attack by the *Bremse* and *Brummer* and last week's attack have also confirmed what a surface force can do.'

Körner, trying to remain calm, was taking all this in, his mind racing on the possibilities. The attacks Hipper had mentioned were on the convoys running between Scotland and Norway. The cruisers *Bremse* and *Brummer* had attacked a convoy in October, sinking most of the merchantmen and their two escorting destroyers. Another attack by destroyers had been mounted just a week ago and had been equally as successful. Hipper's next sentence answered all Körner's mental deliberations.

'I did not advocate any specific ship to the Admiral, but that is an important issue. Talking it over with Walter, we consider *your* ship as the most suitable.' Hipper added quickly, 'Under *your* command, of course. What do you think, Rupprecht?'

Körner was not taken aback by this pronouncement, even though he'd never really contemplated such a possibility since taking command of the *Hindenburg*. However, it did not warrant much thought. There were only five battle cruisers to choose from—the *von der Tann, Seydlitz, Moltke, Derfflinger* and *Hindenburg*. All could undertake the task, but his ship was probably best suited. With both men awaiting his response, he decided to be honest.

'Well, of course, I'm honoured, Sir, to be selected for such a mission. Although, in truth, I'd more or less given up on the likelihood of my report leading to anything. On the right ship,' he continued, 'any one of our battle cruisers could probably undertake the operation, but the *Hindenburg* is the best one, in my view. As I said in my report, fuel and, especially, refuelling are key issues. The *Hindenburg* has more range than the others and her oil-fuel capability may well be an important factor in refuelling.'

'Excellent. Exactly our conclusions, Rupprecht,' said Hipper, with another smile. 'Your ship is the logical choice, ... but you omitted one important consideration: You wrote the report and you are now the captain of the most appropriate ship.'

Though tempted, Körner made no response to his admiral's observation, other than his own slight smile. He also wondered if his service on the *Moltke*, when she visited New York in 1912, could have been a factor in his selection, but he assumed not as neither the admiral nor Bünzlin mentioned it.

'Well, I'm glad we've agreed that ... which I knew you would,' continued Hipper. 'Of course, I am *not* pleased with this!'

Both captains looked anxiously at their admiral, unsure at first whether he seeking to oppose the plan or just angry at the loss of his flagship. He was known not to favour changing his flagship, at least that was the case when he was obliged to leave the sinking *Lützow* during the Skagerrak battle.

'Relax, gentlemen. I'm annoyed that it would mean having to transfer my flag, *again and so soon*,' he joked, at which the other two men, their alarm calmed, smiled politely.

Hipper went on to explain to Körner that he had already tasked Bünzlin with working up the operational plan, taking account of the latest developments, naturally with Körner's input. He asked for the work to be done soon, so it could be ready to put before Scheer early in the new year. He reminded both men that getting it past Scheer was only the first hurdle and that others, not least the Kaiser, would probably want to have their say. He thought that there would be strong objections to such an operation, especially from the Kaiser. To emphasise the difficulty in getting approval, Hipper threw in: 'When the destroyer attack on the convoy was mentioned at Court, it apparently played a poor second fiddle to reports of recent Army successes. So, nothing should be taken for granted. We are doing this because the Admiral has requested it. Nothing may come of it, but I obviously expect a comprehensive assessment to be prepared, one that you're both prepared to take forward, if the order to do so is given.'

Both men nodded to Hipper, understanding that nothing less than their full commitment was required. Perhaps an odd thing to seek, thought Körner, given normal practices and expectations, but he accepted that the war was changing, perhaps even nearing its end, and normal practice may no longer suffice. However, Körner expected that getting the Kaiser's agreement to such a mission would be the most difficult hurdle to overcome. The Kaiser's orders to *his* Fleet had severely restrained its operations. Anything that might lead to defeat or loss, especially of dreadnoughts, or otherwise threaten the Fleet and not preserve it as an intact bargaining chip for the expected peace negotiations at the end of the war, seemed unlikely to win his approval. Körner kept these thoughts to himself.

Bünzlin had said little during the meeting, other than to agree with various statements by Hipper or Körner and to outline his timetable and contact with Körner.

Körner was still intrigued by the circumstances that had led to this decision and, as the meeting's key aspects had been resolved, probed further. 'Admiral, you said this all started from your discussions with Admiral Scheer on the U-boat sinkings. May I ask, what *is* the latest situation?'

'I'm sorry, Rupprecht. I should have explained.' With an audible intake of breath, Hipper continued: 'The latest U-boat figures show a reduction in tons sunk compared to those in the earlier part of the year. As you know, when we resumed unrestricted submarine warfare, the U-boats were very successful, regularly sinking over eight hundred thousand tons a month, with over a million tons on two months. But, while that first six, no seven, months' figures were very encouraging, sinkings for September and October were down to under seven hundred thousand tons. The latest, November, are again down, to near six hundred thousand; the worst yet. Fortunately, the November figures are above, *just above*, the six-hundred-thousand-ton-monthly target. So, if this level of sinkings can be sustained, then we still feel the U-boats can win the war. However, the falling trend is worrying and, in part, has prompted the consideration of other actions that will aid matters. Things are not bad, but it would be irresponsible not to consider contingency measures.'

Körner was aware of the 600,000-ton-monthly target and thought it was being easily achieved. He was not aware of the November figure. He could understand the concern and agreed with the admiral's thinking. Why put all your eggs in one basket, especially when there were other, complementary options?

Hipper continued: 'Gentlemen, if I may be honest with you, as I have been with the Admiral, the original thinking on the six-hundred-thousand-ton-monthly target expected, at that rate of loss, that the English would soon be suffering and, *within six months*, would have to sue for peace. Well, the six months have long since passed and even though, despite the recent fall, we are still averaging over eight hundred thousand tons a month, there's no sign that the English are rushing to the peace table. And, we shouldn't forget, this was all supposed to happen before any Americans reached Europe. Well, that's not happened either. They're here!'

Listening to this, Körner was a bit surprised at his admiral's tone; this subject was clearly something that had gotten under his skin. The admiral had mentioned the U-boat sinking rates before, but he could not recall Hipper being so disappointed on those occasions. Perhaps the admiral's thinking on these matters was a recent affair or there were things that even a flag-captain would not hear from his admiral.

'In view of these facts, I am forced to the conclusion,' said Hipper, 'that either the six-hundred-thousand-ton target or the six months to beat the English are basically not enough, … not enough tonnage, not enough time. Of course, those targets could well be correct and it's simply that the U-boats' claims are just overstated. It wouldn't be the first time that those involved in a battle at sea claim to have sunk more than they actually did.' Hipper took a brief pause, then finished with: 'We could debate the likely influence of each of these factors, but I suspect it's a combination of all of them which has led to the present situation. It's plain to me: we need to sink more; it'll take longer to force the English into peace negotiations; and some U-boat claims are not born out in fact. In view of this, we are indeed right to consider other measures.'

Körner took all this in, but could not resist asking: 'What is the thinking on the cause of the recent drop in sinkings, Admiral?'

'There are probably various factors at play,' replied Hipper, 'but the enemy's introduction of convoys is seen to be the primary reason for the fall. The U-boats have concentrated on areas where convoys are not in operation. Hopefully, that will sustain the required level of sinkings.' With a noticeable drop in tone, Hipper continued his explanation: 'Convoys aren't the only problem. U-boat captains report that the enemy has put out more patrol craft, seems to be dropping more depth-charges than ever and is even operating more aircraft. Sadly, there have also been greater U-boat losses in the last few months.' Hipper finished the impromptu lecture with, 'As I said, sinking England's merchant ships is still seen as the way to win the war, but an Atlantic operation would provide further opportunities to secure victory and must be considered.'

Although Bünzlin was Hipper's Chief of Staff and had more seniority than Körner, on board the *Hindenburg* Körner was the ship's captain and, in that way, the more important of the two. Bünzlin did not let this get to him. He knocked at the cabin door and entered. Körner greeted him warmly, as always. Bünzlin, recalling the young man he'd first seen at Kiao-chau, noted his now receding, short fair hair, looking less blond than all those years ago. The three-centimetre scar on his left cheek was a new addition since China. Bünzlin wondered if some would see the scar as a memento of some duel from Körner's early career, but he knew it was really a small, but very visible indication of how close the English had come to killing him.

In his new position, Bünzlin, intrigued by Körner and his likely role in the Atlantic operation, was easily able to explore Körner's background. He'd concluded that Körner appeared to be a very capable and also a well-connected captain, enjoying Hipper's favour and, he wondered, perhaps even the Kaiser's, following a short posting he'd had in the Imperial Yacht *Hohenzollern*. Körner's file confirmed he was slightly the younger of the two of them. Unlike himself, the son of an admiral, Körner was the son of a Prussian army officer and, interestingly, a Swedish mother. Körner had been married for over twenty years, with three children. He'd joined the service in 1892, progressed through the naval academy and, with his career following the usual route of a combination of ship and shore postings, had risen steadily up through the ranks, as much as the service's seniority-based promotion system would allow. His ship assignments had included command of a small torpedo boat and a destroyer. He'd then served as commander in an armoured cruiser and the battle cruiser *Moltke,* before being given command of the small cruiser *Potsdam* just before the war began. Bünzlin could see that Körner, specialising in gunnery, had improved the gunnery of all the ships he'd held a key position in, always returning a creditable performance in the Kaiser's Cup for naval gunnery. His war service was quite commendable, especially his exploits in the *Potsdam*, as part of Hipper's Scouting Force. Notably, the *Potsdam*'s guns were often the first to hit the enemy. Unusually, his posting to the *Potsdam* had been extended and then she was sunk during Skagerrak, when she was targeted by enemy battle cruisers. Körner, wounded, had been rescued. Recuperating from his wounds had kept him ashore and he'd ended up on Hipper's staff, before being given command of the new *Hindenburg*.

As he'd soaked up Körner's history, Bünzlin couldn't help wondering how things might have been very different. Körner, an undoubtedly able officer, might not now be *Kapitän zur See*, if things had followed a different track all those years ago in Kiao-chau. Back then, they had both been in ships under Admiral Otto von Diederichs, when he captured China's Kiao-chau region in November 1897. There had been no shooting in the takeover, though much manoeuvring between the two sides' forces until the situation was resolved in Germany's favour. Bünzlin believed that Körner, then a *Leutnant zur See*, like himself, had perhaps had a lucky opportunity to capture the limelight and help progress his career. If matters had turned out differently, he also considered Körner might even have faced a court martial. Körner, leading a small landing party from the cruiser *Prinzess Wilhelm*, had temporarily come under the command of Bünzlin's *Oberleutnant*, Friedrich Hamm, who, with Bünzlin, was leading a larger group of armed sailors from the flagship *Kaiser*. The combined force had gone into the port of Tsingtau to secure a key road junction at the southern end of the town and search for a Chinese arsenal, which was believed to be in the same area. On reaching the junction, Hamm directed Körner to take up a holding position to the left of his force. Körner had done so, but later reported that he had found and secured the arsenal. Körner said he had seen some Chinese soldiers and followed them with a handful of men to the arsenal. There had been a brief struggle, claimed Körner, during which, sword in hand, he personally prevented a Chinese officer from suicidally exploding the munitions. At Körner's explanation of events, Bünzlin, no more than an observer of the episode, said nothing, but noticed that Hamm was clearly displeased. He thought Hamm was on the point of remonstrating with Körner, but said nothing after a senior officer openly praised Körner for his quick thinking. From what Hamm later said to him, Bünzlin concluded that Hamm had doubted Körner's story about the Chinaman's intended suicidal action and would have had him court-martialled for abandoning his post.

The Kiao-chau operation resulted in commendations for several officers and crew, with Körner receiving an award and, in due course, no doubt confirmed his later promotion to *Oberleutnant*. They had spoken briefly of Kiao-chau, but Bünzlin never mentioned Hamm's intended action. He was still undecided whether Körner was a calculating risk-taker or just lucky, perhaps both. Either way, he concluded that Körner was the right man for the proposed operation.

This was their third meeting since they'd discussed the operation—now officially called *Georg*—with Hipper on the *Niobe*.

'Rupprecht, my apologies for not getting this revision to you before now,' said Bünzlin, as he handed a dozen or so sheets of paper to Körner. 'My staff have looked again at the issues we discussed at our last meeting.'

Körner invited Bünzlin to sit down, while assuring him that the late receipt was not an issue, though all the time intently scanning the pages. Bünzlin sat quietly while Körner read, realising he was eager to absorb it before continuing their discussion.

Körner perused the document quickly, commenting that this latest version appeared to cover all the issues they'd discussed to date. Bünzlin expected he was keen to note any changes, as they had a specific meeting soon with Admiral Hipper to discuss progress. There were now almost twenty headings, covering the many issues that had to be considered and addressed in planning the proposed operation. Körner raised his head from the papers.

'Well, Walter, we seem to have covered *most* issues,' he said, though with an unspoken *but*.

'Yes,' replied Bünzlin, in a half-serious tone, acknowledging the importance of Körner's undeclared concern, 'but we still do not have a wholly sound solution to the issue of finding convoys for you to attack.'

Körner nodded, his face showing the issue was indeed a concern. Without some way of locating convoys, *Georg* was little more than an idea.

'I met with *Kommodore* Michelsen,' said Bünzlin, pointing to a section on one of the pages. 'As we imagined, he is strongly opposed to any mission which depletes the number of his operational U-boats. He said to take away a dozen boats would be madness ... that was the term he used ... as it would seriously affect the number of enemy ships sunk. He only has forty to fifty U-boats at sea.

'You have to see his point,' continued Bünzlin. 'For similar reasons, he is equally against sending *any* to America. He said he would contest such deployments at the highest levels. Actually, am I being unfair to him? While he was against sending boats to America, he was not averse to them assisting the passage of the colliers, *if* it was on their route to their hunting grounds. In the end, he promised nothing and said he would always push for priority on U-boat operations around Britain.'

'Damn,' mouthed Körner. 'Why? What's his objection to sending boats to America?'

'He seemed well-prepared on that issue,' responded Bünzlin. 'He said to send U-boats to America would inevitably reduce the number of enemy vessels they would sink.'

'We're not looking for his boats to sink ships, just to report their location,' interrupted Körner.

'Well, he says that's not *his* mission. He says he is charged with sinking as much enemy tonnage as will bring down England. He says the time going further out into the Atlantic, especially to and from America would be more valuable if they kept to British waters. He sees that as the place where his boats can be most effective. They can make more round trips and sink more ships than on a long journey across the ocean. I see his logic.'

'Without U-boat reconnaissance, we could go sailing all over the Atlantic and find nothing.'

'I know, Rupprecht, but Michelsen is right about the mission's impact on the number of available U-boats. I can't see how we can get round that. Of course, this is not the end of the matter. He may be obliged to comply with our needs, if Admiral Scheer so orders him. Of course, we may not have it all our way. We mustn't forget that the Admiral is also against U-boats blockading the American coast.'

Körner said nothing to that, but gave a slight exhale and raised his eyebrows, wondering if *Georg* would ever turn into reality.

Sensing Körner's disappointment, Bünzlin threw in: 'We also shouldn't forget that the American convoys are no longer just about supplies to England, they are also the way American soldiers will be getting to the Western Front. Stopping the convoys now has greater meaning.

'Perhaps we should accept that the seaplane option is the easiest one, though,' he paused, as if seeking confirmation from Körner, 'is admittedly not without its own difficulties.'

'Yes,' said Körner, 'you're right. If *Georg* is ever going to become a reality, we may have to fall back on it. As you rightly say, Walter, it certainly has its own difficulties, but, if we cannot persuade them to make enough U-boats available to us, then we must adopt these other means of reconnaissance. I'll be honest, the size of the ocean is perhaps our biggest problem and anything which gives us a way of making it smaller is to be welcomed.'

The two men continued their discussion on this key issue, again touching on the various solutions they'd explored, their advantages and disadvantages. Körner's original report on a battle cruiser mission was written before the introduction of convoys by the English. Then, finding merchant ships on the high sea would have been the same as faced the U-boats, but with merchantmen scattered all over the sea on their way to England, the chance of encountering at least some of them was deemed reasonably good. The introduction of convoys didn't mean there were any fewer ships, just that they were concentrated in widely dispersed groups. The vastness of the ocean made finding a convoy far from easy, perhaps even unlikely.

Körner had quickly agreed that the enemy's convoys required a substantial change to the original battle cruiser sortie. That envisaged an Atlantic raid, though largely just to the west of the U-boats' main operational areas around the British Isles. Now with convoys, the whole of the North Atlantic became the *Hindenburg*'s potential war zone. Furthermore, faced with an escorted convoy, an attacking battle cruiser was considered superior to any U-boat's endeavours. Whereas the U-boat might escape the attentions of the escort, though probably sink only a few of the merchantmen, it was expected that the battle cruiser would not only eliminate any escort (short of dreadnought opposition), but could well sink or damage most of the merchant ships. Even if they scattered, the battle cruiser's speed and long range guns would serve to deal with them.

The problem of finding a convoy remained the crucial factor. A line of light cruisers scouting ahead was the traditional way to guide the big ships onto their quarry. Clearly, it would not be possible to deploy light cruisers for *Georg*. Körner and Bünzlin knew the Fleet could not release enough, never mind the issue of refuelling them all. To replace scout cruisers, Bünzlin's staff had explored all the likely options and a few not so likely, from men on American shores to auxiliary ships lying offshore, all signalling their observations to the *Hindenburg*. The focus narrowed to a few possibilities.

There was a possible solution right to hand, but for various reasons it started off way down the options' list: the *Hindenburg* had actually been designed to carry two seaplanes, which could undertake reconnaissance missions. On paper it seemed a sensible approach, but up to then, while there were ships in the Fleet whose specific task was to carry seaplanes, there had been very limited use of seaplanes by the Fleet's battle cruisers. Nonetheless, the *Hindenburg* plans placed a seaplane on the deck either side of the aft funnel. However, other than the fitting of seaplane handling gear soon after she began her trials, the planes themselves were not yet aboard. Faced with this, attention had naturally swung onto other, possibly more successful alternatives. For example, prompted by the recent, near-7,000-kilometre flight of zeppelin *L59* to Africa and back, long range reconnaissance by the giant airships was thought feasible. Thinking of the reconnaissance already given to the Fleet by their zeppelins, Körner was open to the airship option. However, others questioned their success to date and also voiced concerns about getting enough airships into the mid-Atlantic, their vulnerability to adverse weather and the difficulties of successfully operating several in the middle of an ocean long enough to direct the *Hindenburg* onto a convoy.

Ship-mounted observation balloons proffered greater spotting capability from the ship itself. The English were reportedly using such balloons tethered to their warships, but the additional vision they offered seemed insufficient to Körner to warrant putting such a highly explosive burden on his ship. The balloon, visible to enemy ships, was also a pointer to the *Hindenburg*'s position.

Submarines and, in the end, the ship's own seaplanes, supplemented by intelligence on convoy movements, were deemed to be the most useful and practical approaches to the problem. An extended U-boat line would emulate the scouting light cruiser role, though U-boat lines used in the North Sea to report and attack the English fleet could not be said to have been that successful. Seaplanes carried on the *Hindenburg*, with their altitude, range and speed, could provide a very flexible reconnaissance option, covering a wide front ahead of the ship. Alas, each solution had some problems to overcome.

Ten or more submarines might be required. Trimming the number to five or six significantly reduced their scout-line capability. Stationing U-boats off convoy assembly ports was another approach, but again North Sea experience showed that was no guarantee of success. As with the zeppelins, operating the U-boats perhaps on the other side of the Atlantic was another problem to be addressed. Michelsen, they now knew, would object to any U-boat role which diminished his aim to sink the enemy's merchantmen.

Seaplanes did seem to be the one possibility that could be readily adopted without much resistance from others, though they too were no easy proposition. There were questions about the impact of the proposed planes on the ship's gun-arcs and even the suitability of the planes to be employed, not to mention their effectiveness in Atlantic conditions. That said, there were examples of ship-board planes in the Fleet, especially the auxiliary cruiser *Wolf*, which, even as they discussed the possibility of aircraft, had taken a seaplane on her world-wide mission. There had also been some recent, but very limited experience with a seaplane on the *Derfflinger*, as well as on the *von der Tann*, a few years before, but both were no great examples to cite. However, the English were known to have planes on many of their dreadnoughts. Bünzlin also endorsed the use of seaplanes, citing operations in the Baltic and the enthusiastic support of Prince Heinrich, the Baltic Fleet's CinC, though he accepted the Baltic was not the Atlantic.

So, almost by a process of elimination, it was decided that the *Hindenburg*'s reconnaissance needs would be provided by seaplanes, to be flown from the ship. Körner accepted the arguments for the use of seaplanes, but realised that there would be precious little time to get to grips with the practicalities of operating such planes.

3

Maria

The ship was settling more quickly, listing further to port, her end was near. The large-calibre hits had done for her. He adjusted his stance to counter the increasing list. He had been right to order abandon ship. The order also included him—a promise to his wife that he would never deliberately go down with his ship. He stepped carefully over his Bridge officers' bodies. Amid the devastated surroundings, splattered with blood and body parts, a few showed little evidence of why they had died, but the wounds shrapnel can create were all too evident in others. He was aware of his own pain, but fought through it. He went again to the damaged port side of the Bridge. Through fire, smoke and mist, he looked aft. There was damage everywhere. The mainmast was broken and hanging down towards the sea. The centre funnel was crumpled, its top half bent over to port. Below the punctured funnels, the ship's boats were splintered, smashed. Escaping this destruction, men were abandoning ship. On this port side, he could see that the deck was almost level with the uninviting and choppy, grey sea. Against instruction, men were jumping or lowering themselves down into the water on this side, where they could be trapped by the ship's rigging and superstructure when she would finally roll to port. He made his way down from the starboard side of the Bridge, finding himself at the edge of the deck, looking down at the sea on this rising side. With a sudden movement, the ship healed more to port. He again steadied himself, holding on tight. From an unseen enemy, a salvo of shells straddled the ship, not hitting her, just throwing up huge water spouts. Somehow he was under water. He was desperate to breathe, was almost about to suck in a lungful of sea water, when he broke surface and greedily gulped in air. Disorientated for a moment, he couldn't see the ship. He fought the grip of the cold water, twisted himself round. The ship, about 10 metres off and moving slowly away from him, was well down by the head, her list exposing her red-brown hull. Her list continued relentlessly. Now she was almost on her beam ends. She raised her stern, slowly at first, showing her bronze propellers as she rose, halted for a few seconds, then slipped smoothly below the water. She sank amidst a boiling sea of air, steam and erupting debris. It was all over quite quickly. He felt the scene unreal, an impossible event, something he knew could happen, but never expected it to. His view of the ship's end was intermittently masked by the rising and falling swell, but, as he crested, he looked for others in the cold water. At first, much to his distress, he saw none, but as the waves raised him, he saw some bobbing heads nearby and slowly swam to them.

To his surprise, he heard a bird calling. A faint smile creeping over his lips, he silently accused it of daring to sing in such times as these. He was no ornithologist, but was pleased to know the war had not yet stopped birds thinking of the coming spring. His eyes grew accustomed to the dark. He could make out furniture shapes, the contours of the room. As if on cue, a sliver of early morning light found its way into the room through the all but closed curtains, cutting through the darkness. He felt cold, chilly. His night-shirt was damp. He didn't always relive the *Potsdam*'s end. In fact such dreams had been reducing in frequency, though they usually left him wet-through. He didn't need to dream it—he refused to call it a nightmare—he could remember most of the events quite vividly, though not how he'd got into the water. He persuaded himself that he'd been blown into the water, no other course would have seen him abandon ship before the crew. He knew there were others still on board, trying to escape the would-be tomb. The terror that all his men had been lost and that he was the only survivor had greatly distressed him at the time. It wasn't so, but from his surface viewpoint that was all he could see. The ship should have sucked him down with her, but amazingly she spared him that ending. After what seemed no more than a few minutes, a German torpedo-boat, emerging from a smokescreen, saw his group of survivors and courageously slowed to rescue them—him and thirty-two others. If there were others in the water, they were not saved. There must have been others, there were 375 on board. How long did they suffer? What anguish did they endure as German and British ships swept by? They would understand why ships in battle could not stop, but they must have called out, as loudly as their cold bodies would have allowed. He was lucky, extremely lucky.

When he'd first woken, for a moment he'd thought he was in his cabin on the *Hindenburg* and not in the bedroom of his town house not far from the naval base. Maria, his wife, was next to him, her back to him. He could just discern her gentle breathing. He could not resist lightly running his hand over her nightdress-covered backside, with its soft, but firm globes and alluring cleavage. With this lingering, very tactile experience, he thought of earthly pleasures, but soon also pondered a question he had begun to ask himself in the last year or so: how could men throw away the joys of love and life for the embrace of war and death? Perhaps they took such happy times for granted, gave them little real thought and failed to celebrate them enough or, as men, saw war and fighting as their destiny, even their purpose in life. After all, Germany was encircled by the Entente powers and everyone had spoken of preventive war, if not a continental war. He was as guilty as others. He'd not objected to the war, but readily expected, even sought it, knew it was a likely outcome and the only question was when, not if. Sarajevo might have been the start, but if not that, then most likely some other Balkan spark or perhaps a far-off

31

colonial dispute, all driven by imperial ambitions or treaty commitments, would have lit the powder and—bang—it would have started. He'd accepted the pre-war views that Germany needed to expand its empire, to acquire new territories and colonies for its growing population and must achieve its 'place in the sun', if it was ever to flourish and garner its true place as a world-power. War was seen as the only way, the inevitable way for this to happen. He'd played his own small part: Kiao-chau was a clear statement of German achievement, export opportunities and general contribution to Germany's and the world's development. Tsingtau, the main town of Kiao-chau, with its large and small harbours, had become a prosperous empire town. And yet, all that effort was for naught. Tsingtau had fallen to the Japanese before the war was but a few months old. Indeed, most of Germany's colonies had been lost in short order. The Navy had not been able to prevent it. The most powerful naval force outside German waters had been Admiral von Spee's East Asia Squadron of outstanding cruisers, based at Tsingtau, but it could never defeat the forces arrayed against that distant piece of empire. Spee led them with great skill, crossed an ocean and defeated a British cruiser squadron, but was subsequently destroyed by British battle cruisers sent to avenge that British loss. Körner knew the *Hindenburg* would do the same to any cruisers she encountered.

Being as objective as possible, Körner reluctantly admitted to himself that the naval war had not been a great success for Germany's battle fleet. They had bloodied the enemy, taken the fight to his shores, even killed the enemy in his own bed, but for all that the Fleet's operations seemed inhibited by the threat of a clash with the larger British Grand Fleet. At Skagerrak, they had indeed dealt the enemy a telling blow, with much to be pleased about ship and crew performance, but on reflection he considered Scheer had been lucky to extricate his ships and get them back to base. If the battle had continued into a second day, would the Fleet have survived, he wondered. Wounded and sheltering in the torpedo-boat, Körner saw little of the battle after his ship sank, but the sight of the battle-scarred Fleet in Wilhelmshaven in the weeks following Skagerrak, especially that of the heavily damaged *Seydlitz* sitting deep in the harbour basin, her fo'c'sle almost awash, was something he'd always remember and a sobering insight into the firepower they'd confronted. Whatever his previous thoughts on the matter, it was then clear to him that the Fleet's prospects of winning a major naval battle in the North Sea were unfavourable at best, if he were honest. The British dreadnought numbers were now probably somewhere near double the High Seas Fleet's. The hoped-for opportunity of reducing the Grand Fleet's numerical superiority by destroying a small part of it now seemed very remote, whatever some officers argued. Despite the press and people in the streets cheering the German success, even church bells ringing at the Skagerrak victory, Körner concluded that they had, when confronted by the Grand Fleet's battleships, sought to evade the enemy and when all was said and done had been fortunate to escape without more losses. Following his own appointment to Hipper's staff, he'd had the opportunity to ponder the Fleet's options. He supported the return to unrestricted submarine warfare, but that had not stopped his deliberations about what could yet be done with the Fleet's big ships. The Fleet was a threat to the enemy, even in harbour. It needed to be husbanded, but languishing in harbour was not the desired aim. Scheer had led the Fleet out on a number of occasions after Skagerrak, but without result and certainly there was no wish to provoke a major fleet action.

When Körner first raised the potential of an Atlantic sortie, there were those who rejected it almost out-of-hand as too risky, too difficult, even pointless and, to some, foolish. Hipper was also sceptical, even though he had openly supported the idea back in 1914, but agreed that Körner should do further work on the proposal. Although the concept had received some comment before the war, all, both British and German, dismissed it as impracticable, especially on the refuelling issue.

Körner's own first thoughts on such a sortie had actually been prompted by Maria. He very seldom spoke to her of operations, not just because of security, but because of the worry it might cause her. When Körner had foolishly mentioned to her that crew morale could suffer from their short-range sorties into the North Sea, sometimes less than 100 kilometres out to sea, uncharacteristically, she had exclaimed, with raised voice and no little emotion, that that suited her, more time to see him and much less chance for him to be wounded or worse.

'Leave it to the U-boats,' she'd said, excitedly and surprisingly. 'They are the only way to challenge the English at sea! I don't care if your ship never puts to sea again!'

Her completely unexpected outburst, the sight of her eyes welling up with tears, revealed more than he'd previously thought. She had clearly changed her views of the war and the navy's contribution, especially since he was injured at Skagerrak, and was now being more outspoken about what was important to her, rather than to Germany. She didn't want to win the war at the cost of losing her Rupprecht. Previously she was very supportive of his career and seldom voiced much comment on the war. At first, when the armies were advancing into France, perhaps less so than most Germans, she demonstrated some tempered enthusiasm, but that was very short-lived. The news of deaths of family and friends soon reduced any fervour she had and her comments turned more to the tragedy of it all and hoping it would end soon. She would seldom be drawn to speak on the success or failure of particular German actions, but could be expected to comment on peace-moves or anything that might seem to offer the chance of ending the war. At the time of her outburst, he'd tried, unsuccessfully, to scold her for such comments, though only ended up cuddling her, but her distress had made him think on the bigger picture and begin to ask: why couldn't the big ships join the U-boats in smashing British merchant traffic? Those first thoughts, now enabled by unexpected events, had culminated in *Georg*—something Maria would definitely not want.

Despite all the potential in *Georg*, in Körner's honest opinion—and which he never mentioned to anyone, especially Maria—was that there was clearly more than the usual chance of losing his ship *and* his life in the venture.

Körner chastised himself for such thoughts, full of their defeatist content. He was a naval officer, something he'd committed his whole life to. He was also a Prussian. He would always do the right thing, give his all for victory—it was the only way. It was up to him, like any of the Kaiser's officers, to bring about victory. He must do his utmost. Victory was the only way. Whatever depredations came, they must be endured for victory. But did he still believe that? To contemplate anything else was almost to throw away his life's work, to challenge his own, deep-seated beliefs. To have risen to the command of a great warship was unquestionably a great achievement, a naval officer's life-long ambition, but then, he thought, to be able to put the clock back, to have been wiser. It was easy with hindsight, but could men really not have foreseen? He hadn't. Why should anyone else?

Over the last year this mental debate was occasionally part of Körner's thinking, though seldom at the forefront of his mind. His energies were fully committed to the responsibilities of a *Kapitän zur See*. However, at quieter times, often before rising or when thinking of his family, the questions came. Occasional night-time sweats were the only outward expression of the inner turmoil. Their recurrence he put down to reliving the *Potsdam*'s loss, but also probably to anxieties about the Atlantic mission. He knew not to express such thoughts to anyone, especially Maria, but to endure the mental turmoil, immerse himself in his work, resolve difficulties, not worry about them. The spectre of Germany's defeat was something quite alien and he never really considered it. Indeed, such an outcome was unthinkable, would be unendurable and must lead to change, even anarchy in Germany, with far-reaching changes affecting him and his family, indeed threatening his whole way of life. Food shortages were plainly evident—Germans were all now living on turnips and there were plenty of stories about thousands starving to death. Sadly, he only had to look at the drawn faces and thin bodies of his own family to see the effects of the food shortages. Such things were bad enough, now strikes, peace moves and the threat of mutinies seemed to be moving everyone to a climactic finale. Achieve victory and all would be made better, made whole. There was no turning back. He hoped that everything would return to how it was before, but also pondered if that was likely, even with victory and peace. Nevertheless, German victory was the only way forward.

Thoughts of the *Potsdam*'s end could come all too easily: the shouts and screams of men wounded, dying or trapped below; and the flailing arms of those who got off the ship, but soon disappeared beneath the waves. The loss of so many was difficult to dismiss. They were his responsibility. To be one of the very few who'd survived made him despair and constantly ask why? The *Potsdam* was a very tangible loss, but was it so different to the others the war had laid on him—and Maria?

Maria's two brothers were dead. Both were soldiers. Arnauld, the dashing, handsome Uhlan officer, spoke with much bravado and with real enthusiasm of how the cavalry was going to win the next war. Körner did not question the merits of the use of cavalry, but when he first met the tall Arnauld, resplendent in his brightly coloured, dress uniform, he thought he would not have looked out of place in Blücher's army at Waterloo. Arnauld's war was short. He was killed near the French border in late August 1914, only a few weeks into the war. Reportedly, he'd been brought down by English machine-gun fire—not something cavalry at Waterloo had to face. Although Max Schwenke, Maria's father, a retired businessman and veteran of the Franco-Prussian War, seemed to accept the loss, Arnauld's death was still a real blow to the family. He was seen as a hero, a soldier who'd been killed when Germany was considered to be then only a few weeks or so from outright victory. Körner wondered how Arnauld would have fared now; perhaps he'd be a frustrated horseman, having long since turned foot soldier or, like other cavalrymen, gone off to a new, equally dashing profession as a pilot fighting above the trenches. Maria's other brother, Henning, youngest of the five Schwenke children, was dead too, killed at Verdun. Henning thought war was inevitable, so left his Civil Service office job and joined the ranks in 1913, 'to be prepared' he confided to Körner. Körner remembered him as a kind-hearted, quiet-spoken young man, altogether different from Arnauld. The loss of the family's sons, all now too common to military families where sons gravitated to the armed forces, was a great shock. Thus far, Maria and her two sisters still had their men alive. Körner had been wounded, but largely recovered, though the Körner family had shared in this national death lottery. One of the three Körner brothers was dead. Körner's older brother, Rolf, was in charge of the family estate. Following in his father's footsteps and, perhaps one of the reasons why Körner was allowed to pursue a naval career, Rolf had joined the army, but had been invalided out before the war following serious injuries when he and horse crashed to the ground on manoeuvres. Despite his great difficulty in walking, Rolf was now seeking to rejoin his old regiment, willing to serve in any capacity. Körner's younger brother, Lothar, who, unlike his siblings was no career soldier, but joined up at the start, had spent a very eventful war on the Eastern Front. His occasional letters to Körner spoke of how they'd defeated the Russians time and again, pushing them far back into Russia. He picked up a medal and a field promotion, but in September 1915 was reported missing in action, only about 500 kilometres from the family home in East Prussia. Körner said nothing to his widowed mother to dispel her hopes that he'd be found alive, perhaps a prisoner of the Russians. These very personal losses were nothing but a tiny addition to the millions who'd died, but that didn't really numb the senses or stop the grief. There weren't many quiet times when Körner didn't think of

Lothar. As Arnauld had once said, those who are left to mourn suffer more than the dead soldier ever did.

The personal losses to the Körner and Schwenke families were not isolated affairs. Families all over Germany—all over Europe for that matter—were in mourning. All too many families Maria and he knew personally had suffered the loss of loved ones. Körner never really worried about his own death, other than the impact it would have on Maria and their children. That aspect concerned him greatly. He had witnessed the terrible anguish and sorrow in the families of the many *Potsdam* officers and men who had been lost. He and Maria had met with many and Maria continued to organise charitable events to help the wives and children of those lost. It was hard enough just to get by, without that blow to a family. The hardships of just living were everyday more noticeable, especially for an ordinary sailor's family. Now he feared, as the war drew on, that his own children, his sons, Hans and Manfred, would eventually be called up to the front line.

Their daughter, Viktoria, would not be involved in any fighting, but was not immune to the effects of the war. Now 18, she had taken what originally seemed like an unskilled nursing job in a local hospital. A short intensive training now saw her involved in most nursing duties. However laudable for her to undertake such work, it had exposed her to war wounded and Körner and Maria both thought she had grown up very quickly as a result. Maria had found out that Viktoria had been corresponding with a young wounded flyer she'd met a few months ago in the hospital. In Germany, pilots were regarded as would-be heroes, a new breed of warriors, alas living all too short lives. Körner was not surprised that Viktoria should be attracted to such a man, given the way they were idolized. The normal parental anxieties about their daughter meeting a man had been voiced, but seemed slightly odd in such times, though the war brought new concerns. In truth, Körner knew precious little of aircraft and flying, but was aware that being a fighter pilot was a dangerous occupation. Hopefully, Viktoria hadn't become too attached that his loss could not be endured.

Their eldest son, blonde-haired Hans, nearly 17, would soon take up arms for Germany if the war didn't end shortly. Körner refused to believe that it would still be raging when 12-year-old Manfred came to that age. Hans wanted desperately to be in the navy, like his father, and would very soon enrol as a naval cadet. Manfred had talked enthusiastically about when he too would join the navy, though after Körner was injured he seemed less committed, even strangely quiet about the prospect. Körner felt the weight of all these burdens. If he didn't do his part, indeed his utmost, the bloody war would soon engulf his children. *Georg* was a great risk, but also a great opportunity. He was determined it should be a success.

He could endure his damp night-shirt no longer. It made him cold and uncomfortable. He got up quietly so as not to wake Maria, but as usual she noticed the movement.

᚛

Quietly, Maria turned her head to see what he was about. The thin strip of light getting through the curtains fell on him. His back toward her, she watched him pulling at the clinging night-shirt. As he struggled with the off-white bed-wear, she realised he had been sweating again. He fought to lift the shirt over his head. His wound had injured him more than he would admit. As its long tail moved up, she saw his bottom, something she never tired of seeing. It was still firm, diminutive pieces of muscle, but much smaller than at any time since that first night. His ribs could also be glimpsed. They were new additions to his torso. For most of their marriage, they could easily be felt, but not seen. She worried at this. He had never been so thin. His wounds under his left arm were just coming into view. She still winced at the memory of that first sight of his unbandaged arm and back and his cut face.

As the garment reluctantly gave way in the tug-of-war battle to remove it and gobbled up his head, she glimpsed his genitals—*le paquet*, she called them. That made her think of love-making, an all too infrequent occurrence, not just because Rupprecht was a sailor, though with Tirpitz's North Sea focus, less frequently away from home, but difficult with teenage children around. His captaincy, or was it the war, seemed to be grinding away at that part of their life. The situation now contrasted starkly with that in their early years, when sex used to be a frantic event, squeezed into short shore leaves. As captain of a ship based in Wilhelmshaven, he was often at home. She was undecided whether sex was better because of the navy's enforced and periodic separations or with its practice of officers living ashore with their families rather than on ship made him more like a normal husband and for whom sex was not something that had to happen tonight. She did know she liked him home, in their bed, sex or no. She knew he was returning to his ship.

'Are you all right, my love? Sweating?'

'Yes, a bit,' he replied quietly, lying somewhat and endeavouring to make light of the issue.

She said no more. As he threw the night-shirt to the floor, triumphant in the trial of strength, she eased back the sheets and encouraged him to come back to bed, gently calling him to her side of the bed to avoid the evident dampness he'd left. As his naked body, its man-smell evident, curled up against her, she girdled him with her left arm and leg. In the dim light, she looked up to him, he returned it, knew what it meant, kissed her gently on the lips, then again, harder. Love-making was more functional than romantic, of damp bed-clothes and rucked-up night-dress, undertaken as quietly as their brass bedstead would allow, with both keeping their passions under check in a house full of young people.

They lay quietly, for some time it appeared to Körner. He lay on his back, looking up at the dark ceiling, but mostly kept his eyes closed. Maria's head was on his chest. For the time being, he was removed from the *Hindenburg*, *Georg* and *the War*. His desire for the tender moment to last forever was broken by Maria's soft, slightly muffled voice.

'*Frau* Reinhold says the Kaiser needs to abdicate if the war is ever going to come to an end.'

'My Love, you choose the oddest moments to discuss such matters,' replied Körner, seeking to lessen the subject, rather than defend the Kaiser, as he had done on previous occasions. 'Anyway, what's new about such things? I seem to remember you telling me some time ago that *Frau* Reinhold said the Kaiser must abdicate,'

'Yes,' said Maria, her voice a little sharper, 'though she is not the only person who has said he must go. Many others have said so, apparently quite openly.'

'So? Who?'

'She told the Women's Group that people are now being quite derogatory about him and calling for him and his Government to go. She says, Kaiser or no, he should be subject to the same food restrictions we all have, rather than banqueting all the time. It's said he keeps stables full of horses, each attended to by grooms and stable boys.'

'*Frau* Reinhold and those who speak of such things could get their just desserts for such comments. Your Women's Group should take care what it discusses.'

'She says the police are well aware of what is said, but take no action. They are probably of the same opinion.'

Körner gave an audible sigh, but Maria continued: 'She says the Crown Prince has openly talked about his life after giving up being a royal, though doesn't think his father would know what to do or be able to find work for himself.'

'This is stupid talk,' said Körner, trying to appear riled and now wishing to signal the end of the discussion. 'The Kaiser is *not* going to abdicate. There's no need to debate such issues.'

'Rupprecht, my love, you are at sea, surrounded by officers loyal to the Kaiser, but do such things not get to your ears?' Maria said, still with her head on his chest, but rising to the fight.

Körner could see that it might be easy for this discussion to escalate into a row. He knew that strikes were common-place, with hundreds of thousands of people involved, and that there had been clashes with police. He was quite up to defending the status quo, but given he was returning to the ship and *Georg* and quite probably not returning home for many weeks, he did not wish their parting to be anything but loving. He looked down at Maria, still lying on his chest, her dark hair, dishevelled, enticing. She continued the one-sided discussion, while he concentrated on touching her hair. He ran his fingers through it, silky smooth, letting strands caress his hand. 'Maria, all things will come to pass,' he said, in a much quieter tone. 'We can only play our parts as we see best. I am an officer of the Imperial Navy and must do my duty. I and my officers cannot speculate on the future of the Kaiser or such matters. To do so might well be seen as, well, mutiny … or rebellion, perhaps even treason.' He hoped this would deflect Maria from further discussion, but to encourage that he sought out her lips.

Breakfast was a spartan affair, attended by white-haired, 62-year-old Else Schirmer, the household's maidservant, who'd been with them for over fifteen years. Else was now the Körner's only servant and an integral component of the family. Alfred, their other servant, had long since joined up and, the last they'd heard, was on the Western Front. Maria spoke at length about rations and the plethora of ration cards, the rising cost of food, its scarcity and how those on the farms must be keeping produce back for themselves, to which Körner largely concurred if only to avoid a debate.

Dark-haired Viktoria, in her nursing outfit, said little, her mind seemed elsewhere. Körner engaged her in incidental talk, all the while trying to avoid any gory details about her hospital job. She obliged, saying nothing to distress her mother or brothers, except that the hospital was crammed to bursting with war-wounded. He was proud that she'd taken on such work, at her own request, but worried that she was seeing altogether too much life as a result. She had grown into a beautiful young woman, who should be enjoying life, probably being courted by young men, not seeing them mangled by war.

Hans wolfed down the meagre fare, accepting his father's offer of bread from his plate. Körner knew that since the start of the war, bread wheat flour had been adulterated with large amounts of rye and potato flour. He despaired at what other novel ingredients it might now consist of. As a naval officer and captain, Körner had adequate, indeed too good food on board his ship. Seeing his children eating, he was embarrassed by his own shipboard fare and always concerned at the impact his visits home would have on the family's supplies. Having some wealth, additional food could be obtained, but almost everything, not only food, was now subject to some rationing. A lot of the breakfast discussion was about food, especially what they'd like to eat. Maria thanked and praised Else for queuing for many hours to get various foodstuffs. Else, like a second mother to the children, downplayed her part, though Maria had told Körner that Else had on more than one occasion begun queuing soon after midnight to be there when the shops opened.

Hans questioned Körner about the *Hindenburg*, her speed, her guns and their range, and how she compared with other new battleships in the fleet. Körner gave evasive answers, expecting Manfred to jump in. Manfred said nothing on the subject, but then laughed when Körner replied to Hans in an officious, Tirpitz-like voice, mimicking the great man's forked beard with his hands, that there would be serious consequences to any sailor who gave out such details.

Despite the changes to family life the war had brought, Körner was happy beyond words to be with his loved ones. Of late, he now viewed himself to have been a fairly stern father in former times, probably not unlike his own father, but the war had increasingly made him more aware of the importance of these moments. He could not compare himself to, say, a colonel in the army and the muddy life in the trenches, facing death on a daily basis. He expected that that officer would gladly exchange positions with him, if he knew that a senior naval officer like him had a good chance of reasonably regularly seeing his family or making love to his wife. In a few days, he would take the *Hindenburg* out. This time, differently from all other times, he wondered when he would see them all again.

As the breakfast chatter continued and Else cleared cups and plates from the table, Körner re-ran yesterday's events in his mind. At least they had given him the opportunity for this precious interlude. There had been an important meeting to review the progress on *Georg*, important because Admiral Scheer attended, along with Hipper and other gold braid. Developments to date were presented and questioned, the next steps were also discussed and approved. Various issues were still to be resolved, but, despite reportedly satisfactory U-boat results, victory was still not in sight and meant there was sufficient reason to push forward with *Georg*. Scheer confirmed that approval had at last been obtained from the Kaiser, though a crucial factor had been support from the High Command, who were keen on any action which could inhibit the transportation of American soldiers to the Western Front. Like many in Germany, Körner increasingly viewed the High Command—Field Marshal von Hindenburg (in whose honour the *Hindenburg* had been named) and General Ludendorff—as the true power in the land.

Maria interrupted his thoughts: 'More tea, Rupprecht?'

'Thank you,' he replied with enthusiasm, not wishing to seem too far away, offering up his cup for the *ersatz* concoction. As with the bread, he wondered what type of leaves or other products had been used to make the 'tea'.

As he sipped his drink, he eyed the children, though his thoughts quickly turned back to the *Hindenburg*. He would return to her today. In anticipation of approval for *Georg*, some work on her had been undertaken, which had allowed him to enjoy this brief piece of home life. He could not help going over the meeting and events of recent weeks. The meeting had ended just short of three hours. He'd been asked many questions, none of which he could not answer, but that did not mean everything was satisfactory. In many respects, his task seemed easier than others', though it would be the *Hindenburg*'s achievements out in the

Atlantic that would determine the success of events. He and Schellenberg had worked hard on the preparations for *Georg*, liaising with Bünzlin and his staff and meeting other select players involved in the great enterprise. The plan shaped up quite quickly, going beyond the original work Körner had done, and the real credit for it went to Bünzlin's staff. A full study had been done, working up all its dimensions. It was becoming difficult to keep the operation a complete secret on the *Hindenburg*, without some other support from the ship's officers. Schellenberg was increasingly reporting rumours that were circulating. Despite the secrecy slapped on *Georg*, tongues had obviously been wagging and, of course, different things were happening on the ship. New and unusual visitors had come aboard and it had become necessary to involve some other officers, but without revealing to them the exact nature of *Georg*. The crew must be noticing such developments. With Körner's agreement, Schellenberg let it slip that the ship was shaping up for a training cruise in the Baltic. There was truth in it and it would suppress some of the mess-deck speculation.

As captain, Körner had considerable personal freedom and, to his officers and crew, an almost god-like status. He endeavoured not to abuse his position and the opportunities it presented, for fear it sent the wrong the message to those in his command. He sought an efficient ship, but held back from 'ruling with a rod of iron'. He would punish those who stepped out of line or were clearly not up to scratch, but was keen not to break men's spirit. He was aware of what other captains did, aware that some were virtual tyrants. During the 1917 mutinies, it would appear that one battleship captain had suffered for his approach. He was found dead in a ship's boat, with his head bashed in. Körner was not worried that the same fate awaited him on some dark gangway, but crew morale was always something he watched, even though it was primarily Schellenberg's responsibility. That said, as captain, he was somewhat remote from the crew, as well as his officers, but enjoyed the benefits of coming home whenever he could. A good proportion of the crew had been given leave while the short refit was underway, though by the time they journeyed by rail to various corners of Germany, no doubt making multiple changes at cold, draughty stations, many would have had precious little time with wives and families.

Soon after the war began, Maria started not to ask when Körner might be back home. In any event, he was always evasive on such matters. For example, he had not told her that Hipper had shifted his flag to the *Seydlitz*. He was returning to his ship, that she knew. Maria assisted him with his coat and busied herself with ensuring he looked the part of a great sea captain, straightening his collar and brushing his coat as she felt necessary. Körner did not seek such attention, but was content for her to do such things, if she gained something from them, though was always happy to be well turned out. As he always did on leaving them, Körner lovingly wished each of the children well, kissing Viktoria on the cheek, a grown-up shaking of hands with Hans, but embracing young Manfred.

In the hallway, he looked at Maria, soaking up her beauty, re-imprinting her face and form on his mind. He had not intended such, but unlike previous separations he felt a special desire to take her image, smell, anything about her with him. They embraced as normal on such occasions, though Körner thought Maria's grip of his arm somewhat stronger. They had one quite passionate kiss in the hallway, which Maria cut short when Manfred interrupted them to say good-bye again to his father. As he walked down the street, Körner turned and, seeing Maria and Manfred still in the doorway watching him, gave them a strong wave, unusual for him.

4

Norway

The fog was too thick, visibility less than 100 metres; all ships had been signalled to anchor. Körner was not pleased and not just because of anchoring out at sea. It was not clear how long they would be held here and all the time fuel would be consumed, though he well knew that at this stage such concerns were highly unlikely to be vital to the *Hindenburg*. What was of more concern was that there was the potential for the Fleet sortie to be called off and who could say when the next opportunity might arise for *Georg*, not to mention that all the preparations would have to be revisited, if they could. He tried to remain calm, walking the few steps to the starboard wing of the Command Bridge. There was that eerie silence which accompanied the fog; the sea, almost flat, soundlessly caressed the ship's sides. From the wing, he could see nothing but the blurred shape of a destroyer to starboard. He knew the *Seydlitz*, Hipper's flagship, was ahead, with the *Moltke* astern, but they were lost in the murk. It had been quite remarkable that they had been brought to a halt in this visibility, using only visual signals. Schellenberg approached him.

'The fog could lift at any time, Captain. I think it's already clearer than when we anchored,' said the *Fregattenkapitän*, perhaps sensing Körner's anxiety.

'You're right,' replied Körner, his mood visibly lightening. 'I was thinking of the fuel situation, but really it doesn't matter. We've only been here twenty minutes. The Fleet's appointment with the English cannot be delayed. So,' he lowered his voice, 'we'll either sail soon or the whole enterprise will be cancelled and we may have to go back to the beginning … if we are given the chance.'

Körner went below to his Day Cabin. With the absence of Hipper, he could have moved into the slightly larger Admiral's quarters, but he was comfortable in his quarters. In any event, the quarters for the admiral and his staff were now occupied by additional officers. Dahl provided him with a cup of coffee. As he sipped the hot drink, he gazed at a very small sepia-coloured picture hanging above his desk of Maria and the children, taken a few years before the war. He had taken it from those on the dresser at home, when he moved into the *Hindenburg* to replace the other more recent snaps lost with the *Potsdam*. How the children had grown. Maria, gorgeous as ever, sat in a chair, surrounded by the three children. It was posed and stiff, but was a tangible link to his family.

He looked out of the scuttle, the mist made the glass seem frosted. He had actually hoped fog might help the breakout, but had not really considered it stopping the operation on the start line. He chastised himself, telling himself to focus on the breakout and forget about it being cancelled, though he could not suppress thoughts of the months of preparation and the myriad of subjects that had had to be addressed. Any one of these, if not carefully attended to, might fatally damage *Georg* in preparation or execution. One important setback had occurred.

During the ship's short refit at Kiel, less than a month ago, Bünzlin had joined him to update him on what had transpired while the ship was training in the Baltic. He told Körner the viability of *Georg* had been raised yet again. Körner was not at all surprised to hear that the Kaiser had swung backwards and forwards, always concerned about *his* navy and possible damage to one of *his* dreadnoughts, never mind losing one. Even Scheer, though dedicated to the Fleet supporting the U-boat campaign, still had concerns about action on the American coast. However, with strong encouragement from the High Command, Bünzlin reported that some sense had prevailed and approval given to the Fleet's Norway sortie, with *Georg* proceeding if the outcome of that part of the plan was successful. Körner was pleased that he personally had not had to argue the case for *Georg* and genuinely thanked Bünzlin for all his efforts, though had tried not to ponder the eventual outcome and concentrated on the never-ending tasks ahead.

The Fleet's Norway sortie was Bünzlin's proposal, sparked by the success of the cruiser and destroyer convoy attacks of late 1917. It was selected as an ideal way both to strike again at the enemy's Norway to Scotland convoys and to cover the release of the *Hindenburg* into the Atlantic. Hipper's Scouting Force, with Scheer's battleships nearby, would attack one of the convoys. Destroying another convoy and the escort would be a great victory, especially useful at this time, and complement the army's massive offensive on the Western Front. Once the enemy convoy was destroyed, the Fleet would then depart the scene, head back to base, before the Grand Fleet could intervene. At that point, if not before, the *Hindenburg* would be detached and quickly speed away on an opposite course, with the English, seeking out the Fleet, hopefully looking in the wrong direction.

The planning for *Georg* had continued all these months. Bünzlin and other staff officers had done much of that work, allowing Körner to concentrate on sharpening up the *Hindenburg*. Among other things, this involved intensive training exercises in the Baltic and absorbing additional crew, some with quite specialist knowledge, some others to act as prize crews. On conclusion of their Baltic manoeuvres, the *Hindenburg* had put into Kiel for a final, short refit. The extra crew, Baltic activities and the admittance of more ship's officers into the planning for *Georg* had Schellenberg reporting much speculation amongst the crew on what was going on. He and Körner decided, with a little regret, to restrict the crew to the ship or barracks while they were in Kiel. No point in rumours of *Georg* getting out.

While in Kiel, Körner was able to meet with the captains of the supply ships. They had exercised with the battle cruiser in the Baltic and were then filling their bunkers and taking on other necessities in Kiel, prior to leaving for the Atlantic. The supply ships would replenish the *Hindenburg*'s coal and oil, as well as some ammunition, food and other requirements, and were crucial factors in *Georg*. Unlike other ships that had gone out to attack the enemy's merchant shipping and could sustain themselves with their own resources or through their captives' cargoes, *Georg*'s planning had determined that the *Hindenburg*'s needs were much greater and unlikely to be satisfied through *ad hoc* captures. Consequently, Körner was especially interested in the supply ships' preparations, particularly their breakout and rendezvous arrangements. It went without saying that if the ships failed to make it past the enemy's patrols, then *Georg* was effectively cancelled before the *Hindenburg* sailed.

The supply ships were suitable merchant ships, crewed by navy officers and men. There had been precious little time to identify appropriate ships, but three existing navy colliers were selected and speedily adapted for *Georg*. Although the ships could probably function well enough, crewing was the most difficult issue. Given the time for training, volunteers from the ships' existing crews were used, with additional navy officers and men as necessary. Bünzlin's staff had been working with the ships' captains and convinced Körner that their breakout plans were sound. Although time was short, Bünzlin considered that the new captains had done very well and got their ships and crews ready for the task.

One issue that Körner had also taken to heart and which he had especially stressed to the supply ships' captains when he met them was Bünzlin's concerns about wireless telegraphy. From an early stage Bünzlin had reasoned that the Fleet's wireless use was a risk to operations. Körner knew that concern about the enemy's direction-finding stations had during the last year led to restricted use of wireless by the Fleet; some U-boats were even ordered not to use W/T, except for emergencies. However, Bünzlin had told Körner of a possibly greater concern about wireless usage. When he was in Prince Heinrich's Baltic command, Bünzlin was alerted to their concerns that the Fleet's codes may have been compromised when the cruiser *Magdeburg* was lost in the Baltic at the start of the war. He said Prince Heinrich's protestations had fallen on deaf ears. Körner fully accepted that the direction-finding issue was a concern. It now seemed very likely that, like the few Germany operated, the English had even more stations spread along their longer North Sea coasts and it would be relatively easy to pick up German wireless transmissions and triangulate the sender's position. He was less sold on the possibility that German codes had been compromised. It seemed most improbable. He'd not looked into it in any depth, but was assured by others that there was nothing to worry about. Surely codes would have been changed or otherwise secured, he reckoned, especially after several years. In any event, his ship and the supply ships would operate on codes used by raiders, which were not the normal Fleet codes. However, with so much at stake, Körner had agreed with Bünzlin's proposal that total wireless silence was the best and safest policy, only breaking wireless silence when absolutely necessary or the ship's position was definitely known to the enemy. The Fleet was now adopting wireless silence during sorties. It seemed an entirely sensible tactic. At the very least, such an approach would avoid the very real direction-finding problem. All four ships would operate on new, simple call-signs, but would maintain wireless silence if at all possible, meeting each other at pre-arranged rendezvous positions.

In Kiel, Körner and Bünzlin had also met with *Fregattenkapitän* Karl Nerger, the recently returned and much fêted and decorated hero of the auxiliary cruiser *Wolf.* Nerger had taken his armed merchant ship on a 15-month cruise half-way round the world and back, capturing ships and sowing mines at various places that sank others. Although their missions and ships were quite different, their discussion was most valuable, providing many useful insights for *Georg.* For example, not only had Nerger maintained wireless silence throughout his voyage, but had broken out into the Atlantic by the same route intended for the *Hindenburg.* Körner was especially interested in Nerger's description of the exploits of the *Wolf*'s seaplane that played an important role in the raider's voyage.

Despite all these preparations and precautions, Körner knew that all had not gone well with the breakouts by the supply ships—the first real problem for *Georg.* They had sailed at different times over the last three weeks. All seemed to have gone well with the first two, the *Torsten Meyer* and the *Erda,* at least nothing to the contrary had been heard. A week ago, the last ship, the *Seefahrerin,* appeared to have been lost, perhaps intercepted or captured. A short and garbled message received from the ship raised the alarm, but provided insufficient information, except that she, like the other supply ships, would only break wireless silence if their orders were compromised. Attempts since to contact the *Seefahrerin* had all proved negative. There was considerable debate about what had befallen her. However, with a lack of facts and nothing forthcoming from enemy signals, a mine was thought the most likely cause of her loss. To counter the threats posed by interception at any stage, the supply ships were to scuttle themselves if capture seemed imminent. They were supposed to send a simple signal to indicate their predicament, but either the *Seefahrerin*'s message was not picked up by anyone or she must have been overwhelmed before they had a chance to send one. As with all the supply ships, she was carrying a limited quantity of shells and their propellant charges for the *Hindenburg*'s big guns and there was some discussion about whether this could have exploded and hastened her end.

The *Seefahrerin*'s role in *Georg* saw her going through the Iceland-Faroes gap and waiting off southern Greenland to provide a refuelling option on the *Hindenburg*'s return to Germany. Without her, a hole opened that had to be filled. The loss of a supply ship had been anticipated, but the other two ships were deemed sufficient, though it meant a change in their deployment. Bünzlin's staff had produced options to cope with the loss of any one ship and a revision agreed which allowed *Georg* to proceed, but it was agreed that it could delay the *Hindenburg*'s passage into the Atlantic.

News of the *Seefahrerin* was not just a setback for the *Hindenburg*'s mission, but potentially to the Fleet's covering action, which, of course, also threatened *Georg*. In the few days before the sortie, there was much discussion about its wider implications. Signals sent to the other two ships on the revised proposal for their use, helped to end the debate, but heightened the concern of how to proceed if either of them was lost. In the event of further losses, Körner could abort the mission or seek supplies from captured ships.

So *Georg* was still on, unless other information came to hand. It was considered likely that the *Seefahrerin*'s true mission had not been uncovered. All concluded that if the English were directly responsible for her loss and, short of capturing her intact, they would see her as yet another auxiliary cruiser or even minelayer endeavouring to get out into the Atlantic or waters around Britain. While the *Möwe* and the *Wolf* had both been successful in this, others, the *Greif* and the *Leopard*, were intercepted and lost.

As Körner mulled over this failure, hoping it was not a bad portent, he stared at the bare for'ard bulkhead of his cabin and its single adornment, the photograph of Maria and the children, when the voice pipe's whistle summoned him.

'Schellenberg here, Sir. We're on the move. The flagship has signalled us all to get underway.'

Quite soon, visibility was several kilometres. Eckhardt could now see the First Scouting Group's big ships were all underway, signal flags aloft. A torpedo-boat was approaching their starboard quarter, intending to cross astern of the battle cruiser, he expected. An officer called everyone's attention to the threat of submarines. As he watched the water, half-expecting to see that telltale stream of bubbles, he, sarcastically and silently, wondered how far the Fleet would get this time, though he immediately rebuked himself. The *Hindenburg* had only just rejoined the Fleet from her time in the Baltic. Perhaps things would be different, but when would he get back to the Baltic, he thought. More specifically, when would he get leave to go home—and see Anna? To have been so close and yet so far. The Baltic exercises had been a welcome change from what had been an increasingly restricted situation in Wilhelmshaven and the North Sea. A welcome change, but frustrating. They'd steamed as far as East Prussia. Eckhardt had hoped they'd put in somewhere along the Baltic coast, Danzig perhaps, where he might have been able to get leave to visit his family. As he feared, while they had stopped at several places, mostly sheltered, deserted bays around the island of Rügen, this was only to coal and replenish the ship. The prospect of getting home and especially being so near, rather than the long train journey from Wilhelmshaven, had depressed him. Although he knew the ship would have passed Stolpmünde, on both legs of the voyage, they were far too far out to sea even to catch a glimpse of his home town. When the ship returned to Kiel for several days, like so many of the crew, but especially so, he was infuriated by the order that there was to be no shore leave, though, as always, this restriction didn't affect officers and deck officers. At one point, he'd felt brave enough about putting forward a request to be allowed to visit home, but then easily dissuaded himself. Now he wished he had; at least he wouldn't be kicking himself for not even trying.

To Eckhardt, the only good part of the Baltic operation had been the trip back through the Canal. The Kaiser Wilhelm Canal, Germany's strategic waterway, enabling warships to travel safely from the North Sea to the Baltic, gave the whole crew a measure of relaxation. The 100-kilometre, day-long journey was almost like a river pleasure cruise. Picking up a pilot at the Kiel-Holtenau locks, the ship steamed slowly along the 100-metre-wide canal. Even at their slow speed, the ship's wash beat at the shore, creating three or four waves that seemed to follow them like some tidal bore. At some points, the banks were elevated, well above the Canal, and they also passed under high railway bridges, but for most of the western section, he could view the surrounding flat country, its fields and thatched cottages from his high position. When peasants, especially women, waved at the ship, these were returned enthusiastically by the crew. It was all a tranquil, somewhat unreal situation; a giant warship steaming serenely along a flat-calm, inland waterway was a sight as far as one could imagine from the war at sea. Eckhardt recalled that, for him and the crew, it was only marred by an unnecessary uniform inspection. Couldn't the officers let up for once?

Later that day in the mess deck, while Eckhardt heard some discussion on the pernickety nature of the day's inspection, most of his shipmates were otherwise engaged. At one corner of an adjoining mess table, he noted two of the older men somewhat detached from the others intently debating the finer points of one's latest knitting creation, a decorated sweater. As a fisherman, Eckhardt had some sewing capability, but had never really mastered knitting, often being unable to cast-on. On joining the navy he had been truly surprised to find that many sailors were very adept at knitting, probably even better at it than most women, he thought. However, the main talking point which was generating much heat amongst the men on his table was the ongoing debate about what was in store for the ship.

'Yes! It's obvious we're heading back to Wilhelmshaven. That bloody Deck Officer, Knappe, suggested as much,' said Beyer, a short, thick set, moustachioed, balding and outspoken individual.

'That's bleeding obvious,' Kardorf injected quickly, 'but what are all these extra crew for? If you ask me, there's an operation brewing. Something big, I reckon. We haven't been sailing around the Baltic in preparation for Kiel Week!'

This was readily agreed by all. Eckhardt always viewed Beyer and Kardorf as *the* mess orators, always first to raise concerns, voice opinions on the latest theories or just generally stir up discussion and emotions. However, he couldn't deny that the Baltic exercises, along with new officers and crew who had joined before and since had greatly increased the normal level of rumour and speculation. The four weeks in the Baltic had been non-stop activity, with numerous exercises. There'd been the usual gunnery and damage-control exercises, but also simulated attacks on merchant ships and their escorts, not to mention the inevitable coaling, all in cold, bad weather. They'd also seen zeppelins, though the sight of a zeppelin was nothing new. The giant airships often provided reconnaissance for the Fleet in North Sea sorties. The zeppelins hadn't been the only aerial component of the exercises, the ship now had its own seaplane.

Feeling he should join in with his shipmates' increasingly animated discussion, Eckhardt was on the point of giving his view on things, though he knew he was only likely to reiterate what others had said, when Beyer leaned forward over the mess table, dominating the speaking arena, and, looking around at everyone, spoke quietly, but purposefully:

'Our recent exercises have me worried. They seem out of the ordinary. I reckon they must be in preparation for a sortie against the English.'

This brought comments of agreement from most.

He continued: 'I'm sure none of us fears a fight with the English navy, but this war may well be over soon. If all we hear is true, the army is winning on the Western Front and,' he half-smiled, 'our U-boats are starving England into submission. So, I ask, why should the Fleet seek battle with the English? I don't want to throw my life away needlessly or for that matter die for an officer corps which wants battle just to claim their share of the glory.'

While some concurred with this, Eckhardt noted again that some mumbled their response and some said nothing. He could see that the adjoining mess tables were also now listening in. Before long, the whole mess deck was involved. Eckhardt decided he would keep quiet amongst the hubbub.

Beyer rose to the new audience, enhancing his observations with hand and arm gestures: 'Men! We cannot die needlessly! Who amongst you thinks it's right to die, when we don't have to?'

Whilst he could not fail to agree, Eckhardt thought this brought a mixed response from the mess deck, with some agreeing loudly that a 'death or glory' mission was not for them, whereas some others even favoured another crack at the English. Otto Helmers, a thin, weather-beaten man, moustache-wearing like many, said what some must have been thinking: 'Do you realise that such talk could be seen as … mutiny?'

Beyer shot back: 'You watch your tongue. Is it mutiny to wish *not* to die? That's all we're discussing. Shouldn't men have a say in how they might die?' Before Helmers could respond, Beyer, with a flourish, swung his arms open to the assembled group: 'We love our ship, but,' he paused, 'we love life! Of course, we would fight the English, if, let's say, they attacked us as we left the Canal, but, if we are to go out and attack them so that our officers, our captains, our admirals can claim they played their part in the defeat of the English, I, for one, am against it if it leads to our ships being sunk and our comrades being blown to bits or drowned. Who's with me?'

'Who's with you on what, Beyer?' The booming voice of *Bootsmann*—bosun—Wenzel brought instant quiet to the mess deck, as he entered. The tall, barrel-chested Wenzel was not a man to anger and most men were wary of him. His face, showing his boxing past, was taken as evidence of his aggressiveness. 'And what's all the blasted racket?' said Wenzel, his face almost snarling, with challenge and menace.

'Er, we were just discussing what we might do … when we get back to Wilhelmshaven,' Beyer stuttered out. 'What … tavern we might go to.'

'That's a bloody laugh,' sneered Wenzel. With a raised eyebrow, he then said: 'I understand now. *You* would want to know *who's with me*, as you'll probably be looking to others to pay!'

Wenzel, half-chuckling to himself, looked around, disdainfully, at the dirty-faced assembly. No one ventured further commentary on the matter. The uninvited Wenzel, a look of derision on his face, said something under his breath and slowly turned and left as quickly as he had arrived.

Eckhardt remembered that he had sat quietly as Beyer tried to make light of Wenzel's intrusion and raise the debate again, but there had been no real takers. Wenzel's untimely interruption had poured oil on the water and all now realised that Helmers was right and there was danger in such talk.

The fog had lifted and the ship had picked up speed and changed course. An officer explained that the hold-up had been the danger to all of getting through their minefields in such fog, but Eckhardt was still thinking of Beyer and how this had transpired. When the ship had eased into its position in Wilhelmshaven, he thought little of the various groups of men waiting at the quayside. Hours later, after the obligatory coaling and when he was resting below decks, news had reached them all that several officers had come aboard and shortly afterwards led Beyer off the ship, in chains some said. The 1917 mutinies had been about food and officer indifference and aloofness, but also led to the setting up of the *Soldatenbund*—the Sailors' Councils. The problems of food and officer oppression still existed, but Eckhardt figured that Beyer's outburst was different, more a sort of workers' rights debate. The event, small in its own way, nevertheless stirred up some bad feeling, even if Beyer did not speak for the majority. Everyone expected he would face a court-martial. Would he also face a firing squad, as a few had last year? Helmers was right, but it looked like Beyer might be too. Here, the whole fleet was underway. It hadn't been to sea in such strength since 1916.

Other than a few hours in his Sea Cabin, Körner spent the night on the Bridge. By 5am, he judged the weather as brilliant for action. While there were some thin, white clouds smeared across the pale blue sky, there was ample sunshine and excellent visibility. The horizon was sharply defined. The sea was mostly blue, in comparison to its often grey vista. The wind, which had been a fairly strong, easterly breeze as they journeyed through the night, had now shifted to east-south-east and dropped to Force 4. The small waves, still streaked with white, did nothing to impede the mighty warships. Körner sensed that the officers on the Bridge seemed quite optimistic, even elated, by the Fleet sortie, seemingly with every prospect of a good outcome—and, for those who knew about it, the belief that *Georg* would soon begin in earnest.

Once through their minefields, they had sailed nor'-nor'-west and were now farther north than the Fleet had ever been in the war. From the plot, Körner could see they were almost level with Scapa Flow, over 400 kilometres to the west, that reportedly bleak, but huge anchorage of the Grand Fleet. He had mixed views about Intelligence's views that the bulk of the enemy's fleet was now located further south in the Firth of Forth. To starboard, about ninety kilometres away, lay the beautiful fjords of Norway. The Fleet knew that part of Norway well. Since 1910, almost every year before the war, the Kaiser had visited the fjords in his royal yacht, taking his battle fleet with him. The Fleet was dispersed over several fjords. Körner remembered with fondness the visits to the immense and picture-postcard Hardanger and Sogne Fjords as the *Moltke*'s first officer, where the visiting dreadnoughts were dwarfed by the high fjord walls.

The First Scouting Group, Hipper's battle cruisers, accompanied by the Second Scouting Group's light cruisers and destroyers, were nearly 100 kilometres ahead of Scheer's battle fleet. The ships were at Battle Stations. Everything seemed set for a momentous day. Körner enjoyed the spectacle of the moment. He focused his binoculars on the *Seydlitz*, 300 metres ahead, the sea churning up in her wake, destroyers on her flanks and, far ahead, almost at the horizon, a line of light cruisers searching. He expected a signal at any minute that would tell that they had found the quarry.

'A signal, Sir. From the *Moltke* to the flagship.'

Körner looked around. Bushy-eyebrowed *Leutnant* Reichelt stood, signal message in hand. Not expecting it to be much of concern for him, he asked: 'What's it say, then?'

Reichelt read out the message: 'Starboard engine out of action.'[1]

Without trying to second-guess the message, Körner went to the starboard Bridge wing. Looking aft through his binoculars, he could see the *Moltke*, about 500 metres behind. He endeavoured to gauge any drop in her speed. He had hardly started to discuss this development with Schellenberg, when Reichelt reported another signal lamp message from the battle cruiser: 'Midships engine out of action; water coming in; danger from steam; cause not yet ascertained.'[2]

It was clear the *Moltke* was in difficulty, she was falling behind. More signal lamp exchanges took place between the flagship and the *Moltke*. She now reported her engine room as full of water, but Hipper was obviously not to be stopped in completing his mission. The ailing battle cruiser was ordered to fall back on the battle fleet. An increase in speed was ordered to the rest of the Scouting Group and ships began to pass the *Moltke* and close up the line. Körner could not help wondering if this was all part of the fates conspiring against *Georg*.

Within a few minutes, Reichelt reported yet another signal lamp message, this one from the *von der Tann*: 'Cannot do more than twenty-one knots on account of bad coal, coal consumption fifty-percent higher than usual.'[3]

Schellenberg, anticipating his captain's next question, quickly reported that there were no such problems with the *Hindenburg*'s coal, which for *Georg* was best quality. However, this latest situation was soon followed by a signal from the flagship to all ships to reduce speed to 15 knots, obviously to allow the *von der Tann* to keep up.

'What next?' said Körner, his frustration mounting. Looking over towards far-away Norway, he added, 'I hope the Norse gods are not determined to prevent us going about our business this day.'

'If I know my Thor, Captain,' responded Schellenberg, smiling, 'he would be keen to see some action.'

The search continued, but without any sightings. An hour and a half since those first signals from the *Moltke*, there was another, this time Reichelt reported it as sent by wireless: 'Breakdown serious. Speed only four knots.'[4]

'Well, what was that you said about Thor? Perhaps he does want to see some action,' Körner half-joked to Schellenberg. 'Breaking wireless silence will no doubt bring out the English. They'll know for sure we're out here now.'

'But we still have a lot of sea between us, even if they do come out,' replied Schellenberg.

Nevertheless, even if the English were now alerted, the new development did not stop Hipper; the battle cruisers kept on, searching for their prey. This northerly route also seemed, to Körner, to make *Georg* more likely, but that was dashed when another wireless message came in, saying the *Moltke* was now 'out of control'.[5] At this Hipper turned his ships about. Dashing south, after another hour they came within sight of the *Moltke* and then Scheer's battleships, which were now preparing to assist the stricken ship. Scheer sent his own signal: 'Continue operation.'[6]

So, Hipper turned his ships about, increased speed to 18 knots and resumed his search for the elusive convoy. The weather continued to be excellent for the day's hunting. Despite troubles on the *Moltke*, there still seemed every prospect for a successful outcome to a convoy action, *if* one could be found. While that might have suited Hipper, Körner now all but gave up on *Georg*, believing too many events had happened and too many opportunities had passed to release the

Hindenburg and that his admiral, advised by Bünzlin on board the flagship, must have decided that the ship was too valuable to the Scouting Force. Yet another event: an Admiralty signal pointed to a large group of ships assembling off south-west Norway, which took the light cruisers to almost within sight of the coast, but again without result. It looked as if there was no convoy to be found. Körner thought that, with the weather conditions as they were, the convoy sailing must have been drastically altered or rescheduled, otherwise they must have sighted it. Soon after 2pm, Hipper signalled all ships to follow him south-east. At that point they were not far short of 60 degrees North, abreast of Hardanger Fjord.

Reichelt came up to Körner. He looked quizzically at his captain. 'Signal from the flagship, Sir. It says Georg. Good Luck.'

Körner, re-animated, quickly gave an order. The *Hindenburg* turned to port, pulling out of the line, heading north, passing the other battle cruisers as they went south.

5

Rendezvous

Eckhardt and Schwarz glanced questioningly at each other, though had no permission to discuss then and there all they had just witnessed from their high viewpoint. When the ship left the line, Eckhardt at first imagined it was probably because of orders to move to the rear of the line where the ship's strength would be of value in confronting any pursuit by the English. However, as the ship continued on its northerly course and quickly began to open up a gap with the Scouting Force, he was obliged to think otherwise. He risked a quick look at the officers around him, half-expecting them to explain to their underlings what was happening. While they obviously saw the turn of events, they said nothing, their faces displaying no obvious surprise or other emotion which might suggest they were equally intrigued by what was going on. They must know, he thought. He wanted to ask them, but knew better. As he considered what was happening, he took a last look at the departing ships, now partially obscured by the funnel smoke the *Hindenburg* was pumping out. At a combined speed of well over 30 knots, Hipper's ships were soon hull down and then gone, only their funnel smoke marking their distant presence.

Eckhardt was readily able to deliberate the situation by himself, without others' input. On reflection, he had plenty of information that previously seemed uncoordinated, but with each new piece of the puzzle in place he had at least an indication of the bigger picture. The ongoing mess-deck debates, fuelled by much speculation and loose-lipped titbits from those thought to be in the know, had correctly pointed to a sortie, though expectedly as part of a Fleet operation, as they'd never sailed into the North Sea alone throughout the war. Even the loss of flagship status could now be seen as part of what was now transpiring. The last coaling, only a day before departure from Wilhelmshaven, had not seemed particularly out of the ordinary, but the call to load the bunkers 'till they burst'— to the fears of those trimming them inside—now indicated a need for maximum range. Perhaps nothing too unusual, but now steaming alone, out of the North Sea, he realised they must be on a mission beyond normal expectations. A long-range operation would also explain the other supplies of additional food and clothing they'd taken on board. After their Baltic training, these factors were at first taken as a new standard of provisioning or, as more facts became known, as a requirement for the expected Fleet sortie.

The seaplane that now sat in its canvas box on the Boat Deck was, on reflection, also seen as further evidence of something special afoot. In the weeks before they'd sailed for the Baltic, word quickly reached Eckhardt that some crewmen from the *Santa Elena*, one of the Fleet's few seaplane carriers, only recently transferred from the Baltic to Wilhelmshaven, had come aboard to assist in the construction of a canvas-covered structure on the port side of the Boat Deck, stretching back between the funnels. It seemed no easy task and had required the relocation and landing of some of the ship's boats. He went on leave for a few days—wasted, as it transpired, as there proved insufficient time to get home—but by his return, the box, a *hangar*, was complete. It was not dissimilar to the two box-shaped ones that could be seen on the *Santa Elena*, though Eckhardt thought the *Hindenburg*'s looked a bit more flimsy than those on the converted merchantman. Its top and fore and aft sides seemed robust, quite solid, though the port and starboard walls were more curtain-like affairs. It was obvious, he and his mates debated, that a plane would be housed there, though no one at that stage read much into it, as seaplanes had occasionally been carried by other battle cruisers. There was further discussion, but no surprise, when news reached them that some officers and men had come aboard as pilots and maintenance crew for the plane. The speculations continued afresh with news that a dismantled plane, delivered in various large crates, had also been brought aboard. The arrival of the real thing, an actual flying plane, was something that did get everyone talking, but again it generated no great insight into what was ahead.

Late one afternoon, as the battle cruiser waited in Voslapp Roads, just outside Wilhelmshaven, a single-engined biplane had alighted near the ship. Like those who could, Eckhardt had watched with interest as the blue, grey and black-camouflaged, twin-float plane taxied up to the ship's port side. A line was attached and a derrick raised the plane with its two-man crew up onto the ship. This finally convinced the few sceptics about the reasons for the structure that had been erected on the Boat Deck, along with a new, long-arm derrick. During the following weeks, as they exercised in the Baltic, the plane had been used on many occasions, disappearing into the distance and returning after several hours. The crew became quite attached to their '*Little Ludo*', as a few called it after Field Marshal Hindenburg's sidekick General Ludendorff, watching its take-offs and landings with interest, though many were somewhat doubtful about its real value.

Amongst all this crew debate, Helmers, perhaps now buoyed up by his mutiny prediction, had voiced the amazing idea that they were off into the Atlantic, perhaps to attack ships off the American coast or even to bombard American cities, like they had when the Fleet bombarded English coastal towns in 1914. He was roundly shouted down, even ridiculed, by the mess deck for such 'daft' thinking. Eckhardt had certainly smiled and then joined in the scoffing at these suggestions. He agreed that the Atlantic, never mind America, was 'too far' and for what purpose? His own ideas, now refined by recent events, suggested some strike at the enemy, but the what and where eluded him. His best thoughts were that the *Hindenburg* was some kind of decoy or bait to draw the English fleet away or split it up, allowing the Fleet to ambush a small part of it or strike elsewhere.

␩

After an hour and a half, Körner ordered course altered a point to westward, but kept speed at 18 knots. This adjustment to the ship's heading paralleled the Norwegian coast about 100 kilometres away. He wanted to get away from Norwegian waters quickly and, therefore, could not reduce to a more economical cruising speed, but was content that others were responsible for monitoring and reporting to him on the ship's fuel consumption. The Norway-Shetland gap was not much more than 150 sea miles. Still quite a bit of sea, as he looked at it, but that much closer to the enemy. Once he was passed that imaginary line, he could think again about reducing speed.

From the port side of the Bridge, he swung his binoculars across the western horizon, imagining he might see something his look-outs didn't. There was nothing. The sea was empty. The weather was much the same as it had been all day: moderate easterly wind, largely clear sky and good visibility, with a rising barometer. Now, he joked to himself, he needed the fog they'd run into when they left Wilhelmshaven.

Till they reached the Norwegian Sea, Körner kept the ship at a high state of readiness: everyone remained at their posts, look-outs straining to ensure they saw everything, telegraphists listening for any transmission that might indicate a nearby ship and gun crews ready to engage the enemy. All during the war, the English had maintained blockade patrols across these seas to prevent merchant ships bringing sustenance to Germany. Intelligence and U-boat reports indicated that the patrols had been reduced since America's entry into the war, as all traffic now leaving that country was reportedly checked for contraband and approved before sailing. Körner could take no chances. He had to ensure that nothing prevented the breakout. While he deplored the clear weather, it also gave his look-outs ample opportunity to spot a ship at the earliest moment, perhaps allowing him to turn away before being sighted in turn.

Four hours later nothing had been reported. There had been no sightings and wireless transmissions had revealed nothing of concern. Then the ship swung hard to starboard. Körner, in his Sea Cabin at the rear of the Bridge, quickly came out.

'A periscope was reported off the port quarter, Captain, so I ordered a turn to bring our stern towards the sighting,' explained Schellenberg. 'No further sighting on the contact.'

Perhaps it was the mission or a view that his personal input was required, but Körner could not resist looking aft. Despite the evening hour, the light was still good. He could see nothing. The sea seemed calm enough to make sighting a periscope relatively easy. Like so many submarine sightings, a frequent occurrence in this war, he reckoned most were probably illusory. They were most likely just an odd wave spray, a piece of wood—both he and Schellenberg had seen brooms floating, handle upright, in the water, giving an excellent impression of a periscope—or, in the current circumstances, just look-outs being extra keen. It also seemed unlikely to him that the English would remove their submarines from their normal hunting grounds in the North Sea, but he had earlier convinced himself that it would be folly to ignore the possibility of the undersea threat.

'Well done ... and please pass that on to the look-out,' smiled Körner. 'It may well be nothing, but we'll keep on this heading for another twenty minutes, before resuming our course.' Körner then took Schellenberg to a quiet corner of the Bridge. 'As we've heard nothing about the English catching the Fleet, they must be safely on their way back to Wilhelmshaven. Equally, there seems nothing as yet to indicate that the English have discerned that we are no longer with the Fleet or that we are at sea. That is all for the good, but I realise that the crew must be asking what's going on?'

Schellenberg nodded, but added, 'Actually, while there have been rumours circulating for some time about our mission, since we broke away from the Fleet, I haven't encountered anything that questions our change of course. Nevertheless, as time draws on there must increasingly be more debate about what we're up to. Some word of our plans may well slip out.'

Körner expected as much, sailors being sailors. 'Some officers are fully in the picture, others less so,' he said, 'but the men have no real insight into why the ship is heading north ... and alone. It's not my way to keep the crew informed about proposed plans, but, given the unique circumstances, we need all to be fully committed and for morale to be maintained at a high level. Who knows what lies ahead? I propose to speak to all officers, so that they can brief their men.'

Schellenberg readily concurred with Körner's proposal to make a general announcement of what was planned. He agreed that it was warranted by the situation.

There was no need to rush the matter, but within the hour, while Schellenberg and some other officers watched over the sea and ship, Körner met most of the rest in the officers' mess in the *Oberdeck* superstructure. The Paymaster's staff had prepared a short note for issue to each of them, summarising what he was to say. Körner intended only to give a short commentary on the mission that, in addition to the note, he thought would reduce the opportunity for inaccurate feedback or unwarranted embellishment when they passed on his message. It was a crowded session, with most standing, but all waited quietly and attentively, as Körner spoke.

'Gentlemen. Some of you are aware of the reason why we are steaming north on our own, others of you perhaps less so. As you will appreciate, our plans demanded as much secrecy as possible and for that reason they have been kept from you ... and the crew.' He paused for a few moments, then said, 'We are now engaged in Operation *Georg*. The purpose of *Georg* is to disrupt the enemy's convoy system.' He noticed a few raised eyebrows on the faces of some of the young midshipmen. Disbelief or interest, fear or elation, he wondered. 'We are now heading to rendezvous with our supply ships. Two supply ships have been sent out ahead of us.' He saw no reason to inform them of the *Seefahrerin*'s loss. 'We will refuel from them. We shall then sail into the Atlantic and seek out and attack the enemy's convoys. This will undoubtedly affect the enemy's convoy traffic and further depress the English morale ... and it will offer new opportunities to our U-boats and the Fleet.' He held his hands behind his back and looked purposively at his audience. Then, going beyond the prepared note, said, 'This is a unique mission for the Fleet and a singular honour for our ship. We were selected as *the* best ship for such a mission. Not surprisingly, in my opinion.' Körner looked around, pleased to see some smiles and nodding heads at this. 'With this mission,' he continued, 'we can play a great part in winning the war. It goes without saying that there will be challenges ahead, but I am confident that this ship, its officers and men can deal with all of them. Under the circumstances, it's not possible to assemble the crew on the Quarter Deck and explain all this to them, so I ask you to pass on the information to your men. The crew, indeed all of us, will have to endure hardships we don't normally encounter. I'm thinking here of the many more days and nights we'll be at sea than normal and that, for example, the men will be using their hammocks all that time and not getting the extra comfort of being housed ashore when we're in harbour. If they can endure all that the coming time can throw at us, they will have participated in an operation that will help Germany bring this war to a glorious and victorious end.'

P

Eckhardt reported for his Afternoon Watch, in the middle section of the three-layer Spotting Top. As usual on any of his watches, he assessed the state of the ship and sea. All seemed in order, with main turrets fore and aft, as if on manoeuvres. He judged her speed to be thirteen or fourteen knots, about their best cruising speed. The ship's heading was still a half-point north of west by north. They'd been on this course since a change during yesterday's Second Dog Watch.

They were now well beyond the boundaries of the North Sea. It was undoubtedly cold, but Eckhardt was surprised that the weather was not as bad or as cold as he'd expected. The wind was now more south-easterly, though perhaps a little stronger than yesterday, he judged. The following sea was showing numerous whitecaps, with spray, but no great waves. The sea's colour was slate-grey, compared to yesterday's blue. The sky ahead was largely clear, but to port some distant clouds seemed, with the prevailing wind, to threaten a change of weather in the next day or so.

They'd had two sunrises since leaving the Fleet off Norway. The mess deck grumbles that first night about why they were heading north had, unsurprisingly, not been entirely put to bed by the revelations given out by their officer the next morning. Eckhardt was not shocked by the news that he was on a ship heading out into the Atlantic. He had already figured out that they were on some special mission. Between watches, the difficulties of the task, mainly about finding a convoy to attack, had occasionally come to mind. Despite the differences with previous missions, primarily that they were always part of squadron of big ships, he just took it for granted that they would get home safely. Most of the mess deck had voiced similar opinions and, like Eckhardt, many felt all right, if not good, about the mission, which at least had a real sense of purpose after so many past let-downs. A few voiced some concern and he heard comments like 'bloody waste of time' and 'convoys is U-boat work'. Another reminded them that single ship sorties, whether by warships or auxiliary cruisers were little more than suicide missions, whatever they achieved in the way of sinking enemy ships. Eckhardt knew there was some truth in that, though not always. While all the warships abroad in 1914 had sooner or later been sunk, the auxiliary cruisers *Möwe* and *Wolf* had both been successful *and* returned home. Despite these comments, most spoke positively if not enthusiastically about the possibilities of the operation—'a chance to strike the English'—and of great confidence in the ship. Even the Kaiser got the odd favourable mention from some die-hard royalists, when it was suggested he must've personally OK'd the mission. Helmers was now really seen as some sort of fortune-teller, but surprisingly could not be drawn by 'what's next?'

Things had calmed down to some extent, though everyone was keyed up about the mission and especially keen to ensure he played his part well. There had been a couple of scares, both submarine sightings. The first on that first evening, the second yesterday. The first had not been confirmed by other look-outs; the second had—a whale. The look-out was given a ribbing for this bit of visual detection, though Eckhardt thought he too would have probably raised the alarm if he'd seen it. Porpoises had often led to periscope alarms. He actually regretted not being aloft at the time. In all his years as a Baltic fisherman, he'd never seen a real whale and this one was reportedly a large one, but at least it did put a smile on everyone. Watching the sea can be boring. The whale thoughts made Eckhardt smile about his father's claim to have seen a big whale in the Baltic, but the other fishermen just humoured him or suggested he should have caught it. Thinking of his father led to thoughts about his mother, home ... and Anna, but *Oberleutnant* Fassbinder's voice reminded him of his duty.

'Attention! We are expecting to rendezvous with our supply ships today. So keep a sharp eye out, *all round*! There is also the prospect of sea ice ahead, so report any possible sighting.' Then, a small smile evident, Fassbinder said, 'Pack ice is reportedly an interesting sight, but not something we want to get too close to. So shout out. You may see a change in the sky, a lightening perhaps, due to sunlight reflecting off the ice.'

This news was good for Eckhardt; he felt a renewed purpose, keen to sight the ships and the ice. He'd seen sea ice before, in some sheltered Baltic bays, around the Bight coasts and harbours or in the Kiel Canal and Kiel Fjord. He knew nothing about these northern seas they were now in, but just expected sea ice would be more likely and much more formidable.

For the rest of his watch Eckhardt scanned the sea, but no ice was seen and no ships. Comments around him suggested the excitement generated by the prospect of meeting their supply ships was beginning to wane as the time rolled on. He felt the same. The ship changed course on several occasions, making periodic turns to starboard, suggesting a rendezvous point was being circled. While he expected a sighting of the ships to be made before long, as time passed he also began to consider the possibility that they were never going to appear. What then, he thought. When Schwarz's blonde head appeared through a deck hatch in the Spotting Top, Eckhardt knew his watch was coming to an end. He was glad to be going below, feeling cold and tired. He made his way carefully down the starboard leg of the tripod mast, the wind tugging at him. From the searchlight platform below the Spotting Top he descended through the various Bridge levels, the Upper Bridge, the Admiral's Bridge and then the Command Bridge. There he encountered the captain and the first officer standing to the starboard side away from other officers and deep in conversation. He saluted and continued his way down to his mess deck.

⚑

'Nothing reported, Sir. No sighting and no wireless messages,' said Schellenberg. 'The Navigator's original estimate that they could be here by 1500 hours was conditional on them leaving Jan Mayen as soon as the signal from Nauen was first transmitted.' Schellenberg knew that there was no specific time for the rendezvous. They had picked up the 'RDE' signal the previous evening, presumably not long after the Fleet had got back to Wilhelmshaven. This short, pre-arranged signal, repeated over a number of hours, told the battle cruiser and the supply ships to head for RDE—the agreed rendezvous site between Jan Mayen and Iceland. None would acknowledge receipt of the message, maintaining wireless silence. As previously established, all would head for the rendezvous, *unless* something prevented it, when a signal would be transmitted by the ship concerned and captain Körner would then decide how to proceed. While the Nauen transmitter, near Berlin, had a truly enormous range, the same could not be said of ship-borne W/T equipment. However, the proximity of Jan Mayen should not create a problem. They had arrived at 14.30, some 18 hours after the signal was received. Schellenberg agreed with the navigator that it would be nearing sunset when the supply ships got the RDE signal. 'They should have got underway immediately, so we could expect them soon.'

'Well, hopefully,' was Körner's reply. 'We have no option but to wait. We can't move too far from the rendezvous point, but we'll continue to circle it. A ten-kilometre radius should allow us to gain some extra coverage, while still keeping near.' Körner tried not to dwell on all the factors that could delay the ships—the weather, engine problems or even enemy action. He considered their captains to be competent officers, so, unless a signal was received to the contrary, he expected them to arrive. One ship could have failed to pick up the RDE signal, but surely not both of them. Likewise, enemy action or whatever stopped the *Seefahrerin* from signalling was unlikely to sink both the others before they could get off a wireless signal. There was a possibility that wireless reception, affected by the snow and ice, could be poor at Jan Mayen. Anyway, all that was idle speculation. He could send his own, low power wireless signal, to reduce its distance, but he was very keen to maintain wireless silence. For now, he could wait. He joined Schellenberg and the other Bridge officers and look-outs in searching the horizon with their binoculars.

After they'd all made at least a couple of sweeps of the horizon, Schellenberg spoke: 'Well, surely, here's a chance to use the seaplane.'

'Is the sea too rough?' replied Körner. His response was not based on any great insight into seaplanes, despite their Baltic exercises, though he had once seen a plane fail to get airborne in much calmer conditions than now prevailed. 'But let's ask our intrepid aviators,' he said, smiling. 'I was assured that it was perhaps the best type available, better than Nerger had on the *Wolf*.'

Kapitänleutnant Klaus Brandmann, the short, but seemingly self-assured officer in charge of the seaplane section, was summoned to the Bridge. Brandmann was one of three officers and a petty officer who actually crewed the planes. The planes were maintained by a small number of mechanics, under a non-flying warrant officer, though could also draw on the ship's workshops. All the air personnel, aircrews and support, plus the two planes, had been assigned from the aircraft mothership *Santa Elena*. Notwithstanding the authority of *Georg*, the defeat of Russia had shifted resources to the west and meant there was no problem in getting these men and the planes.

Brandmann and most of the air contingent had joined the ship before the crated plane arrived, to get things ready. Brandmann and *Leutnant* Kühl reported to Körner on joining the ship. To Körner, Brandmann, one of the two pilots, seemed competent and enthusiastic. When the mission was fully explained to him, he fairly effervesced about how his planes could assist. Kühl, an observer/gunner, said little during their few meetings and Körner didn't know what to make of him. The other pilot, *Leutnant* Geiger flew the other plane to the ship. Geiger seemed quite a contrast to Kühl. For one thing he was more outgoing, but also tall and, in Körner's limited views on such matters, quite handsome. Brandmann spoke highly of his officers and men, saying they were the best on the *Santa Elena*.

Their aircraft, which Körner had known from early on were both the Friedrichshafen aircraft construction company's model FF49, were housed in the large, rectangular hangar erected on the Boat Deck, greatly disrupting the storage of most of the boats normally accommodated there. When first slated for the *Hindenburg*, Körner openly admitted that he knew little of planes, but was encouraged by their potential to see 'beyond the horizon'. Nerger's description of his plane's exploits had also enthused Körner about the real benefits of a plane. When the decision was made to employ the ship's seaplanes as the primary reconnaissance method to ensure adequate search capabilities, Körner had wanted the planned two aircraft complement. However, the intended twin-engined, Gotha seaplanes proved to be too fragile, apparently being easily damaged on alighting on the water. Other similar planes were in the production pipeline, but were either never made in any great numbers or otherwise deemed unsuitable for ship-board operations. Naturally, attention moved to proven seaplanes, for example Friedrichshafen's single-engine FF33, as used on the *Wolf,* and settled on its successor, the FF49, which was reported to have good capabilities. Alas, resolving the plane type did not solve all their concerns, especially the disquiet about siting the planes on the upper deck, either side of the ship's aft funnel. Körner had always been worried about how that position would affect the operation of turret Caesar, fearing one blast from its guns on a forward bearing could well destroy the plane or blow it overboard. Furthermore, it was one thing to carry seaplanes on an exposed deck for a day or so around the North Sea, but a totally different affair when faced with a much longer voyage across the Atlantic, where it would be subject to waves and weather and, importantly, where regular maintenance of the plane would be required. This led to the hangar and which housed only one fully assembled, operational plane, along with the crated-up plane ready for assembly if necessary.

Körner was quietly pleased with the plane, but he worried that the Baltic, where it had shown its capabilities, was no Atlantic and, he feared, that would limit its usefulness. With most of the decisions on the planes resolved, he had sought to put aside his previous lack of enthusiasm for all things aerial and, as with as any new addition to his ship, endeavoured to get to grips with the seaplane's details. He'd read up on its technical data, but, when it first alighted near the ship, like many of the crew, it was his first sight of their biplane. He noted the large, slightly angled-back wings were connected to each other by a dozen struts, further strengthened with a criss-cross of wires. The aerodynamic nose cone of the two-bladed propeller gave a pleasing, stream-lined appearance that continued on down to its large rudder. Its floats, with their own array of spars and wires, were a considerable appendage and extended from out beyond the propeller to half-way back along the length of the plane. In what seemed like cramped conditions, he saw the heads of its two-man crew poking out from the fuselage. He admired their courage.

'There is quite a wind, but the waves are not too great,' said Brandmann, in non-too nautical terms for Körner and Schellenberg, 'but we should be able to lift off.'

'That's good news, *Kapitänleutnant*,' replied Körner. 'I'll be honest, I did suggest to the *Fregattenkapitän* that you might say just the opposite.'

No sooner had Körner said this than he regretted it. Surely such a comment would do nothing for the pilot's morale or paint a negative picture of his captain's attitude towards the airmen and their plane. However, on the contrary, Brandmann appeared not to be taken aback by it. If anything, a slight smile seemed to form on his lips.

'Captain, the forty-nine, or rather this version, the *forty-nine c*, is quite a robust aircraft. We've found that it can take off and land in quite rough seas. Oh, yes Sir,' smiled Brandmann, obviously confident in the plane's capabilities, 'this is a very good seaplane.'

Brandmann hurried away, but it was still a while before things happened. With Körner, Schellenberg and others somewhat apprehensively looking-on from the Bridge, the hangar front was pulled back. A wire was attached from a derrick and slowly the undoubtedly aerial craft moved forward until the wings were free of its shelter. After a few attempts at spinning the propeller, the engine coughed into life. There was much engine noise, as the propeller spun ever faster, and soon it was signalled that the plane was ready to be lowered onto the sea. Körner still feared being stationary and a sitting target, but, if he was ever to use the plane, he knew he must bring his ship to a halt. It seemed unlikely there would be any nearby submarine, hiding, waiting for just such an opportunity, but he was naturally concerned. With scores of pairs of eyes scanning the waters for that hidden menace, the ship was brought to a halt. In the lee of the ship, the plane was lowered onto the water, the lifting tackle cast off and, with Brandmann at the controls, it motored away from the ship, revving its engine. Before the plane had even attempted to fly, Körner had his ship underway.

There had been no really rough weather for the plane to contend with in the Baltic and all take-offs and landings had been from sheltered waters. So, apprehensive eyes stared at it, now well astern of the ship, as it shaped up to take off. Half-expecting it to be undone by each wave it had to confront, Körner watched the aircraft gather speed, now looking quite small against the backdrop of sea and sky. The waves did bounce the plane, but it seemed to relish the motion, surging forward to the next wave. As had been the case in the Baltic, the actual take-off took little time. A white wake began to build, with spray gathering under the large floats. The pointed ends of the floats began to rise with more and more protruding beyond the white water and then, when one might have expected it to have to go a lot faster and travel further along the surface, it lifted and was free of the water's grip. Even so, the ascent seemed painfully slow, but very soon the plane was above the ship. The pilot circled the *Hindenburg* and headed off in the expected direction of the supply ships, to the collective smiles and relief of those on the Bridge.

The successful launch of the plane seemed to make most on the Bridge confident about finding the supply ships. Körner kept his own counsel on the matter, as he watched the plane disappear away to the north-west. Over the weeks, he had been pleased to have his views on aircraft changed. He had been something of a sceptic, largely out of ignorance, but he knew that their limited Baltic training experiences were yet to be shown to be practical capabilities. A lot was riding on reconnaissance by the plane; it had become a key factor in the success of *Georg*. He silently wished Brandmann *Good Luck*.

Despite the use of the plane, the prospect of not meeting the supply ships was still unsettling, but Körner tried to put it to the back of his mind, hoping the combination of good seamanship on both the *Hindenburg* and the supply ships, now supplemented by Brandmann's efforts, would lead to a meeting of the ships.

He had been trained to plan for just about any situation, but life wasn't that simple. He and Bünzlin had joked that Schlieffen's planning for the attack on France was easier than theirs. *Georg*'s planning catered for failure to meet up with the supply ships before the first refuelling, though it would very much depend on the situation. He could take fuel from captured ships, but that was easier said than done, especially in these waters north of Iceland with limited ship traffic. A serious delay in refuelling could affect *Georg*'s execution. Without refuelling, he would return to Germany; it was as simple as that. He consoled himself that it was too early to start worrying about refuelling. If the supply ships could not be found, they still had plenty of fuel for the return journey, even at higher speed, and there were no indications that the enemy knew about the breakout. He retired to his Sea Cabin; there was nothing to be gained by his pacing the Bridge. He lay down and was soon asleep. He thought he'd been asleep for only a moment, when Battle Stations sounded. He hoped for some sighting, even if it was the enemy, he jested to himself.

The ship was at Battle Stations, slowly increasing speed, but ready to engage all comers. Quickly back on the Bridge, Körner was told a ship had been sighted. He stared intently in the direction of the other binoculars. The light level was falling. In an hour or so, the sun would set. Three points off the starboard bow, he saw a dark ship and, lurking beyond her, another. They *must* be the supply ships, a thought endorsed by his officers' comments, but he noted the first gunnery officer still had, correctly, the ship's guns focusing on them. They were still a long way off, perhaps 15,000 metres, but he made out a single, tall funnel on the nearest ship. Even at this distance, its outline suggested a merchant ship. To Körner's query, Schellenberg replied, 'No, nothing from the plane, Sir.'

The *Hindenburg* circled the much smaller merchantmen, now only a few hundred metres away. Recognition signals had been exchanged and now signal lights flashed back and forth. Körner watched as sailors on his ship waved to the merchant ships, though wondered whether they could see in the last rays of the day the waving of the figures lining the supply ships' decks. He was mightily relieved to have successfully rendezvoused with the supply ships and especially pleased he didn't have to consider the other worries he'd earlier mulled over. He had greetings and congratulatory messages sent to the ships. Amid the good feelings generated by the rendezvous, he realised that, perhaps amazingly, *Georg* continued to run to plan. They could not rely on luck, he told himself. He recognised that the war had thrown a fair bit of good fortune his way and for once worried that it was not infinite.

'The plane, Sir,' an officer enthusiastically reported to Körner, pointing astern, away from the supply ships.

Körner looked astern to see the plane approaching them. In a few minutes, its black crosses easily visible, it flew over the battle cruiser and then circled the three ships. It had been less than two hours since it took off. With the light failing, recovery of the seaplane was given first priority. All eyes were turned to the sea, watching for a possible submarine. Signals were then flashed and, as the ship slowed, the grey plane touched down hardly thirty metres away, all but merging with the grey sea, with its forward motion coming quickly to a halt. The recovery was quick, further encouraging Körner that operating a seaplane from a big ship was practicable. As to being valuable, he was disappointed that *it* had not found the supply ships. Schellenberg had taken on the additional burden of being responsible for seaplane operations, the machines and the officers and men. He would report on any apparent failure.

Körner would've preferred to have a face-to-face discussion with the supply ships' captains on the next step, but, with the fading light and believing he just couldn't risk stopping his ship any more times that day, he denied himself such a meeting on the *Hindenburg*. So, the flashing light exchange continued, assessing the supply ships' capabilities and condition and informing them of his immediate intentions. They mentioned 'delay leaving GRI'—GRI being the code for the island Jan Mayen, their sanctuary before being summoned to the rendezvous—and the *Torsten Meyer* reported an engine problem that had affected her speed. Other than the ships' best speed, Körner sought no further explanation about the *Torsten Meyer*, though it confirmed which ship they would refuel from first. He was now keen to get quickly to the refuelling point, but that was still over 250 sea miles away and their speed would be limited by the colliers. They had a service speed of 12 knots, but, alas, as *Torsten* Meyer could now only maintain 10 knots that would be the ships' speed. At least the three ships were now together. Within an hour of the rendezvous, the ships, with the battle cruiser leading, were on a westerly course.

As the little flotilla steamed through the night, initially the sky was clear and the star-show was truly magnificent, but, with the moon yet to rise, the countless bright spots above provided no illumination at sea level. Keeping track of the supply ships challenged one's eyesight. The black shape of the *Erda* was at times completely lost in the equally black sea. The *Torsten Meyer*, about half a mile farther astern, was even more indistinct. Visibility got much worse when clouds rolled over them, bringing rain and some sleet. The wind, now more easterly and astern, also picked up. Even in the dark, it was possible to see the long waves that ran alongside them, with ghostly white crests everywhere and spray in the air. Körner feared the ships could be dispersed in the rough weather, but he would not use the *Hindenburg* as a shepherd in the darkness. The supply ships had the course, knew their destination and the speed required. If necessary, he would round them up at daybreak.

Körner kept the *Hindenburg* at a high degree of readiness, with half of the guns' crews closed up, while the rest slept nearby in their hammocks. Their course had them only 70 sea miles north of Iceland and a similar distance from the expected edge of the Greenland pack ice away to the north west. Any ship travelling around the north of Iceland might encounter them, *if* their courses were near enough. With any luck, the war, the convoy system itself and the weather and ice at this time of year would all militate against merchant ships being in these waters. They could well expect, however, to encounter fishermen going about their business on Iceland's bountiful seas.

As the first dawn light tentatively scratched at the horizon, the two merchant ships were still in sight though, as Körner half-expected, they were no longer in a tight formation. The *Erda* was still dead astern, but now about a kilometre away. The *Torsten Meyer* had drifted off to starboard and was about two kilometres away, but already manoeuvring to get back on station. The battle cruiser turned to starboard and checked both. Within a hour they were all back in a tighter group. He noted that the colliers put out quite a bit of smoke as they maintained the required 10 knots, which unfortunately could signal the presence of the little fleet.

꙳

Battle Stations! Eckhardt ran to his secondary station on the Bridge. The sky was still dark, overcast and menacing, with occasional rain squalls. The wind was also stronger, now striking their port beam, as they sailed south. Despite the pre-dawn darkness, he could see the vague outline of land ahead; it excited him. This must be the refuelling point, he reasoned. His mess deck had endlessly debated the *when and where* since they'd met up with the colliers over a day ago. While the meeting of the ships on the high sea was good for morale, no one looked forward to the coaling ahead. All accepted it was a necessary part of a modern steam navy and clearly a very important factor in them getting home—whenever that would be—but that didn't mean anyone relished the filthy business of coaling.

The ship picked up speed and soon left the two colliers astern. Eckhardt couldn't see much detail of the land, but, as the light level increased, its outline became clearer, showing what appeared to be a low range of hills or possibly mountains, extending from left to right. The rising sun silhouetted them, but, when the ship was still several kilometres out from it, the land immediately ahead stood out, appearing to be detached and darker than the higher ground beyond. In its centre was a high peak, pyramid-like in shape, and Eckhardt could make out another shorter, but sharper peak slightly to the right of the main one. The ship made a starboard turn, moving across this dark outcrop. Bridge officers' comments confirmed his belief that this was the refuelling point.

'We should see the bay shortly, just beyond the headland,' said an officer near him. Then, directed at all: 'Watch out for any ships in the bay.'

Taking his cue from the direction of others' binoculars, Eckhardt focused his on the same bearing, still trying to penetrate the coastal darkness. The rising sun came to his aid and with each minute he could see more detail. Soon it was evident that the coast ahead was in fact a complete wall of vertical cliffs, reaching up hundreds and hundreds of metres. The high summit he had first made out could now be seen to be the highest point of the cliff wall, which, to port, curved away as far as he could see and on the other side all the way to the supposed bay entrance. Here and there the cliff wall had what looked to be a series of spectacular cathedral-like buttresses holding up this massive natural structure. The whole vision was improbable, even mythical. He could see numerous large gulls soaring almost effortlessly up and down the cliff face. He made out a near vertical line to the right, darker than the land beyond. It must be the headland, the bay.

Still over three kilometres out, they moved west across the mouth of the bay. The tension was palpable. All guns were pointing into the bay, ready to overwhelm any enemy ship that might foolishly challenge the *Hindenburg*. Eckhardt quickly swept his glasses around the bay, trying to probe each nook and cranny of what appeared to be a very large body of water, perhaps three or four kilometres wide and stretching away south. The mouth of the bay had high cliffs on both sides, but beyond that were mountains and valleys on each flank and, against a backdrop of distant mountains, there seemed to be lower ground at the far end. There was snow on all the surrounding higher ground, but this thinned out at lower levels revealing a brown, bare and inhospitable landscape. Horizontal lines of rock strata were to be seen on all the cliff faces, each starkly picked out by the snow. Without consciously analysing it, Eckhardt felt good about the waters of the bay; they were flat calm, shielded from the rolling sea and wind by the bay's great eastern rampart that swept round like a giant protective arm. No one reported any sighting. The bay looked completely deserted, empty of ships.

They continued west at high speed, leaving the bay, but soon encountered another great inlet, similar, but wider and more open than the first. Nothing was seen to cause alarm there either. Again, this land seemed to have been abandoned to nature. The ship turned to starboard and returned to the first bay, to see the two colliers slowly entering it. Eckhardt expected to follow them in, but the ship continued on to check out the land to the west. This soon curved away from them to the south and within a few minutes the ship turned to port and went out to sea. He didn't understand what was going on—nothing new there. He hadn't understood a course reversal the previous day, for a time believing, like others, that the operation was cancelled and they were returning to Germany. Eckhardt's curiosity could not be held back, so, not without trepidation, he asked a young officer near him, 'What's happening, *Leutnant*? Are we leaving the colliers?'

The *leutnant*, trying to wear a stern face to the seaman's enquiry, but failing to fight back a slight smile, replied, 'No, we're not leaving them. They're just going to reconnoitre the bay for us.'

'Thank you, Sir.' Eckhardt wanted to ask more about the bay and what was going to happen, but, as the *leutnant* proffered no more, he felt he'd used up his asking cards for now. He looked back at the bay, to see the stern of the rear ship disappear behind its high walls.

6

Rosyth

It was something of a family tradition that the sons of the Earl of Harrogate would join the navy or army. In more recent times the diplomatic service or politics were deemed acceptable, but the armed services were still seen to offer a fitting career. All the respectable families benefited from having a general or admiral in their ranks.

Fair-haired, tall and good-looking, the Honourable Edward George Framlington, the Earl's second son, had not disappointed in joining the Senior Service. At 24, he was a lieutenant and had seen action, but for a time it didn't look as though he'd get much further or even get to sea again. Jutland had all but put paid to his career, or so it had seemed. Serving on the light cruiser *Calliope*, his war was interrupted when his ship first tangled with German torpedo boats and then some battleships. A shell fragment had injured his right leg. At one stage there was even the fear that he might lose it, but fortunately that turned out to be a false alarm. However, he was still left with a bit of a weak limb and he was glad his war wound was covered by his trouser leg. After nine months' convalescence, he could get by well enough.

Deemed fit enough to return to duty, he was initially given a paper-pushing job ashore, in Portsmouth, assisting a Rear-Admiral who enjoyed the title of 'Captain of Dockyard'. Such work was not at all what he wanted, determined to play what he thought to be a more meaningful part in the war. After almost a year of that job, he sought a change, but nothing suitable seemed in the offing. The Earl, calling in some favours, managed to assist the process and got his son a posting working for another admiral, but this time on a ship.

Framlington took the long rail journey to Rosyth to join the staff of 54-year-old, Acting Vice-Admiral Arthur Backhouse-Smith. He was well pleased with his appointment. He found the admiral—'Smitty' to friends or equals—to be quite a jovial, but nonetheless exacting task master. He actually reported to Lieutenant-Commander John Cox and would be responsible for secretarial and signals work. Cox was a pleasant-enough chap, but a stickler for efficient practice. After a couple of early failings, which fortunately didn't bring too much criticism, he coped well with the demands and foibles of both Cox and the admiral.

Smitty's command was the Light Cruiser Force, including the First Cruiser Squadron and its big cruisers HMS *Courageous* (the flagship) and *Glorious*.

Unconcerned about another cruiser assignment, Framlington looked forward to joining the *Courageous*, but initially wondered about her real capabilities. With her long profile, she had a certain beauty, though perhaps not every sailor's idea of a handsome ship. On the other hand, there were things about her that seemed strange to him.

He'd been told that the *Courageous* and *Glorious* were 'light battle cruisers'. There was no denying some of their battle cruiser credentials—large (almost 800 feet long and nearly 20,000 tons), very fast (over 30 knots) and mounting 15in guns—but he accepted that such bare statistics can hide a lot. While the *Courageous* was seriously larger than the *Calliope*, he heard she had no more belt armour, perhaps even less, than his old ship, only a few inches thick, precious little, even for a battle cruiser. As for the 15in armament, such guns were as big as any mounted on the Fleet's dreadnoughts, but there were only four of them. Not exactly the 'all-big-gun' arrangement one had come to expect. With so few big guns—a twin-gun turret at each end of the ship—it was obvious that hitting anything was going to be more difficult than, say, with an eight-gun-armed ship. When Commander Cox told him that they had originally been described as 'large light cruisers', Framlington did not demur from that description. Despite these initial misgivings, he soon warmed to her, loving her great speed. He also drew comfort from the knowledge that the ships had been in a recent battle, a running fight with German cruisers, from which they'd more or less emerged satisfactorily, though with few accolades. He was not one to approve of her unofficial nickname—*Outrageous*.

Since April 1917, Rosyth was the Grand Fleet's new base. Admiral Beatty, the CinC, had relocated the Fleet there from Scapa Flow, so as to be closer to the enemy. Seemed reasonable, thought Framlington; his not to reason why. From a personal point of view, Rosyth, near Edinburgh, civilisation *and* women, would always get his vote over the cold, bleak and isolated Flow. However, compared to Scapa Flow, the Fleet appeared well packed into the Firth of Forth, with most of the big ships above the famous rail bridge, though getting to sea swiftly, night or day, seemed to pose no problem.

In spite of being at Rosyth, the Fleet's pride took a bit of a dent when they missed what seemed a golden opportunity to bring the enemy fleet to battle in late April 1918. The Germans had once again sought to strike at the Scandinavian convoys, though this time not with just a couple of cruisers or destroyers, but with their whole battle fleet. Alas, their operation was not discovered until they had reached Norwegian waters. The Grand Fleet sortied *en masse*—over 30 dreadnoughts and a hundred other warships—with the First Cruiser Squadron up ahead and Framlington full of eagerness, but nothing came of it. The enemy managed to get south of the Fleet's eastward drive across the North Sea and escape back to its Wilhelmshaven base. Fortunately the enemy had missed the convoy, but some on the *Courageous* thought that little compensation against the lost chance of a decisive fleet action. It was a most disappointing episode—made worse by subsequent revelations.

Some days later, Smitty called his cruiser and flotilla captains to his flagship. Where possible, he was always keen to discuss upcoming operations and to take stock of any issues arising from the Squadron's recent activities. Not surprisingly, the German foray and the failure to bring them to action was the main focus of the meeting. Framlington was there, taking notes, pushing paper. He'd also hung a map of the Atlantic alongside the usual one of the North Sea. Did anyone register the addition?

The assembly, seated at a large table, debated the events of the German operation, concluding that the Light Forces had done all asked of them. No one seemed especially pleased at that, as it didn't reduce the disappointment of the enemy escaping their attentions.

'Well, gentlemen, we may have *another* problem,' said the admiral, his emphasis registering with everyone. 'The Admiralty isn't absolutely sure, but the enemy's little venture the other day may have produced an unexpected development.' He didn't leave them time to ponder that, quickly adding: 'The battle cruiser *Hindenburg* may have broken out into the Atlantic.'

Framlington noted a few changed expressions, raised eyebrows and the odd, noticeable exhale and quiet murmur from the admiral's audience. Being on the admiral's staff, Framlington already knew about it, but his first reaction had been similar. He knew that various raiders, disguised merchantmen, had slipped out over the years. Some had been intercepted, the last in 1917. This time, a major warship—Germany's latest battle cruiser—had got by them; yet another reason to feel the Fleet had failed in its duty, even if, so far, nothing untoward had happened.

After dropping his startling bit of news, the admiral raised his hand slightly, cutting off any immediate questions. 'She would have used the operation as cover,' he continued, 'taking the opportunity to head off into the Atlantic, while our attention was on their fleet rushing south, back to their base.'

He fell silent for a second, which some took as a cue to ask questions.

'Sir, if she has broken out, do we have any indication of her possible whereabouts?' asked Captain Harding of the *Chester*.

Other murmurings endorsed the need to know that.

'Yes, assuming she has broken out, that is *the* most important question.' said the admiral. 'Well, so far, there's nothing to go on. We have had no sightings and no other intelligence about her location. She may well be keeping absolutely silent, making no wireless signals. That now seems to be their practice. There is the possibility,' he threw in, 'that the Admiralty's suspicions may prove to be totally wrong and she is in fact languishing in Wilhelmshaven or some other harbour.

'However, let's not get our hopes up,' he said, his tone more serious. 'The Admiralty's intelligence suggests it's more than likely she has actually broken out into the Atlantic, intent on attacking our convoys.'

With this, Framlington again registered some reaction from the assembled group, no words, just facial movements, raised or frowning eyebrows, suggesting a mixture of concern and disappointment.

'As to exactly where she might be,' Smitty said, turning to look at Framlington's Atlantic map, 'as you'll appreciate,' his arm making a languid sweep over the map, 'that will depend on a whole range of factors, including her speed, course chosen, whether she is able to refuel, etcetera, etcetera.

'Actually, on fuel, that could well be a key factor. She may seek to attack convoys at any point on their routes across the Atlantic,' his hand circling areas of the map, 'to the west of Ireland, in the central ocean area or even off the coast of America. She may be able to strike off the west of Ireland without refuelling, but obviously there she most risks being brought to action. If she sails to the western side of the Atlantic, then, she may avoid our big ships, but she would definitely need refuelling. The Admiralty's latest thinking is that, fortunately, she may not have enough fuel to even reach the Canadian, let alone the American coast and the closer she tries to get to America the less time she'll have to find convoys. Of course, her range would depend on whether she's supported by colliers or is able to capture any and, equally, whether she can find a quiet place to coal. On the other hand, we think the *Hindenburg*, their latest class of battle cruiser, also uses oil fuel, so capturing an oil tanker and possibly refuelling at sea are possibilities.'

At that point the admiral indicated that Commander Cox take over. Stepping up to the map and using a pencil as a pointer, Cox illustrated the courses the *Hindenburg* might have taken: 'If the sortie of the High Seas Fleet was undertaken, at least in part, to cover her break-out, she would have left them about here.' His pencil touched the map near the coast of Norway, almost opposite the Shetland Isles. 'From there, she had various options for breaking out into the Atlantic.'

Framlington glanced from the map to the others around the table. He noted that all their eyes were glued to the pencil's movements, as it began to trace invisible lines on the map.

'It's thought unlikely, given the proximity of Scapa Flow, even with the fewer ships now based there,' said Cox, 'that she would have gone through the Orkneys-Shetlands gap, preferring instead the waters between the Shetlands and the Faroes or the Faroes-Iceland gap.' He paused, then moved the pencil above Iceland. 'It's not impossible that she could have journeyed north of Iceland and entered the Atlantic via the Denmark Strait. That wouldn't be surprising. It's suspected that other raiders have used that route.'

Turning to face his listeners, he continued, 'So, she could be heading for the far side of the Atlantic, aiming to attack convoys near their starting points, or indeed,' his pencil sweeping back towards the British Isles, 'as the Admiral has said, she may be heading for this side, to the waters west of Britain and Ireland.'

The admiral stood up. Cox instantly fell silent.

72

'Er, thank you, Commander,' said Smitty. 'There are pros and cons about all the various options the Commander has outlined, but I don't propose we go into them. If she's out there, we should know her intentions soon enough.'

'Agreed, Sir, but may I ask what action is proposed to stop her?' asked another captain.

'Before discussing that further, perhaps I should say the possibility of such a break-out has actually been expected for some time and plans have been drawn up to deal with such an eventuality.'

Framlington noted a few expressions of surprise in the audience at the admiral's revelation. Did they think the Admiralty were asleep on such matters, he wondered, though he too had been somewhat surprised when he heard of the planning already done.

'Well, assuming she's broken out,' the admiral continued, 'some preventive measures are already being taken on convoys, their routing, their escorts; these things can be done relatively easily. The Americans have not sent all their big ships over to join us, so they will seek to engage her if she does indeed venture right over to their waters.

'As to what we and the Fleet can do, we must wait for that bit of news which will tell us where she is. But, for now, it's been decided that our big ships won't be gallivanting all over the ocean trying to find her. That could just dilute our force and leave us open to attack elsewhere, ... which is probably part of their strategy. So, we need to be on our guard for just such an eventuality. Given the difficulty of finding a lone ship in the Atlantic, the plans which have been drawn up envisage us tackling her when she eventually tries to get back to Germany.'

This brought a few, but only a few, nods and murmurs of agreement.

'While we'll not be complacent, *far from it*,' stressed the admiral, 'let's look at this for what it is. One ship, however capable, will have her work cut out to achieve anything. In my opinion,' his attitude and tone dismissive, 'this is a poor move by the Germans. They think breaking out into the Atlantic will change matters. It will probably achieve little or nothing and, in the end, they'll lose a valuable warship. Good for us, bad for them.'

Framlington noted a few nods from the audience. He noted a gradual change in the admiral's demeanour. From what had started out as almost a friendly, matter-of-fact lecture on the latest situation, like one given by the teacher to a bunch of school boys awaiting their homework, it had moved to one of steely determination to bring the enemy to book.

'The Atlantic is a big place,' the admiral continued. 'If the German ship is lucky, she may find and sink some ships, but she can't stay out there forever. She will have to refuel, if she can, and, probably sooner rather than later, will try to get back to Germany. Whatever happens, we'll get her.

'I have no doubt,' he said, his voice much quieter, 'that, if she has made it to the Atlantic, she will be brought to action ... and sunk.'

7

Hornvik

Körner was relieved when one of the supply ships was seen coming out of the bay. He turned the *Hindenburg* towards it. A signal lamp flashed from the ship.

'It's the *Erda*, Sir,' reported Schellenberg. 'She says: Soundings taken, buoys positioned. *Torsten Meyer* awaits you.'

'Excellent,' replied Körner. He was anxious to begin refuelling and get the giant *Hindenburg* tucked up out of sight of any passing traffic which may be hugging the coast. Coming to this remote corner of Iceland and at this time of year was paying off, he thought, though things had not gone exactly to plan so far. It was intended to have the seaplane investigate the bay and the surrounding coasts first, but on this occasion the conditions were judged to be too difficult for a take-off. He had no option but to approach the bay with the ships.

The supply ships had taken almost two hours to complete the task of checking the depth of the bay, somewhat more than expected. Although anecdotal evidence suggested the bay was deep enough for the battle cruiser, they could not proceed without some confirmation of its depths. *Georg* planning, thorough as ever, expected the supply ships to confirm depths at several points and mark a 10-metre-deep line. Even so, he'd agreed with Schellenberg that the *Hindenburg* would still feel its way into the bay, checking depths as they proceeded. 'Make to the *Erda*: Well done. Happy to trade places with you. Keep in visual touch at all times.'

Along with most of the Bridge officers, Körner watched the *Erda* pass them, noting her merchant ship lines. She had a bluff-bow, with raised fo'c'sle and poop decks. Her higher central superstructure was crowned with two tall ventilators alongside her tall funnel, and, fore and aft of this, her shelter decks with their cargo hatches and high masts with their large derricks. She would keep watch offshore, supplementing the seaplane's reconnaissance flights. As they watched the *Erda*, to his right Körner saw the tall figure of white-haired *Oberleutnant* Kehlmann in conversation with the much shorter and youthful-looking Gärtner. The journey to Iceland had involved some course changes to arrive at dawn, but despite all that, the navigation had been good, which he acknowledged he'd not commented on. '*Herr* Gärtner. Sorry, I meant to say earlier: Very well done in getting us here; right on target.'

'Thank you, Sir,' replied a very pleased Gärtner.

'*Oberleutnant.*'

Kehlmann immediately stepped forward to Körner and Schellenberg. 'Captain.'

'You mentioned there were a few farmsteads around Hornvik. How many do you remember?' asked Körner, quite reverentially.

By the look on his craggy face, Kehlmann was racking his memory. 'I think it was three, Captain,' he ventured. 'Perhaps four. But there could be more by now.'

'Yes, quite so. Do you think any will have telegraph or telephone?'

'It's many years since I was here, Captain, but I doubt it.' Then, reminding himself, 'Nineteen-oh-four was the last time I anchored in Hornvik and I think that was before Iceland had *any* telegraph or telephone systems.' Kehlmann then offered, 'This is a very remote part of Iceland and, as I recall, the people here are very poor, scratching a basic living. I doubt they'd have the telegraph or even if telegraph wires had reached this far.'

'I agree, but we can't leave anything to chance. If someone has the telegraph … or, God forbid, a telephone, we need to know. If a message got out too soon about our stay here, it would alert the English and reduce the element of surprise that we still seem to have.' Körner turned to Gärtner. 'Sorry not to have thought of this sooner, but could you take on the task of checking out the farms around the bay to see if they have telegraph or telephones?'

'Yes, Captain,' replied Gärtner, stepping forward to the side of Kehlmann. 'Do you wish us to go into the farms … make contact with the farmers?'

'Preferably not, but I leave it to you. Try to do what you can from the ship or boats. Best to keep the numbers ashore to a minimum and, where possible, keep our distance from any people.'

Gärtner looked at Kehlmann, but then checked himself and spoke to Körner without discussing it with his subordinate. 'We can presumably check for telegraph poles and perhaps wireless aerials from the ship.' Gärtner asked Kehlmann: '*Oberleutnant*, can we see all the farms from the bay?'

'Yes, that should be possible, but it's a wide bay … depends where we anchor.'

'Good. Well, I leave it all to you,' interrupted Körner.

'*Herr* Kehlmann, how's your Icelandic?' Gärtner joked to the tall seaman.

One outcome of that discussion, thought Körner, was it would probably save Kehlmann from any part in the forthcoming coaling. He was pleased that he'd decided to get Kehlmann assigned to *Georg*. At 59, Rolf Kehlmann was the oldest man aboard. Kehlmann had made a life of the sea and sailed the Icelandic and Greenland waters extensively, initially for sealing and then fishing. He was also the only man aboard who'd been to this part of Iceland. He was captain of his own trawler when the war intervened. Bünzlin had found him and, though he provided much useful intelligence in the planning of *Georg*, Bünzlin agreed with Körner that he could provide useful information as the operation continued. As a reservist, it was easy to get him on board, but Kehlmann was happy to do his bit.

He was appointed to Gärtner's navigation division. Körner increasingly viewed him as having played a decisive part in the planning of *Georg*. It had largely been his knowledge of these waters and this Icelandic bay they were now entering—Hornvik—which had resolved the debate on where to refuel.

Some of Bünzlin's staff had pushed for Jan Mayen as the refuelling point. The fifty-kilometre-long, volcanic island of Jan Mayen, 450 kilometres from Greenland, had much to commend it. Primarily, it was remote, uninhabited and belonged to no one, so affording a secret refuelling place and one not likely to cause an international incident with, say, a neutral power like Norway or Denmark. Of course, all realised that Jan Mayen was no picnic spot. Available information gave no obvious refuelling point, no especially protected bay or inlet. There was even concern that there may not be enough water under the keel to get the battle cruiser close enough inshore. But it was Kehlmann's fairly intimate knowledge of that remote island which decided matters. He was quite possibly the only man in Germany who'd actually been to Jan Mayen. As a young seaman, he was on a ship which supported an Austro-Hungarian polar expedition that went to the island in 1882 and stayed for a year. He confirmed that, lying beyond the Arctic Circle, it was not only very cold, but, most worryingly, at this time of year it could well be ice-bound, still in the grip of the winter's sea ice possibly stretching all the way from Greenland. He did agree that it was a suitable place for the supply ships to wait for the break-out.

Other refuelling options were Greenland, Iceland or even the Faroes. Körner had looked enviously at the map of Greenland, which showed an extensive array of suitable fjords on her long east coast, but Kehlmann told him they were, especially at this time of the year, iced-up or inaccessible because of offshore sea ice. The Faroes also offered good refuelling waters, but would almost certainly mean the early loss of surprise and were deemed too close to English bases, only 250 sea miles from Scapa Flow. Iceland had suitable fjords, even some remote ones. There was naturally the fear that using Iceland risked losing the element of surprise. Unlike Jan Mayen, all these other lands also belonged to Denmark, which might threaten conflict with the Hague Conventions on warships in a neutral's waters.

These matters were extensively considered by Bünzlin's men, with Körner's input. Kehlmann's contribution to these debates was crucial. He said he'd used Hornvik bay on three occasions, sheltering from fierce storms. He knew little about its depth, though did know that away from the shore it was not shallow. He said it was a very out-of-the-way, bleak area, but not as cold as Jan Mayen. It had no towns or villages nearby. He'd mentioned that there were a few isolated farms, but that Hornvik was a truly remote area and the farmers were unlikely to have easy contact with the outside. He believed there should be ample time to coal and leave long before any alarm was raised. Bünzlin had further investigations made, including information provided by their embassy in Denmark and even some from a few other old sea dogs, which confirmed Hornvik's suitability as a refuelling site. Notably, there probably were few people in that area of Iceland. Indeed, the whole island was very sparsely populated, reportedly with perhaps a total population of only some 100,000 people. The telegraph and telephones were not widespread, with no such systems in place before 1906 and even now thought to be only located in and around the capital, Reykjavik, some 250 kilometres to the south. Using Iceland for refuelling could mean problems for relations with neutral Denmark, but didn't seem likely to be a concern, especially at this stage of the war. Denmark, although a professed neutral, had agreed to Germany's request to mine its own waters right at the start of the war and had since allowed obvious territorial violations, so, wary of the threat of German invasion, was considered unlikely to react precipitately. Anyway, the stay would be less than twenty-four hours, permitted under the Hague Convention, and unlikely to be an issue with an Iceland known to be pushing for its own independence from Denmark. Importantly, neither Denmark nor Iceland had any forces able to prevent the *Hindenburg* from refuelling in Hornvik bay. All matters considered, the bay seemed an ideal site. Furthermore, it was only a day's sailing from the North Atlantic.

As the *Hindenburg*'s bow entered the bay, Körner could see the high, near-vertical cliffs at its mouth gave way to a snow-covered vista of high, steep-sided peaks, with shallow valleys. The *Torsten Meyer* was in the eastern part of the bay, a languid column of thin smoke rising from her funnel. She was not anchored, but moving very slowly, waiting for the battle cruiser to anchor first. Nearby, her small cutter was being rowed, trying to keep up with the ship. He imagined it had been involved in the depth checking.

Körner reduced speed. They had moved a kilometre or so into the bay before he and his officers could see the buoys laid by the *Erda* and *Torsten Meyer*. There were only eight, four along the eastern side, showing that deep water came close to the high cliffs on that side, and the others defining a shallow arc ahead, away from the wide shore at the bay's southern end. He took comfort from the sailor in the chains taking soundings. Still a kilometre or so from the colliers' buoys, using the props he manoeuvred the ship to a position where her bows were facing the sea and dropped anchor. They were stationary, the first time in six days. The ship lay in calm water less than a kilometre from the bay's eastern side and about one and half kilometres from the mouth. There was a good view of the sea and the *Erda* cruising offshore. A constant eye would be kept on her.

He watched as the *Torsten Meyer* secured along their starboard side and the coaling began. He heard Schellenberg speaking to the assembled crew through a megaphone about the importance of this coaling, extolling them to do their utmost, but needing to be ready to fight the ship. The men, all wearing their worst or oldest clothing, swarmed all over the collier and soon, amid clouds of coal dust, her derricks were lifting numerous bags across nets between the two ships and onto the warship's decks where they were barrowed and manhandled down the chutes and into the coal bunkers. The empty bags then returned to the collier for the process to begin again and again, until it became a continuous cycle of toil, sweat and all-pervading black dust. Normally there would have been preparations beforehand to make the process go even faster and protect the ship and crew from the intrusion of the coal, which would invade through every orifice, large and small, to leave its black calling-card everywhere, but on this occasion that had not been as extensive as they would have liked. Although most men were engaged in the black task, some were helping with other supplies, moving crates, boxes and other containers into the battle cruiser. Thank goodness, he thought, that they were largely shielded from the wind and the rain was now little more than the odd shower.

Moving to the port side of the Bridge, he took one more look around the bay. Away to the south, at the head of the bay, he could see a few buildings on the sole area of flat land; one of Kehlmann's farms, he imagined. He searched for telegraph poles, finding none. He could see they had what looked like a couple of large rowing boats, both pulled up on the shore. He put his binoculars down and looked around the ship, contenting himself that things seemed to be going well. He also saw the ship's steam boat and a motorboat were in the water being prepared for patrol and tasks ashore. He knew that if and when the ship had to leave the bay, anyone not aboard would have to fend for themselves.

Above the noise of the coaling, he heard the whirring clamour of the seaplane's engine. When he looked, the plane was already moving away from the ship's port side, out into the bay. The water was still; he expected to see an easy take-off.

⚑

Not surprisingly, Eckhardt was disappointed that Schwarz and not him was selected for Spotting Top duty, watching for signals from the collier at sea or shore parties. He listened to the first officer's loud-hailer message, but didn't need to be told how important this coaling was. Everyone understood the situation; it was self-evident that they had to complete it quickly and get out of the bay and away from Iceland. The band, also dressed in their coaling clothes, started up. He enjoyed their music, especially at times like this. Along with about half the *Hindenburg*'s crew, he was detailed to work initially in the collier's hold. Nets covered the whole gap between the ships and, with danger from the swinging derricks above, he crossed over to her, though before he descended into her, he noted a few figures on the shore, presumably locals, Icelanders, from the couple of buildings higher up the sloping hills. He wondered what they thought about the giant warship in their bay. It looked as if they were waving. He could not stop himself thinking: don't they know there's a war on?

Soon he was deep in the *Torsten Meyer*'s aftmost, number four hold filling bag after bloody bag and quickly enveloped in a coal-dust cloud. Before long, everyone around him was as black as coal miners, as no doubt he was, and all periodically spitting and clearing their throats. He tried to keep the coal dust out of his nose by stuffing bits of greased cotton wool up his nostrils and put grease around his eyes, but it was a hopeless venture. He tried not to rub his eyes, but the coal dust was everywhere and even his mouth tasted of coal. He often thought that coaling meant he must've *eaten* his fair share of the damned stuff and half-joked that even his shit looked black. He was pleased that the *Hindenburg* was also an oil-burner, which meant less coal had to be shovelled.

The coaling continued for many hours, broken by welcome short breaks for coal-dust-covered drinks and sandwiches. During these brief respites, Eckhardt, up from the dark hold, could see that the battle cruiser's decks were getting thick with coal dust, with black footprints and barrow tracks everywhere. It would be easy to view it all as a disorganised, black mess, but everyone had years of experience and well established practices, routines and skills made it a smooth operation. Accompanied by much swearing for any bungling performance and, where necessary, some direction by officers, the oversize bags were quickly filled, ensuring any pieces of coal that were too large for the coal chutes were first smashed up. A load of a dozen or more bags were hoisted by each derrick from collier to ship where an endless train of barrow men, more skilful than any railway station porter, moved each bag around the deck to the appropriate coal chute, depositing it so its open end fell neatly at the mouth of the chute. Below, red-eyed trimmers and stokers had the unenviable and dirtiest job of ensuring all the coal bunkers were filled. The empty bags were just as efficiently passed swiftly back to the collier.

Back in Wilhelmshaven, Eckhardt knew they would've easily shifted 200 tons an hour, perhaps more. Would they match that, he heard some of his black gang discussing. Despite the task in hand, all were working quite feverishly, spurred on no doubt by the situation and the first officer's exhortations. Some had said there were pre-war coaling records of nearly 400 tons an hour. When he thought back to his first coaling, he half-smiled, thinking then that it was something to approach with interest, even enthusiasm and just another job for a sailor, but that attitude very soon died. Coaling was nothing but a thoroughly filthy, back-breaking job and, with the potential for heavy bags of coal swinging between the ships dropping on you, a dangerous one. Eckhardt worked as hard as his shipmates, but, when the blade of his shovel was stopped short yet again by the unyielding coal mass, he silently cursed that anyone who pursued records in coaling ship needed their head examined.

The engine noise was deafening, above the small windscreen the airflow buffeted him and he was cold, but he was in his element and, as always, captivated by the panorama below. *Leutnant* Karl Geiger would privately accept his naval career had not been going anywhere, until he was encouraged to apply for pilot training. That was his best move since joining the navy. Surprising even himself, he had proved to be a good flyer. He had even been decorated for his aerial exploits in the Baltic, which he doubted would ever've happened if he'd kept his feet on the deck. High up, the Earth always looked so beautiful. It was a shame war came along to interfere with such sights.

He peered through his oil-smeared, dirty goggles at the sea and the white-brown landscape stretching away to port. His reconnaissance flight was intended to scout the Icelandic waters to the west and east of Hornvik bay, reporting any craft which might threaten to surprise or report the *Hindenburg*. His orders were to fly west first about thirty to forty kilometres investigating the waters beyond Hornvik. He was to keep at least a kilometre from the shore and, if possible, to avoid flying over any ships, villages or farms, lest the plane's German insignia be recognised. It was not clear if there were indeed any aircraft in Iceland, so any sighting of his would be expected to raise questions about the plane. After flying west, he would turn back and inspect the waters to the east of Hornvik.

He realised he had an important task to undertake, even without *Kapitänleutnant* Brandmann, his commanding officer, repeatedly stressing it in briefing him. He was disappointed with Brandmann to get such an instruction; he was no inexperienced officer or a novice flyer. He considered his record in the Baltic as good as anyone's. Then again, much to his chagrin and questioning his own expertise, his first attempt at a take-off was not a success and he wondered if Brandmann would comment on it. He'd been keen to get aloft, but misjudged the calm water near the ship, which prevented the plane from getting 'unstuck'. His observer sitting in the rear cockpit, *Flugmeister*—Flying Petty Officer—Günther Falbe, quickly identified more suitable waters over on the western side of the bay. There the wind had stirred up the water, providing small waves which he used successfully to get the plane airborne.

The journey would not take long, travelling at their speed of 100 kilometres an hour. Geiger had a small pencil map of the coast ahead, which showed the few bays they would encounter. Brandmann had said they were not to go farther than the Straumnes head, where the coast turned more south-west. To go beyond that, he'd been warned, could take him into more populated areas.

After flying out over the *Erda*, Geiger first went out to sea and began to climb, intending to take the plane up to nearly 2,000 metres, but still well below the clouds. Although no opposition was expected, the two men could not fail to watch for fighters. Falbe swung his machine gun slowly across the sky behind them. Apart from the usual air turbulence which could cause the plane to fall alarmingly, Geiger eventually reached the desired altitude. He then turned the plane west and they soon saw the great bay they'd seen from the ship earlier that day. It was much wider than Hornvik and extended as far south. Whilst it looked like one large bay, the map showed it to be two. Geiger didn't even attempt to pronounce either of their Icelandic names. From their altitude, little seemed hidden from view, but, to ensure nothing was missed, Geiger banked the plane and paralleled the shoreline. Like Hornvik, this bay had some flat areas, intersected by stark, snow-swept, oddly shaped mountains, one of which came right to the water's edge in a steep cliff and defined the two bays. Falbe immediately pointed out what seemed to be some isolated farm buildings.

When aloft, communication with each other was down to shouting or using various hand signals. 'They must have seen the ship!' screamed Geiger, to which Falbe raised a gloved thumb. He let the plane glide down several hundred metres to getter a better view of what were scattered farm buildings. He saw nothing to indicate any cause for concern, some boats, perhaps large rowing boats, could be seen on the shore, but no telegraph wires. They did not tarry and, following the shoreline, headed west, flying above a ridge of the same brown and white-coloured mountains that tumbled steeply or in some places vertically into the sea. On both bays' flat ground, he'd seen several farms, though even from this height they looked poor affairs. He marked dots on his map to indicate their location.

At their speed, they were soon at the next headland. A sharp-faced mountain seemed not that far below them as they turned into the next, quite different bay. Unlike the previous ten or twelve kilometre-wide bay, this one was only about two kilometres wide. The high mountains that defined its seaward end opened up to a flat landscape, with a large lake in a valley that stretched away to the south-east. Nothing was seen, as they pressed on.

Ahead was Straumnes, the third headland from Hornvik. Before they reached it, another valley, almost full of a lake, disappeared away to their left. Falbe, tapping Geiger's shoulder, pointed to another farm, at the far side on flat land, below a steep-sided mountain. Again, they saw nothing to arouse their concerns. A small row boat was on the seashore, but no telegraph poles could be seen. Geiger turned the plane sharply towards the Straumnes headland, flying alongside another high mountain, its steep lower slopes completely covered with scree.

As they rounded the headland, Geiger immediately saw a ship close into the shore. For a moment he was shocked by it, but almost immediately realised that it was actually aground on the rocks. It seemed to be at least fifty metres long and, he reckoned, must be some sort of coaster. He saw it was rusty and ravaged by the sea, but the paint on its hull, superstructure and tall, single funnel showed it was obviously a new wreck. He flew lower and could see white cross-shapes and what looked like letters on the hull. They were sufficiently intact for Geiger to figure out that they spelt DANMARK. He wondered if it was a victim of the war or had just run aground. A tap on his shoulder and bellowed words in his right ear made him turn his gaze away from the land; Falbe was pointing at small shapes—ships—many kilometres out to sea.

Despite his orders, he needed to get closer to be able to assess what craft they'd encountered. He swung towards them. The ships were only about fifteen or so kilometres offshore and the two airmen were soon able to see that they were small sailing craft, five of them, probably fishing boats. Mostly, they had their bows to the east, but no great sail showing, so he concluded they must be fishing. Even keeping several kilometres away, Geiger expected the fishermen must have seen the plane, there was nothing to hide it from them. Marking the position of the boats, he signalled Falbe that he was returning to the *Hindenburg* and not going to wireless this finding.

As they turned, Falbe again drew his pilot's attention to the north. A thin, broken white line seemed to stretch across the distant horizon. Geiger was unmoved by it, but Falbe shouted: 'Ice!'

By increasing speed and taking a more direct route, after hardly twenty minutes Hornvik was in sight. Geiger could see the *Erda* steaming slowly about a kilometre north of the bay. Aiming to bring the plane into the mouth of the bay, he went into a shallow glide and was soon skirting alongside the long western cliff face. As the bay unfolded, he could see the ship ahead, still with the *Torsten Meyer* alongside. He was only about fifty metres from the highest part of the cliff wall whose crest was now above the plane. They had seen seabirds throughout their flight, usually below them, but suddenly the sky seemed full of white flashing shapes milling about them, as birds swarmed around the cliff face. It all happened so quickly. The thump was almost inaudible, but he suddenly felt the plane swing to the right. As the plane slipped sideways towards the cliff, it seemed obvious to him they were going to hit the rocky wall. Inexplicably, for an instant he did nothing, then rather than turn to port, away from the danger, he turned the plane further to starboard. They swung round, coming within a few metres of the terrifying brown rocks; he felt the updraft catch the plane, tipping her port wing higher. In a moment, the plane was heading back into the bay.

⚑

In the large stateroom, across the passageway from his Day Cabin, Körner sat at the head of the room's long table. On the table were a few mugs of coffee, with a couple of ashtrays readily demonstrating how the room had acquired its blue fog. Two rolled-up maps pointed down the table. To Körner's left sat *Kapitänleutnant* Ulrich Eckel, the *Torsten Meyer*'s balding captain. Traces of black around Eckel's eyes and on his hands showed that he'd been close to the coaling. Next to Eckel sat *Leutnant* Alfred Lohr of the *Erda*. The young, fair-haired officer seemed confident enough and not intimidated by a meeting with the warship's captain. With the *Erda* guarding the anchorage, Körner accepted that her captain, the bearded Klaus Harberer, had left his second-in-command to discuss any matters with him. Despite the coaling from the *Torsten Meyer* which had been going on for several hours, both supply ships would continue to have important roles during the rest of *Georg* and Körner wanted to discuss their next moves. On Körner's right sat

Gärtner, Kehlmann and *Korvettenkapitän* Erich von Schönert. A serious-looking, but approachable individual, Schönert was a representative from Bünzlin's staff, who had worked on *Georg*'s planning. Given his previous experience, he was assigned to the ship as Signals Officer, with additional responsibility for intelligence operations, including a special code-breaking unit.

Körner's initial thoughts on the meeting were to have separate discussions with each supply ship's captain. He intended that, as they would have quite separate missions, they did not need to know each other's, especially if the capture of one might in some way jeopardise the other, but given time constraints and similar issues to cover, he went ahead with a joint meeting. Körner had opened the gathering by asking about the supply ships' seaworthiness. Both officers affirmed that their ships were well able to continue to support the *Hindenburg*. 'But what of your engine problem, *Kapitänleutnant*?' Körner asked Eckel. 'Is it corrected? Likely to recur?'

Eckel had earlier explained how his ship had developed a steam leak just when they were leaving Jan Mayen. 'The problem was never great, Captain, but unfortunately it affected our speed. Now we've had the time here, the problem has been resolved.' He added, 'Your engineer was most helpful.'

Körner was not wholly convinced by Eckel's confidence, but Faber, the *Hindenburg*'s chief engineer, had sent one of his staff to look at the matter and reported back that all seemed satisfactory.

'Well, I'm glad to hear that,' said Körner, trying not to give any unnecessary air of concern. 'All our ships need to be fully operational.' He continued, addressing both supply ships' officers, 'Your orders covered sailing to Jan Mayen and the rendezvous with us. From that point you were to take orders from me. While you lacked detail about future moves, no doubt it will come as no surprise to know that our next move is for the *Hindenburg* to break-out into the Atlantic.' Their faces appeared to confirm this. 'I have here,' holding two envelopes in his hand, 'your orders, which I'll summarise now and try and answer any questions you may have.

'I don't know if any of my officers have mentioned it … no matter … but we fear that our other supply ship, the *Seefahrerin*, has probably been lost. You may have picked up the signals trying to contact her.'

Lohr showed no knowledge, though Eckel confirmed that his wireless office had noted the calls to her and imagined she was lost.

'We know nothing about her whereabouts, so are proceeding that she is lost. I'm sure you accept that that means your ships are now even more essential to the success of the operation and, *Leutnant*, your ship must now fulfil the *Seefahrerin*'s role.'

The two men said nothing in response, but Körner noted the slight, but clearly affirmative nod given by Lohr.

'Once the refuelling is completed,' he quickly continued, 'I intend to leave this bay soon afterwards.' Handing Eckel the envelope containing his orders,

Körner said, 'When we all leave here later today, you will take the *Torsten Meyer* back to Jan Mayen. You will remain there until you have orders to the contrary. If all goes well, we may not need to call on your services again, … but, if necessary, you will be an important reserve.'

Eckel gave no indication of concern at the news. 'We can do that, Captain,' he smiled. 'Will wireless silence continue?'

'Yes,' replied Körner, his tone indicating surprise at such a question. Continued wireless silence was in Eckel's orders, but he thought he had better emphasise the reason for this. 'I consider that the longer we maintain wireless silence, the more chance we have of successfully completing our mission. Once we break it, for whatever reason, we should expect the English to locate us and have the opportunity to marshal their forces against us.'

Concerned about the importance of wireless silence, Körner looked at both the supply ship men and continued his discourse. 'I know that our ships' wireless-telegraphy equipment has a limited range, but under favourable circumstances may reach far enough. So, I say again, you should not break wireless silence until you hear from the *Hindenburg* or the Fleet … or you are attacked by the enemy. If an enemy ship looks likely to capture you, you are to break wireless silence *immediately* and send the plain language, triple-A message, repeating it as long as possible,' which they all knew was the agreed, simple morse signal that the ship was threatened by the enemy. 'Of course, you will scuttle your ship before capture. Even if you are under fire, endeavour to keep signalling for as long as you can. Likewise, if some other problem arises that prevents you from fulfilling your orders, you should signal that. Is that understood?'

'Aye, Sir,' was both men's instant response.

Finishing off his instructions to Eckel, he asked, 'I am told that supplies have been transferred from your ship and coaling is nearly finished,' though, whatever Eckel said, he would seek confirmation of coal and oil fuel taken aboard from Schellenberg.

'Yes, Sir,' answered Eckel. 'Oiling is complete, coaling almost. Food and other items transferred.'

'What is your remaining oil and coal?'

'I calculate we'll have about 800 tons of coal and some 150 tons of oil.'

Körner knew that the three supply ships were differently configured in their oil and coal cargoes and while some changes had been possible in developing them for *Georg*, time did not allow for comprehensive alterations. 'Enough coal, … but not enough oil to fill our tanks,' he said, 'though it should allow us sufficient for a fast run home from Jan Mayen. Our main intention for the journey back to Germany will be to refuel from the *Erda*, but even that will depend on events.' Körner looked at Gärtner, who gave a slow, single nod, signifying that the fuel situation either way would be satisfactory.

'Well, we will welcome you, if you need to visit us at Jan Mayen, but will be just as pleased if the *Erda* satisfies your needs,' said Eckel, trying to make light of the subject. 'Hopefully,' he went on, unbidden, 'if you do come to us, the weather will have improved. Jan Mayen is an amazing sight, but is a God-forsaken place ... and, of course, cold. It's easy to understand why it's uninhabited, indeed, not yet owned by anyone, though no doubt someone will plant their flag there soon enough,' concluded Eckel.

The *Hindenburg* officers smiled politely at these unrequested observations, but, other than Kehlmann, had no real insight into Jan Mayen's topography or weather, beyond what they'd read. Eckel had already spoken to Körner about the sea ice conditions at the island before the meeting, but Körner, still debating about the merits of refuelling there, sought yet more information.

'When we first got to the island,' said Eckel, 'we attempted to sail around it, but found the Greenland Sea ice had completely enveloped its western coast. The sea beyond, as far as could be seen, was frozen,' he said, a degree of despair in his words.

'Hopefully, as I've been informed,' said Körner, 'April generally sees the greatest extent of the ice, so it shouldn't get any worse,' which brought a few smiles, though he noted Kehlmann's eyebrows rose slightly, perhaps suggesting nothing should be taken for granted. 'Did you identify any suitable refuelling sites?'

'At least on the eastern shore,' replied Eckel, 'there are no fjords or major inlets like Hornvik, though there are some small bays and headlands which could offer a sheltered position, against west or north winds. A stretch of shore near the southern end of the island would probably serve well, depending on the depth of water. We will take soundings.'

Körner thanked Eckel and then handed the *Erda*'s envelope to an obviously eager Lohr. '*Leutnant*, your Captain's orders require you to replace the *Seefahrerin*. You will proceed through the Denmark Strait with us and take up position to refuel us in one of Greenland's western fjords. *Oberleutnant* Kehlmann,' gesturing to the older officer, 'will accompany you and assist in the direction to the fjord.'

Lohr gave a single, respectful nod to Kehlmann who smiled back at him. Körner could not help thinking that Kehlmann might well be older than Lohr's father. He hoped the *Oberleutnant*'s presence would not disrupt the *Erda*'s command structure, but had clearly set out Kehlmann's status in the orders.

Körner gave no more information about why Kehlmann had been assigned to the *Erda*. Kehlmann had briefed the *Seefahrerin*'s captain on the selected Greenland fjord and, in the changing circumstances, he and Gärtner had concluded that he would now be better on the *Erda*. Kehlmann had always argued he was no great expert on Greenland's west coast, but his knowledge was better than anyone else's and would again be most useful. He'd confirmed that, at this time of year, much of Greenland's south-western coast would be ice-free, but many of the fjords were gateways to glaciers and, like many others, were full of loose ice. Using Greenland as a refuelling option was one of the concerns in *Georg*'s planning. Nothing like Hornvik seemed available and information was sparse. Kehlmann had selected one he'd been to during his travels, which could be used for refuelling, though he'd confirmed that the whole coastline was a veritable fretwork of fjords and inlets. Depending on the ice situation, many of these would easily be able to hide the giant battle cruiser and her supply ship. Körner had expected the degree of uncertainty about a Greenland refuelling site, in comparison to Hornvik or Jan Mayen, would be one of the elements of *Georg* which Admiral Scheer would strongly challenge, as he routinely expected detailed plans supporting all operations. However, surprisingly, he'd raised no objection, perhaps because the planned second refuelling had specified Jan Mayen over Greenland.

Refuelling at Jan Mayen on the return leg back to Germany had various benefits, but, as the voyage progressed, Körner had debated the pros and cons of Jan Mayen and Greenland with Schellenberg, Gärtner and Kehlmann. Their discussions, which centred on the advisability of retracing their path through the potentially ice-strewn Denmark Strait, not to mention Royal Navy patrols, were now further influenced by the *Torsten Meyer*'s engine problems and her captain's views on the wintry island. Körner had decided to opt for a Greenland refuelling and passage home across the broad Atlantic, south of Iceland. The discretion on such matters was his; he was not bound to use any of the planned refuelling points.

'We will lead you through the Strait,' Körner said to Lohr. 'We will try to keep as far from Iceland as possible, but there may well be ice.' He knew of the airmen's sighting of what looked like possible ice not far to the north of Iceland, but said nothing of it. 'So keep a keen watch for that and our signals. If we encounter any ships, we will have to gauge matters as they happen, but, again, watch for our signals.'

'Aye, Sir.'

Can you maintain twelve knots?'

'Yes, Sir. That is our nominal service speed. Our maximum speed is nearly fifteen knots, but, even if we could achieve that, we couldn't sustain it for any great period,' said Lohr, trying to be helpful.

'Well, that's good to know. Who knows how things may turn out, but, if necessary, you may have to ask your stokers to do their utmost,' said Körner, with a slight smile. He continued, 'At the designated point … it's in the orders … we will detach you to make your own way to Greenland. Under the *Oberleutnant*'s guidance, you will proceed to the refuelling fjord. You will then rendezvous with us and lead us back to the fjord.'

Turning to Gärtner, Körner said, '*Herr* Gärtner, could you please point out the fjord and the rendezvous point.' It may have been better to ask Kehlmann to point out the fjord's location, but Körner, mindful of the hierarchy, deferred to Gärtner.

Gärtner did not defer to his subordinate. He leaned forward and unrolled one of the maps, holding the corners down with the empty mugs. The map showed the

North Atlantic, Canada, Greenland and Iceland. He pushed the other map to Lohr. 'This map is for you, in case you don't have one of the area,' he said.

On his open map and with little comment, Gärtner, using his middle finger, traced the ships' intended course. He moved quickly and lightly around the northwest corner of Iceland, continued down the Denmark Strait to Greenland's southernmost point, clearly labelled with the interesting and somewhat disconcerting name *Kap Abschied*—Cape Farewell—then around to the western coast. Although the map stretched across much of the table, it was really of too small a scale to show much detail of Greenland, though it was obvious to all that Greenland's coast was littered with fjords and inlets. Gärtner's finger came to a halt some centimetres along the south-western coast.

'The selected fjord is here,' said Gärtner, now using a sharp pencil to indicate the coastal area between places on the map labelled as *Lichtenfels* and *Frederikshaab*, 'almost six hundred kilometres from Cape Farewell.' Turning to Kehlmann, he asked him to describe the fjord and the prevailing ice conditions.

'This part of the Greenland's western coast could well have thick sea ice,' said Kehlmann, indicating the south-western tip of Greenland, 'but further up the coast, the fjords are considered to be ice-free, even at this time of the year. I have been to the chosen fjord. We never found out its name. It's about two kilometres wide and, like many of Greenland's fjords, very long, perhaps ten or twenty kilometres long, providing plenty of scope for refuelling sites. Many Greenland fjords,' continued Kehlmann, 'have a glacier at their head, which produces considerable ice moving down them. Our fjord has no glacier and probably no great ice. Nevertheless, we shall have to proceed carefully, keeping a special ice watch. Currents could force ice floes into it or might well block the entrance. We will check it out before rendezvousing with the *Hindenburg*. As you can see, there are many fjords and inlets, so even if our fjord is impassable, we should readily find other suitable sites for the refuelling.'

At that point, Kehlmann looked to Gärtner, indicating that he had finished speaking. Gärtner needed no invitation.

'The rendezvous point, 'W, S, E', is here,' said Gärtner, his pencil tapping the map a couple of times. 'Sixty north, fifty-one west, about two hundred kilometres south-west of the fjord. From there we can easily return with you to it for the refuelling. As the *Oberleutnant* has indicated, the fjord or nearby waters should provide various sheltered locations for refuelling and will probably have deep water, though you should take some soundings, as you have here.' Lohr nodded to most of these statements by Gärtner. 'The *Oberleutnant* has told us that there'll no doubt be eskimos in the vicinity, indeed possibly quite a few, but we doubt the locals will be any more of a problem than we've encountered here in Hornvik.'

Körner saw that the mention of eskimos brought smiles to some faces, but not to Kehlmann. Körner took that as meaning that the old sailor had, unlike the others, some knowledge and quite possibly respect for these Greenland natives.

Gärtner continued, addressing his comments to Lohr. 'We envisage striking the enemy in this area,' his pencil moving south and, without marking the map's surface, described a large oval shape from Nova Scotia to the mid-Atlantic, 'which is about two thousand kilometres away. That means it would take us, say at fourteen knots, all of four to five days to reach you. Any questions?'

'No,' said Lohr, 'that seems clear enough, though,' adding, 'I'm glad we'll have the *Oberleutnant* with us.' This brought a few smiles, not least to Kehlmann's usually unmoving face. Lohr then asked, 'With cold air from Greenland, any warm sea could create fog?' Seeking approval, he said, 'We will use our siren, if there's a visibility problem.'

'Yes, good point,' said Körner. 'We must meet up and, short of using wireless, that seems as good a way as any of making contact, if the weather is foul. However, as our exact arrival time is not that predictable, I would counsel against its use. We may not be there; others may,' he quipped. Lohr looked a bit crestfallen, which was not Körner's intention. 'As you'll find in your orders,' he continued, 'while I'm reluctant to break wireless silence, we may have to do so, if we can't find each other. A low power call may be necessary, but let's hope it doesn't come to that. Weather permitting, we can also use the seaplane to locate you.'

After a slight pause, Körner said, 'Maintaining wireless silence will mean we cannot signal when to make for the rendezvous. Instead, we estimate you should aim to be at the rendezvous ten days after we part company off Greenland. You should then cruise that area, until you hear otherwise.' By that Körner meant if something had happened to stop the *Hindenburg* getting to WSE, but he didn't elaborate. 'This is not an ideal situation, far from it, but if wireless silence is to be maintained ....' He said no more. Lohr seemed to understand; it was all in their orders.

Körner allowed questions to continue for some minutes. These touched on the fjord, but also about possible visitors from *Frederikshaab* and other towns or settlements to the south of it, an issue which continued to bother Körner. After some final points, not least about the two supply ships changing positions so that the *Erda* could collect Lohr and Kehlmann, the meeting came to an end. Körner wished the two supply ship officers good luck.

⚐

Eckhardt and his mess-mates were trying, with varying degrees of success, to clean themselves up after their coal-moving endeavours. Everywhere, even on the mess deck, showed the black signature of coaling, a fine film of darkness on every surface. Eckhardt grumbled to those in earshot that, given their circumstances, they and the ship would never be clean again until they got back to Germany, which was readily agreed, though they knew that the decks would soon be hosed down, washing away their black coating and in due course they would also wash their bodies clean of the stuff. Word came down that the first officer was well-pleased with everyone's efforts during the coaling and that over 200 tons an hour had been shifted. This was all met with a mixed response; faint praise, thought some. The collective view was simpler than that and settled more on 'thank God that's over'.

They didn't need to be told that the ship would not linger much longer in this Icelandic bay, but after cleaning up the ship and themselves, a belated meal was promised. Other than interludes for bread and drinks, the coaling had disrupted the normal ship routine. The day's 12 o'clock meal was postponed—for once everyone understood why—and all the men now looked forward to it. The mess deck was prepared, tables dropped and utensils prepared. The call to Battle Stations stopped the meal preparations. No one questioned it, other than the odd 'what now?'

Eckhardt made for the Spotting Top and was well out of breath when he reached his post. The *Torsten Meyer* had long since moved out of the giant bay, almost as soon as coaling was completed, and he could see the *Erda* off their port beam, in the process of raising a boat. The *Hindenburg* had begun to move, her big-gun turrets moving slightly, as if sniffing out a target, ready to deal harshly with any threat. Eckhardt swung his binoculars to the bay's mouth. There was nothing but empty sea.

'What's up?' he said quietly to nearby Schwarz.

'The *Torsten Meyer*,' the look-out responded. 'She's signalled that she's seen a ship.'

Again, Eckhardt swept his glasses across the mouth of the bay and far out to sea, but could see nothing of the *Torsten Meyer* or her sighting. Soon, the battle cruiser was closing on the bay's mouth. He could feel his heart beating, imagining the enemy was waiting for them, warships surrounding their only escape route. There was nothing for it; the ship couldn't be trapped in the bay. His view was all on the fast approaching open sea beyond the cliffs, but out of the corner of his eye he glimpsed the *Erda*, now off the starboard quarter, Hornvik's steep slopes towering above her. Her wake showing she was getting underway. The sight of activity around her boat davits had him wondering if all the men on jobs around the bay had been recovered.

⚑

Körner was at the front of the Command Bridge, right up against the canvas screen. Until any shooting started, he would not consider going inside the armoured conning tower. After Battle Stations was sounded, once Körner had reached the Bridge, Schellenberg had gone to the aft control position. Before he left, he'd informed Körner of the *Torsten Meyer*'s message, that she'd sighted a ship to the east and was going to investigate.

Körner was disappointed with Eckel. It was not his job to engage the enemy; his ship was not equipped for that. Körner quickly pushed such thoughts to the back of his mind, as his ship approached the mouth of Hornvik bay and he searched the horizon for the supply ship and the enemy. The sky was overcast and the northern horizon dark with rain squalls. The wind was coming from the south, almost astern of them, and the coastal sea, in the lee of the high cliffs, looked remarkably calm.

The ship's bows pierced the sea outside the quiet bay waters. Almost immediately the sighting of a ship away to starboard was called. While Körner prepared to order a course change to bring all the ship's big guns to bear on the possible target, he focused his binoculars in that direction. Looking beyond the steep cliffs, which formed the eastern arm of Hornvik bay, he saw a ship—it was the *Torsten Meyer*. She was hardly a kilometre or so offshore and stern-on to the *Hindenburg*. She appeared to be stopped. Near her starboard side was a small craft. It looked like a sailing boat, a twin-mast affair. Judging by the state of the sails, it was being shielded from the wind by the merchantman's bulk. Körner saw a light winking from the merchantman's superstructure. A young officer reported to him.

'The *Torsten Meyer* reports that they have stopped a fishing boat.'

Kehlmann had alerted them to expect fishing boats along the north coast. Their presence had been confirmed by the seaplane's all but disastrous flight, but this one was not the first they'd actually encountered. During the previous night, as their course angled them closer to Iceland, they'd seen a few dim lights away to the south-east. They considered them to be two, perhaps three, fishing boats, who, unlike the German trio, were not worried about keeping their ships darkened. They were far off and Körner did not consider they warranted a course change or other action. Even though such fishing boats probably didn't have any wireless, the *Hindenburg*'s wireless operators listened out for tell-tale messages that the German ships had been seen and, thankfully, heard none.

Körner had a message sent to the *Torsten Meyer* asking if any others were visible, to which the supply ship fortunately said no. While he didn't think the newcomer would have been any more a threat to their security than the farmsteads in Hornvik, he could not rebuke Eckel, who presumably intended to inhibit the fishermen from seeing into Hornvik bay. As it transpired, they no doubt got an eye-boggling close-up view of the giant warship, as she sailed passed the *Torsten Meyer* and her captive. Körner could see that the fishing boat, with some sails down, was now alongside the supply ship. He would leave it to Eckel what to do with them. The battle cruiser made a slow starboard turn till Körner was rewarded by the sight of the *Erda* emerging from Hornvik bay. Once the *Erda* had closed up, with a final exchange of good luck messages with the *Torsten Meyer*, Körner took the battle cruiser north, away from Hornvik, endeavouring to mislead anyone watching from the shore—or Eckel's unwanted guests—of his ship's Atlantic course.

8

Denmark Strait

Although sunset was several hours away, the overcast conditions threw darkness onto the sea and intermittent rain squalls and mist reduced visibility to little more than seven or eight kilometres. Iceland soon disappeared from view. At that point Körner turned the *Hindenburg* and the *Erda* west, on through the Denmark Strait and towards the open Atlantic.

Körner stared aft at the supply ship following about 400 metres astern. As ordered, she was keeping slightly to port of the ruffled, but smooth-looking, white water of the battle cruiser's wake, so as not to impair her speed. The warship easily slipped along at 12 knots, her funnel smoke at a minimum. This contrasted with the merchant ship's smoke which produced a dark cloud blown off to starboard. There was nothing that could be done about her smoke, which might easily be seen far off if visibility improved. He could not predict what would happen if they were sighted, it would depend on who saw them. He concentrated his mind on getting safely through the Strait.

While the *Erda* inhibited a high speed dash through the Strait, he accepted that the real prospect of ice, especially with limited visibility and the evening drawing on, necessitated a reduced speed that would allow his look-outs time to alert the ship about any sea ice.

Gärtner had reported that the ice gap between Greenland and Iceland could be expected to be at its minimum in the Strait, perhaps forty sea miles, though he said Kehlmann knew of some years when it was much less—at worst, the Greenland ice could reach Iceland. Although Körner was concerned about ice, he drew some comfort from the fact that Nerger had used the Denmark Strait to take his ship into the Atlantic in December, but reminded himself that it was the following few months which usually saw the worst ice conditions. Körner's ice worries were also augmented by the seaplane observations, which suggested possible ice to the north of their present course.

It would have been good to employ the seaplane on the journey ahead, but the day's events had at least postponed that. Körner had not seen the plane come close to disaster, but was quickly updated by Schellenberg. A seagull was now reckoned to have struck the plane's starboard upper wing, damaging the wing and almost bringing down the plane. Another had hit the radiator and it looked like a third had challenged the propeller. Thankfully, the pilot was able to avoid crashing and managed a hard, but safe landing in Hornvik bay. He and his observer were unharmed. Brandmann said that the damage to the wing could be repaired and the radiator replaced, but they and an engine problem had curtailed further flights, leaving Körner to rely on the supply ships to watch over the sea outside the bay. Schellenberg had reported that repairs were underway, but would not be completed for quite some hours. Even if the repairs were done quickly, given the lateness of the hour and the misty conditions, no reconnaissance flights could be contemplated until the morning. Körner had tentatively asked about the possibility of assembling and using the crated plane, but Schellenberg responded that it would probably take as long as the repair and, of course, that they did not have sufficient hangar space to manage two seaplanes.

Körner was in the Chart Room next to his Sea Cabin with Gärtner when two ketch-rigged sailing boats were reported—probably fishing boats, like the one encountered off Hornvik. They were about eight kilometres off, at the edge of visibility, sails billowing, running before the wind and paralleling the ship's course. Körner was annoyed with himself for not putting more sea room between the *Hindenburg* and Iceland, but gave no thought to rounding up the fishing boats and instead turned the ships away. Very soon the little boats were out of sight, but he thought it would be too much to hope for that the fishermen hadn't seen them. Probably—hopefully—lacking wireless, they'd have to return to shore to report their encounter. 'How long before they're back in port?' he asked Gärtner.

The navigator checked his charts. 'The nearest big port is …,' he struggled with the pronunciation, 'Isa…fjord…ur, in the largest fjord on this stretch of coast, just to the south of here. It's about sixty kilometres away. It would take them some time to get there. I doubt they can do, say, more than eight knots, but the wind would be against them, so I think we have eight, perhaps ten hours, before they'll get back. Given their course, they may not be intent on returning to port just yet.'

'Yes, good. Perhaps they'll concentrate on their fishing and not bother about us,' replied Körner, smiling, but his tone showed his disappointment at the sighting and he doubted they would forget to mention sighting a large warship.

Soon enough the battle cruiser and her merchant ship attendant changed their westerly course to a south-westerly one. In another six or seven hours, Iceland would start to fall away to port, leaving them with a clear run into the Atlantic. Plenty of time, Körner thought, to get away from these waters before news of them leaked out. Well, that was what he hoped for.

'Ice, dead ahead!'

Körner and Gärtner, again studying the maps, emerged from the Chart Room. Schellenberg, binoculars raised, was looking ahead. Körner was about to ask him for the exact location of the ice, but stopped himself when he saw the thin white line lying across their intended course. He could see that the ice, still some seven or eight kilometres off, stretched out before them as far as the limited visibility allowed. At this distance, the sea, appearing even darker against the white ice, also seemed calmer.

'Spotting Top reports ice ahead, Sir, though it appears to be broken ice, ice floes, not a solid ice pack,' said Schellenberg.

'Well, hopefully it's not too thick or there are gaps we can get through,' replied Körner. 'Alert the *Erda*.'

As the distance reduced, it seemed the ice was quite dense and extensive to Körner, extending across much of the horizon. The individual ice floes appeared to be a mix, some large, some small, mostly flat shapes, though some clearly had pronounced ridges and other projections that suggested they were thicker. No pieces appeared to have ridden up on top of others, suggesting no untoward pressure in the ice field. Körner and Schellenberg considered that they could probably negotiate this ice. They often had to cope with winter sea ice off Wilhelmshaven and Körner knew Nerger had coped with ice during his passages in the Denmark Strait and survived, so the *Hindenburg*, even her consort, should be able to get through without damage. However, he had no desire especially this far from base to tangle with any large piece of ice, which might damage, say, a propeller. He turned the ship to port, regrettably towards Iceland, keeping the ice off their starboard beam. He expected the ice to the east to be easier to negotiate.

Soon Schellenberg again reported, his voice encouraging. 'Captain, Spotting Top reports that the ice is thinning.'

'Thank goodness. I thought we were going to have to sail back to Iceland to get around it,' said Körner, attempting a humorous response. Schellenberg smiled politely. They were both nevertheless pleased that it had only been fifteen minutes since they were turned by the ice.

Körner conned the ship himself from the higher levels above the Command Bridge to get a better view. At reduced speed, he took her through what was now clearly dispersed, loose ice, though occasional impacts and scraping noises may have made some a bit apprehensive. Looking astern, he saw that the *Erda* seemed to be having no problem negotiating the gap created by the big ship. A signal light exchange confirmed she'd come through unscathed, but no sooner had he begun to feel pleased about getting both ships safely through when ice was again reported. Another band, again ice floes, barred their path, less than fifteen kilometres from the first. Fortunately, this line proved to be looser than the other and they negotiated it as easily.

'Will there be any more?' asked Körner, more thinking aloud than seeking an answer from Schellenberg.

No more ice was seen. They kept on, heading south-west by south, through those high latitudes' short night and into the new day. The wind picked up a notch, now coming at their port quarter. This argued with the grey-blue sea and periodically managed to put a wave onto the deck. The dark weather front continued above them, probably held at bay by cold Greenland air away to their starboard beam. Körner did not complain. Its low clouds and occasional rain could shield them from view.

After their tiring and long day of coaling and Battle Stations, Körner stood the ship down to give the crew a chance to recuperate, trusting to no surprise ocean encounters. The *Erda* plodded on behind them, still keeping near the big ship's white wake, her funnel smoke now chasing the battle cruiser and occasionally all but hiding her from their view. All went well. The misty Denmark Strait was behind them and they were well south of Iceland, though the map still showed Greenland as a barrier to any westward movement. Soon the ships would separate, the *Hindenburg* turning due south, while the *Erda* turned west for her Greenland appointment. During the transit of the Strait, Körner had been on the Bridge most of the time, catching short rests in his Sea Cabin. Now, busy again, he, Schellenberg and Gärtner, in the Chart Room's limited space, discussed the forthcoming course change and future options. Schönert pushed his head around the door, interrupting their deliberations. They could all see his face displayed an urgent issue.

'Captain, we have intercepted an important signal.' He said no more, but handed a small piece of paper to Körner. 'We intercepted this, in clear, from a Newfoundland station.'

Körner took but a few seconds to read the note. Its content was clear. The English knew—or at least suspected—they had broken out into the Atlantic. Having read it, his eyes returned to a few of the pencil words: *Enemy battle cruiser may be operating in Atlantic.*

╠╛

Körner made his way down to his Day Cabin to ponder this latest development, on this occasion seeking a bit more privacy than his Sea Cabin afforded. A few junior officers stood to one side as he went along the port-side passageway past the officers' mess and other officers' cabins. His quarters were located at the port, aft side of the main superstructure. He thought of the seaplane now housed directly above him, hoping it could be fully repaired. His quarters were, as to be expected for a ship's captain, comfortable and, with the exception of the admiral's quarters, larger than any other officer's. They were by no means large or extravagant and the furniture and fittings were spartan. His bedroom and bathroom were aft of the larger study, which was about four and a half metres by at least three. He sat at his small desk, looking at various small-scale maps of the North Atlantic and America, though whenever he looked up his eyes inevitably went to the picture of Maria and the children. Savouring their features and memories of them, he wondered how they were and hoped all was well with them. There was a knock at the cabin door, startling him for a moment, feeling guilty of being lost in thoughts other than of the ship. It was Schellenberg. Körner had asked him to join him. Dahl, using the Captain's Pantry opposite, duly brought them coffees. Neither man had had much time to consider the Newfoundland signal, least of all discuss it with the other senior officers; time was pressing. Körner thought a considered, though early decision was required, so had asked Schellenberg to meet him in his cabin to talk about the options. They had already reached the original point for course changes and separating from the *Erda*. Her captain had been signalled to await new orders.

'This was to be expected,' opened Körner. 'Refuelling in Iceland was always likely to reveal our presence to the English. The only issue was to be one of timing.'

'I agree, Sir,' replied Schellenberg, 'though to what degree does this affect our plans? I recall little specific about how this likely development should be tackled.'

'To be honest, Peter, Captain Bünzlin and I did consider that total secrecy, or rather our never being discovered, was unlikely. As I said, the only real issue was *when*. If early on in the mission, say before refuelling, then the whole mission would probably be abandoned and we'd return to Germany; if afterwards, then continue. In any event, the decision would depend on the circumstances and would ultimately be my decision.' Körner sat back in his chair, his voice calm. 'Given where we are now, I intend to continue with the mission.' Schellenberg gave a slight nod. 'In which case, I concur with you: how does this affect our planned actions?'

'Of course,' he continued, 'the message suggests that the enemy only *suspects* we're in the Atlantic. But I think we would be wise to conclude that they believe we *are* at large, which, if it already hasn't, must sooner or later be confirmed from England. However, they don't know exactly *where* we are, … which is still to our advantage. Starting from that premise, we need to consider what, if anything, should we do differently?'

'Giving it some limited thought,' said Schellenberg, 'my first inclination would be to change our plans for the *Erda*. If the English have their wits about them, given our use of Hornvik, they would likely explore other refuelling sites. These might well include Greenland, as well as Iceland, and, as we did, they'll probably not worry too much about Danish sensitivities. I think the *Erda* should keep well clear of the Greenland coast until we are ready to rendezvous with her. We can then make for the planned fjord.'

After a few seconds mulling over the idea, Körner said, 'Yes, Peter. I'm inclined to agree. She may well be able to hide in the fjord, but her discovery would obviously affect our options. I doubt the English can search the whole coast, though they're bound to focus on the ice-free coast.' Then he quickly added, 'Of course, if she keeps clear of the Greenland coast, she may well be safer, but we've lost our chance to check out the refuelling fjord.' Körner could not but think of his decision to select Greenland over Jan Mayen and whether it was now sound, even though their earlier discussions on the matter had concluded that Jan Mayen was the riskier option, with the possibilities of the English patrolling the Denmark Strait and checking out Jan Mayen.

'I agree, Sir, but we didn't check out Hornvik. I suspect we'll be able to do as we did there.'

'Yes, quite so, Peter,' said Körner. He thought the situation might not be quite the same, given the limited information they had about the fjord, but he was inclined to accept his first officer's view. Whether the English would be able to organise the necessary resources for such a search was also a question, but he agreed that there were risks in the *Erda* making landfall days before they arrived to refuel. 'We'll get the plane to check out the fjord before we approach it. We'll order the *Erda* to keep at sea, until she gets the call for the rendezvous.' Körner unrolled the North Atlantic map. 'If she keeps south of Greenland,' his finger circling the large area of sea between Greenland and Newfoundland, 'she should be able to keep out of harm's way, till we need her. Perhaps we also need a new rendezvous? Can you please discuss that with the Navigator and prepare new orders for her.'

'Aye, Sir,' replied Schellenberg.

'Have we sorted out the *Erda* too quickly?' said Körner, smiling, hoping he was not tempting fate by such a comment. Schellenberg only smiled back.

The navigator was summoned and told of the new requirements. When he was gone, Körner continued the debate. There were various issues that had been considered in the planning of *Georg*, but had been discussed further by him and Schellenberg during the voyage. The news of their apparent discovery just added another dimension to their discussions.

'Well, one things for certain,' said Körner, 'we can expect the English to be taking steps to try and stop us, but what?' Uncharacteristically, Körner spoke first about his own ideas. 'I expect the English will take additional steps to protect their convoys. They must reason we intend to strike at them.' Schellenberg nodded agreement. 'If I were them,' he paused, looking at the map, 'I'd shift the convoy routes south, put more sea room between them and us. It might take them longer to reach England, but it would be safer. It's a logical step to take and would, in truth, inhibit our mission. I doubt they will stop convoys … they are too valuable to their war effort … but we should expect some re-routeing of convoys and … probably also an increase in convoy escorts.'

'That does seem logical, Sir,' said Schellenberg, who rested two fingers on his strong chin in contemplation. 'Our planned route sees us sailing due south, slightly east of thirty degrees west, down to about fifty north. If the English do swing their convoys further south,' Schellenberg's fingers moved from his chin to the map and traced a southerly curve on it, 'perhaps towards, perhaps even south of the Azores. That might add a thousand or more kilometres to their journey, but that *would* make them a difficult target for us. It would of course also take them well south of fifty north. On that basis, we might well be wasting our time to continue with that part of the plan.' Sweeping his finger back to Newfoundland and the Canadian coast, he then said, 'May I suggest that we sail directly for America and seek to attack their convoys nearer their assembly ports. Any change to their normal sailing routes will be less marked there.'

Like Schellenberg, Körner knew the intelligence for *Georg* suggested that every few days convoys from American and Canadian ports were expected to cross the thirty degree meridian on their way to England, which would provide an opportunity to sight and attack a convoy in the 30 west, 50 north area. But, faced with more southerly routeing, such convoys would be absent from those waters. Schellenberg was right; it would be a waste of time. Moving in towards America favoured finding a convoy or, as the *Georg* options provided for, they could still strike at an assembly port—most likely Halifax, half-way down the coast of Nova Scotia. Such a strike would be aiming to sink ships, not bombard Halifax itself, but that alternative could not be ruled out. If they had to shoot at Halifax, their gunnery would be aided by the seaplane's observations. A bombardment would not only damage the port's facilities, but would also be expected to create a panic which would spread along the whole coast.

'Peter, excellent. I agree,' said Körner. He had such ideas himself, but he did not wish to appear to be diminishing his first officer's proposal by saying anything like he'd thought of it first. 'Finding convoys in the open ocean was always the most difficult element of *Georg*. By moving more directly towards the coast of America, we may yet still encounter a convoy, perhaps before the English can change their operations, and, as the plan envisaged, if we don't find a convoy, we will attack Halifax. It may add to our planned journey, but we had anticipated such a move.' Then, surprising Schellenberg, he asked: 'What of the seaplane?' though it was but a few hours since Schellenberg's last update.

'Brandmann reports that repairs are all but complete,' said Schellenberg. 'Matters were dragged out by the nature of the damage, but all seems to have gone well.' Anticipating his captain's next question, he added: 'Brandmann considers the sea is presently too rough to launch the plane.'

So, thought Körner, robust as Brandmann considers the plane, it has its limits. 'And the latest on the pilot and observer?'

'They are OK. Thankfully, they only suffered little more than some bruises, though they were no doubt shaken up by the event. Brandmann thinks the *Leutnant* did very well in the circumstances to get the plane down safely.'

⚑

Körner privately still wondered if he'd made the right decisions about the changes to the plans. In part, it was due to the apparent ease with which they'd decided matters. In any event, he mentally confirmed Schellenberg's value as the ship's first officer and fully expected him to be made *Kapitän zur See* in due course.

Their plans were altered, however. In their haste they had not considered everything. Gärtner drew their attention to the Grand Banks, with its famous fogs and fishing, not to mention any remaining ice around Newfoundland. Körner readily agreed to the navigator's proposal to keep further east of the whole area. The Grand Banks would probably have many fishing boats on them and while any fog would shield the battle cruiser, it could also hide enemy ships, not to mention icebergs. Gärtner's new course, not far from due south to avoid the Banks' easternmost fishing grounds, also still permitted a sweep of the convoy routes originally planned under *Georg*. The distances were still considerable and continued to limit their speed. At normal cruising speed, they could get back to the *Erda* or, if necessary, the *Torsten Meyer* at Jan Mayen. Gärtner's calculations showed it was even possible to get back to Germany without refuelling, but that any high speed sailing would challenge their fuel reserves. No one ever imagined *Georg* would be easy.

The battle cruiser slowed, allowing the *Erda* to catch up. With the two ships abreast of each other, the supply ship was signalled with her new orders to keep to sea and in keeping with the original ten-day timescale to make for a new, more southerly rendezvous: 'PRA', over 200 kilometres south of 'WSE', the previous rendezvous point. As farewell and good luck messages were exchanged between the two ships, the *Hindenburg* came to her new course, 'south by west, three-quarters west' and stepped up to 14 knots. Looking back at the merchantman, Körner noted that the *Erda*'s bow wave almost immediately began to subside, as she no doubt reduced her speed and gave her hard-worked stokers a deserved rest.

He kept an occasional eye on the little merchant ship, as the distance between them grew. In the faint light of the evening, soon she was a grey silhouette near the distant horizon. After the days of continuous overcast, with intermittent rain and mist affecting visibility, this day had ushered in change. The sea was less boisterous, the wind, now more from the north, was much reduced and the cloudy skies were being left behind. Ahead the darkening sky seemed clearer with broken, thinner clouds. Visibility was improved, though suffered as the light faded. When he looked again, their steamship consort of late was gone, with just the battle cruiser's wake pointing to where she had once been.

They were alone. What had gone before seemed as nothing compared to what they still had to do. They had not yet seen, never mind fought the enemy. Körner called a meeting of his senior officers. He had met with each of them frequently, but thus far seldom as a complete group. Most knew what was going on through discussions with him and Schellenberg and from their own responsibilities. While he had utmost faith in them, it would be useful to discuss the way forward with all them, binding them into the mission and his expectations and allowing some conversation on the next steps.

It was dark outside when they met in the stateroom. The ever-dutiful Dahl had provided coffee, but knew the signals and left them alone. The coffee cups, like odd-shaped buoys marking out a channel on a flat sea, mingled with a few ashtrays. To be expected and with Körner's agreement, blue-grey smoke soon filled the poorly lit room.

Although Körner gestured to his officers to sit down, they seemed to delay until he took his seat at the head of the table. Schellenberg sat to Körner's immediate right, along with *Korvettenkäpitane* Gärtner and black-haired Kruse. Robert Kruse's prominent nose seemed to fit well with his 'Guns' label. To Körner's left were the ship's three other *Korvettenkäpitane*. Heinrich Faber, *MarineOberstabsingenieur*—the ship's Engineer—was the oldest of the group. His pale complexion almost matched his near-white hair. Körner often wondered if his below-decks life was the cause of his colouring. Next to Faber sat Werner von Lang, the somewhat aristocratic *Zahlmeister*—Paymaster—his thin moustache adding to the patrician impression about him. Schönert, perhaps emphasising his late-comer status, sat at the end of the left-hand group. All their eyes were on Körner. He returned their gaze, making fleeting eye-contact with each. He knew they'd worked tirelessly to get the ship ready for *Georg* and had continued their hard efforts since they'd sailed. Kruse, for example, had kept up a relentless regime of personal tours and daily checks of his guns and men to ensure they'd be ready when the time came. As first gunnery officer, a very large proportion of the *Hindenburg*'s crew came under his command.

'Gentlemen,' Körner's usual opening address to any group of officers. 'You will have heard that the English think we are in the Atlantic.' A range of eyebrow movements and a couple of smiles greeted this. 'In the light of that, I've made some changes to our plans and wanted to explain these to you. But first, I want to take this opportunity to thank you for your work so far. You've each done very well. Please pass on my thanks to your men.'

This also produced some slight smiles, but Körner moved on. It wasn't that he didn't mean what he said, only that it was not his way to shower praise or to single out individuals in such gatherings. He set out the latest events and what he and Schellenberg had of late decided.

'Erich's team intercepted the signal which indicates that the enemy suspects we are in the Atlantic. Whilst, as yet, they may be suspicious, the wording suggests it's still open to doubt. However, our refuelling in Iceland was always likely at some point to get back to the English, so my inclination is to accept that our presence is known and I have taken that into account in deciding our next course of action.' This produced various nods. 'As you may have expected,' Körner continued, 'this information has not altered the aim of our mission ... to attack the enemy's convoy system. We must, however, expect that the enemy will in short order take action to make things more difficult for us. I doubt they will stop convoys, but we should anticipate some re-routeing of convoys ... probably more to the south ... and also an increase in convoy escorts.'

Again there were some nods. No one spoke; the captain was speaking and had not invited comments.

'Peter and I have discussed the news of our discovery and concluded that the enemy's likely moves warrant some changes to our plans. We still have a degree of surprise. The English may not be sure we're at sea and, even if they feel sure we're in the Atlantic, they don't know exactly where we are.' Körner stopped for a moment, gauging the faces of his subordinates. He saw nothing which suggested they disagreed with his views, though he would probably have been surprised if anyone had. 'The first step we've taken is to alter the rendezvous with the *Erda*. She was due to move close into the Greenland shore, to check out our fjord, but, in view of the signal, the English may search likely refuelling anchorages. So, we have ordered her to keep to sea, until the rendezvous, which has also been moved further south, well offshore.

'We have also decided to steam more directly for the American coast than was originally intended, though,' smiling at Gärtner, 'first, we'll need to keep well to the east of the Newfoundland fishing grounds, the Grand Banks. If the enemy does re-route his convoys, a more direct route could yet produce results before they have been able to fully implement any changes. In truth, this is not a great change to the original plan and was always an option.

'There's still the chance to intercept a convoy at sea, but, if not ... and as originally envisaged ... we will strike at one of the enemy's assembly ports. For that option, I have selected Halifax on the Nova Scotian coast. We may well encounter ships near the port, perhaps even a convoy, but, if not, we will close and shell the port.' Looking directly at Kruse, Körner said, 'Robert, please consider that possibility and draw up plans to attack Halifax.'

'Yes, Captain,' replied Kruse, making a pencil entry in a small notebook.

'By these changes,' continued Körner, 'the time saved may allow us to catch the English ... or is it the Canadians ... off guard. Alas, because of the distances involved, we must keep to our best cruising speed, which will obviously take us longer. Wolfgang has worked out that, if we end up going all the way to Halifax, we will still have enough fuel to get back to either of our supply ships or, if necessary, sail directly for home. However, if we do go back to Germany without refuelling, there would be no room for any high-speed steaming. So, depending on how things go, my intention is to seek to refuel after attacking Halifax or a convoy.

'Well, in a nutshell, that's our plan. Do you have any comments?' concluded Körner, half-expecting nothing but acceptance. He noted that their faces seemed to convey broad agreement, though he saw a wrinkled brow and the earlier smiles had disappeared.

Lang spoke first. He never seemed to be put off by the occasion. 'Captain,' he said, adeptly knocking his cigarette end into an ashtray, 'I understand the changes, though, as you say, they are little removed from our original intentions. I have two immediate observations, if I may.'

Körner gave a slight open hand gesture, indicating Lang should put his points.

'If we do go to Halifax, as an assembly port, might we encounter a gathering of warships? Any idea what we might encounter?'

Körner immediately chastised himself. He knew *Georg* had not resolved this pertinent issue, largely because of a lack of facts. He wondered if that was truly Lang's question or perhaps it was more about the *Hindenburg* coping well with numerous attackers.

'Very good point, Werner,' said Körner, to be seen to acknowledge the Paymaster's question. 'I should emphasise that we are still intending to attack convoys and that an attack on Halifax itself will only proceed if we find none. But, if that becomes necessary, it is possible we'll encounter warships there, though how many or indeed what type of warships remains to be seen. Each convoy will probably have its own escort and, if convoys leave frequently, there is a chance that some would be in the vicinity. We believe most convoys are thought to have cruisers as escort.' He quickly added: 'There is the possibility they would seek to use battleships, if they really think we are around … but they would most probably be pre-dreadnoughts.' He looked at Schönert. 'Erich, what's the latest intelligence on the issue?'

Schönert seemed to hesitate before answering, then said, 'Much as you've said, Captain. All we have is the estimation that every few days a convoy leaves one or other Canadian or American port. In the Nova Scotia area, they'd leave from Halifax and Sydney, … though Sydney is considered to be ice-bound at this time of year.

'Their convoys are thought to be escorted to our War Zone around the British Isles, most probably by one or perhaps two armoured cruisers and possibly some auxiliary cruisers, where they pick up a strong cruiser-destroyer escort to bring them into port. On that basis, there must be cruisers moving to and from each port. If Halifax has, say, weekly convoys, there could be a couple of cruisers at hand. We might also expect some smaller warships, though perhaps only coastal patrol types. The Royal Navy's North American station is thought to have at least two older armoured cruisers. We have no information on American warships, but there may be some in the area. Our latest assessments do not include battleships, though I agree with you, Captain, one might imagine that, faced with the threat of attack by a battle cruiser, they would seek to use them. However, as you say, these would most probably be pre-dreadnoughts. The Americans believe in a concentrated battle fleet strategy and would probably not split up their dreadnoughts and may well keep them in their own home waters … unless it was to counter a specific threat to their activities. Similarly, I don't think they'll send single dreadnoughts to a Canadian port. They are much more likely to concentrate such warships near their own home ports, Boston or New York, for example.'

After letting all that sink in, Schönert then revealed, 'We do know that Halifax suffered what appears to have been a devastating explosion late last year, probably an ammunition dump or ship. This may have affected their harbour defences, but doesn't seem to have stopped their convoys.'

'Thank you, Erich. Very useful,' said Körner. He turned his gaze back to Lang. 'Well, Werner, we may have to cope with a couple of warships, perhaps old cruisers, but we can't rule out the possibility of battleships, though probably only pre-dreadnoughts. It's not possible to give a definitive view of what we'll do if and when we encounter enemy warships. We'll have to assess it at the time, but I'll just say I feel confident in this ship and her crew, whatever we come up against.' Smiling, Körner ended it there. He had no intention of debating how he'd actually deal with a squadron of armoured cruisers or battleships. He threw in: 'We shall time our attack at Halifax for dawn, putting the rising sun behind us, hopefully making their gunners' task more difficult.'

Lang seemed content, but said no more, till Körner prompted him about his other *observation*.

'Sorry, Captain,' he said, 'I asked about Halifax in part because I have a concern about whether we can indeed find a convoy at sea.'

Körner resisted nodding to this comment, even though he had harboured such thoughts himself for a long time.

'We have been at sea for over a week,' continued Lang, 'and not sighted anything bigger than a fishing boat. Of course, we were not seeking anything then, but it serves to demonstrate how difficult our task is. Even though a convoy would be quite large, in terms of the hectares of sea it would cover, I fear we will not encounter one unless we know its actual course and position. I know the seaplane is intended to help us overcome this dilemma, but, if I may be so bold, I will not be surprised if it does not find a convoy for us. Its performance so far has not been, shall I say, spectacular. It failed to find the supply ships; is, it would seem, unable to take off in anything but a relatively calm sea; and now has been brought down by a seagull.'

Körner could tell by the looks on his officers' faces that they all had similar views on the matter of finding a convoy and possibly also about the worth of the seaplane. Finding a convoy had come to be *the* key concern in all *Georg*'s planning and which had singularly failed to be satisfactorily addressed. The seaplane was the approach selected from a string of options, though, he accepted, it was yet to show that it was worth carrying one right across the Atlantic. He did not want to go over them with his officers, but was very mindful of the considerations whereby, for example, U-boats and zeppelins had eventually given way to the decision to employ a seaplane. That decision was ultimately based on operational experience, most notably from success of the seaplane forces in the Baltic and Nerger's use of the *Wolf*'s seaplane, which had shown that a plane could serve as a very useful reconnaissance tool. Indeed, the Atlantic mission itself owed much to the seaplane decision, in that strong support from Prince Heinrich, unexpectedly persuading his brother, the Kaiser, of the merits of such an aircraft, was an important reason in getting approval for *Georg*.

These thoughts didn't provide Körner with a good response for Lang. He felt Lang's comments were something of a challenge, given Körner's role in the decision-making processes. He did not like to be challenged. He was the captain, with an important and unique mission, which he was determined to fulfil. He looked intently at Lang, though aware of the others.

'Werner, I understand your concerns. I assume you are not seeking to debate how the decision was made to have an aircraft onboard, or revisit the pros and cons of the use of aircraft in our mission,' he said, his voice normal, steady and calm. Even if Lang was keen to raise such issues, it was clearly not the time. He noted a slight tightening of Lang's forehead. 'Given we have a mission to accomplish, we must use all our resources. The plane is the only method we have available that can materially extend our search capabilities and I intend to use it to the full.' Lang made no move to comment. 'The plane has been repaired,' said Körner, glancing at Schellenberg, who nodded. 'Accepting that the weather and sea state are important factors in using the plane, we shall send it aloft to scout the seas ahead whenever possible. It obviously extends our vision, which must help us locate a convoy.'

'Gentlemen,' he continued, 'with or without the plane's assistance in finding a convoy, if we encounter one, we will attack it. If we do not find a convoy, we will close with the Canadian coast and bombard Halifax, one of the enemy's convoy assembly ports. As regards enemy warships who oppose us, as I've said, we must gauge the situation at the time, but my inclination is to sink them or drive them off before continuing with our mission.' He decided not to add that, if outgunned, they would use the *Hindenburg*'s likely superior speed to good effect. Debating a retreat was not appropriate.

'So,' he summarised, 'either having attacked a convoy or, if necessary, attacked a convoy port, we will have served our purpose of damaging the enemy's convoy system, in large part by creating alarm and forcing him to adopt even more robust convoy arrangements. We could expect this to cause at least some delay and disruption to their convoys, but probably also result in them sending out hunting groups … looking for us … or further increasing the number of warships attached to convoys. Any of these measures could well assist our war aims, by interfering with the enemy's convoy arrangements and possibly taxing his resources and dispersing his warships. These could open up new opportunities for our U-boats and the Fleet.' He also added: 'We might achieve some of these things by just allowing ourselves to be seen off the North American coast, but I doubt that would have the same effect as an attack on the enemy.'

This statement by Körner seemed to end the discussion between them. At least, no one spoke further about the plane.

Eckhardt and his crewmates were at ease with their situation, the excitement of earlier days gone or subsumed by their duties. Many were just pleased to be away from the confined and icy Icelandic waters. Rumours abounded. A few had the majority of support: it was too difficult to find convoys, so they would soon be heading back to Germany; they were going to meet up with U-boats to locate and attack convoys; or they were going into the Atlantic where their mere presence would disrupt the convoys. Each seemed to have some logic and merit and each had come from what the men supposed to be a trusted source, for example, an officer, officers' steward, yeoman or wireless operator. The rumour that the English knew they were 'out' had caused some alarm, but the expected inevitability of that and the vastness of the Atlantic seemed to lessen the concerns it raised. However, as he listened to the men's discussions, chipping in the odd agreement, each rumour seemed plausible, but also to be open to other interpretation.

'We can't be going back to Germany,' said an animated Schwarz, dismissing the idea with a flick of his wrist.

'Oh, yeah? Stands to reason, we're going back,' said Müller. 'Now that the blasted English know we've broken out into the Atlantic, the game's up! They'll set their ships on us once they know where we are. If we attack a convoy … if we can find one that is … then word of that will soon get back; they'll know where we are and will soon be chasing us. They only need to follow us with their small ships, while calling in their big boys. You watch,' said Müller, a bit of smirk on his thin face and a twitch from his excuse for a Kaiser-like moustache. 'Stands to reason. We need to keep low and get back to Germany, sharpish. If we keep out of sight ... which should be easy out here ... with any luck, we'll get back safely to the North Sea *and* Germany.'

'So, why are we going *south*?' responded Schwarz, a touch of sarcasm in his voice.

'Well, stands to reason,' said Müller, without hesitation. 'We've got to put some distance between us and Iceland. Sailing round that God-forsaken island will soon alert the bloody English where we are. We need to get into open water, away from any likely shipping lanes. Once we're free enough, we'll swing round and make for home. Stands to reason.'

The debate went on, with other men adding their views to the mix. To Eckhardt, both Schwarz and Müller were right. They were heading south—though, interestingly, a touch west of south—but now the enemy was alerted to their presence, he'd be waiting for them to strike and then bring in all his ships. But they were a good day's steaming south of Iceland, over 500 kilometres away. Surely the ship's heading would have been changed by now. If not and intent on attacking a convoy, how'd they find one? They couldn't find one off Norway, with the whole Fleet looking for it, so what chance alone in the Atlantic?

Eckhardt gave general assent to both men's comments and, he realised, to much of what was said about the other rumours. Even as a young man, he shunned confrontation—except when emboldened with drink. His life at home and as a fisherman had been under the direction of his fairly strict and uncompromising father. He was prepared to acknowledge *to himself* that that early life had left him with an acquiescent and somewhat self-critical manner. The navy and the war were slowly changing that, making him more of his own man, but he still felt reticent about arguing his point of view. That didn't mean he couldn't reason matters out by himself. He thought that *Georg* was still underway and the captain was intent on convoy attack or perhaps just causing disruption. He thought a link up with several U-boats might provide a way of intercepting a convoy or, as others debated, that the seaplane would find one.

9

Halifax

With the aid of a 1906 English map, Kruse explained his proposal for an attack on Halifax to his captain. The map before them showed the *Maritime Provinces of Canada*, with Nova Scotia, edged in orange, stretching right across its lower half. Körner noted with interest that every couple of millimetres along the province's Atlantic coast, each cape, head and island was named, the fine script curving into the sea. Almost hidden by this curtain of seaboard wording were sprinkled coastal towns and ports. Most had traditional English names, *Dartmouth*, *Liverpool*, *Medway*, but he also saw *Lunenburg* and *New Italy*, showing there were other places the land's immigrants had come from. Halifax, about two-thirds of the way down Nova Scotia's Atlantic coast, was differently and appropriately highlighted, as the province's capital, in bold, capital letters. The wording on a dotted line sweeping out from Halifax across the sea to the eastern edge of the map caught his eye: *Liverpool to Halifax 2485*.

Kruse admitted to favouring this English piece of cartography, because it showed Halifax to a larger scale in a separate box at the corner of the map. He drew Körner's attention to the inset. 'As you know, Captain, Halifax itself is set back from the open sea, about twelve kilometres. Bedford Basin,' his finger traced the narrowing harbour waters up past Halifax into a large body of water north of the city, 'is further … and, I'd venture, a very good area for convoy assembly.'

Körner noted that the pink-coloured city blocks of Halifax were indeed well inland, up a long channel flanked by islands and headlands. The channel reduced to about a kilometre or so wide as it passed Halifax, where it carried the apt title *Narrows*. The nearest piece of open sea lay ten or so kilometres from the city, but was nevertheless labelled *Halifax Harbour*. That area contained a few fathom lines that signified shallower water. It was immediately obvious that bombarding Halifax would be no simple affair. However, the *Hindenburg*'s guns could reach targets 20,000 metres away, so Halifax was still vulnerable, but long range shooting was never simple.

'From the available intelligence, including records of visits by our own warships some years ago, there are coastal batteries here and here,' continued Kruse, as his finger pointed out various coastal and island sites. 'Their guns are thought to be fifteen-point-twos, though they could well have added to their defences since the start of the war. They may have installed larger guns, even added minefields or submarine barriers.'

'What larger guns do you think?' asked Körner.

'It's difficult to say. I would be surprised to encounter thirty-point-fives, ...'

'I'm sure we'd all be very surprised by twelve-inch guns,' interrupted Körner.

'Er, quite so,' said Kruse, with a slight smile.

Körner noted his gunnery officer's slightly hesitant response. He could not say if that was because his use of the enemy's inches, instead of the metric equivalent, or perhaps because he was unsure about the nature of Körner's 'surprise' comment. He was about to clarify, but Kruse continued.

'From what we know of English coastal defences, any larger guns would probably be nine-point-two-inch,' said Kruse, demonstrating his own ease of dealing in inches. 'Given the shape of the harbour,' he continued, 'the narrow channels, islands and the like, plus the shore guns and possible minefields, it would be wise to fire at longer range from deep water.'

Körner simply nodded. His mind went back to the first months of the war, December 1914, when the *Potsdam* escorted the battle cruisers in their bombardment of the English coast. The situation there was very different to Halifax. The big ships had opened fire on Hartlepool from only a few kilometres out, pouring in a thousand shells in some forty minutes. Despite such firepower, even that action had not been one-sided and the ships were hit several times in return by shore batteries. He knew he could not afford to expend a large amount of his ammunition, in case they subsequently had to fight their way home, and naturally he would not wish the ship to be damaged. Again he acknowledged that *Georg* continued to test them.

'If we made two runs across the bay,' Kruse's finger moved across the *Halifax Harbour* area, 'we could fire some two hundred shells, from about eighteen thousand metres. We can't target any specific area with confidence, but given the size and the longer, north-south layout of Halifax, we should get most into the town. That should create some disturbance,' said Kruse. Almost as an afterthought, he added, 'The secondary guns will deal with any shore batteries.'

Körner agreed. Hundreds of 30.5cm shells falling into the town must, he accepted, cause significant damage and quite probably panic amongst its inhabitants. However, his mind was again on other implications of the bombardment—not the validity of bombarding Halifax, which was a protected port and therefore a legitimate target under the Hague convention—but whether using 200 shells, over a quarter of the ship's main armament ammunition, would weaken the ship's ability to deal with future opponents. He'd heard that Spee's ships at the Falklands had run out of ammunition before they were sunk, because of the number of shells they expended at their earlier victory at Coronel.

As the two men continued their discussion of the problems presented in such an attack, not least the well-held view that ships were always at a disadvantage when confronting shore batteries, and the benefit of spotting by the seaplane, the speaking tube whistle, that herald of limited vocabulary, interrupted them. It was Schellenberg. Körner had intended that Schellenberg would be present to hear Kruse's plan, but other issues required him elsewhere. He and others would soon be briefed on it.

'Schellenberg here, Sir. The seaplane has returned. They've sighted a ship … er, two ships.' There was no hint of excitement in Schellenberg's voice.

'Where?'

'Seventy-five kilometres west. They're sailing ships,' said Schellenberg.

In a few minutes, Körner joined him on the Bridge. Schellenberg showed him the note of the plane's signal: *Two sails 75KM W course W.* Körner gave the order to recover the plane.

⚐

The seaplane circled the battle cruiser, though Eckhardt had not been able to decipher much of the messages in its winking light. As the ship slowed, he would have liked to watch the recovery process, but the uncompromising order for everyone, not just look-outs, to watch for submarines snapped his head round. Most of the crew now realised and welcomed that the seaplane could provide them with information about what targets and threats lay beyond their vision. That said, the launching and recovery of the seaplane equally gave most some cause for concern. To bring their great ship to a halt each time was to expose her to torpedo attack from an unseen enemy. No one expected a submarine to be this far out to sea, patrolling just on the off chance of such an opportunity. He had never been in a submarine, but knew they saw the world through their periscope. To happen on a stationary dreadnought, he thought, must make her captain quiver at the sight through his spy tube, probably like seeing a naked woman through a key hole. While the ship came to a near halt, he searched the swell, watching for any telltale sign of the undersea menace. He realised that, even if he saw something, by the time he gave the alarm, by the time the ship began moving or the guns started firing, it could be too late.

Eckhardt had experienced being torpedoed. In 1915, in the Baltic, the *Moltke* had been hit by one. It struck near the bow, but he felt it even at his Battle Station on one of the aft 8.8cm guns. The battle cruiser had coped very well with the resulting damage; only a few men were killed, though some hundreds of tons of water flooded into the ship. However, the ship pulled out of the operation it was on and the damage took a month to repair. If the *Hindenburg* was hit by a torpedo, even though she was larger than the *Moltke*, he reasoned she must be damaged, but would it have severe consequences for their mission and, God forbid, even jeopardise their return to Germany? He didn't waste his concentration on such thoughts, but continued to scan the blue-grey water, skimming over the shining

108

surface, for the danger signs—a feather of fine spray as a periscope cut through the water or, more frighteningly, a row of bubbles from the torpedo itself. Very soon, he felt the ship moving and without realising it breathed a small sigh of relief, accompanied by a trace of a smile.

Eckhardt had heard gossip that since the plane had been repaired, following what most were calling its near-fatal incident in Hornvik, the weather or some technical issue or even pilot problem had prevented its regular use. Now, to just about everyone's delight, this was the plane's third flight in two days. Each time it returned, it flew around the ship several times playing its own part in searching the sea before it alighted on the water. He knew it had machine guns, though suggestions it also had small bombs proved false, so it probably couldn't do much to worry a submarine, but it was a valuable assistance nonetheless. Yesterday's two flights found nothing, generating some comments about the plane's worthlessness. It would not be long, he imagined, before the results of today's search filtered back to the Spotting Top.

Pu

The pilot, accompanied by Brandmann, reported to the Bridge. Squeezed into the Chart Room, a somewhat excited Geiger, his face greased, oiled and smoke-blackened, pointed out the approximate position of the sailing ships to Körner, Schellenberg, Gärtner and Brandmann. The navigator confirmed the position as near the eastern edge of the Grand Banks.

'To judge by their sails and effect on the water, they were both moving slowly, perhaps five knots, perhaps even less. But, please excuse me on that, Captain, my expertise in gauging sailing ship speeds is sadly deficient,' said Geiger, trying to get everyone to accept his shortcoming without too much criticism.

'Well, perhaps so,' said Körner, meaning the sailing ships' speed, then realising they might think he was referring to the *leutnant*'s lack of expertise. 'With their sails spread, they may well have been setting off home, who knows, perhaps preparing to race each other home, or just moving to new positions on the Banks,' he continued, without seeking to clarify his last comment. 'You think they were heading west?'

'Er, yes, Sir,' said Geiger, though his voice displayed some uncertainty. 'As instructed, I kept well back, several kilometres. I didn't wait too long, before returning to the ship, though not directly. The weather was a bit misty at sea level, nearer the Banks.'

Körner acknowledged the likelihood of misty conditions, which probably prevailed on the Banks, given the rise in the barometer over the last twenty-four hours, accompanied by light winds and calm seas. The men continued to discuss the sailing ships, thought certainly from Geiger's description to be Grand Bank fishing schooners, and the implications for them and *Georg*.

During the night, their course had been altered to south-west, skirting the fishing grounds. 'We will continue on this course,' declared Körner. 'Even if they saw your plane, I doubt they could identify it from a distance. Even though I imagine there can't be too many planes around this area, we will proceed with our mission. I doubt there will be any fishing schooners well away from the Grand Banks, but we'll take the risk. With good visibility, we should see their mastheads far enough away to warn us.'

When the impromptu meeting had broken up, Körner walked around the Bridge, taking in a quick visual appraisal of the ship and sea. Ending up at the port aft corner of the Bridge, outside his Sea Cabin, his view astern took in the ungainly seaplane hangar that sat between the funnels. Also, just below his position were two of the ship's four 8.8cm guns. In comparison to the ship's other guns, they were small weapons and, unlike the bigger guns, were open to the elements and relied on their thin, curved gun-shields to protect their crews from enemy fire. As 'quick-firing guns', they could deliver a high rate of fire against attacking destroyers or torpedo-boats, but as the war drew on it was as a defence against aircraft that they warranted their place on the ship. However, Körner always wondered if they could actually shoot down an aircraft and, worryingly, whether the enemy's own aerial defence weapons would be more successful against their seaplane.

Such thoughts only temporarily crowded out the multitude of issues his mind was considering. The Command Bridge was no large area, but Körner knew that when he stood at this part of the Bridge the other officers tended to keep clear of him, observing tradition and knowing he needed that space to contemplate matters. In some ships, this *captain's area* was on the starboard side of the Bridge, on the *Hindenburg* it was the port side. Here he would only be approached if there was a need for his input. Schellenberg came forward.

'We've received a signal, Sir,' said Schellenberg, unfolding a piece of paper and offering it to his captain.

Körner, with a little apprehension, took the paper. Since detaching the *Erda*, the last three days had been largely routine as far as the running of the ship was concerned, but that first wireless message suggesting the English knew of the *Hindenburg*'s breakout had then been followed by others. These served further to confirm that the enemy was reacting to the possibility, or perhaps the strong probability, of a German warship in the Atlantic. A station in Newfoundland had broadcast a signal in clear which warned shipping to be alert for a *battleship off Iceland*. Other signals they'd picked up during the last two days had also suggested increased discussion by the enemy about their whereabouts. Most were in code, but Schönert's experts had gleaned that the *Hindenburg* was probably being discussed.

In many ways, the signals sent to them from Nauen had caused Körner some disappointment. He had agreed with Bünzlin that there would be no wireless signals from Germany or the Fleet to the *Hindenburg*, unless they contained especially relevant information about the enemy's activities, perhaps germane to the movements of warships and convoys. He worried unnecessarily, he hoped. The signals were in code, but there was always the concern that messages directed at a particular ship—a ship that was supposed to be in the Baltic or Wilhelmshaven— might aid the enemy in some way. Just as Schönert's men could get some useful data from the enemy's transmissions, it seemed likely that the English might well be able to harvest enough from messages to him to conclude that the *Hindenburg* was at sea, rather than still with the Fleet. The transmissions they'd been sent were also proving not to be particularly helpful, being largely concerned with the enemy's suspicions about the *Hindenburg*, usually from intercepted signals, or opinions on convoys, for example, that they may be 'routed further south'. Of course, the *Hindenburg* had made no response to any, not that their W/T could have been picked up by Germany.

Körner read the signal, which was the Fleet's latest reckoning on convoy movements, and gave it back to Schellenberg. 'It confirms our views that a convoy may leave each of the main assembly ports about every week.'

'Yes,' replied Schellenberg, 'though without more specific information that only means we could miss one by up to a week.'

'Quite so,' said Körner. Lowering his voice, though no one else was nearby, he then said, 'Without new, factual information or other material insights, I see no alternative but to continue on our current plan to approach Halifax and attack any shipping there or bombard the town.' Werner von Lang's opinions about the plane again came to mind; finding two fishing boats was not furthering *Georg*. He returned to Halifax. 'On that matter, the Gunnery Officer and I have just gone over his preliminary bombardment plan. There are a few things to resolve,' continued Körner, thinking primarily of the contest between ships and shore batteries, 'but I would prefer to sink ships!'

'I second that, Sir,' responded Schellenberg.

'Well, my discussion with Robert did remind me that we are now crossing the normal Great Circle route from Halifax to England, so, with any luck, a convoy may well come into our sights,' smiled Körner, but wondered if that was tempting fate. 'Anyway,' he continued, 'we will continue on towards Halifax. When the Grand Banks allow, I intend to alter course and begin our run in to Halifax. We could cruise here for another day or so, which might fool the English about our intentions, but I doubt it. We might as well attack as soon as possible. Please ask the Navigator to do his calculations.'

'Aye, Sir.'

Then, with his mind again swinging back to convoys, Körner said, 'If the weather continues to be good enough, I think we should also take the opportunity to use the plane as much as possible, especially as we run in towards the coast and now that we're approaching the Great Circle routes.'

'I agree, Sir,' said Schellenberg. 'I have discussed this with Brandmann. We could go for more flights, two a day, or possibly one of longer duration. These would test plane and pilot, not just the strain on both, but the possibility that the pilot cannot find his way back to the ship probably increases.'

Körner expected no less. As to the risk of failing to locate the ship, he did not want to lose the plane or crew, but, obviously, the benefits of having the plane wouldn't be realised if it wasn't flown. 'In war, we must take risks.'

Formal responsibility for the ground crew rested with Kühl, but either *leutnant* oversaw the launch and recovery arrangements when the other was flying. When he was to fly, Geiger never failed to discuss the launch with Kühl. So, before he started his own pre-flight routine, Geiger had a few words with Kühl about the intended launch procedure. While there could always be specific issues to deal with, he really did it as much for Kühl's benefit as his own. He knew that Kühl especially liked to observe the correct protocols and also because he always wanted to maintain good relations with his fellow officer.

With that little exercise in etiquette done, Geiger inspected the plane. Content, he pulled on his large fur-lined gloves, ones he had purchased himself, and got into the cockpit and completed his pre-flight checks of his cockpit equipment and the plane's controls and gauges. Before proceeding to the engine, he turned his head slightly to the side and he asked: 'You OK, Günther?'

'I'm fine, Sir. Everything checked, all OK,' replied Falbe, the slightly older of the two men, who was in the rear cockpit.

They both then sat without further comment, as the hangar, such as it was, was opened and peeled back by several of the ground crew to reveal a largely blue sky. The sun had only just cleared the horizon. The sea seemed all but calm. High barometer readings, with their calm seas, light winds and good visibility, had been with them for several days now, facilitating much flying. Geiger was quite tired from his regular flights, but he knew the plane was now seen by most as an important part of *Georg*. He and Brandmann generally took turns in flying the seaplane missions, even getting the plane into the air twice on a few days. This was the fourth consecutive day of flying, thanks to the ground crew and especially the good weather and calm sea. Despite this, the flights had not been trouble free. On one, he had, thankfully, hardly gone a couple of kilometres from the ship when there was a fuel leak and he had to return straight away. On another, Brandmann had had engine failure soon after being set down on the water. Occasionally, the sea state had proved too rough either to attempt a launch or to take off. The fitters and riggers were kept busy servicing the plane after each flight and keeping it airworthy. Various parts of the crated plane were increasingly employed as spares; the engine had already been replaced. Now he was faced with a long flight, the longest they'd undertaken so far. Despite his understanding of the effect of wind, Brandmann had especially called his attention to the wind on such a long flight, which, although light, could well affect his navigation and getting successfully back to the ship.

When the hangar was clear of the plane, Falbe stood up on the fuselage, perching on the gap between the two cockpits. With the upper wing blocking his view, Geiger couldn't see much of what then transpired, but knew the routine well. Falbe would extract the lifting cable from its slot in the upper wing, then get hold of the derrick's hook that was hanging above the plane. Keeping a tight grip on both, he would slip the cable over the hook. This was a straightforward task when the plane was on board the ship, but far from easy on the surface of the sea when there was any kind of wave action, not to mention the hook swaying back and forth. If the observer fell into the sea at that point or later when he had to hook up the plane for recovery, Geiger knew he would be unable to continue either way. In such circumstances and depending on the sea state, Geiger had the awkward option of reaching behind and endeavouring to hold onto one of Falbe's legs, though that probably wouldn't prevent him falling if he started to go over.

Guided by the ground crew, the derrick lifted the plane slightly forward, nearer the edge of the Boat Deck. One of the crew then stepped up in front of the near-three-metre-long propeller. After a set exchange of words with the pilot, he primed the engine with a couple of half-turns of the propeller. With a further, simple question and answer between him and Geiger, he pulled sharply downwards on the horizontally-positioned propeller and, not surprisingly, at once stepped smartly back. Sometimes more turns were needed to start the engine, but this time, especially as the engine had previously been started and run up by one of the fitters and was already warm, it immediately coughed and the propeller began to spin. Slowly at first, with Geiger doing his bit to coax the whole thing into life, the blades were soon spinning faster into virtual invisibility. Taking his time, nursing the engine, Geiger gradually revved it up little by little, aiming to test the engine's power and capability. Once he was sure it was running satisfactorily and tested to high revolutions, he reduced its speed. He then signalled for the derrick to begin the lift from ship to sea.

From the very beginning of their posting to the *Hindenburg*, the first officer had stressed that the launch and recovery processes were to be as quick as possible, endorsing the captain's concern about the dangers facing a stationary ship. This message was repeatedly stressed to Brandmann, who passed it on down the line. Naturally Geiger appreciated the need for efficient and speedy practice and was keen to comply. Launching procedures on the stationary *Santa Elena*, while sound, did not focus on record-breaking routines and their limited time with the *Hindenburg* in the Baltic had also not offered much scope to improve matters greatly. With continuing practice during the mission, the onboard elements had been honed to a fine degree, but matching them, the raising and lowering of the seaplane and its takeoff and landing, to the slowing and speeding up of the ship was crucial. So Brandmann pushed for each launch and recovery to be a model of good practice and, if possible, 'better than the last'. A tight order, but Geiger took the issue seriously. There had not yet been a call for an especially rapid launch, but the time from receipt of the order to launch and the plane taking off could be anything from twenty to thirty minutes. Geiger's best launch time was some ten minutes from being hoisted up by the derrick and the plane lifting off from the sea.

Once the plane was prepared, signals were made and the ship began to reduce speed. As soon as it had started to lose way and stopped producing waves that was the point to begin lowering the plane onto the water. Geiger was pleased thus far with this particular launch. He reckoned the sea state would also facilitate matters and focused on a quick getaway from the ship's side.

As soon as the plane was on the surface, Falbe, who had continued his balancing act during the whole descent, released the derrick hook from the plane, successfully timing the event to cope with the small, rising and falling swell. Falbe dropped back down into the aft cockpit, but his work was not over. He then quickly released a line that ran from his cockpit back to a couple of sailors who were carefully using it as necessary to keep the plane's tail towards the ship. Once this had fallen away, Falbe shouted and Geiger quickly increased power to get some urgent, forward movement away from the ship. Geiger always feared the worst at this point that, despite his onboard engine routine, the engine would fail or generate insufficient power to get away from the ship. This had happened once, but fortunately without the plane hitting the ship's side or being caught in the ship's wake. Nothing untoward happened on this occasion and the engine performed well and Geiger was able to get the plane smartly away from the ship. He did not look back to the ship, as she would slowly begin to raise her own speed. The sea was near ideal, with some limited wave action. Turning into the light wind, he took longer to build up speed, but inevitably the floats began to lift and they were airborne. He reckoned it had been a near-perfect launch, not taking much more than his previous best time. Pleased, he shouted a 'well done' to Falbe.

By the time Geiger had circled and gained some altitude, the ship was building up speed and continuing on its near-west course. He approached from astern, flying along its length to confirm its heading, and then set off slightly to starboard, gaining more altitude as he went. This flight could be as much as five hours and, he knew, would seriously task his navigation skills. He would fly for two hours, on a course fifteen degrees starboard of the ship's, before turning to port for an hour and then turning back towards the ship. The return flight should be shorter, given the ship's movement towards them.

Although the course had been laid out in defined degrees, his navigation work was cut out for him as his small compass, mounted on gimbals, constantly bobbled around. The triangular course would cover the sea either side of the ship's course for two hundred kilometres ahead and about a hundred across. When added to the extra distance they could see from their height and the clear weather, the flight should give good advance warning of anything ahead. Subject to a whole variety of factors, including, he smiled to himself, magnetic interference to his compass, he and Falbe should return safely to the ship. Given the shorter leg back to the ship, there should be ample fuel to check out any sightings and to search for the battle cruiser, if they did not rendezvous as intended with her. Importantly, by flying at up to one thousand metres, in the good visibility conditions that existed, they could in theory see a very long way. He'd been told a plane at a thousand metres could see over a hundred kilometres, though the conditions were never that good in his experience. However, even if he and his observer could only see forty or fifty kilometres, they should still find the ship on the return leg. If they got into difficulties, they could send a wireless signal which it was hoped the ship could focus on and rescue them. In keeping with Captain Körner's strict orders on the matter, the ship would not wireless them and they were also not to use their wireless, unless necessitated by important sightings or problems with the plane. Of course, there was no guarantee the wireless would work, as sometimes occurred. If they crashed into the sea, he mused, none of that would be of concern. He looked ahead, the sky was mostly an azure blue. Although, high above there were wispy cloud trails stretching right across the blue, at lower levels there was hardly a cloud to be seen. The sea below them was a smooth, darker hue.

As the minutes and kilometres droned by in the loud, all-embracing, but easily ignored noise of the powerful Benz engine, his mind touched on the differences between his flights from the *Hindenburg* and those from the aircraft mothership *Santa Elena* in the Baltic. Although he might fly over open sea and out of sight of land and the *Santa Elena*, which was usually in some sheltered anchorage, he reckoned he could always find her once he made landfall, subject to making the correct decision to turn left or right. The Atlantic was a wholly different game. He checked his heading and other instruments for the umpteenth time.

The weather was a fantastic bonus. For several days, the ship had journeyed under a high pressure anti-cyclone. It provided light winds and clear conditions, at times providing excellent visibility. There was the risk of fog at sea level, but they'd avoided such problems thus far.

As usual, there were precious few, shouted words between him and Falbe. He acknowledged his observer's intention to check that his flexibly mounted machine-gun was working, loosing off a burst astern. This prompted him to fire some from his forward-facing, fixed gun. The Spandau-made gun worked, its rat-a-tat noise announcing the rapid discharge of twenty or so rounds. To combat the guns freezing up, they would fire them occasionally. He also hoped his would not jam in action, though his real preference was that they wouldn't need their weapons today. He'd had very limited experience in fighting other planes and, if he was honest, didn't relish the prospect. His operational flying had been largely one of reconnaissance and, even though he felt he was a good flyer, he was wary of engaging other planes, especially land-based ones which were not handicapped by a pair of large floats. He had been credited with shooting down a Russian plane, though the bullets for that success had all come from his observer's gun. The initial elation was tempered by the sight of the enemy plane spiralling uncontrollably earthwards. His limited aerial combat had certainly confirmed to him that 'dog-fighting' was an exhilarating, though terrifying experience. He didn't expect any aerial encounters this far out at sea, well hopefully not, but they would both keep searching the skies, as well as the sea.

This longer flight raised important questions about navigation and finding the ship. The one thing he tried not to think about was *pissing*! Too often, when he did think about it, he would immediately feel the urge coming on. His normal approach was a last-minute visit to the heads before a flight. If necessary and to avoid a wet and possibly frozen crotch, he had a tin can, but he didn't look forward to using it, given the almost insurmountable difficulties involved, especially with the cramped cockpit, the numbing cold and the multiple layers of clothing he wore. Aiming was perhaps the trickiest aspect, often resulting in it going all over the floor of his cockpit.

It was coming up to the two-hour point and all was going well with the plane. They'd had one sighting, which on closer inspection they concluded to be a group of whales. Other than that the blue sea went on forever. They were a long way from land. Geiger knew that Halifax was about six hundred kilometres away to the north-west, though there was little Sable Island, some one hundred and fifty kilometres to their right. This small, forty-kilometre-long, thin crescent of sand had been brought to his attention by Brandmann. He had to keep away from it, lest seen and reported by some sharp-eyed lighthouse keeper. He knew from Brandmann that a more direct course to the north of the island had been the captain's desire for the ship, but continuing fears about encountering Grand Banks' fishing boats and coming too close to the island itself had led to a change. The ship was now following a course well to the south of Sable Island, before turning for a night approach to Halifax and arriving at dawn. He and Brandmann knew this because they had been tasked with determining the flight on that morning, especially the issues of take off in the pre-dawn darkness and how best to help the ship in the proposed bombardment. For now, he was intent on today's flight.

At the turning point, he raised his left hand to alert his observer and swung the plane onto its new course. Hardly ten minutes later, Falbe tapped his shoulder and shouted in his ear.

'To starboard, Sir!'

Geiger looked to the right, but could see no obvious object. To improve his vision, he eased his dirty goggles up to his brow. Far off, indistinct but unmistakeably something, a small black smudge could be seen just aft of starboard.

'A ship!' bellowed Falbe.

Geiger made no response, but turned the plane towards his crewman's sighting. As they flew towards it, the shape of the darkness changed. It was black near the sea's surface and greyer, thinner, higher up. It's movement was near vertical in the weak airs. It must be smoke from a coal-burning ship, he reasoned. 'Yes,' he belatedly shouted to Falbe, 'it looks like a ship!'

He estimated the ship to be about thirty or even forty kilometres away. He was very conscious of his orders to avoid being recognised, but would need to get closer to see what it was and determine its heading. After his failure to gauge the fishing schooners' speed sufficiently accurately, he felt compelled to set the record straight with this sighting. He decided to get closer. He gained altitude and kept his approach so the sun was behind him, seeking to blind the ship's look-outs or at least silhouette the plane to them.

At ten kilometres, Geiger, using Falbe's binoculars, could see clearly that it was a merchant ship, with a single, tall funnel surmounting a compact and central superstructure. At about seven, what was most noticeable was that the whole ship, hull, upper works and funnel, was sporting a most bizarre paint scheme, presumably for camouflage he thought. It was not painted to try and blend in with its background, but was a striking montage of strong lines and shapes painted in bold colours. He could see black, white and blue. He did not understand the rationale behind this, as it stuck out so well. It was the first such camouflaged ship he'd ever seen.

Maintaining his distance from the ship, he made a careful assessment of her course and speed. He estimated her speed as slow, perhaps seven or eight, certainly no more than nine knots, and that she was on a nor-westerly course. Halifax bound, he wondered. He considered this single ship and its course away from the *Hindenburg* posed no threat to the big ship and did not warrant use of the wireless—though at this distance he doubted that the plane's wireless signal would reach the *Hindenburg*. His initial reaction was to return immediately to the *Hindenburg* with the news, but decided that was not necessary and, conscious of his standing orders to avoid giving away the battle cruiser's position, he turned to port, away from the ship, and flew south, pursuing their previous course. To turn back immediately would accomplish little and could expose the *Hindenburg* to danger. He saw the merchant ship as no threat to the *Hindenburg* and as an unlikely target for her, even if it could be overtaken. Unless its look-outs were asleep or more focused on the sea than the sky, he reckoned they would probably have seen the plane in the clear blue sky and might well report it. If they reported the course the plane followed, at least that should not point to the *Hindenburg*. He shouted a 'well done' to Falbe and told him they would continue with their reconnaissance mission.

Quite soon, the ship was left behind. When Falbe shouted that he could no longer see the merchantman, Geiger settled down to complete the flight and looked forward to reporting the sighting. He would continue on this heading, a little east of south, for another hour, when he would swing to port and head back to the battle cruiser.

Looking ahead, he could see nothing but sea and the horizon looked clear. His view directly forward was inhibited by the engine's cylinder head which protruded from the fuselage. However, he was well used to the obstruction and slight alterations of flight allowed him to see most of the sky and sea ahead.

The time passed slowly. In the clear sky, there was little sensation of forward movement, other than the wind in his face. He checked his heading and his watch. The course change was coming up. Again he held up his hand and shouted, 'Turning!' though without checking whether Falbe, who would probably be looking aft, caught the message. Once they'd turned, he checked the heading and the time and, with gloved, very cold fingers, felt in the map case, hanging to his right, for his small note pad to enter the details. Then he went over his pencil scratchings of their course and the alterations arising from the earlier sighting. His calculations suggested they should sight their ship in about an hour and a quarter, perhaps an hour and a half, assuming she'd been able to maintain her course and speed.

'Günther!' No response. '*Flugmeister*!' he shouted back over his left shoulder. 'We should see the ship in about an hour and a half.' Still no response, except when Falbe respectfully tapped his right shoulder. He ignored the tap, thinking it was just Falbe's acknowledgement, but on the second tap, he jerked his head round to glimpse him out of his right eye. Falbe had his binoculars up and was looking out to starboard.

'There, Sir!' shouted Falbe, his right arm pointing away to the horizon stretching out beyond the starboard wings.

Geiger eased his goggles up and stared intently in the direction of his crewman's still extended arm. At the horizon, he could see a dark stroke-like shape stretched along what looked like barely five or ten centimetres of that distant line. The words formed on his lips, but Falbe's loud words came first.

'Is that a convoy, Sir?' he shouted, as he offered the small binoculars to his officer.

Geiger was reluctant to answer straight away, in case that somehow put a hex on it, made it a mirage or just another single steamer, and he endeavoured with limited success to hold the binoculars steady with one hand. If it hadn't been such a clear day, they probably wouldn't have seen it or else would have dismissed it as a cloud or rain curtain. 'It might be,' he ventured quietly, then realised Falbe probably couldn't hear him. He stuck his thumb up. 'We better go and see!' he shouted, but, no sooner had he pointed the plane towards the hoped-for convoy, than he had second thoughts. He again struggled with his note pad.

Turning his head back to Falbe, he shouted, 'Günther, we may not have enough fuel to get back!' Falbe made no response. Geiger thought he should justify his concern. 'Whatever that is, if it's a hundred kilometres away, we'll definitely end up in the sea!' Again, he heard nothing from Falbe. He turned around as far as he could. The seasoned Petty Officer was looking at him, but he couldn't really discern any message on his goggle-covered face. Was he expecting him to justify his rank, take responsibility and make a telling decision, he wondered. He again reviewed his fuel calculations. There were two crucial issues: how far was it to the convoy—*if* it was a convoy—and would the *Hindenburg* be at the expected the rendezvous point? It was clear that the convoy was beyond the horizon, perhaps a hundred kilometres away. They could not get back to the ship after such a flight.

'Right. We'll keep going for …,' he hesitated, 'thirty minutes … and I'll get us some more height! We must turn back then! We can refuel and come back and check it out.' If Falbe said anything to this, he didn't hear it.

He began the slow climb, as he flew towards the dark strip. The allotted minutes came all too soon. They were then at nearly two thousand metres. Geiger swung the plane round, so they both could see to starboard, uninhibited by the propeller, engine and wings. They were looking towards the sun and the sea was silvered towards the horizon, but they could both see the dark cloud, a tempting sixty or so kilometres away. They were familiar with the funnel smoke from small Baltic convoys; this had all the hallmarks of being a convoy and perhaps a large one at that.

'It *must* be a convoy, *Leutnant*!' shouted Falbe, his words partially lost in the cold wind.

'Yes!' replied Geiger loudly, feeling a real sense of excitement rising within him.

If they continued towards the target, Geiger knew they must end up in the sea. He had no faith that the ship would find them or that their wireless messages would even get through. They must get back. As he'd said, they could refuel and be back in a few hours. Any duty or desire he felt to confirm that it was a convoy had to be balanced against the near-certainty that they would die in the process and still fail to get the news to the ship.

Geiger looked carefully at his compass and tried to get an accurate bearing on the sighting and even daring to gauge its direction of travel. He scribbled these on his note pad, along with the time. After a last look at the dark shape, he turned the plane away onto what he estimated *and prayed* was the right direction back to the ship. The detour to check on the garishly-coloured merchantman and now this one had probably used up their reserve fuel and seriously challenged his navigation skills. He just hoped this further delay hadn't pushed them too far. Thank God the wind was not strong today, he thought, or it could have really caused him problems. Even so, as Brandmann had reminded him, it could yet have moved him more than he estimated. He looked carefully and repeatedly at his instruments, especially ensuring that the tachometer showed the best cruising revolutions. He was not worried yet, but, for a second, the thought of ditching did come to mind. The plane flew on, always heading for the line where the blues of the sky and sea met. He made a mental note to discuss with Brandmann the feasibility and wisdom of such long, maximum-duration flights.

After twenty minutes, Geiger revisited his pad. His navigation was now more guesswork and luck. He toyed with breaking wireless silence, but then thought, as his luck would have to run out at some stage, that the wireless would probably fail to work. Once again, Petty Officer Falbe proved he had the better eyesight and fully justified his observer status. His left arm snaked out past Geiger, pointing to port. 'The ship!' he shouted.

Geiger saw it, a lone, dark shape. It had to be the battle cruiser. He gave an emphatic thumb signal and turned towards it. He kept moving his eyes from the ship to his instruments. The fuel gauge looked perilously near empty. They had not flown far, when the big ship's distinctive profile was confirmed. He was mightily relieved. He dropped towards the ship. He realised that if not for the good visibility and Falbe's uncanny eyesight, his navigation, now clearly not up to all the various course changes they'd made, had put him on a heading that was taking them well astern of the ship. He concentrated on getting back to the ship and not on what might have happened.

The fuel gauge still worried him as he approached the giant warship. He half-expected to hear the engine begin to cough and splutter. There was no time for discussing what signals to send, getting down was his priority. He did not risk circling her, hoping Falbe was checking for submarines, as he wasn't. The *Hindenburg* was already slowing and turning to give her avian child a protected lee to land upon. Geiger quickly had her down, without mishap on the near smooth sea, neatly avoiding the ship's bow and stern waves. He turned quickly towards the ship, her superstructure beginning to tower over them. Guided by Falbe, he moved the plane forward to get underneath the derrick hook, matching his speed to that of the slowing ship. He had precious little room to operate; the wing tip was only three or four metres from the hull. Falbe, out of his seat and doing his gymnastics act, grabbed the hook on the second attempt. Once the plane began to leave the water, Geiger, with a tremendous feeling of relief, shut off the engine. It was only later that he appreciated just how lucky they'd been. The fuel remaining was reported to be only a few litres.

꩜

Informed that the plane was in sight, Geiger rushed to the Boat Deck, ostensibly to supervise the recovery, but his real eagerness was in hearing what Brandmann had found. The plane circled the battle cruiser, as she reduced speed, its signal lamp flashing. It seemed that everyone except Geiger was watching the sea for submarines. He stared at the plane as it came into land, apprehensive that some mishap might befall it. It was now over three hours since it had taken off.

His report of the freighter and especially the possible convoy had, not surprisingly, caused considerable debate on the Bridge. The discussion, something of a rerun of his previous discovery flight, saw Captain Körner, First Officer Schellenberg and Commander Gärtner, plus Brandmann and him, all deliberating the facts and possibilities of his sightings. Despite the lack of absolute confirmation, Geiger's opinion that it was a convoy was accepted. Nevertheless, there was some debate about what would happen if there was *no* convoy and how that would affect the attack on Halifax. A convoy was the preferred target, but Halifax was real and its location known. Finally, it was *Fregattenkäpitan* Schellenberg's assessment of the various facts that swung matters and the captain had agreed to the second flight and the *Hindenburg*'s change of course and speed towards the possible convoy.

The *Fregattenkäpitan* had seen the single merchantman as a key element in the drama. He'd calmly asked: Why had this lone ship been sailing to Halifax? If it was steaming to join up with the next convoy, then why approach from that direction? Perhaps it was sailing alone, he'd offered, detached much earlier from a dispersed, westbound convoy. Or, alternatively, it was a freighter which had suffered some problem that had led to an inability to keep up with the rest of a Europe-bound convoy and had been sent back to Halifax, while the convoy continued on. If so, it was a pointer, of sorts, to the convoy. It was acknowledged that both of Geiger's sightings seemed on the same bearing to Halifax. At the time, Geiger had not considered any link, but thought it all seemed logical.

The debate and a problem with the plane had delayed the second flight by nearly two hours. As before, the day's second flight was undertaken by the other pilot. With Brandmann at the controls, the plane had set off in search of the convoy. Had the *Kapitänleutnant* found it?

The recovery went well and, as the plane rose up to the Boat Deck, Geiger studied the pilot's face for some sign that he had found the convoy. He saw no reaction, so resigned himself that Brandmann had had no success, but then the black-faced Brandmann looked directly at him and raised a thumb.

In a few minutes both pilots were hurrying to the Bridge.

'Didn't you read our signals?' said Brandmann.

'No, Sir. My morse is not good enough,' said a frustrated Geiger, though noting what looked like disapproval from Brandmann.

Although Geiger tactfully badgered his superior about the convoy, Brandmann said little on the Boat Deck or in the passageways and ladders leading to the Bridge, other than, 'We found it!'

Once again, the two airmen, the captain, first officer and navigator were squeezed into the Chart Room. Outranked by everyone, Geiger said little unless asked, but he soaked up Brandmann's report and the subsequent discussion. He was keen to know what role he'd play.

The news that Brandmann had found Geiger's convoy produced smiles all round, not least on Geiger's face. The captain's 'Excellent!' response seemed to sum up everyone's views. Brandmann, his face looking blacker than Geiger's after a flight, set out what he and his observer had found. After over an hour, they'd spotted smoke almost exactly as calculated by the navigation team, which turned out to be the convoy. Geiger noted that the navigator's face had a smug expression, perhaps pleased in having correctly predicted the convoy's course and position, though he quickly turned back to his maps, no doubt recalculating positions and courses.

Brandmann continued his report: they'd kept their distance, though were able to conclude that the convoy comprised twenty or more ships, steaming west at 10 or 12 knots. The ships were sailing in a box-like formation of five or six columns. As Geiger had reported with his single freighter, Brandmann said all the ships seemed to be similarly painted with black and white lines and shapes.

'What escort did the convoy have?' asked the captain, obviously expecting that to be a core element of Brandmann's account.

'Er, yes, the escort,' replied Brandmann. 'We concluded that there was one naval escort, a large, four-funnelled ship.' Before he was asked, he said, 'By her funnels, a cruiser, I would say.'

Geiger knew that his and Brandmann's ship recognition was limited largely to Russian and German navies. Schellenberg quickly agreed, saying that four funnels would signify a cruiser, most likely an armoured cruiser. While this debate was no doubt of interest to all, Geiger could see the captain had other issues on his mind.

'Only one ship?' the captain enquired. Geiger thought his voice suggested he'd expected more.

'That was all we saw or could see, Captain,' said Brandmann, his tone clearly defensive. 'We kept our distance from the convoy and the convoy was putting up quite a lot of funnel smoke. If there were any other warships, we couldn't make them out.'

'Do you think they saw you?' asked Schellenberg.

'I would be surprised if they didn't,' replied Brandmann, not evidencing any concern about it. 'We were never closer than about ten kilometres, but the sky was virtually free of clouds.' Then he added a qualification. 'Whether they are skilled at watching for planes, who can say?'

The captain offered no opinion on that, but Geiger heard him say to Schellenberg about the need to monitor wireless traffic. Then the captain looked again at Brandmann, though his comments were for all. 'If they did see you ... and are suspicious ... they would be wise to change course.' Geiger saw Gärtner give a slow nod to this. 'If they do make a radical change of course, we may find ourselves no closer to them,' continued the captain, calm, showing no visible concern, but signalling that the job was far from finished. There was discussion about possible wireless signals from the convoy, but none had been intercepted. The captain then said, 'Well, *Herr* Gärtner, when will we be able to engage the convoy?'

All eyes turned to the navigator.

'Captain, I was just looking at the plot. Interesting to note that, if they are travelling on a south-east course, they crossed our course about six hours ahead of us. *So* close. We would have missed them, if not for *Leutnant* Geiger's discovery.'

'Quite so,' said the captain. 'The plane has been a very useful addition to our capabilities, but when could we be in gun range?'

Geiger thought the navigator looked somewhat chastised by this, but quickly recovered his composure.

'Captain, assuming they have kept to the reported course and speed, at this time, we are approximately ninety kilometres almost dead astern of the convoy. At our present twenty knots and their twelve, we will be in gun range in some five hours. Of course, that will be after sunset.'

'Quite so,' repeated the captain. He was quiet for a couple of seconds, but then announced to all: 'We will engage the convoy at dawn.' To Geiger and Brandmann, he added, 'Allowing you time to relocate them.'

10

USS Seattle

Satisfied with the dawn drill, David G. Benham, captain of the USS *Seattle*, a 14,500 ton armoured cruiser, gave the order to secure the ship from General Quarters. He was as keen as any of the crew to get back to his bunk.

He went aft to his Day Cabin along the boat deck, the ship's funnels towering some fifty feet above him. From that deck he had a good view of the ships around his own vessel. Some 200 yards off the starboard beam was the Royal Navy cruiser HMS *Leviathan*. Her profile was not dissimilar to the *Seattle*'s, especially her four tall funnels and two tall masts. In line with many British ships, she wore a truly complicated dazzle camouflage scheme of differing, bold shapes and multiple colours. He wondered if it would serve her more effectively than the simpler, less colourful and altogether more block-like composition sported by his own ship. While he knew the two ships' outlines, even their dimensions and tonnage, were very similar, there were important differences between them, most noticeably with their main armaments. Although both ships mounted large-calibre guns, typical of big armoured cruisers, his ship's were clearly superior, with four 10in against the British ship's two 9.2in.

Stretching to port and starboard and astern of both warships were several columns of merchant ships. There were a variety of ship shapes to be seen amongst them. Some were large, twin-funnelled affairs, but most were typical, straight-stem, single-funnel merchantmen. Two of the larger ships were carrying a small number of troops, but this was not deemed a troop convoy. Like the warships, all were wearing their war-paint of black, white, blues, sandy-yellows and other colours in a variety of bold shapes. Everyone was endeavouring to steam at the required speed of eleven and one-half knots and the darker western sky just about obscured their many funnel smoke columns. All these ships—now twenty-four, after one turned back with engine problems—comprised convoy 'HC1', *en route* from Halifax to England.

HC1 was the first of a new 'medium-speed' convoy scheme. The HC—'Home from Canada'—convoys were intended to replace Halifax's faster 'HX' convoys, which had recently been reorganised to start from New York. However, US ships were slated to join the HC convoys and the *Seattle* had just escorted most of those now in HC1 up the coast from New York to Halifax. It all seemed a bit odd to Benham; something about easing the burden on New York harbour.

The *Leviathan* and the *Seattle* were positioned at the head of two of the central columns of the convoy. Benham could also glimpse quite some way astern, at the rear of the convoy, the armed merchant cruiser *Arlanza*. She did have several 6in guns, but was not a real warship to him. He knew most of the merchant ships each mounted at least a single gun, but, with the concerns about a German raider, the two armoured cruisers would be their primary defence.

Plans to deal with a raiding German battle cruiser, relying on US battleships, were in place, but a decision had been taken to sail the convoy as scheduled. The *Leviathan* had been the intended, sole escort, but, for added protection and as the *Seattle* was then at Halifax, Benham's ship was ordered to join the convoy for some or all of the ocean crossing. There were some question marks about the speed and turn of events, but the fact that some of the few troops on board were American also lent weight to the *Seattle*'s inclusion. The British cruiser's captain, John Inglethorpe, was designated as the senior officer. Benham, not normally one to challenge authority, accepted the situation, though felt some discomfort, given that Inglethorpe was about ten years his junior. Benham had had little contact with the Royal Navy, outside of occasional pre-war courtesy visits by British warships. He had certainly never had any real time to get to know any British officers. Inglethorpe was not only younger than him, but *was* the senior captain. He put this down to the two navies' systems; USN officers tended to be older than their RN counterparts. From their all-too-few meetings, Inglethorpe had not turned out to be the complete upper-class, 'I'm superior to you' Royal Navy-type Benham expected, though his English accent could easily give one that impression. He did put Benham at his ease from the start, treating him as an equal and welcoming the American cruiser *and* her 10in guns, with such comments as 'fine ship' and 'impressive guns', not at all patronising. As Inglethorpe did not mention his own war experiences, Benham felt no need to evidence that he too had been in a naval battle, albeit back in '98, at Santiago on the *Oregon*.

Just as he was about to go below, ensign White, half-running, came up behind him. The 'Sir!' stopped him on the first tread.

'Yes, Mr White.'

'Commander's compliments, Sir. Foremast look-outs report smoke to the north-west *and*,' with an extra note of surprise in the young officer's voice, 'an *airplane* has also been seen. Other ships have reported the same.'

Walking briskly back to the bridge, he was met by his exec, the tall, 40-year-old Commander Richard Lee.

'Captain, we have smoke to the north-west and a seaplane has been seen circling the convoy. The wireless room has also picked up some signals, simple letters and numbers. It could be coming from the plane. The signals could be about the convoy.'

Benham, unresponsive, went to the port side of the bridge and raised his binoculars. He couldn't see anything of the smoke, but he wasn't surprised, being much closer to the sea than those on the foremast's high platform. 'Where's the plane?'

Lee looked about the sky, obviously having difficulty, when a junior officer pointed it out over the port bow. Acknowledging the assistance, Lee directed the captain's gaze onto the dark speck far up in the light easterly sky. Benham studied the distant object, again without comment.

'Why do you think the signals were about us?'

'As best we can figure it,' said Lee, 'they appear to be short messages, just a few letters and numbers, but could well be about the convoy's size, speed and heading and possibly our location. The letters are quite probably for German words, according to Lieutenant Miller.'

Benham knew that Lieutenant (jg) Frank Miller's parents were German and he could speak German fluently.

'Seems quite likely,' said Lee, 'that the messages are for the owner of the smoke.' He then added, 'Quite likely the German raider we've been alerted to,' which Benham took as more as a belief than a suggestion or question.

'Yes, seems entirely possible,' said Benham. 'Anything from the *Leviathan*?'

'Yes. They also report the smoke and airplane.'

'Sound General Quarters, Mr Lee.'

Before the crew had got to their stations, a lieutenant reported to the captain. 'Signal from the *Leviathan*, Sir.' With a slight nod from his captain, the young man read out the message: 'Looks like we have company. Follow me. Twenty-one knots.'

Benham looked over at the English ship. She was slowly moving ahead of the convoy, bit by bit putting on speed, with more white water at her bow and stern and more smoke pouring out of her tall funnels. It was dense and grey-black, appearing tinged with brown. He could also see she now had several large white ensigns flying. 'Full speed ahead! Follow the *Leviathan*!'

The decision to sail with the convoy had left precious little time for him to liaise with 'Jack' Inglethorpe, but he knew what the *Leviathan*'s captain was doing. Their first discussion confirmed, as expected, that their shared concern was the German battle cruiser, which Inglethorpe said was thought to be the *Hindenburg*, a Derfflinger-class battle cruiser, all 28,000 tons of her, armed with eight 12in guns. Nothing had been seen or heard of her since she was reported in Icelandic waters. Inglethorpe said information suggested she had refuelled, so might well push south to attack the Atlantic-crossing routes. Sailing the convoy five hundred miles south of the normal route to England was considered wise, putting additional distance between them and a German raider and reducing the risk of interception.

Inglethorpe's basic approach to confronting an enemy battle cruiser was simple enough: protect the convoy. He did think there were benefits to be gained in damaging the enemy, so that she could not continue with her mission, but considered that the safety of the convoy must take priority. His plan of action was to put the *Leviathan* (and now the *Seattle*) between the convoy and any raider, protecting it and, if necessary, giving it time to escape or disperse. He said he would seek to close the distance if the enemy gunfire was beyond the range of his own 9.2in guns. In such circumstances, they agreed that the *Seattle*'s longer-ranging and heavier-hitting guns should be used to cover the *Leviathan*, if she had to close the range. Alas, thus far, there had been no detailed decision about their tactics, other than such matters would depend on the circumstances. Inglethorpe didn't offer anything about the likely outcome of a battle between armoured cruisers and a battle cruiser, though it was plain to Benham that the Royal Navy captain viewed it as something he might in other circumstances have sought to avoid, but that didn't seem remotely possible, if it jeopardised the safety of the convoy. His comments left Benham in no doubt that he had adopted a policy of 'they will have to get through us to get at the convoy.'

The USA and Benham might still be seen as newcomers to this war, but he'd kept pace with its naval events. He knew that, so far, armoured cruisers had suffered badly when pitched against dreadnought firepower. The Falklands, Dogger Bank and Jutland battles had each seen armoured cruisers overwhelmed by battleships or battle cruisers. Putting armoured cruisers in the battle line may have worked well enough for the Japanese in the final clash with the Russians at Tsushima back in 1905, but that was an altogether different, pre-dreadnought affair. There was nothing in this war to date to suggest that armoured cruisers could successfully fight the new, *all-big-gun* warships. It would seem that they could neither withstand hits from such a foe's big guns, nor inflict any material damage with their own.

Despite this recent history, Benham didn't think there was any inevitability about the outcome of combat with a battle cruiser. His ship's 10in guns could probably fire as far as any German ship and the weight of her shells—each 510lbs—could well inflict significant damage. Acting in concert with the *Leviathan*, there was all to play for. Naval warfare is not all about ship statistics, he reckoned.

The *Seattle* was soon following in the *Leviathan*'s wake, about four hundred yards astern, as the two ships manoeuvred across the face of the convoy, with both ships now approaching about eighteen knots. The *Seattle*'s maximum speed was now little more than that, even if the *Leviathan* could still manage a few more knots. An officer reported that the convoy had made a starboard turn. Benham just noted the fact. No doubt the *Arlanza*, taking responsibility for convoy headings, was manoeuvring it to keep the threat astern of the merchantmen. Frustratingly, he still couldn't see anything of the ship that was causing all this reaction. Ships in the port columns of the convoy and voluminous smoke from the British cruiser were all but blocking his view of the horizon ahead. 'What does foremast see now?' he called out.

A few minutes later, the response was, 'Ship upperworks on horizon, about twenty thousand yards!'

The two allied ships were coming around the port for'ard corner of the convoy; soon they would confront their opponent. 'Signal from *Leviathan*, Sir. ... Warship in sight.'

'Well, that's most useful information,' said Benham, with an obvious degree of sarcasm, 'but I can't see *anything*.' The *Seattle* was still following the cruiser, whose abundant smoke was drifting to port across the likely line of sight. Without further clarification, he could only assume the enemy was dead ahead—a very bad tactical approach. Inglethorpe must, he thought, soon turn to port not only to clear their gun arcs, but also to avoid the risk of having his 'T' crossed—the classic naval manoeuvre which saw one side sailing across their opponent's course and engaging him with all their broadside guns, while only the forward-facing guns of the enemy's leading ship could return fire. He did not want to disobey the orders of his designated senior, but could not permit his ship to be kept in the dark about the enemy. He considered he should take action along that already discussed with Inglethorpe. He hadn't pondered the situation for more than a moment when a message from the foremast came through that the newcomer had opened fire. At least that cleared away any lingering doubts about the interloper's Teutonic origins and hostile intentions.

Benham couldn't see the horizon dead ahead for the *Leviathan*'s smoke, but, perhaps 400 yards ahead of the British ship's starboard bow, he saw huge, high and snow-white shell splashes rise up from the calm sea. Some 200 feet high, the splashes stood up for a few moments, before collapsing back into the sea. They had not long disappeared when they were replaced by another salvo, this time closer to their target. It was all very different to Santiago. These shell impacts convinced him, he had to be able to see their enemy. As he gave the order, 'Starboard two points!', he saw the next spread of shells surround the British ship, with splashes on either side of her. The German ship had straddled her in short order. He'd read reports of the accuracy of German ships' gunnery. There was no time to take it in; his ship was moving slowly to starboard and he expected he would soon get his own view of their opponent. At that, whatever signals the British cruiser had sent, he ordered a report to be wirelessed: *Am engaging enemy warship attacking convoy HC1.*

The next enemy salvo found the British ship. A line of white water spouts, rising well above her tall masts and funnels, fell across the old cruiser. There was also a wicked red flash to be seen on the cruiser and large pieces of debris rising up into the air. Benham saw part of what looked like a ship's boat catapult over the side. That hit was replaced by thick smoke and further water spouts and another hit as the enemy's accurate fire continued to find the *Leviathan*. Through the smoke and flame, Benham, binoculars up, caught sight of the cruiser's aft main turret; smoke was either coming from the area around it or the turret itself.

The next salvo once more crashed into the British ship. A red flash—a hit—on board her could be seen, accompanied by more smoke and some flames.

One of the German's shells, probably overshooting its target, landed about 150 yards off the *Seattle*'s port bow. The towering mass of white water that erupted momentarily diverted his eyes from the British cruiser's plight. At that wayward miss, he accepted that a shell could strike the *Seattle* at any moment and he retired to the cramped conning tower. Its small space was never considered suitable for managing the ship in battle, but its nine-inch armour afforded as much protection as anywhere else on the ship.

As the *Seattle* began to move to starboard, Benham, peering through the conning tower's too-small viewing slits, could see that the British cruiser had taken a fearful battering. Smoke and flames were coming from much of her starboard casemates, upper deck and superstructure. Her funnels were still standing, though he thought he could see smoke issuing from shrapnel holes in them. Amazingly, despite the obvious damage she'd taken, her engines seemed intact, as she continued to surge through the sea. He couldn't see any fire from her guns. They were either out of action—a possibility with the look of damage she'd sustained—or they were still out of range. 'What's the range?' he called.

'Eighteen thousand yards,' was smartly relayed to him.

He knew Inglethorpe would drive to close the enemy, seeking to bring the range down to at least fifteen thousand yards. He must take the pressure off the British ship. He looked ahead, taking his cue from the direction of the forward turret's guns. There, off the port bow, lay the enemy. Through his binoculars, he could see a long, clearly dreadnought-profiled ship, grey and menacing. Her funnel smoke showing her undoubted high speed, as she moved from left to right near the distant horizon. Orange flashes impressively rippled down her side. 'Open fire!' The *Seattle*'s forward turret let fly, first one gun, then the other. In the short interval between salvoes, with his view partially obscured by gun smoke, he waited for what seemed an age, but was no more than twenty or so seconds, for the shells to end their flight. Almost a ship's length to the left of the target, a high white splash, then another. Benham hoped for much better, though this was only their opening shots. 'Starboard, six points!' He knew he could not fight the German with only two guns and must bring the aft turret into action. This course took him away from the British cruiser, but would allow him the best chance of covering her advance.

Prompted by one of his officer's calls, he allowed himself a quick glance at the *Leviathan*. She had at last opened fire; he saw the flame from her forward, single nine-point-two. Hardly had that gun fired, when he saw her straddled again. He turned back to his own battle. The *Seattle* was now broadside on to her opponent. Her two main turrets could now both see the target and had begun to pump out shells, the shock of each reverberating through the ship.

A yeoman called out, '*Leviathan* on fire!'

Benham couldn't be deflected from his own fight. He again peered at the German; the flashes down her long hull showed her firing did not seem to be affected by her opponents' guns. The range was now reported as down to 14,000 yards; there was every prospect of hitting her. Some white splashes appeared to land alongside the German ship. He couldn't resist shouting, 'Good shooting!' As he watched, his view was completely blocked by water spouts near his ship. They were clear evidence that the enemy's guns had shifted onto the *Seattle*.

A couple of minutes later, splashes again blanked out most of his view and, as they fell down, the closest deposited tons of water onto his ship, its spray sweeping over the conning tower. With the noise of battle, their own guns firing and the enemy's frequent straddles, Benham didn't feel the first hit, but soon reports of damage and casualties from it came in. He definitely felt the next hits; each time, the whole ship shook. The damage reports painted an increasingly worrying picture. The enemy's big shells caused carnage when they hit and even hull damage from near misses. One of the *Seattle*'s 10in guns had been affected, a recoil problem, but it was in the ship's engine rooms where most damage, with some flooding, had occurred. Her speed began to fall away quickly. Soon she could only manage 12 knots. She continued to fire back, though without any indication that her shells were hitting the German ship. Benham ordered a further two point turn away from the enemy, to increase the range and so hopefully reduce the effectiveness of the enemy's gunfire. This order was hardly given when Benham was informed that the *Seattle*'s forward turret was out of action. The aft turret continued to fire, but there were still no reports of any hits on the German. The enemy's next salvo must have hit the ship, as Benham again felt a distinct tremor. Soon, reports came in of serious flooding. The ship slowly began to list to port. The pumps weren't able to stem the flow and there was certainly no time even to think about shifting coal. He ordered counter-flooding, which temporarily brought respite.

Shells continued to drop all around the now wounded cruiser, when one struck the conning tower. To the men within, there was a terrific crash as the shell exploded. The thick armour did its job, though some men inside were grievously injured by splinters coming through the viewing slits. Luckily, Benham was unharmed, though, like everyone, the shock of the blast knocked him down. As he got to his feet, he thought the armour on the inside of the conning tower seemed slightly distorted. Thick, choking smoke had also entered through the slits. As well as making breathing difficult, it severely limited what he could see through them. Fewer reports were coming in, but all were indicating an alarming situation. Perhaps unwisely, he left the apparent safety of the conning tower to get a better appreciation of the situation. Stepping through the inches-thick armoured hatch, he first encountered bloody, gut-wrenching, dismembered bodies littering the surrounding area and then saw a great, blackened gouge on the conning tower where the shell had hit. Looking forward, the foredeck was a mass of smoke and flame, with a large jagged hole near the bow. Immediately below him, he saw that the forward main turret, trained to port, had a fire-blackened face plate.

The main deck directly in front of its giant guns was smashed up, with much smoke issuing from below. It was obvious the turret wasn't in operation. The turret wasn't turning, nor were the guns moving up or down. A couple of men were inspecting the damage, with one bent over, looking down into the hole next to the turret. Benham imagined that a shell, probably easily ripping through the deck, had struck the turret's armoured barbette, perhaps somehow jamming the whole structure. He was about to call down to the men, when shell spouts erupted around the ship and water cascaded down over him, half-knocking him back. Fairly soaked and tasting salt water on his lips, he regained his balance. When he looked down again, the men were gone; the turret was still immobile. Turning aft, he could see that the fore funnel was seriously damaged and the whole thing no longer completely upright, with deformed and smoking metal plates extending half way up it. The other three funnels, along with the large ventilators beside each of them, looked as though they too were riddled with holes. The port side of the boat deck was a mass of destruction. None of the ship's boats there seemed undamaged. Above all, wherever he looked, there was thick smoke and flames.

The commander emerged at the top of a ladder. His face was black from smoke, but he looked unhurt. They both instinctively half-cringed for a moment as another salvo roared in, with at least one shell clearly hitting the ship. Benham knew that he would only have left his aft conning position if he had to. Before he could enquire about matters, the commander reported. 'Captain. Extensive flooding! There's several feet of water in the engine rooms.'

'What of the guns?' he said, meaning the aft turret.

'Aft turret's still firing. I don't know about the fore turret.'

'It looks as though it's out of action,' said Benham, without emotion. He didn't ask about their 6in secondaries, most having been removed to arm other ships. The remaining four—two on each beam—were unlikely to influence the battle, even if the range was favourable to them. 'Can we bring the flooding under control?'

'Last report from Damage Control just said that damage was considerable and they were working to stop the flooding.'

As if to tell them how she was suffering, the ship suddenly listed further to port.

'Richard, go below and assess the damage. We have to keep her underway,' he said, then quickly added, '… and afloat. Report back as quickly as possible.'

'Aye, Captain,' said the commander, as he turned and disappeared down the ladder.

As he looked aft for another assessment of the damage, far astern, at least a couple of miles away, Benham glimpsed the *Leviathan*. She appeared to be moving slowly, but the main image was one of a ship covered by mass of smoke from stem to stern. Shell splashes rose around her—the enemy's fire had been split between the two cruisers—but, in all that dismal scene, he saw her guns firing. More shell spouts did their best to block his view of her. He turned away to look at their enemy. She continued on her easterly course, even at this distance looking powerful and indomitable, firing her guns rapidly. He noted a few shell splashes from his or the *Leviathan*'s guns, though well wide of the mark. He hoped even one hit would cause her captain some concern, but, being honest with himself, expected it would probably take several hits to alter matters.

He went back to the conning tower, was going through the armoured hatch, when some of another salvo must have landed on board. The ship trembled again. He fell back onto the deck. Helped to his feet, he thought he'd bashed his elbow, but when he rubbed it, there was blood on his hand. It was then he realised that the ship had slowed, still moving, but was no longer under way. Another shell struck home. Splinters flew everywhere, tearing through the superstructure and cutting down some of the men around him. Miraculously, he had escaped serious injury. The list increased and she began to settle by the stern. Worse, fire was reported to be threatening the forward magazine. He gave the order for it to be flooded. The fact that the forward turret was out of action gave him no comfort in the decision. Shortly after, he realised he couldn't hear any of the *Seattle*'s guns firing.

Despite having no guns and being a sitting target, his only thoughts were about saving his ship. There was no word from Lee and communications were failing, voice pipes and telephones cut. He sent men off to find out what was happening throughout the ship. Enemy shells continued to rain down. Again, the list increased. The deck was now at quite a steep angle. Unless the flooding was stopped, she might well capsize. As some of the men returned with their damage assessments, he felt he had no option. Flooding was truly extensive and could not be stopped. The sea was almost up to the quarter deck. She could soon capsize. He needed no one to tell him: 'Abandon ship!' It was something he had never imagined, never wanted to call.

The order was quickly transmitted. Amid the smoke and fire, men gradually emerged from below deck, several wounded, many with clothing missing or burnt and torn, faces blackened. All this time, the enemy never let up, seemingly determined, as long as she was afloat, to sink her. Yet another hit caused more death and destruction. Benham's invulnerability came to an end; a wound to his calf brought him down. In an orderly manner, men went into the cold water. After some protest, Benham was helped over the side, but insisted on being the last man to leave. As no boats were launched, Benham and the survivors gradually fanned out away from their sinking ship.

He watched the smoking *Seattle* raise her bow slightly, but then roll over onto her beam ends. After a few minutes, she continued her turn and then sank stern first, her bow temporarily rising to the sky. The boiling sea, strewn with wreckage and survivors, marked her grave. It had only been a little over forty minutes since she opened fire.

Struggling to cope with the waves that periodically washed over him, Benham could not see his enemy from his lowly viewpoint. He thought he heard her big guns firing, but the absence of shell splashes suggested they had shifted to another target. Although he was desperately cold and feeling very tired, his thoughts turned back to his men and his ship. When the *Seattle* was launched, she was christened the *Washington*, but not so long ago had surrendered that name to one of the new, planned dreadnoughts. Some thought it bad luck to change a ship's name.

11

Greenland

From his usual position on the port side of the Bridge, Körner stared out to sea. After much fog of preceding days, visibility was now good. There was some broken light grey cloud overhead, though he saw a band of solid, darker cloud stretching out before them, approaching from the north-east. The air was cold, near freezing or felt so, in part because of the gentle to moderate northerly breeze. The sea state was good for the plane to take off, but, even with his limited grasp of aeronautical skills, Körner could see that the oncoming cloud would cover them in the next hour or so and might interfere with the plane's flight. He could also see Schellenberg looking at the clouds and wondered if he would at least mention the oft-said concern about difficulties that posed for the pilot in relocating the battle cruiser. Körner gave the order to make the flight. They had come a long way since attacking the convoy. To have the best chance of getting back to Germany, they had to refuel. They must find the *Erda*.

In the aftermath of the action, Gärtner had reported that there was enough fuel to sail directly to Germany, but that there would be little scope for any high speed steaming. Now, after diverting to meet the *Erda*, the fuel situation, if anything, was worse. Körner could not countenance trying to get all the way home at 14 knots or indeed running out of fuel like some other German warships had in the early stages of the war. The ignominy of those prospects was too much to bear. They must find the *Erda*. As well as fuel, foodstuffs were also a concern. Although there had been some pre-war ocean voyages by the Fleet's big ships and the *Hindenburg* had a greater radius than others, the main focus of Germany's dreadnoughts was fighting in the North Sea. Long sea voyages and crew habitability and other comforts were deemed less important. *Georg* also challenged the navy's normal boundaries.

Another bonus from meeting the *Erda* would be to replenish their ammunition. The action against the convoy, especially dealing with the escorting warships, had been a heavy drain on the ship's ammunition. While Körner had rightly praised Kruse for the excellence of the ship's gunnery, there had been a downside. As he expected, an important statistic of the action had been the number of main armament shells fired: 311, not far from half the original complement. Each of the supply ships had been loaded with a small number, only thirty to forty, of the

30.5 shells and their propellant charges. Nonetheless, he would gratefully accept even this limited quantity. Equally, he would be very pleased to get back home without having to fire another shot.

In preparation for the seaplane flight, Körner's usual apprehension about submarine attack had him believing his own eyesight would be an almost essential addition to the required scrutiny. His ship's safety was paramount and he never took it for granted. He scanned the cold waters, flecked with a few whitecaps, checking out any odd-looking waves with his binoculars. There were no alarm calls. The ship slowed and the now well-tried seaplane launching process got underway. Soon the ship was moving off and he watched the plane taxi away, though suddenly it seemed to come to a halt. Looking through his binoculars, as the plane drifted astern, he could see that its propeller was not turning. No problem, this was not the first time such a launch setback had arisen. The drill was for a boat to row out and for someone to spin the propeller, allowing the plane to proceed on its mission; a disappointing, but thankfully infrequent occurrence.

The ship circled the lonely-looking seaplane, slowed again and the cutter was lowered. Soon the oared boat approached the plane, which bobbed lazily on the small waves, and made its way to the front of the plane ready to begin the process of bringing the engine to life. Körner and Schellenberg watched the process. While others of the boat crew held onto the plane's floats, one, with evident balancing expertise, stood up in the stern of the boat in front of the propeller. Rather him than me, thought Körner, conscious of the lethal potential of the whirling blades. The ship and plane were both moving, however, and for a while the plane remained tail-on, all but hiding the dangerous process from Körner. As the line of sight cleared, it was apparent that the seaman had regained his seat in the boat. A line was made fast to the struts and the boat began to pull the plane back towards the ship. Körner looked quizzically at Schellenberg.

'It must have been too rough to start the propeller or perhaps there is an engine problem,' suggested Schellenberg, stepping nearer his captain. Körner gave a slight nod in response.

The battle cruiser came to a halt again, but towing the plane back to the side of the ship took some time, too long in Körner's view. His usual anxiety at being stationary was getting on top of him. He momentarily switched his attention to other command matters, while the propeller was spun in the lee of the ship or, if need be, the plane was hoisted aboard. When he looked back, the plane was being raised, men were waiting with long poles, ready to fend off the plane if it threatened to collide with the ship, but that was all in vain. As it reached the Boat Deck it was also clear that the end of the plane's upper wing was damaged, crumpled like paper. Disappointed and tempted to curse, he said nothing, as the order was given to get under way once the boat was being raised.

As Körner looked at the disabled seaplane, hardly a dozen or so metres astern of him, he saw Brandmann and his observer climbing down from their cockpit and others of the air contingent, including Geiger, getting ready to inspect and no doubt repair the damage. Schellenberg would soon report on how long that would take, but it was obvious that the plane was not going to help in locating the *Erda*, well not for some hours at least.

They would stay at the rendezvous point. They could miss the supply ship if they went off searching for her, especially if the weather front reduced visibility. Adjusting the ship's speed to arrive after dawn, they'd already been at the rendezvous for some hours, criss-crossing the local area since. Körner expected the *Erda* to be seen at any moment, but wondered how she'd fared since they'd parted company. Had she successfully avoided contact with the enemy during the many days since? Nothing had been heard, probably a good sign, he thought, but that was no guarantee. With the imposed W/T silence, they were relying on the previously agreed rendezvous arrangements. Following their separation in the Denmark Strait, the *Erda* would make for the PRA rendezvous after ten days, checking on it thereafter; this was the twelfth day.

If the *Erda* was sunk or captured, then he'd already agreed with Schellenberg to head for Jan Mayen and the *Torsten Meyer*. They might also be able to get coal or oil from any ships they captured, but, after encountering no lone merchant ships so far, that seemed an unlikely prospect. He hoped his decision not to capture any of the convoy's ships would not prove to be a costly mistake. If the *Erda* had been discovered, captured or sunk, then enemy ships might even be close by. Anyway, despite the possible danger, after an hour at the rendezvous, he stood the ship down from Battle Stations.

During the journey to the rendezvous a submarine periscope was reported, resulting in a sharp alteration of course, but there were no further sightings. Other than that the passage was uneventful, if the weather was discounted. After the days of blue skies and good visibility up to the convoy action, the weather had inevitably changed. They'd soon encountered rough weather, with strong winds, high seas, rain and heavy overcast skies. Other than some damage to the canvas hangar, though fortunately not to the seaplane, the ship rode it all well and, to be expected, Körner was grateful for the poor visibility the falling barometer brought with it. Around Newfoundland they'd found themselves in fog, thick and white, as bad as anything experienced in the North Sea. In an area where icebergs were to be expected, it had challenged everyone's eyesight. Several icebergs were seen, including one blue-white giant, leaving no one in any doubt about how the *Titanic* had come off worse. All were given a very wide berth.

Körner had spent some time reviewing reports from his officers and held discussions on how their command areas had functioned in the battle (which Schellenberg said the crew were reportedly calling *die Schlacht vor der Sable-Insel*—the Battle off Sable Island). He still marvelled at the outcome of the action, not least that there'd been no damage to the ship and no casualties. Morale, never low, was now reported as excellent.

While it was fresh in his mind, he had drafted his Combat Report.* He'd never considered he was any good at putting together such post-action documents. He contented himself that this was only his first thoughts and would be further developed with more detail from his officers and data from the ship's War Diary.

Throughout the drafting, even though it was a short document, he found himself looking more at the little picture of Maria and the children than at the Report. As he had on many previous occasions, he wondered how they all were and especially how Maria was managing, though he also knew she would cope well. His concern was mainly that when he had left her, she might well have expected to see him soon. He had given her no indication about *Georg*. Except when in the Baltic, he could well return home sometimes in only a few days, such was the Fleet's routine. They had endured some longer separations, so this shouldn't be a great concern at this stage. Bünzlin had said he would pass on any approved messages or communications. Unlike any previous time during the war and given the scope of *Georg*, before the ship sailed he had given some thought to his death and what that would mean to Maria. Now at sea, he gave no thought to the possibility of death or of not getting home. He was going to get home; he would bring his ship and crew into Wilhelmshaven.

Schönert, holding a piece of paper, appeared at his side.

'Sir, a signal from Nauen,' said Schönert, a slight smile on his face.

After the action, Körner was now less displeased by such W/T traffic. The action would have confirmed to everyone that a German warship was off the coast of North America, but exactly where was hopefully still unknown. With any luck, convoy survivor reports that it was last seen on a south-easterly course, possibly towards the Azores, a potential refuelling point, might have sent the enemy searching in completely the wrong direction.

Schönert's W/T team had picked up various enemy signals about the action, some in code, some in clear. These acknowledged that a convoy had been attacked by a raider. Largely, few details were given, though the scale of the action and enemy reaction could be gauged by the volume of W/T traffic. If the *Hindenburg*'s W/T had been capable of reaching Germany, Körner would have sent the appropriate signals announcing the attack. There would be no need to worry about the enemy's direction-finding at that point. Nevertheless, the Fleet must have picked up some information of the action. The ship had received various Fleet messages since the action, most continuing with the updates on likely enemy shipping, including possible warship moves along the American coast, but evidence that the Admiralty knew something about the action came in a simple summary of enemy reports, including that there had been an attack on a convoy

---

* See Appendix.

which was 'defended by British and American warships'. Later signals identified the convoy's cruisers as the English *Leviathan* and the American *Seattle*.

Körner took this latest communication from Schönert, failing to register his officer's smile. The message was specifically addressed to the EG Captain—EG being the *Hindenburg*'s call sign for *Georg*. He read the decoded message: *His Majesty sends you his congratulations on your successful convoy action. He is very proud of your achievements and watches your exploits with great interest. His Majesty has invested you with the Commander's Cross with swords of the Royal House Order of Hohenzollern for the great victory. He also awards 300 Iron Crosses second class for your officers and men who merit special recognition for their part in the action. Distribution to be at your discretion. Good luck and God speed. Müller*

Körner had met short-haired, thin-lipped Admiral Georg von Müller, when he'd visited the ship to speak to Hipper. Interestingly, Körner knew that Müller, like him, had a Swedish connection, the admiral having been born there, though nothing was said of it between them. As Chief of the Naval Cabinet, Müller enjoyed—if that was the correct word—close contact with the Kaiser. Körner stood silently for a few seconds, re-reading the communication, when Schönert spoke.

'May I be the first to offer my congratulations, Sir.'

'Er, thank you,' replied Körner, in truth feeling a little embarrassed. Praise from the Kaiser was truly uplifting. However, while the medal was indeed an honour, he knew that the 'with swords' meant it was being awarded for bravery in action. What bravery had he exhibited? He'd been in the action, but other than being the ship's captain and at times being in the conning tower, protected by thick, thirty-five-centimetre armour, he had done little except issue various orders. As Schellenberg and Gärtner soon became involved in the congratulations, he put his thoughts to one side. The four joked about how the Admiralty had found out about the convoy action; certainly there had been no signals from the *Hindenburg*. Körner threw little into the discussion, though the others offered several ideas including intercepted enemy signals and reports from neutrals or even spies.

The mass award of Iron Crosses was not unusual. Körner knew that the Kaiser had made a similar award to Spee following his success at Coronel. Taking Schellenberg aside, he said, 'The distribution of these three hundred crosses, not easily done. In a way, too many and too few. Please seek recommendations from all the *korvettenkapitäne* on their men and compile a list. I'll have my own to add to it.'

'Aye, Sir,' said Schellenberg, who then left the Bridge.

The allocation of medals sparked Körner into considering who in his immediate group and others, like the pilots, should be honoured with the medal. All bar Lang of his *korvettenkapitäne* already held the Iron Cross second class, some also had the first class medal. While that could be easily addressed through the Kaiser's gracious award, he would ensure that in due course all were recommended for the Iron Cross *first class*. His thoughts on medals were interrupted by Schellenberg, now returned.

'Sir, the repairs to the plane may take some time, probably the rest of the day. As we thought, the plane's wing was damaged by striking the ship. A combination of swell and lack of experience at towing the plane seems to be the cause. As well as the damage to the wing,' he continued, 'there was a fuel problem. That's why the engine cut out.'

After two hours below, Eckhardt returned to the Spotting Top. In the increasingly cold weather, like others around him, he was soon blowing into his cupped hands and rubbing his hands and arms to warm himself up and keep awake. The news about the seaplane's failed take-off and then the wing damage quickly reached all in the Spotting Top and, without the plane aloft, look-outs were reminded, unnecessarily to Eckhardt's thinking, to keep a sharp eye out, not just for the supply ship, but also for English warships that might be in the vicinity. The plane's problems attracted the odd comment. However, it did little to dampen the crew's morale, at an all-time high after the convoy action. They felt confident they could cope with anything.

Eckhardt had also heard of the Kaiser's medals, news of which had flashed round the ship and seemed to go down well with the men. Initially he had the temerity to think he might be a recipient, but just as quickly discounted it as there was no good reason why he should receive a medal; he figured he'd done nothing to merit being recommended for one. He focused his attention back onto the sea.

His watch passed slowly, matching the ship's slow speed. After about an hour, he reckoned that the visibility had reduced. The dark clouds had brought a band of rain, then showers with some sleet, at times seriously cutting back how far he could see. The wind had also picked up a notch, kicking up more white-topped waves. As usual, he saw illusory ships' bows in every white wave that broke at the far edge of visibility. This kept him on his toes, though as time passed his mind easily strayed onto other things: would they get home without further action, would he get leave and, as always, would Anna still love him? Another bow wave, …. 'Ship! To starboard!' he called, loud, but restrained. 'Starboard Beam!' he corrected.

As he continued to watch and update on his sighting, the great ship came alive. Battle Stations sounded and in a few minutes the ship began to assume the purpose for which she had been built. Cruising as they were, there was only a marginal increase in her speed, but reassuringly her big-gun turrets quickly came round to challenge the newcomer. The distant vessel was soon identified as a merchant ship, though the question of friend or foe took a few anxious moments to answer, before tensions were soon relieved when word spread throughout the battle cruiser that the merchantman was indeed their supply ship, the *Erda*.

The sight of the *Erda* was a good fillip. There was no cheering, but it brought on some animated chatter, as well as smiles to everyone, before long being banished by an order to maintain look-out.

Soon enough the two ships closed on one another. To Eckhardt, the collier exhibited no change in appearance since they had parted company many days ago. Like everyone, he was pleased to team up once again with some of their countrymen. It was only one ship, but it made them think they were not all alone. He even accepted with no great distress that this would soon mean another bout of coaling, especially as that might probably mean they would be heading home. They could not stay out here forever.

The two ships steamed passed each other, about fifty metres apart. Eckhardt could see sailors on the *Erda* waving. While he thought their arm movements were not especially energetic, no doubt they too were pleased to see their compatriots. When he could, he endeavoured to read the flashing lights now coming from the merchantman. He gleaned there were greetings and what seemed like comments about the battle cruiser's triumph—how did they know, he asked himself. The next signals he could only partially read or not at all as the big ship altered position to port and put him looking away from the collier. Then, little more than fifteen minutes after the rendezvous, the *Erda* took station about three hundred metres astern of the battle cruiser and both ships proceeded north at what he estimated to be ten knots. Eckhardt was a little surprised to find that occasionally the big ship varied her heading, adopting a periodic zigzag course. Submarines! He would always bow to the officers' view of needing to guard against submarine attack, even at their slow speed, but just couldn't envisage one being in these remote waters, though, admonishing himself, just as quickly remembered that a periscope sighting had recently been made.

He noted that the supply ship did not comply with the zigzag course changes. An officer said something about her not being able to manage the extra knots. The two ships kept up this slow advance. As Eckhardt finished his watch, there was nothing to see apart from the grey waters, though, as the skies cleared, the visibility improved and some colour returned to the sea.

Mess-deck rumour had it that they were headed back to Iceland to refuel, though most recent talk seemed to be focusing on Greenland. A few suggested that they'd use some remote estuary or inlet along the north-east coast of Canada, but that had been pooh-poohed, as being too close for comfort. Their northerly heading now strongly indicated Greenland.

As Geiger expected to take up the plane on the next flight, he visited the hangar on several occasions to check on the repairs to the plane. Although Kühl was responsible, Warrant Officer Erich Brandt was the real authority in the hangar, supervising and directing the ground crew. Approaching midnight, even though there was no real night at those latitudes and time of year, Geiger again went to the cold and draughty hangar. He found the balding Brandt wiping his oil-covered hands on a dirty piece of cloth, his face and scalp also streaked with oil and dirt, but the 43-year-old immediately snapped to attention as Geiger entered.

Responding to Geiger's enquiry about progress, Brandt said, 'The wing repairs are complete, *Leutnant*.' The seasoned veteran's voice seemed to evidence that the job was indeed done and he would not be challenged on it. The engine fuel problem had been sorted out some hours ago. Brandt summed up all their work with: 'The seaplane is ready for its next flight, Sir.' At times Brandt could label a particular repair as likely to be difficult, even daunting, but, so far, he had never failed to deal successfully with one. Brandt and his crew fully merited their Iron Cross recommendations.

'Well done, Warrant Officer. Very well done,' replied Geiger, as he strode onto the hangar deck to take a look at the plane, showing particular interest in the plane's repaired wing tip. Notwithstanding the various unpainted patches the fuselage had acquired over the course of the voyage, the wing tip and the plane for that matter looked as good as new to him. 'An excellent job,' said Geiger, loud enough to overcome the cold wind finding its way through or under the canvas screens, but also so the crew would hear him. Brandt confirmed that the repair had once again been possible by using parts from the crated plane. He emphasised to Geiger that any future damage that could not be met from that source might well tax their resourcefulness. Geiger acknowledged the issue, but finished with another 'well done' and bid them all a good night's sleep. They'd earned it, working all day. Soon enough they would be up to assist with the morning flight, weather permitting. As he made his way below, Geiger accepted and not for the first time that Brandt and his men had worked wonders, perhaps miracles, in keeping the plane airworthy. Warrant Officer Brandt was an essential component in this aerial enterprise. He and his men had a hard enough task, made all the more difficult in the ship's improvised and cold hangar. Geiger also reflected on the fact that while Brandmann and his two officers might be in charge, they relied on Brandt to manage the men and undertake maintenance and repairs. If they wanted some specific action on the plane, they so ordered it, but depended on Brandt to get it done. He might sometimes moan about the difficulties in keeping the plane airworthy, but Geiger knew that the plane's success owed much to Brandt.

He had descended one deck from the hangar, when he felt the ship turning. There had been several turns during their northerly course as the battle cruiser periodically zigzagged. However, this alteration of course was different; Geiger felt the ship do what seemed like a complete turn to port, reversing course.

Curious, he diverted from his descent and emerged on the port side, just for'ard of turret Caesar. None the wiser, but bitterly cold, he thought to go below and leave the Bridge officers to decide on the ship's course, when his eyes picked out a line, a faint white line, off to port. Intrigued, he questioned a *fähnrich* who was about to ascend a ladder to the nearby aft control position.

'Ice,' was the young midshipman's hurried reply, as he climbed to his post.

Geiger stared at the white line, stretching as far aft and ahead as he could see.

卐

Schellenberg reported to Körner. 'The plane's repairs are complete, Captain. It is ready to fly. The pilot will scout fifty kilometres north and south of our position. If there are suitable channels leading to the coast, he will also check them out.'

'Thank you, Peter,' said Körner. He said no more, but turned to look again at the ice, hoping that the plane would soon find the ice was not as extensive as it appeared and that there were suitable channels to get them to Kehlmann's refuelling fjord. Körner had come quickly to the Bridge when first notified of the ice barring their path. There was no option but to check out its extent, search for an opening. The Spotting Top had soon reported it as a complete ice-barrier. The navigator judged it to run parallel to the Greenland coast and there was some debate about how far back it stretched, perhaps to the shore, even though that was about one hundred kilometres distant. The plane would soon resolve the situation.

The battle cruiser and her supply ship cruised back and forth, along the edge of the ice, while the plane was prepared. It was very cold, but, to Körner, the light northerly airs, clear blue skies and gentle swell all seemed to point to excellent flying conditions. They should know within a couple of hours what ice conditions they faced. To Körner, the ice indeed looked solid enough and extended as far as he could see north and south and, quite probably, it did reach all the way to Greenland. Even if the plane found gaps or passages, these would have to be navigable. He wanted to refuel and, as often happened in the Bight in winter, he was confident of the ship's ability to negotiate sea ice, within reason, but this wasn't the Bight and he was wary of getting trapped in the ice or caught there by the enemy.

While the two ships cruised along the ice edge, there were frequent reports of loose ice, some large pieces, some close. While a fair distance from the ship, one solitary, near rectangular slab looked quite menacing and generated some comment on the Bridge. At perhaps a good forty or fifty metres long, it was smaller than the bergs they'd seen before, but still something to be wary of. Körner noted it had an almost flat top, brilliant white in the sunlight, with one end angled up like a ship's bow. Its five-metre-high sides, ragged in places, smooth and rounded elsewhere, showed some grey, but appeared shot-through with varying intensities of sky-blue veining. He watched it as it passed, moving steadily north, about a kilometre away from the ice sheet.

142

The ice situation led to an exchange with Kehlmann on the *Erda*, with the two ships steaming abreast of each other for a short while. Kehlmann had little to add to the debate. He said the Greenland ice, such as it appeared, was 'completely unexpected', not something he'd encountered before at this time of the year. Normally, May saw the coastal ice breaking up, he shouted through a megaphone—with the crew listening in—and he thought there may well be breaks and passages.

Körner, with Schellenberg at his side, watched the seaplane launching. Everything went well, with no repeat of the previous day's events. The plane flew off north, clearly following the ice edge. Körner watched it till it was a distant speck in the clear blue sky. The plane had proved its worth on previous occasions; this was yet another important flight.

During the flight, Geiger had remained near the hangar. He had his flying gear ready, in case there was a need to go aloft quickly on its return. As soon as it was spotted, his eyes, like those of Falbe, Brandt and the others of the ground crew, were glued to the plane. It had been a good two hours since take-off. As it flew around the battle cruiser, it flashed messages, which he relied on Falbe to decipher.

'Ice … unbroken … no way through,' relayed his observer.

Geiger gave a quick 'thanks' for the somewhat depressing information. This news was little different to the message it had flashed to the ship about an hour earlier, when it returned from the northern leg of its mission and then continued off south. From what he could see of the ice from the ship, he was not surprised at the reconnaissance outcome. The ice sheet, largely a white panorama, tinged with grey and blue colours, appeared solid enough, stretching off as far as he could see. Actually, he'd observed that it was not a single, solid ice block, but a vast array of large, white, irregularly-shaped plates, joined to each other by grey slush-looking mass that filled any apparent gaps. The ice edge itself was not a uniform, continuous edge, but here and there snaked in and out. There were some dark areas, perhaps open water or just thinner ice, but there was clearly no easy passage through it. He imagined the ship might well be able to push through it, especially some of the dark cracks, but surely not all the way to the coast of distant, out-of-sight Greenland. It was too risky.

Geiger exchanged a few words with Brandt about the process once the plane had been recovered, but their conversation died off quickly, as both focused on the plane as it began to come in from astern to set down near the port side of the slowing ship. Everyone was supposed to be watching for submarines, but the air contingent considered their primary responsibility lay with the plane. The weather was still very good and Geiger judged the sea state to be close to ideal for a landing. He found no fault with the plane's descent, but, when it touched the water and jumped a little, momentarily lifting from the water, he felt his eyebrows rise as well. When the plane dropped back to the surface again, Geiger thought the port float seemed to stab into the water and, before he could give it any further consideration, the plane's lower port wing also made contact and then in an instant the whole machine half-spun round to the left and flipped right over into the sea, the scene instantly veiled in a large cloud of white spray.

While Geiger, hands tightly gripping the deck guardrail, was almost dumbstruck at the calamitous sight, he was enveloped by an outpouring of gasps and profanities from Falbe, Brandt and the rest of the ground crew. He looked anxiously at the upside-down plane, which, rocked by the occasional small wave, was obviously sinking. The forward part of the plane and the wings had already disappeared, leaving only the tail section and floats above water. In no time, they also lowered themselves further into the water, until only the aft sections of the upturned floats and the end of the tail could be seen at the surface. He realised that the floats were all that was keeping the plane from sinking completely. Amidst all that, he could see no sign of Brandmann or his observer, Kühl. How to rescue them?

For a moment he felt quite impotent, being so close, yet so far. He looked to the deck immediately below where the cutter, manned and hanging in the davits, waited for such an emergency. He didn't have to shout. Someone there had quickly taken the initiative and the boat was already dropping towards the sea. The battle cruiser was hardly moving, but, while the plane had landed only fifty metres abreast of the ship, her slow forward movement soon left the plane astern. This meant the boat crew had at least a one-hundred-metre pull to the pitiful plane, but he hoped it should present no problem to them.

As the boat, temporarily hidden from him by the ship's side, came into view, Geiger watched its obviously well-drilled crew, moving as one with powerful, synchronised strokes, their oars biting into the peaceful waters, as they pulled easily towards the plane. The battle cruiser also began to move, putting yet more distance between him and the plane. He grumbled inwardly at this, looking for'ard to the Bridge for a moment, though without real purpose. Did he think his look of dismay, even anger, would change the minds of those there? He knew only too well that the captain would not allow the ship to be exposed to torpedo attack by remaining at a standstill for too long.

Geiger looked back at the plane, its floats and tail still evident, though periodically obscured by even the small waves out there. He hoped the buoyancy afforded by the twin floats would suffice to keep the plane at the surface until the crew could be rescued. He wondered if that state of affairs would continue, but quickly reasoned that, providing they had not been damaged in the crash, the normal watertight integrity of the floats, with their internal bulkheads, might keep the plane from sinking. Through binoculars provided by Falbe, he saw a figure at the rear of the far float. 'I can see someone!' he called to the assembled ground crew, most of whom didn't have access to binoculars, but would be able to see well enough. He could not, however, determine if it was Brandmann or Kühl, as the figure, one arm crooked across the top of the float, disappeared with each wave, so kept quiet on that fact, but gave a limited commentary on what he could see. 'The boat's alongside, … they're pulling him aboard, … one of the boat crew has gone into the water.' Frustratingly, he could see no more, as the boat itself partially blocked his view of the rescue.

Geiger, pleased that the crew would now be saved, then dared to ponder the recovery of the plane. If it would keep afloat long enough, there was probably a chance to lift it out of the water. Perhaps it was salvageable. It would obviously have suffered some damage in the crash, as so often happened in such events. But, who knows, Brandt and his men could perform another miracle and get it to fly once again. The derrick, which had been ready to undertake the normal recovery, was still manned and projecting over the ship's side. It could yet be used, if the ship could get alongside the plane, but, he wondered, would the captain risk his ship in such a move?

'Warrant Officer!' he half-shouted, mostly to get the ground crew's full attention, 'Ensure that the derrick is ready to pick up the plane sharply, if we have a chance to get it alongside.'

Brandt's wide eyes seemed to indicate surprise at the prospect, but he simply responded, 'Aye, aye, Sir!'

'I'm going up to the Bridge.'

⚐

Körner had seen plenty of death and destruction in this war, but was not inured to it. The plane crash was not at all in the same vein as, say, a ship sinking, but was tragic nonetheless. The plane—and its crew—was important to him. He kept his binoculars on the scene. He could see that both members of the plane's crew had been rescued, but couldn't gauge their condition. The boat had pulled away from the stricken plane, whose floats were still occasionally to be glimpsed. The battle cruiser had circled the crash site while the boat crew undertook the rescue. He brought the slowing ship as close as possible, while most eyes scanned the sea for the feared submarine attack. He did not expect submarines to be in this area, but it was always better to be safe than sorry in his view. The *Erda* had closed up and offered help, but was just told to 'stand by'.

Recovery of the boat took longer than hoisting a seaplane aboard; something wrong there, mused Körner. From his view of the men in the boat, both of the seaplane crew could be in a bad way, showing no obvious signs of movement. He'd asked for an immediate update on their condition. Schellenberg, who'd witnessed the crash with Körner, had stepped away to deal with some matter. Now he was back, with *Leutnant* Geiger at his side.

'Captain, are we to recover the plane?' said Schellenberg, his voice giving no suggestion that that was his own desire.

Körner turned, sensing that the question probably came from Geiger, and could see from the tall *leutnant*'s face that he was obviously looking for a 'yes'. '*Is the plane recoverable?*' he asked, looking more at Geiger. 'Won't it have sustained considerable damage?' Körner thought he saw Geiger's chest expand as he rose up to his full, impressive height.

'Captain, until the plane is recovered, we just won't know,' said the young pilot. 'For now, it's still afloat. I see no obvious damage.'

Körner noted the way the tall *leutnant* had calmly responded, with perhaps just a tinge of emotion, though clearly denying the likely situation. Obviously damage could only be guessed at, but it was a flimsy machine and unlikely to avoid serious damage in such a crash. He thought for a moment before responding. The plane had been extremely useful, especially in finding the convoy. Could they get along without it? Probably, was his snap conclusion, but were they getting ahead of themselves? 'Well, I would be surprised if it hasn't been damaged, perhaps seriously, by such a crash-landing. Anyway,' he quickly added, 'what about the other plane? Can't it be assembled?'

Körner saw that Geiger first glanced at Schellenberg before responding.

'Possibly not, Sir,' said the *leutnant*. 'Parts from the crated-up plane have been used to repair the other, *including* the engine. There is quite a bit remaining, but it may not amount to a *whole* plane. It would be prudent to recover that one,' his slight head movement suggesting the plane in the sea, 'to ensure we have the best chance of assembling a flyable machine. If I may suggest, Sir, we should take speedy action, as the plane may well sink.'

Through Schellenberg's updates, Körner knew something of their repair practices, though, he now realised, the question of how that affected the viability of the other plane's assembly had not registered on him. He had just always thought they would have one airworthy plane, if the other was lost.

At Geiger's warning that the plane could sink, he and his two officers swung around and checked on the plane. His binoculared-view showed the occasional glimpse of the plane's floats and tail. Rather than waste precious time debating the pros and cons of why they should recover the plane, he announced: 'All right, let's try and salvage it.'

After a few minute's further discussion on the process, Geiger left the Bridge, while Körner brought his ship closer to the plane. The *Erda* was also signalled to be ready to assist.

Although intent on recovering the plane, Körner debated the situation further with Schellenberg. His first officer, whilst supportive of the need, raised doubts about the recovery, fearing the upturned plane would not only be difficult to raise from the water, but agreed that it may also be severely damaged. Their discussion was interrupted by a sick berth attendant.

'Captain,' the clean-shaven man said with obvious reverence. 'Message from the Surgeon. The Surgeon reports that one of the airmen, … *Kapitänleutnant* Brandmann, … is dead.' There was a small, but noticeable pause, then he continued, 'The other officer is suffering from exposure, but the Surgeon thinks he will survive.'

So, the first loss, thought Körner. He nodded to the young man for the information, feeling unable to thank him out loud for it.

Geiger, sitting in the back of the cutter, was now wet and cold, but his attention was all on the recovery. He could see that he had been right to seek immediate action; the plane's port float and lower wing were slightly raised, showing that it may be sinking. The seamen pulled quickly towards the plane, spray from their oars occasionally adding to Geiger's discomfort. He took little notice of the *Hindenburg* and the *Erda* steaming slowly around behind them.

On reaching the plane, with a brave sailor over the side, it did not take long to secure it to the boat, which Geiger hoped would keep it afloat. He quietly thanked goodness for the benign sea state. Summoned forward, the *Erda* came up to raise the plane. Geiger wanted the plane lifted onto the battle cruiser, but could not persuade Captain Körner to risk the warship. The captain's apprehension of presenting a stationary target for any great length of time had worked against Geiger's arguments to raise the plane onto the *Hindenburg* where it would be better placed to aid the assembly of the other plane.

The *Erda*'s derrick was well up to the task, but the lift proved problematical and, to Geiger, would contribute further damage to the machine that was slowly lifted from the sea. Unable to attach the plane to its normal lifting point, the floats were first pulled together and then, no doubt, water pressure on the wings damaged them too. The craft that emerged from the water had taken on a slightly inverted v-like shape, with the upper wing looking like it had suffered most from the crash. To Geiger, as it came up, most of the plane appeared to be there. The engine was still in place, even the propeller seemed to have survived the impact. Once he was aboard the supply ship, he supervised the plane's gentle lowering to the deck. After a further examination, it could only be covered with a tarpaulin and secured, until a suitable opportunity to transfer the wreckage arose. Geiger, accompanied by *Oberleutnant* Kehlmann, then returned to the cutter and the pull back to the *Hindenburg*.

Once back aboard the battle cruiser, Schellenberg met him and, with only a curt comment about the successful recovery of the plane, informed him about Brandmann. 'Please go and see how your colleague is … and, if possible, find out what they saw during their flight. We read their signals, but see if there's more to report.'

Geiger, still wet from the boat journeys, descended the few decks to the sick bay. He reported to the surgeon. To Geiger, *Kapitänleutnant* Manekeller, looked very much a doctor than a ship's officer, but he acknowledged the surgeon's rank. 'Sir, the First Officer wants me to get the observer's report. Is he able to talk?'

'Yes,' replied Manekeller, 'though *Leutnant* Kühl was very lucky that the ship's boat got to him when it did. If the rescue had been any slower,' suggested the surgeon, 'then he too might have died from immersion in the freezing water. We're endeavouring to get some heat into him.'

Manekeller gestured to the pilot to go into the sick bay to see his air colleague, but Geiger, intrigued, asked, 'Did the *Kapitänleutnant* die from exposure?'

'No,' said the surgeon, 'he drowned. He hit his head. This may have knocked him unconscious or he just was unable to free himself from the plane.'

Geiger, sobered by this news, entered the small sick bay. The first cot was occupied by a sailor, with Kühl in the next. The *leutnant*, half-sitting up, seemed to be thoroughly wrapped up, with a couple of metal hot water bottles on top of his many blankets, one at his feet, the other resting in his crotch. An attendant was helping him down a steaming hot drink. Between sips of the liquid, he gave a half-nod and half-smile towards Geiger. The attendant moved away to allow Geiger in. Geiger felt he should make some witty or uplifting remark, but with Brandmann dead and Kühl looking pale and at death's door, his ideas fizzled out. 'Good to see you're on the mend,' tried Geiger.

Kühl responded with a very quiet, 'Yes, … I'll soon be up.'

'Sorry to bother you, Ernst, but the First Officer, the Captain, … they're keen to know if you have anything to report. Did you see any breaks in the ice? Any way through?'

His voice feeble, Kühl replied, 'No. Just ice, solid ice.'

As their somewhat tentative discussion continued, Geiger kept thinking that it could well have been him and Falbe in the plane. Geiger had expected the next flight would be his, but Brandmann, making light of it, joked that it was still his turn, as yesterday's engine failure meant he'd never even got into the air. Geiger hadn't argued.

12

Eskimo

Geiger approached the hangar from the starboard side of the Boat Deck, savouring the weak sun on his back. Astern, he saw the *Erda*, plodding along, though with quite a bow wave and a lot of funnel smoke. After he'd reported Kühl's observation that they'd found no gaps in the ice, the captain ordered both ships onto a south-east course. The order Geiger was given was simple enough: assemble the other plane. That might be an order easily given, but he wondered whether it would be as easily achieved.

He found his men still in the cold hangar, standing around, some just looking out to sea through the partially open, curtained entrance. Without the plane, the canvas hangar was all but empty, except for the crates containing the other plane. These, most already opened, along with other, various aircraft parts, were set against the rear and side walls. Brandt called the men to attention. Geiger summoned the warrant officer to come closer.

'They know about the *Kapitänleutnant*, Sir,' said Brandt in a quiet voice.

Geiger gave a slight nod to this and said, equally quietly, not wanting the others to hear, 'The Captain wants the other plane assembled.' Then, even quieter, 'Can we do it?'

Brandt hesitated for a moment, then said: 'We can give it our best shot, Sir, though,' he paused, 'even drawing parts from the recovered plane, we may not have everything we need.'

Geiger half-expected such a response from his warrant officer. He fervently hoped Brandt was just giving his usual, guarded response and really meant 'yes, it can be done'. He knew from his time on the *Santa Elena* that a plane could be comprehensively dismantled in a day, but accepted Brandt's cautionary observation that to assemble a complete and *flyable* plane, especially where they might not have all the necessary or fully functioning parts, could be a tall order.

Geiger then stood back, looking at the whole group, the six men, making eye contact with each. Other than Brandt, the others' faces suggested them to be a dejected, downhearted bunch. Who could blame them? Like him, they'd witnessed the crash and knew of the loss of their commanding officer, but, then again, he wondered, did they care or had they seen it all before? Did they, like him, ask what had happened, what had actually caused the crash? He'd speculated on whether Brandmann had hit a piece of ice. To him there was no evidence for it at the time, but several different sized pieces had been seen that morning. Perhaps they weren't greatly moved by such events or hadn't even given it much, if any, thought; it was tragic, but there'd been similar happenings on the *Santa Elena*.

Endeavouring to justify his officer status, he spoke with a raised voice: 'Men! As you know, the *Kapitänleutnant* was killed in the crash.' He said nothing about how Brandmann had actually died. He also said nothing about the plane crash itself; they'd all witnessed it. 'The good news is that *Leutnant* Kühl is alive and expected to make a full recovery.' No sooner had he said that when he wondered if he would be challenging the fates with such a pronouncement. Well, too late, he thought. 'As you know, we've recovered the plane. It's on the *Erda*.' He paused, still no visible change in their demeanour or expressions. Why should there be? These were sailors of the Imperial Navy, who were trained to focus on the officer to their front. 'We've been charged,' he continued, still speaking a bit too loudly, 'with assembling the other plane.' He again saw no change in the faces. 'I know that we have, for some time now, been using that plane, the crated one,' waving his hand in the general direction of the crates, 'to keep the other one in the air, but I know you'll be able to assemble a new plane. If necessary, we can use parts from the plane on the *Erda*. It's damaged, but I suspect much of it is useable.

'I doubt I have to tell you that having a plane has proved to be immensely useful to the ship on this mission. It's no falsehood to say that without the plane, we would never have found, never mind attacked, the convoy. And, above all, it has been *your* efforts, *your* skills, *your* expertise that have kept the plane aloft.

'So it should come as no surprise to hear that the Captain wants the other plane assembled as quickly as possible!'

Even after what he hoped would be taken as praise, he could still discern no change in the men's faces. Why was he even hoping for it? He did not need anyone, least of all the faces of his men, to tell him that he was no great orator or motivator of men. By default, he was now in charge of this small group and was plainly not doing enough to rebuild their spirits. He silently recalled the reasons why he'd made the move to airplanes. He decided to bring his speech to a close.

'We're soon to return to Germany,' he said without really knowing what was ahead, but guessing that that must be the next stage of operation *Georg*, 'and just as soon will be deservedly returned to our homes and loved ones.'

With the men dismissed, he again spoke separately with Brandt about the expected timescale, getting no firm answer other than perhaps a minimum of two days, *if* they have access to the *Erda*'s plane. Whether it would then fly would be the issue.

⚑

As usual, there was little communication to the men about the latest situation, never mind any intended actions, but there was, equally as usual, enough information to hand to generate ample mess-deck discussion and speculation about the ship's apparent change in fortunes. The plane crash and the loss of the pilot, the southerly course and delay in refuelling, not to mention the endless ice edge that paralleled their course, had all quickly contributed to a dampening down of the otherwise high morale generated by the convoy action. However, despite the day's events, Eckhardt was not worried and encountered no evident despair or concern from others about getting back to Germany. The crew still placed their faith in the ship, its speed and magnificent gunnery, though most realised the plane had been an asset. Even those who all along had questioned its value did not dismiss its loss as being of no consequence, but, not surprisingly, were now sceptical about producing another plane from the clearly damaged plane that was raised from the sea. As a look-out, Eckhardt knew better than most that without a plane they were now back to how far they could see from the ship, perhaps twenty kilometres, instead of the hundreds a plane could provide. He, for one, hoped rumours of getting a plane into the air would come true.

The look-outs were told to report any break or 'bay' in the ice. Periodic changes in the ice edge were sighted, with some large indentations, but none which offered an evident course to the Greenland shore and possible coaling. None of the bays seen appeared large enough. For once, Eckhardt was keen to see the filthy refuelling process begin, understanding the ship's predicament about the need to fill the bunkers to get home. At least the weather remained good for them. The sea was quite calm and mostly untouched by a light wind blowing almost from the port beam. It was undoubtedly cold, but sunny, with a largely blue sky and good visibility. Then again, he thought, was that the sort of weather they now required?

⌛

From the port side of the Command Bridge, Körner too was staring at the Greenland ice and, not surprisingly, also thinking of refuelling. Occasionally, he swung his binoculars onto the *Erda*, following about 400 metres astern, her smoke little affected by the light winds. Limited by the merchant ship's slow speed, after some hours steaming south, they were still over 250 sea miles and many hours from Cape Farewell, the southernmost tip of Greenland and the turning point for Iceland or Jan Mayen; Germany was no longer feasible. Not long after the decision to head south, Gärtner had brought the predicted, but nevertheless gloomy news that getting back to Germany without refuelling was now out of the question, at any speed. Throughout the mission there had been times when Körner was concerned about one matter or another. Now, these all seemed as nothing compared to their present, difficult situation. Without fuel, his mighty ship would be all but useless, certainly unable to escape if the enemy came in sight and leaving him with the unenviable decision of whether to order a fight to the inevitable end or, to save lives, the scuttling of the ship.

As on their journey north the previous day, he still adopted a zigzag course, but kept the ship close to the ice, only about seven or eight kilometres away. This didn't allow much freedom for manoeuvre, but he had to be able to keep the ice in sight. Notwithstanding the ice's discouraging, even mocking presence, sea mile after sea mile, he still hoped to be able to refuel somewhere in Greenland. He had asked Kehlmann, now back aboard the *Hindenburg*, about the likely Greenland ice conditions ahead. The old seadog's response was not encouraging. Although his own experiences pointed to the likelihood of some ice-free anchorages, he was concerned, given the ice situation that confronted them.

As a consequence, Körner had held a meeting with Gärtner and Schellenberg to consider where they might take on coal and oil. If not Greenland, then Iceland and Jan Mayen were the only alternatives, though Schellenberg had quickly suggested another option. He reminded Körner that in the waters off Iceland Nerger had refuelled *at sea*. A difficult enough task for his ship, the *Wolf*, but to Körner an impossible one for the *Hindenburg*, which required considerably more fuel than Nerger's single-screw merchant ship, hours of calm water and no enemy interruption. Schellenberg still felt that the calm sea offered the possibility of refuelling by putting the *Erda* against the ice edge, with the battle cruiser to seaward of her. Challenged by Körner, he had accepted that his idea could well deliver some fuel, certainly the oil, but in any swell the ice and the battle cruiser may well damage the merchant ship, perhaps fatally, before enough coal could be transferred. Nevertheless, the Spotting Top was told to report suitable 'ice bays'. They must be prepared to be flexible and not pass up any potential answer to their problem.

Having dealt with Schellenberg's ice bay suggestion, their attention focussed on Jan Mayen and Iceland. Körner had listened patiently while his two officers then debated the advantages and disadvantages of the two main refuelling options. Although a desolate place—something in its favour—Jan Mayen offered a known location, with the added benefit of the *Torsten Meyer* in place. However, that meant another passage of the Denmark Strait. All had agreed that getting through the Strait safely and unobserved would be quite a task, though it would be easier if the seaplane was available. Despite success in dealing with the Strait's ice on their previous journey through it and the hoped-for recession of the ice at this time of the year, the unexpected magnitude of the Greenland ice raised concerns that they might find even more ice barring their path. One thing seemed likely: enemy patrols. There was general agreement that the English must surely have checked out Hornvik bay and could also be expected to have introduced patrols to watch the Strait in case it was used as a return route by the battle cruiser. Schellenberg added another interesting twist to their deliberations: Schönert's men had not picked up any W/T traffic that would indicate enemy activity in the area. This was also backed up by the Admiralty signals which gave no warnings of enemy ships north of Iceland. Körner, however, had thought it unlikely there would be no enemy ships in those waters and expected contact if they ventured there. He accepted they could probably force their way through any ice in the Strait, though it may drive them nearer to Iceland. All thought that any enemy patrols could probably be dealt with, but any warships they didn't sink or avoid would undoubtedly follow them and draw in others. Factors like fog could help, but were just too uncertain upon which to formulate any plan. Iceland seemed to offer more options. It had many, most likely ice-free, fjords. Hornvik had been ideal, but could not be chanced again, though the island's northern coasts presented many other fjords and suitable bays. Of course, they would also require a Denmark Strait transit. The much closer western fjords were thought too close to Reykjavik and the majority of Iceland's main population centres. The southern shore was almost devoid of fjords or bays. The handful of fjords at the island's easternmost extremity seemed to fit the bill and, also, by keeping well to the south of Iceland, could probably be approached without detection. However, their main drawbacks were their proximity to Scapa Flow, less than 500 sea miles, and the known telegraph links with Europe in that area.

All had accepted that whatever destination was selected, the need for the plane in searching the waters ahead was an obvious advantage. Although monitoring of the plane assembly was in place, Schellenberg re-affirmed that he would keep Körner appraised of its progress.

After almost an hour's discussion, Körner was not comfortable with the outcome, but that reflected the dilemma they faced. There was no surprise that they had decided that Greenland was the much preferred refuelling option, though the question of exactly where would depend on the ice. Keeping a close watch on the Greenland sea ice would continue. If no Greenland site, including Schellenberg's open-ice suggestion, presented itself by Cape Farewell, then they would sail for Iceland's western fjords, primarily because of the shorter distance to them, even if they had factors against them. The prospect of passage through the Denmark Strait argued against the other Icelandic fjords and Jan Mayen. This was somewhat disconcerting, as all three were also acutely aware that *Georg*'s recommended homeward route was the Denmark Strait. Although clearly a related matter, Körner deferred a decision on the route home, until they had refuelled.

The meeting concluded with Körner charging Gärtner with further work to select the exact Iceland fjord to be used. He then retired to his Day Cabin, intending to catch up on some sleep after the eventful night and morning, but he slept fitfully. At one waking, he busied himself with the Iron Cross list Schellenberg had submitted for his consideration. He was more than happy with Kruse's suggestions, reflecting the excellent gunnery during the action. He was also pleased to see the plane's air and ground crews well represented. He had indicated that the nominations could go beyond those directly involved in the convoy action and include those who had been deemed to contribute to the success of the action. This allowed both air crew and those who kept the plane operational to be considered for the decoration. Alas, he did not see how he could extend this to those on the *Erda* and *Torsten Meyer*. They had obviously contributed to the success of the mission so far, but had not been involved in the convoy action. He would see that they were rewarded once back in Germany. For now, his only concern with the list before him was the high proportion of officers, in comparison to the rank and file, who were proposed. He noted this for Schellenberg's attention. Similarly, where the difference in one of the ship's departments seemed marked or a department's numbers low or even absent, he asked Schellenberg to look into it. He hoped there would be an opportunity to thank each man personally, rather than just post the final list.

There was a knock at the cabin door. It was Schellenberg. 'Sir, we're ready.'

Schellenberg led the way, out to the *Batterie* deck aft, starboard side. There, mid-way between the two aft turrets, Körner saw the small burial party waiting, now at attention, for his attendance. Nearer the ship's side was the firing party and opposite were various officers and crew. He noted the presence of the air contingent, Geiger and his men. Before him was the pilot's canvas-wrapped and flag-covered body. He did not see them, but knew the white and red-crossed church service pennant would be aloft and ship's flag at half-mast.

The service was a very brief affair. He said the required words and then the volleys were fired. The ship had not been slowed, but had, temporarily, kept to a straight course. Only now sensing the cold air on his face, Körner watched, with checked emotion, as the weighted, white shape slid over the side.

Another day, another watch, another climb to the Spotting Top. As he climbed, Eckhardt noted the increase in wind speed and the cloudier skies. During the limited night hours, there had been little chance to assess the ice-barrier, as it was now described by everyone, though there had been a change of course, but only because the position of the ice changed, as it conformed to Greenland's changing coastline. Through his binoculars, Eckhardt could easily judge that the ice appeared as formidable as ever and equally depressing. Would it never end? He wanted to suggest they tackle it, push their way through. The lower deck's considerations had continued unabated and all knew coaling was now essential to their survival. Their view: risks must be taken.

He heard two officers discussing that Cape Farewell was still about five hours away and that that would 'decide matters'. He wondered what that meant, unsure, but guessing that the ship might then swing up Greenland's eastern coast or perhaps leave these waters, but where for? With these thoughts in his mind, he kept to his task: scanning the ice-barrier.

A look-out reported land off the port bow, but it was soon seen that it was just some offshore islands. The ice girdled them and forced a change in course to skirt them to the south. Despite the ice and snow, the islands could readily be picked out. There were many of them, guarding this part of the coast now about fifteen or twenty kilometres beyond. Most were flat affairs, probably just slabs of rock of varying sizes, though one or two were quite large and stuck up about forty or fifty metres high. Anyway, none was ice free or, for that matter, something anyone wanted to get much closer to. After an hour, their number and size began to diminish. There was a bit of excitement when a look-out announced he could see movement on the last group of islands, but on closer inspection it turned out to be seals. It was the end of Eckhardt's watch.

'Ice receding!' came the shout.

At such a call, everyone, a crowd of binoculared faces, stared to port. Eckhardt, no desire to go below, could readily see that, almost unbelievably and completely unexpectedly, the ice-barrier had all but petered out as they moved passed the last rocky islets. Who knew why or for that matter cared, but the sea now appeared to have restored its link with the coast, seeming to reach right up to the great range of massive mountains that formed this part of Greenland. Amidst further debate about the ice, Eckhardt noticed that no one challenged the sighting or congratulated the look-out for that matter. No doubt everyone wanted it to be a way to the coast, a way to a refuelling site. Would it be a false hope? No, the range finder in the upper stage of the Spotting Top confirmed it. This was quickly followed by voice pipe exchanges that led to a new course for the two ships, port towards the land.

◊

Back on the Bridge since dawn, Körner was as stirred as any of his officers about the 'ice receding' message from the Spotting Top. He heard Schellenberg, standing next to him, make some comment about the change in the ice, but, other than a mumbled acknowledgement, Körner said nothing. After the many hours of staring at the ice-barrier, his thoughts were now monopolised by the new vista and whether this would turn out to be a golden opportunity, perhaps a last-chance one at that, to refuel their ship in Greenland. He could see for himself that while the ice-barrier as such was gone, there was still much sea ice to be seen all around. There were many pieces of loose ice adrift and littering the sea between them and the distant land, making it quite white in places, elsewhere the ice looked much more dispersed. The white shapes ranged greatly in size, mostly small and flat and no problem to the ship, but some were larger and some were even small iceberg-like affairs. At least the ice they were now faced with was not the impenetrable obstacle they had confronted for so many long hours and that gave hope. Körner quickly dismissed thoughts of why the ice had relinquished its stranglehold on their options, imagining the lengthening hours of sunlight and perhaps the greater influence of the Atlantic in this southern extremity of Greenland had all played their part in the change. 'Er, sorry, Peter,' turning his head to Schellenberg, seeking to apologise to his first officer. 'You were saying?'

'I was just saying, Sir, that this is a remarkable change of circumstances,' responded Schellenberg.

'Yes, … and welcome. Let's hope it provides a chance to refuel,' said Körner, looking astern to see the *Erda* following their new course.

Drawing Gärtner into their conversation, Körner asked, 'What's the coast like here, *Herr* Gärtner? Any good refuelling sites?'

'Difficult to be certain, Sir. We have few detailed maps of this area. I suspect, as with most of Greenland, there will be numerous fjords and bays, some very large,' was Gärtner's immediate response. 'They would probably all suffice … depending on any ice.'

Disappointed with this answer, knowing he should have asked a more specific question, Körner kept a straight face and looked for himself. From the Bridge it was difficult to see the detail of the land before him, but Körner could see what looked like valleys or, more likely, fjords ahead. Somewhat theatrically, he pointed at what appeared to be a large gap in the mountains off the starboard bow. 'Is *that one* suitable?' he asked, feeling some aggression in his tone.

Whether Gärtner felt reprimanded by this question was unclear to Körner. 'I'll check, Sir.' He swung around and retreated to the Chart Room. In two or three minutes, he emerged, accompanied by Kehlmann and one of his junior officers who was carrying various maps. Without looking at the maps, he then announced that there were questions about the accuracy of their charts of this area, some dating from the end of the last century, but he confirmed that Körner's suggestion seemed promising. Indeed, the gap in the mountains appeared to be one of several large fjords on the south-west coast, which, Gärtner said, threaded their way through to some larger ones that emerged on Greenland's east coast, north of Cape Farewell. Gärtner's young *leutnant*, Ernst Winter, showed the maps to Körner and Schellenberg, indicating the maze of fjords in the area, which all seemed to confirm Gärtner's assertions. Kehlmann, when asked, said he could add nothing to aid the deliberations, as he had not been there before.

As favourable reports on the ice continued, Körner gave the order to explore. There was the concern about being surprised with no sea room, but he could not turn down this refuelling chance. He ordered Battle Stations, just in case. Gärtner then added a further consideration.

'Sir, there are *towns* nearby.'

'What? Where?' was Körner's immediate reaction, as he was not expecting such news.

Gärtner showed him an old Danish map that covered the immediate area, pointing to two dots with names, which indicated habitation. 'That one,' pointing to a dot almost north of the ship's position, 'is named *Frederiksdal*. It's about eighteen kilometres away. The other,' his finger moving a few centimetres to the right, 'called ... *Ilua* ... is presently about ...'

'About fifteen kilometres, north-east,' said Winter, rescuing his commander.

Gärtner added, 'I'm afraid I have no information about the size of these towns, but, given Greenland's small population, I suspect they will probably not be large. Indeed, to call them towns may not be warranted.'

While Gärtner and Schellenberg discussed the likely size of the towns and especially the accuracy of their maps, Körner said nothing, switching his gaze in the direction of one town, then the other. At this distance, he could see nothing of the towns or anything, like smoke or ships, to indicate their presence. In truth, while he could see the coast, its mountains, valleys and likely fjords around the first town, the view towards the second town was seriously obscured by mist.

Gärtner, responding to a question by Schellenberg, said, '*Friedrichsthal* is shown on another map to be in this area of southern Greenland, but its scale is much, much smaller and it cannot be used to confirm the accuracy of the town's location. It's obviously the same town, just shown in Danish on one map, in German on the other.'

Kehlmann chipped in to confirm it, saying that the German name obviously linked to the Moravian missionaries that were in the area until around the turn of the century, when they left and the Danes took over.

'Well, gentlemen,' said Körner, his interruption stopping dead his officers' debate, 'whether the maps are accurate or not or whether they're towns or villages or even Danish or not, I don't think we're in a position to let the possibility of encountering some of the local inhabitants turn us away from this opportunity to refuel.'

All readily agreed with their captain. There was some further discussion about whether to take the ship to either of the towns and refuel there, checking out whether they had any W/T, or to stay away from them. There was the possibility that the inhabitants would see the ships' smoke.

Thinking that over, Körner put his hand to his chin, immediately aware that he could benefit from a shave. 'That may be so,' he said, 'but I would like to keep them at arm's length, if we can. If they have a wireless, they *may* signal our presence *if* they see our smoke, but we should expect them to, if we sail right up to their town. We can listen for any wireless signals.' He looked to Schellenberg and Gärtner, expecting them to question this strategy, but they did not challenge it. 'OK. For now, we should keep an eye out for any eskimos,' he half-joked, 'but we'll endeavour to use that fjord,'—the one he had previously suggested—'for refuelling. The quicker we're done, the quicker we'll be out of here.' To his first officer, he said, 'Please alert Commander von Schönert about possible wireless messages.'

The ship easily pushed aside any small drift ice, but avoided the larger, blue-tinted ice blocks which were moving very slowly out to sea. Still watching for the expected eskimos, everyone's attention was, for a few moments, focused on some seals, basking on a large ice floe almost dead ahead. They were all at least man-sized, grey and black coloured. With the ship nearing their floating platform, all but one brave creature slid off easily into the sea.

As the ships closed on the selected fjord, one of three branching off from the sea at that point, Körner slowed the warship and had the *Erda* signalled to move up. Even though fjords could be expected to be exceptionally deep, they had to feel their way and Körner wanted her to assist in the process.

The junction of the three fjords was about ten kilometres wide, with near-equal-sized entrances to each. Despite the wind, the mist away to the east continued to inhibit their views of the fjords to starboard—and Gärtner's second town. The fjord Körner had selected, unnamed on any of their maps, was bounded on their starboard side by a string of small, generally low-lying islands, though which built up to one over 300 metres high. Beyond them Körner could see that the ground rose up a steep, more rounded mountain, with even higher mountains beyond. To port was another island, much larger than those on the other side. Its fjord wall was steep and high, with a summit perhaps of a thousand metres. Again, beyond that mountain could be seen higher and even more jagged peaks. Wherever the slope of the ground was not too steep, there was snow, starkly white. The rest was dark brown and barren. The fjord could be seen to stretch a long way back, but, in addition to the drift ice and ice blocks which dotted its surface, a distant white line across it suggested there might be a greater density of ice awaiting any deeper incursion.

If he'd ever harboured any doubts about the plane's value, Körner now realised the benefit it could have provided in checking out this and other nearby fjords, though he knew it could not have checked their depths. Schellenberg quickly pointed out a possible refuelling site at the south end of the large port-side island, but after a little discussion and further consideration of the Danish map, they pressed on. Farther inland might well provide some spot that was not as easily seen from the sea. Körner sent the *Erda* on ahead, instructing her captain, Harberer, to check out the depth in suitable refuelling sites on the port side. With the aid of one of her boats, the battle cruiser would check out the starboard side. Gärtner's old map suggested sheltered channels between islands and the mainland on both sides of the fjord that looked promising, allowing Körner to believe that these waters would deliver an acceptable refuelling site. For once, he seemed comfortable that no submarines or other vessels were likely to threaten his ship, so had little concern when he stopped and lowered one of the ship's motorboats to help with the soundings. While the small boat proceeded along the islands to starboard, the *Hindenburg* steamed very slowly up and down the centre of the fjord, where, as expected, the water was shown to be exceptionally deep. However, progress by the *Erda* and the motorboat was slow, with many soundings being taken. Their movement was also inhibited by the ice. The small pieces were no real threat to the warship and her collier, though the motorboat kept clear of them, but the larger ice blocks, fortunately few in number and slow-moving, were monitored closely and given a wide berth by all. The tops of some were ten metres above water, but everyone knew that the ice you saw above the sea was as nothing compared to that below sea level.

The first part of the fjord, before the mainland was reached, was about seven kilometres long. Both survey vessels signalled more than adequate water depth for the battle cruiser, but Körner and his Bridge officers saw no suitable coaling site, especially where the ships would not be exposed to collision with a big ice block, however unlikely that might be. The motorboat soon reported one suitable bay amongst the islands to starboard, but Körner thought that while it was protected from ice block collisions, it gave no manoeuvring room. He quipped to Schellenberg that they'd have to go astern to get out of it.

Other than that, the main islands on both sides of the fjord seemed to offer no sheltered anchorage. At the northern end of the last and by far the largest of the starboard-side islands, the motorboat began to check out a channel leading into the next branch fjord, soon signalling sufficient depth of water. From the Bridge, Körner could see it offered something of a sheltered stretch of water between the island and the mountains on its north side and contained no large ice blocks. Small islands appeared to block its far end, but it looked promising.

The *Erda* reported that she intended to check out the channel behind the large port-side island and Körner had to shift the *Hindenburg*'s position to monitor the merchant ship's movements. From this position, Körner got an even better view of the main fjord. It went almost due north for fifteen or more kilometres. Although now strewn with ice of various sizes, he wondered if the summer weather might well clear the waterway and make the fjord navigable for large ships like the *Hindenburg*. What caught his attention were the high peaks on either side. Their pointed summits, stretching up to the sky, seemed immune to the effects of wind and weather.

The *Erda*'s channel, about a kilometre wide, appeared to extend several kilometres to the south-west and pointed back to the open sea. There was also a wide bay on the south side, which the *Erda* initially made for. On the face of it, Körner thought the channel's topography made it good for a likely refuelling spot, but noted it contained a few large ice blocks making their way out to sea. While Körner discussed the suitability of this waterway with his officers, Gärtner reminded Körner that *Frederiksdal*, a 'settlement', as he now labelled it, lay to the west, just over the intervening mountains, and barely six or seven kilometres away by sea. Körner thanked him, but added that wherever they selected would probably be closer to one or other of the towns. As if to interfere with their deliberations, it started to snow.

The *Erda*'s bay seemed ideal, but the ice blocks in the channel raised concerns; the motorboat's easterly waters were selected. The *Erda* was recalled and the two ships steamed back across the fjord. The motorboat's officer, a midshipman, had signalled that the centre of the selected waterway, a wide and kilometre-long bay, was thirty metres deep.

Körner, talking to Schellenberg about the anchorage, was suddenly surprised by the report of 'Eskimos, port side!' Like almost everyone on the Bridge, he turned and raised his binoculars. A long way off, perhaps two thousand metres away up the fjord, he saw small, dark shapes moving gracefully between the ice floes. At that distance, all he could make out were that there were no more than three of them, in what appeared to be small, one-man canoes, low to the water and somehow propelled along smoothly. Other than some childhood knowledge, largely about igloos, he was quite ignorant of eskimo ways. He then noted that one eskimo canoe had stopped moving and imagined the occupant was looking at the two German ships. Körner wondered what he might be making of the *Hindenburg*.

The sighting promoted some banter. Gärtner observed that as they appeared to be travelling west, the eskimos were possibly heading to the western settlement. Whether their arrival there would trigger wireless signals was discussed, but, as no other threat could be imagined, attention quickly switched back to the task in hand. Körner was well pleased to be free of the ice-barrier and now able to begin the crucial task of refuelling, but disappointed that it had still taken almost seven hours since they had turned towards the land to approach, select and survey these waters. The *Hindenburg* moved into the bay, taking her own soundings, and dropped anchor; soon the *Erda* made fast along her port side. The crews were sent for a meal and, if they had any other thoughts, told to prepare for coaling.

᛭

The aircrew, following Geiger's lead, had taken a few minutes to peer inquisitively at the eskimos, though little could really be seen at that distance. Brandt summoned his men back to the plane. The warrant officer's call also jogged Geiger and he also turned away from the eskimos. Before him, in the dark hangar, phoenix-like, was the *new* seaplane. The men had worked almost non-stop since the decision to assemble the plane, with only small breaks for sleep, food and warmth. Geiger had assisted in the building process, though largely in an advisory capacity, but, like them, his face, hands and clothes were smeared in oil, grease and dirt. All that effort had clearly produced a seaplane, but had not yet resulted in a *flyable* machine. One of the floats needed further work and the tail was still to be finished, as was the engine, but it had been evident from an early stage of the assembly they would need to make use of the other plane. There was still no guarantee that that would complete the job.

As the *Erda* had come alongside, Geiger and three others were waiting to board her and get the plane lifted up to the hangar. Much to Geiger's relief, the process went better than he expected and the long-arm derrick on the battle cruiser was soon lifting the damaged plane up onto the deck at the front of the hangar. Schellenberg had told him that, if coaling was delayed because of problems in lifting the plane off the *Erda*, it could result in it being discarded, 'dropped overboard!' Geiger and his men were excused from coaling to concentrate on the plane. Naturally, they preferred that arrangement.

As the battle cruiser's men assembled for coaling, they were first called to the quarterdeck. To ensure the *Erda*'s crew could also hear him, Körner climbed onto the roof of Dora, the aft turret. Hundreds of silent heads were looking at him, their faces not yet filthy. The great land mass off their port side afforded some shelter from the wind, but, with the temperature hovering just above zero, a few spots of sleet dotted the turret roof. He did not pull his great coat shut.

'Men!' his voiced raised. 'I know you do not like coaling ship, ... but once you have finished this filthy, but never more important task, we shall be sailing ... for Germany!' He paused, looking around, taking in as many faces as possible. 'I'm proud of you all!' he shouted. 'You have sailed this ship well and won a great victory for our country! You have sunk enemy ships, disrupted the enemy's Atlantic convoys and prevented many American soldiers from reaching the Western Front!' Again, he paused, again turning to see everyone. 'In only a few days, we shall be back in Wilhelmshaven, where you will all get much deserved leave!'

The clatter of coaling penetrated through Körner's Day Cabin walls and its accompanying black dust cloud soon darkened its scuttles. Through one of the small round glass openings, he could just glimpse the steep slopes of the land to the north. White, brown and grey, but also blue-black in places, it looked both foreboding, yet impressive. He had agreed with Schellenberg to post look-outs at several places on the land surrounding the bay, to get a good view of the sea approaches. They did not want to be surprised, whether by ships *or* eskimos.

There were some officers and men on vital tasks, but the vast majority of the crew were engaged in coaling. Periodically, Schellenberg reported on progress of transferring sustenance from the *Erda* to the warship.

'Progress is very good, Captain,' said Schellenberg, as he entered the cabin, black dust on his face. 'Oil fuel is being transferred. Coaling is going very well; the men are excelling themselves. I think everyone understands the importance of this particular refuelling.'

'That's all very good news, Peter.'

'Sir, the Gunnery Officer has asked me, have you made a decision about the shells?'

They had agreed to concentrate all their efforts on the refuelling before bringing over the main armament shells. However, Körner had raised a question about how those few shells should be distributed amongst the turrets. The convoy action had seen the forward guns firing more shells than the aft ones. Wondering about any future clash of arms, he'd asked himself whether the extra shells should go to the aft guns, in the expectation that the ship might well be presenting her stern to enemy ships. However, he also wondered whether he would be tempting fate by any such action. He decided to be logical.

'There are relatively few shells—thirty-eight—not even five shells per gun. However, while we may run into enemy warships, I doubt we will be seeking action. So, let's put them in the aft magazines.'

As Schellenberg turned to leave, Körner asked about the plane.

'*Leutnant* Geiger reports good progress, though the engine may need some more work on it. They have assembled it, but are still endeavouring to get it to work. The original engine was replaced quite soon and repairing it with parts from the one which has been in the sea has no doubt caused its own problems. Geiger says another twenty-four hours before any flying.'

'If that plane isn't flying soon, it may not get a chance to,' said Körner. 'Please inform the *leutnant* that we need his plane aloft when we leave this anchorage. Dawn tomorrow.'

🏴

Eckhardt shivered and, not for the first time, stamped his feet and blew into his gloved hands. He turned expectantly to midshipman Jahncke, who looked equally cold. He wanted to ask how long it would be till the boat came for them, but thought it unwise to put that to his teenage officer. Catching the midshipman's eye, he felt he had to say something. His first offering was: 'Let's hope there are no polar bears, Sir.'

'Well, I certainly hope not,' said Jahncke. Then, smiling, he added, 'Are you keeping that rifle warm? Don't want it to freeze up, if a bear *does* come by.'

In an exaggerated manner, Eckhardt pulled the long weapon close to him to show his understanding. All joking apart, the mention of bears got him thinking about what would happen if a bear did attack them. Would his Mauser rifle stop a polar bear, reputedly a giant creature? He was no marksman and had never fired the gun in anger. As soon as they'd come to their rocky look-out post, he'd loaded a clip of five bullets into the rifle's magazine and, with the satisfying noise of the bolt closing, chambered one round, then put the large safety catch to its central, upright position. In the event of a bear attack, he expected—hoped—that he'd have enough time to flick the safety catch to the left, 'ready to fire' position. As he handled the weapon, checking the safety catch again and holding it up, looking along the barrel at possible bear-hiding places, he saw Jahncke eyeing what he was doing. 'Just in case,' said Eckhardt, half-seeking approval, but Jahncke said nothing. Eckhardt stood up and took a nonchalant look around them, very much hoping not to see a bear nearby, though every white mound bothered him. He had been pleased to be told of his look-out duty, thereby relieving him of some or hopefully all of the coaling he would have been obliged to undertake. However, when handed the gun 'to guard against polar bears', he was somewhat taken aback, suddenly wondering whether coaling was the better assignment.

He and Jahncke had been brought to the far shore of the fjord to the east of the anchorage in one of the ship's boats. Managing to get onto the solid ground without getting wet, they'd clambered over its weathered rocks and negotiated some thick patches of snow in seeking a good vantage point. Eckhardt had been content to keep nearer the water, where there was better shelter from the wind and a good view of the sea. Jahncke, playing his officer role, reminded him that they had to be able to see the ship, in case a message had to be passed back by signal flag. Eckhardt thought his selected point met their needs, but bowed to the youthful officer's authority. They'd made their way up the slope to a higher point, some twenty-five or thirty metres above the sea. The climb was not steep, but the state of the ground obliged them to step carefully and negotiate some deep fissures in the rocky surface. Jahncke seemed content, though Eckhardt mumbled to himself about the exposed nature of the position. Through his binoculars he could see the ship some two kilometres away. From here they also had a good view of the sea. Another look-out team was stationed in the fjord the ships had steamed through. The two teams would ensure nothing could approach the ship unseen from the sea. Jahncke had told him that another team, perhaps themselves, could have been sent up to the top of the high island south of the ship or the high ground north of the anchorage. However, the island was deemed too difficult to climb and the other's view of the sea inhibited. Either one, he'd joked, would probably have been a lot colder than their current assignment.

Despite the midshipman's obvious devotion to duty and pleasure in his little command post, Eckhardt could soon discern that Jahncke, who he reckoned could only be about eighteen years old, was feeling the cold as much as him. Jahncke took little persuasion when it started to snow, albeit lightly, in quickly accepting Eckhardt's suggestion that they should seek shelter in a large cleft in the rocks he'd noticed lower down the slope, which provided reasonable protection from the snow and wind. They couldn't see the ship from there, but could still see the sea. They drank the hot, well quite warm, drink from the Thermos they'd brought with them. It was good and held the cold at bay.

Given the cold weather, they were only scheduled to stay for an hour or so. It was one of the longest hours Eckhardt could recall. Every five minutes or so, he ventured out of their rocky alcove to check on the ship *and* for bears. The ship looked fine to him, though he could see that the voyage was taking its toll on the warship's paintwork. Through his binoculars he could see that the paint on her hull was far from pristine, with large areas near the bows dark, no longer looking as if they had any dark-grey paint on them. He could also see that the *Erda* was still alongside, the air around the ships looking dark, so, he figured, coaling must still be underway. He then saw the sight that most gladdened him: the motorboat was heading their way. Uplifted, he gingerly scrambled back to the midshipman. His focus was mainly on the rocks as he made his way down the slope. Looking up, he saw boats. Eskimos.

Rousing the midshipman, they both emerged from their safe haven to get a better view. Almost due south, close to the shore were five boats. Four small, one-man canoes and a larger canoe with several crew. They were still a kilometre or more away. A quick check on the motorboat's progress showed it was not much farther away, but should get to them first. Eckhardt was apprehensive, having no knowledge of eskimos, imagining them to be everything from simple, primitive nomads to unpredictable savages. He was pleased he had the rifle.

As they got back to the water's edge, the motorboat approached them. Jahncke, his replacement, a Petty Officer, and Petersen, the motorboat's midshipman, then went into a bit of a huddle discussing the eskimos, still some distance away, but obviously coming their way. Eckhardt exchanged a few words on the canoeists with his replacement, Gustav Weber, though all the while both men kept their eyes on the approaching flotilla.

Eckhardt could see that the one-man boats were sleek affairs, pointed at both ends, about four or five metres long and a beam little wider than the occupant's body. The canoes sat very low in the water, the freeboard looking hardly more than fifteen centimetres. He could see that each of them was completely enclosed, the deck area covered in right up to the man's waist, who must have been sitting on the bottom of the boat. The man, using a double-ended oar, propelled the canoe with ease, moving it forward very smoothly. Eckhardt could also see that the men had various pieces of equipment on the top of their canoes, including what looked like spears *and* rifles.

Once 'they've got rifles' was announced, Petersen called the men to be ready, but not to shoot unless he ordered it. Weber pointed his gun in the eskimos' direction; Eckhardt just held his across his chest, but eased the safety catch to the left position.

As they got nearer, the eskimos looked quite oriental to Eckhardt, round-faced, with leathery, dark skin or were they just dirty? He had expected them probably to be dressed from head to foot in fur clothing, but, other than some fur lining around their headwear, they all seemed to be wearing brown smock-like clothes.

As the canoes approached, he had a good look at the large one. This was an altogether different boat, being about six or seven metres long, more than a metre wide and more boat-like in shape and operation. Unlike the one-man canoes, it was open-topped and had several, high-positioned thwarts. Light seemed to show through its sides, suggesting it was thin material, possibly made from skins, thought Eckhardt. It was crewed by six men, each using a one-bladed paddle.

About fifteen metres away, one of the large canoe's crew stood up and raised his hand, an obvious greeting signal. Petersen tentatively raised his hand in response. The eskimo, with what looked like a smile, said something which no one understood. He then spoke in something that sounded like a Scandinavian tongue to Eckhardt.

To Eckhardt's surprise, Petersen responded with like-sounding words. Normally, his opinions of midshipmen largely centred on whether or not they had started to shave and he certainly did not think they would be able to decide on what to do about the eskimos. However, suitably impressed by Petersen's obvious linguistic skills, his estimation of the young man rose a notch. The eskimo and the midshipman continued their slightly stilted exchange for several minutes, with the eskimo making some wide sweeping gestures with his hand and pointing both in the direction of the *Hindenburg* and out to sea.

'We have to get back to the ship. From what I can understand,' said Petersen, 'he says he has seen another ship here ... recently!'

13

Cape Farewell

'The plane is *largely* complete, Sir,' Geiger reported to *Fregattenkäpitan* Schellenberg, though immediately sensed from the movement of the first officer's eyebrows that it was not what he wanted to hear. The assembly of the body of the plane was complete. There were still a few applications of dope on some areas of newly stretched fabric yet to dry, but that was nothing to worry about. Only the engine was delaying matters. He decided that there was no point in lying about the situation. 'The engine's the real sticking point, Sir. It's a combination of fuel and ignition problems,' he offered. 'I'm sure we can overcome them.'

'But when, *Leutnant*?' responded Schellenberg.

By the first officer's tone, Geiger could not be certain if he was being asked a genuine question or whether the words were merely a sarcastic comment about his failure to get the plane ready. He didn't know how to reply, worried about how it might be taken. The first officer had always seemed a fair officer, but wasn't known as one to tolerate poor performance. The answer to his question was *soon*, *later* or *never*, but Geiger truly didn't know which was most likely. He risked a target: 'Sir, I expect the engine will be working by the end of the day.'

'Well, you better get on with it,' was his terse reply. 'Let's hope,' he added, 'the eskimo's ship doesn't pay us a visit before then. Let me know progress in an hour!'

Geiger made his way back to the hangar. The first officer was obviously none too happy about progress and hadn't indicated any sympathy for the problems Geiger and his men faced. Geiger appreciated that the ship reportedly seen by an eskimo was just the sort of thing the plane would have been especially helpful in resolving one way or another; and he accepted that to leave these waters without a reconnaissance of what might be lying offshore could place the ship at a great disadvantage. The end result of all that was Geiger felt like he personally was putting the ship in jeopardy.

All through this long war, Geiger had never really been in command of anything more than the plane he was flying. Now circumstances had not only put him in charge of the ship's whole air contingent, planes and men, but had also done so in the middle of a mission where he thought the plane had become an important, if not crucial element in its success. In terms of seniority, he had a few months over Ernst Kühl, thank heavens, and rightly should succeed to the command after Brandmann's death, but promotion was not uppermost in his mind when the first officer had detailed him to the task.

It was left to Geiger to tell Kühl, still recovering, that Schellenberg had put him in charge of the air contingent. Kühl gave no indication that he disagreed with the decision. It was a logical result, if for no other reason than seniority. Arguably a mistake, Brandmann had never formally assigned either man as his second-in-command. The two young officers had quite different air roles, one a pilot and the other an observer. When they weren't flying, Kühl also had formal responsibility for the ground crew and Geiger liaised with the various parts of the ship for their other needs.

While Geiger was now formally in command, nothing was said about such matters as promotion or moving into Brandmann's cabin, which he'd shared with a ship's officer of the same rank. Mainly because he feared a rebuff, Geiger had not raised these specific issues with the first officer. Consequently, he and Kühl continued to share their small cabin on the *Hindenburg*.

Despite knowing each other for over a year on the *Santa Elena* and now in even closer company, Geiger still did not consider their relations to be especially cordial. Pleasantries would be exchanged, they might even share a laugh, but he thought Kühl a bit of a cold fish, sometimes outspoken, sometimes aloof, though always with an air of superiority. Occasionally on the seaplane mothership, Kühl had accompanied Geiger on flights. Geiger had no complaints about Kühl's execution of his duties, though sometimes Kühl had made suggestions that seemed more like orders. It had never come to anything, but Geiger wondered if Kühl really wanted to be in charge, perhaps be promoted or perhaps be the pilot. It was on one of these flights when they—well, Kühl—shot down a Russian plane. He'd always felt that Brandmann had considered Kühl to be a very good observer and gunner and most often teamed up with him. Geiger knew little of Kühl's background, except that he was from the Baden city of Freiburg and, from the odd comment, possibly came from well-off stock.

It was a short journey to the hanger, but Geiger's mind was on the engine problem. As he'd reported to the first officer, with the assembly of the plane's fuselage, wings and floats complete, only the engine was holding up a test flight. It had refused to run properly, soon coughing and spluttering to a halt each time, despite the best efforts of whoever was in the cockpit trying to coax it into life. This engine was originally in the first, now wrecked, plane, but had developed various, niggling problems that collectively led to it being replaced early on in the mission with the crated engine. At least it hadn't been under water. Brandt accepted that its problems had not been successfully tackled in the interim and equally accepted responsibility for the failure to do so, apologising to Geiger. Brandt had worked tirelessly throughout the mission and Geiger would not accept the warrant officer's self-criticism or apportion any blame. Some parts culled from the wrecked plane's engine had had to be used, so he reasoned they were most probably contributing to the problem, but one thing he did know: he relied on Brandt to deal with such problems.

Coming out onto the Boat Deck, the music of the ship's band caught his ear; it competed favourably with the sounds generated by the coaling process, though did little to raise his own spirits. Alas, he knew the music wouldn't be alone in penetrating the ship's recesses; the inevitable coal dust would find its way into the hangar and onto the plane, including any still-wet dope. As if to check his thinking, he ran his finger along the gunwale of one of the ship's boats, clearing a small track in the fine and almost invisible black stuff. There was little he could do about it. He'd had the port-side hangar curtain closed, but opened the starboard one, allowing light in and hopefully a little warmth from the weak sun.

He was half a dozen paces from the hangar opening, when the noises of the coaling and the band were suddenly and completely drowned out by the unmistakeable coughing, cracking and whirring noises of the aircraft engine starting. He was not surprised. They'd tried the engine numerous times in the last few hours and he'd given no orders to hold off while he went to the Bridge.

This time, it was soon obvious to Geiger that something was very different: the engine sounded better and hadn't yet coughed to a stop. He dared to think that Brandt had worked his usual miracle. His pace quickened and, as he stepped into the hangar, the plane's port side towards him, to his left he saw smiles on the dirty faces of Brandt and his crew as they stood in front of the all but invisible, spinning propeller. As he walked forward, he could just see the face of fitter Grützmacher in the cockpit, not smiling, but tensioned, as he worked to keep the two-metre-long, six-cylinder Benz engine in front of him going.

Geiger joined the others in front of the plane, with a smile at Brandt. He looked again at Grützmacher. The young fitter's face now brighter, happier, showing that he too was comfortable, even pleased with the engine's performance. Geiger could tell from the sound that Grützmacher was maintaining a steady pace, not applying any great power at this stage. For more than a minute they all stood watching, then Brandt signalled Grützmacher to switch off. As the propeller slowed and the engine noise quickly died away, Geiger spoke, now feeling good about the prospect of reporting their success to the first officer. It did cross his mind that getting the engine to work might have been a one-off and that it wouldn't start again, but he quickly chose to ignore that prospect. 'Well done, men! Very well done! A brilliant job!' He had been with them throughout the assembly, even assisted and taken his turn in the cockpit, but it was the ground crew who deserved all the praise. 'The Captain,' he lied, 'just asked me how things were going. He must have heard the engine! Let's try her again!'

168

Körner was on the Bridge to watch the coaling, seeking assurances on its progress, though just as often scouring the surrounding waters, especially the fjord the ships had come through. He hadn't actually noticed that the plane's engine was now successfully running, assuming the periodic engine noises emanating from the hangar were just more attempts to get it started. While he was pleased when Schellenberg relayed the good news, he was disappointed to hear that they could not proceed with a test flight until coaling was finished and the two ships separated to allow the plane to get into the water. It was only one more part of the jigsaw that must be completed to enable them to leave Greenland. Of course, the puzzle had had another piece added in the shape of the ship sighted by the eskimo. He might have been inclined to dismiss it, but, given what *Fähnrich* Petersen had reported, that could be folly. Thank goodness Petersen spoke Danish; thank goodness the eskimo did. It had been difficult to confirm the actual day the eskimo had seen the ship, but perhaps three days ago. If but for the refuelling stop, the ship—of unknown type—and the *Hindenburg* might well have encountered each other.

As a result of the eskimo sighting, he'd agreed with Schellenberg's proposal to add to the number of look-out positions. Each possible approach waterway was already covered, but all were at comparatively low-lying positions and Schellenberg wanted a higher position to be able to see well out to sea. The large island to the south of them offered as good a vantage post as any, being about 300 to 400 metres high, but how to get men up its steep slopes was an obvious problem. Anyway, he'd left it to Schellenberg to resolve.

'Sir,' reported Schellenberg, 'my assessment is that we should have taken on at least two thousand tons of coal by nightfall and all our oil. While that won't have filled the bunkers, having discussed it with the Navigator, I'm satisfied it should be sufficient to regain Wilhelmshaven.'

'Good, good,' replied Körner, glad to hear that coaling would soon be finished. 'I do not want to tarry here any longer. I would like to sail soon after coaling is over, but with the prospect of encountering ships, we will hold off until the plane has scouted the waters ahead.'

Eckhardt did not escape his turn with the shovel, nor another look-out spell. Indeed, the day had turned out to be a very busy one and leaving everyone, like him, filthy and totally exhausted. After an hour warming up, he and *Fähnrich* Jahncke had again returned to their cold look-out post. The eskimos seemed well gone, reportedly rewarded with blankets and schnapps, but he and the young midshipman kept a better and three-sixty-degree watch this time, in case anything, eskimo *or* polar bear, came up behind their rock shelter. Returning to the ship, it was not long before he was shovelling coal and, later, moving other supplies and ammunition from the *Erda*. At that time of the year, in those higher latitudes, it seemed light for most of the day. He was one of the last to be dismissed.

As he went through the post-coaling, washing routine, rumour came that they were soon to leave, even before dawn. That didn't happen, but he was roused from his hammock all too soon for him. He was detailed to undertake another look-out duty ashore.

He wore as much as he could get on, shouldered a Mauser and made his way to a motor launch on the starboard side. Too early for breakfast, yet he was given a Thermos and small rucksack containing some food, largely bread and sausage. Despite the early hour, it was quite light, but desperately cold. He and Jahncke had been teamed up yet again, but this time were headed for a different location. The launch moved astern of the battle cruiser and Eckhardt saw that the *Erda* had been cast off, taking up a position some two or three hundred metres astern of the big ship. The channel the ships had journeyed up the day before was only disturbed by the noise of the boat's motor. There was little wind and the black fjord waters were entirely still. While the sun was yet to impact on the towering rocky islands on both sides, Eckhardt could easily make out their steep walls and some pieces of ice on the fjord surface. At a slow speed and with several course alterations to avoid various ice floes, they reached their assigned position, another large rocky outcrop. Eckhardt noted the frozen faces of the men they relieved, one with frost in his moustache.

Despite the cold, the weather looked promising. To Eckhardt it looked as if it was shaping up to be a pleasant enough day, with a largely clear blue sky and light, northerly winds. As they made their way across the hard surface of their new look-out post, Jahncke gave a cursory signal for Eckhardt to follow, pointing to a higher position. Here we go again, thought Eckhardt.

'*Fregattenkapitän* Schellenberg wants us to get as good a seaward view as possible. We should get higher, so we can see farther. They are taking the eskimo's sighting seriously,' said Jahncke.

Jahncke also said something about the need to keep alert to which Eckhardt gave a half-nod, taking such a requirement as obvious and sick of the way officers felt the need to remind their sailors. Thinking of the eskimo, he was jealous of the schnapps that had been given to him and wouldn't have minded a blanket or two either.

They scrambled over the unyielding, rising terrain of what was a small island, which, much like their first look-out post, was a generally smooth, domed affair and similarly cut deeply by numerous fissures. Most of these could be stepped or jumped over, though some were full of snow, which made them wary of any snow coverings lest they hide a leg-breaking crevice. Some two hundred metres back from the shore line they were close to the island's high point, about forty or fifty metres above the sea. When they stopped and turned to look back seawards, Eckhardt doubted the slightly higher position had improved things over their previous look-out post, but the open sea, less than ten kilometres away, stretched out before them. One thing which was different from their other post, which lay someway off to the east, was that they couldn't see the *Hindenburg*. How were they going to signal her, he wondered, but said nothing. Perhaps rifle shots would suffice.

As they'd done before, they soon sought shelter, finding a suitable crevice on the fjord side. It was not at all a comfortable billet, but its size and shape offered somewhere they could both sit down, allowing the light wind to pass over their heads. From there they periodically poked their heads out or Eckardt walked round the top of the barren island. Being on an island, Eckhardt felt better protected from the threat of eskimos or polar bears, though knew the sea around them was no barrier to either. He kept his rifle at the ready, determined not to be surprised, but soon tucked into his food and drink nevertheless.

As their hour drew to its end, the discomfort of the cold, only held at bay by the lack of any serious wind, had Eckhardt looking as much up the fjord as out to sea, hoping to see, if not hear, the motor launch. They'd seen nothing, no ships, eskimos or bears. He even began to doubt there were any bears. Eckhardt sat down in their little hidey hole, but Jahncke, binoculars up, was looking out to sea. Eckhardt, anticipating some comment to patrol their rocky castle, lifted himself out of the crevice. He too swung his binoculars across the distant horizon, not trusting the young midshipman's look-out skills. He saw no ships, but he did hear one. The boat was coming for them. Thank goodness!

The first thing both of them noticed, as they waited at the water's edge, was that there were no replacements for them in the boat. Jahncke commented on it, to which Eckhardt nodded. It probably meant that the ship was preparing to sail. Eckhardt was pleased about the impending departure, soon confirmed by the boat's crew. Looking at the fjord, its mountains, snow and deep waters, he likened it to Norway, but, he joked with Jahncke and the boat's crew, he was more than happy for the eskimos or the Danes to keep Greenland: 'They're welcome to it!'

It was only about five or six kilometres back to the ship. As she came in sight, he immediately saw evidence that the ship was preparing to sail. Boats were being hoisted aboard and much more smoke was issuing from the funnels. The *Erda* was still some way off, bows pointing to the sea. He heard a new engine noise; the seaplane suddenly zoomed low over the battle cruiser's stern. He turned and watched it fly back down the fjord, towards the sea.

Geiger gently lifted the plane's nose. This flight had two purposes: they were on a reconnaissance mission, but it was also a test flight. He had to check out the surrounding waters, but also had to ensure the plane was in all respects functioning properly. There was no time for two separate flights. Brandt still had concerns and said he would like to have had a short, but separate test flight. Geiger had pointed out that time was against them and this one would have to suffice, seeking, unsuccessfully, to placate him with: 'flying is a dangerous pastime.' He agreed to take it carefully.

The plane had been lowered into the water and, still attached to the crane, the integrity of the floats was tested. Then the engine was started and run up; even after the onboard tests, it was Geiger's main concern. With Brandt looking on and advising, he was eventually content that all seemed well and it was time to take their plane up. Easier said than done. There was much ice on the surface of the dark waters. Coupled with the lack of wind, it took another fifteen or twenty minutes surveying the waters and taxiing back and forth across the fjord, searching for a sufficient stretch of ice-free water to take off. A few unsuccessful attempts were made, but close to the western side, there seemed enough clear water and wind to make another attempt and at last Geiger was able to get aloft. If all went well, they would rendezvous with the ships nearer the sea, where, hopefully, there should be enough clear water to land safely.

As they were facing almost north when they took off, Geiger had flown the plane in that direction, up the fjord. Even ten or more kilometres from the sea the fjord was still wide here, perhaps two kilometres, with peaks over a thousand metres high rising above them on both sides. As had been said on the ship, this fjord seemed to stretch far inland, but he had no business in that direction and soon took a wide starboard turn and headed back to the ships. Falbe, alert as ever, had pointed out eskimo canoes to the west, not far from where they'd taken off. Geiger instructed him to flash a message to the *Hindenburg*. Flying low over the ships, he then took the plane south, down the fjord towards the sea.

Geiger aimed down the fjord, soon passing the various large and small islands that flanked it and in less than ten minutes the land lay behind them and they were over the quite startling, blue water. Flying down the fjord, he had gained altitude gradually, reaching 500 metres. The visibility was good and at that height he estimated the horizon to be at least thirty or forty kilometres away. Thankfully, the plane was handling well and he felt less anxious that something untoward was going to happen, but still took things carefully, scrutinising his gauges and listening out for any worrying change in the engine noise.

Their reconnaissance mission was to check the surrounding waters, especially those leading off towards Cape Farewell, only about forty kilometres away. Geiger first circled, giving him and Falbe plenty of time to check out the immediate waters. Seeing no smoke or ships, he turned south-east, following the coast. They would soon reach the Cape. The first officer had told him again of the eskimo sighting and that any ship might well be to the south-east of them. The first officer thought they could well have expected to see a ship travelling north along the coast, as they travelled south the previous day, hence the focus on the waters to the south, the *Hindenburg*'s intended course. After surveying the Cape

Farewell area, he was to rendezvous with the battle cruiser as she and the *Erda* reached the open sea.

A navigation officer had provided Geiger with a rough, hand-drawn map of the coast down to the Cape. It showed several fjords. Indeed the whole coast appeared to have more fjords than Norway. He reasoned that any of these fjords could easily accommodate a steam ship, but if the eskimo had seen one in the last few days, by now it could equally be far out to sea, indeed far away from Greenland.

After flying for a few minutes, they crossed the seaward end of a large peninsula, about six or seven kilometres wide, and, like everywhere else, its terrain was brown, snow-streaked and rocky. Beyond that they found, unsurprisingly, another ice-speckled fjord stretching away on their port side. It had a very broad, ten-kilometre-wide mouth, narrowing to a point where two fjords branched away. Geiger's attention was drawn to the far, eastern shore, where the low, morning sun was casting large and dark shadows. He was wondering if the darkness could hide a ship, when Falbe shouted: 'Boats!'

Geiger quickly made out the small shapes of numerous boats, probably eskimo canoes, some kilometres in from the western, seaward end of the fjord. His eyes moved to the nearby shore. Beneath steep, mountainous slopes, there was a low-lying, small piece of land jutting into the fjord and just beyond it there looked to be some small buildings. He acknowledged Falbe's sighting, pencilling the location on his map. Although he could see no large vessel, freighter or warship, there or in the shadows, he swung tightly around and descended to get a closer look at the dwellings, checking for signs of wireless aerials. From a lower altitude, he could definitely see a couple of buildings and several figures walking around. They'd obviously seen the plane, as most stopped and stood still, perhaps mesmerised by the sight. As he expected, he saw no evidence of aerials. He turned back towards the Cape. The engine spluttered and power fell off, but only for a second or two, then returned to its normal rhythm. Geiger was alarmed. Normally he would have not been unduly worried, but the possibility of engine problems had been on his mind and this was in the way of a test flight. He couldn't be sure, but it was either fuel or spark related. What to do? He reckoned they were only ten or so kilometres from Cape Farewell, just over the next fjord. As the problem seemed to have abated and thinking of his mission, he decided to fly on, though concentrated hard on the engine, listening intently to it, while keeping an eye on his instruments.

The fjord's eastern shore had four- or five-hundred-metre-high cliffs. Having come down a couple of hundred metres, he swung out to sea, rather than press the engine in climbing over them. Again, this land mass was another sizeable promontory. Its high cliffs continued on to its most southerly point. He kept away from them, now somewhat wary of cliff-dwelling birds, though saw none. Clearing the last cliffs, he circled back to port and the next fjord came into view.

This was smaller than the previous one, but still a wide-mouthed affair, with various small valleys leading off on either side. Ignoring its ice floes, it seemed a good refuelling fjord, he pondered.

He looked ahead. Before them, across the fjord, stood what was undoubtedly Cape Farewell. It was a clear and separate nodule of rounded rock, barely joined to the land behind it. It was less than 300 metres high, a slight bump in comparison to its craggy, mountainous neighbours. Flying hardly 100 metres above it, he took the plane on and into the next fjord. He was looking ahead, but concentrating on the engine, unfairly relying on Falbe to survey the waters below them.

Geiger immediately saw that the coast had swung sharply to the north-east; it really was the Cape and the southernmost tip of Greenland. He could see no ships ahead or out to sea. With no orders to go farther, he was happy to get back to the ship. They had been flying for about thirty minutes. He turned the plane and soon flew back over Cape Farewell.

Thinking about the rendezvous and, despite his earlier concerns, it was nevertheless quite a shock when the engine suddenly stuttered, then ran smoothly for a few seconds, then coughed again. There was obviously something wrong, but would it persist? Gently on the controls, he tried to rescue what looked liked a difficult situation. After a few more seconds, the engine was missing, worse this time, power falling away. Quite abruptly, it cut out, the propeller blur slowing into a solid blade. Nothing he tried could get it to restart. 'We're going down!' he shouted.

He kept the plane's nose up as much as he could, trying to slow the rate of descent to give him a chance to check out the water below. From 300 metres up, he could see there was much ice on the fjord surface, including some very large, flat pieces, but there also appeared to be some good gaps. For half-a-second, Brandmann's crash came into his mind, but he quickly concentrated on his own situation. The water looked smooth enough, with a light wind from their starboard side. He turned slowly into the wind and chose a line avoiding obvious big pieces of ice and glided down, as gently as possible. They hit the water, harder than he hoped, bounced once and were down. Without the engine, the plane was fairly rapidly brought to a halt by the action of water on the floats, but not before they had collided with a small ice floe. Alarmingly, the impact caused the plane to slew round. There was nothing he could have done about it; he had no real steering capability, no engine, insufficient wind on the rudder and ailerons. Anyway, getting down alive was the main aim and for now he could not focus on the ice impact. Despite the cold, he was sweating profusely and could feel his heart beating furiously. Exhausted by the experience, his head slumped forward.

'Are you all right, Sir!' shouted Falbe, his hand gently touching Geiger's shoulder.

'Yes, yes,' he gasped, raising his head. 'You?'

'I'm OK!' Then, in a quieter tone, the petty officer added, 'Well done, Sir. Well done.'

It had all happened so quickly. In little more than a minute or two they had touched down. For a moment, Geiger forgot about the shock of the event and looked around. They were about two kilometres into the fjord and less than one from the nearest shore over to the west. High peaks filled every view ahead of them. Away to the far right, he could see the Cape's island mound. As with everything they'd seen in this part of Greenland, the land was a picture of impressive brown and white shapes. It also looked incredibly desolate and foreboding. He didn't notice the cold; it had been colder aloft. The floating plane tended to keep its nose into the wind, but, astern, over his shoulder he caught sight of the sea, in contrast to the land, a flat expanse and a glorious blue. Whatever the views, he quickly turned his attention to their immediate problems of the engine and the float.

⚐

The battle cruiser started to go astern. Battle Stations had been sounded. Eckhardt, once again deprived of a good meal, was back in the Spotting Top. He could see the supply ship some distance away, further back up the fjord, but with her bow pointing towards the sea. She looked to be fairly well surrounded by ice floes. Soon the *Hindenburg* had a similar, seaward heading and, with the *Erda* following, began to move slowly forward between the strings of large and small islands they had passed only the day before. Several eskimo canoes were reported to starboard, no doubt seeking free schnapps and blankets, he reckoned. From his position covering the port side, he saw the island where he and midshipman Jahncke had only recently spent a freezing and uncomfortable hour. At least the bright day he had forecast had come about. One or two thin, wispy clouds were all that marred the blue sky.

Everyone was keyed up. There were expectations of enemy warships barring their path. At least the good visibility should allow none to approach them unseen. The plane had supposedly checked out these waters and there were no reported ship sightings. The ship was still ready for anything. The large land mass to starboard, said to be an island, could well hide a sneak attack behind it and, probably in response, the ship's course changed a few degrees to port and he saw the forward turrets swing over ready to engage any attack from that direction. Eckhardt could see no threat from the port side and wanted to swing his binoculars to starboard, but most others were looking for that danger.

Soon the great ship cleared the rocky southern end of the island and nothing was seen but the full expanse of blue sea ahead. Greenland was behind them. Eckhardt panned his binoculars across the wide horizon. He could see nothing untoward, no ships, their upperworks, masts or smoke. If there were any ships out there, they were far off. He heard officers discussing an increase in speed, but only to ten knots or so, and course due south. Presently he could see the *Erda*'s bow wave increasing as she too put on speed. Eckhardt noted that the warship was not zigzagging.

Another half an hour and the ships were well out to sea and still there was nothing to be seen. The sea had a gentle swell, but a strengthening northerly wind added to its surface motion. The ships reversed course, turning to port, the *Erda* following in the battle cruiser's wake. Then after ten minutes the *Hindenburg* led round onto a south-easterly course.

'Watch for the plane!' came the order.

'The plane was supposed to meet us here,' said another look-out to Eckhardt.

꒰

'No, Sir. There has been no signal from the plane,' reported Schellenberg. 'They still have fuel for some hours yet, but the instruction was to rendezvous with us near the mouth of the fjord.'

Körner said nothing, just gave a slight nod, acknowledging Schellenberg's comment.

Schellenberg continued: 'It should have only taken an hour at most to fly down to the Cape and back. Either they have flown farther on to investigate something ... or have had some problem, mechanical failure perhaps. It was the plane's first flight. I would doubt they could have suffered from enemy action.'

'Who's to say?' ventured Körner. 'But, if they haven't extended their flight for some reason, I agree that a problem with the plane is the more likely.'

'In which case, they will probably not make it to the rendezvous and have come down somewhere ... possibly somewhere along their intended route,' suggested Schellenberg.

'Well, let's go and see if we can find them.'

In short order, the ships were sailing down the coast, with the *Hindenburg* about five kilometres offshore and the *Erda* a further five away on the battle cruiser's starboard beam. Körner was matter of fact about the aircrew's chances: they will be found along the route to the Cape, but beyond that point the ships will leave Greenland waters without them. The battle cruiser's speed was increased steadily to sixteen knots and the *Erda* quickly fell away.

꒰

It took no special insight for Geiger to know that their chances of survival were slim if they could not get out of their predicament. The two airmen said nothing to each other about that element of their situation. The cold was just tolerable by virtue of their flying clothing and grease-covered faces. Even so, Geiger was now definitely cold. The plane's skin provided a little protection from the light wind and in the sunshine one could believe you were warm.

There had been no time to send out a signal, the descent was so quick. Even so, Falbe's Morse skills could probably have got a simple message off, but Geiger's flying preferences had prevented it—a point he now thoroughly regretted. He didn't like to fly with the long aerial extended because of drag and the danger of it being caught on some part of the plane. Now that they were down, they could neither transmit nor receive signals.

Initially, Geiger did not think their situation was insuperable, though knew it might prove to be more than simply fix the engine and take off. Any difficulties in restarting the engine and taking off amongst the ice floes would have to wait until he'd figured out what had caused the engine to stop, but he knew his first concern was the float. Without inspection, the jarring impact worried him, but he had hoped that it would prove to be superficial, perhaps little more than a glancing blow. Sticking his head over the edge of the cockpit, he could see from its depth in the water that things didn't look good with the starboard float. He climbed down to inspect it, but even before he stood on the float, it was obvious some damage had been sustained. The leading end of the float, normally twenty or more centimetres above the water, was almost level with it. Water had obviously got into the float. There was no indication that it was continuing to sink, so he figured the internal bulkhead must have contained any flooding. Gingerly edging forward, he saw that the end of the float, now under water, looked bashed and bent. It was immediately clear, even if they fixed the engine, taking off could be difficult, if not impossible, even fatal.

'Looks like we might be stuck here,' he called out to Falbe. 'The float's damaged, obviously holed. Fortunately, it looks like the flooding is not getting any worse.'

'Can we take off?' asked Falbe, his tone expecting the worst.

'Well, we could try … but I'm bound to say we would be lucky to get her unstuck. It will depend on whether the forward motion lifts the float up or whether it will increase any flooding.' He kept his worst thoughts to himself.

'I suppose I need to check the actual damage,' though he did not relish plunging his arms into the freezing water, so added, 'but let's see if we can get the engine to work first. I could end up pretty wet for nothing.'

Their combined efforts indicated a fuel or ignition problem, either the fuel pump or one or both of the engine's two carburettors. Whatever, it was quite possibly a recurrence of the engine problem that had delayed completion of the plane. Neither man was that knowledgeable about the technicalities involved, though concluded that the problem didn't appear to be a simple one. They both joked that they should have brought Brandt along. Falbe endeavoured unsuccessfully to take things apart, though Geiger feared they couldn't fix it if Brandt had had such difficulties. They tried to start the engine, to see if that would draw the fuel through, but that was also difficult. The floats were over three metres apart and positioned outside of the propeller arc. Falbe had to stand behind the propeller to swing it, there was no chance of balancing on one float in front of it. Anyway, he managed to swing the propeller, but repeated swings produced nothing. After an hour since the forced landing, Geiger called a halt to their efforts and both men settled back into their cockpits to conserve their heat. At least the float seemed to hold up, thank God, sinking no farther. He didn't want to contemplate what to do if it went under. The float wasn't their only problem. Alas, the intended short flight had led to no hot drinks or food being taken onboard beforehand, though Falbe had fortunately brought a small water bottle with him.

The wind and tide moved the plane around the fjord a little, at one point coming within a few hundred metres of the shore, though thankfully not out to sea. Soon the plane was almost surrounded by ice, all small pieces. Although concerned about damaging contact with the ice around them, Geiger would have liked to bump up—gently—against one of the larger ice floes or the small and flat rocky islands they could see near the fjord's mouth. There they might be able to undertake further checks and even offer a safer position to spin the propeller. The ice floes could also provide a way to the shore, but any immersion in the water would almost certainly be fatal in these temperatures. His mind kept returning to the damage to the float. He didn't dare going down again to check it out, in case his weight just made things worse. There was little to do, but hope the ship came looking for them. They knew the plane's course. They must sail along the coast. It was on their way to Germany.

It did not take long for dialogue between the two men to dwindle away. The ensuing silence was then all but complete bar the tinkling noise of water slapping the floats. It was easy to feel a degree of loneliness and despair. It was too early to give up hope of rescue, but Geiger felt he should not rely on it. Should they leave the plane or stay with it?

'I propose we wait a couple of hours, to see if the ship finds us. If she doesn't show by then, we'll have to take matters into our own hands.'

Falbe said nothing.

'It's a shame we didn't come down in the next fjord, where we saw those eskimos. They could probably have been persuaded to help us,' Geiger joked with Falbe, who he imagined was, like him, sitting hunkered well down in his cockpit. 'Who knows, they saw us, they may yet paddle around the headland.'

'Well, if the ship doesn't show, perhaps *we'll* just paddle into the next fjord,' responded Falbe.

'A good idea!'

Both men offered up a few other ideas about what action they could take, some comical, producing restrained laughs.

In accordance with standing orders, they'd fired flares every half hour. Falbe reported they still had five, three white, two red, so enough for a couple more hours. It wouldn't matter if they got through all of them; the cold could well have seen them off by then. Geiger decided to keep one or two back, though time seemed against them.

'When the ship does show,' said Geiger, trying to raise both their hopes, 'you'd better be ready with that flare pistol. But if they don't see them, we'll also fire the guns. They should see the tracers.'

'It'll be a regular fireworks show.'

After Battle Stations was stood down, Eckhardt and the other look-outs were kept at their posts. As he scoured the coast opposite, with some coffee he devoured some bread as if he'd never eaten before, not allowing even one crumb to escape his mouth.

'It could be anywhere,' said Schwarz, binoculars up. 'They could've come down inland. We'd never see them.'

'Yes,' mumbled Eckhardt. Similar thoughts had crossed his mind, but he tried to dismiss them, wanting to be hopeful. 'We can only check the coast. We're close enough … I hope.'

At twenty knots, they were moving quickly along the dramatic coast, one of changing shapes, both worn down and sharp-topped mountains, all brown and white, interspersed with fjords. Eckhardt could not argue with course changes when low-lying, off-shore islands and rough water, suggesting shallower water, forced them farther out to sea. His binoculars moved rapidly over the islands and equally up at the mountain tops and peering down valleys, wondering about what the wreckage of a plane looked like or if smoke or even the debris from a crash would be seen. Fortunately, the bright sunshine made the work easier, illuminating details better.

'Eskimos!'

Some observant soul had seen them. Eckhardt had to be directed to them. At that distance, they were no more than faint pencil shapes scratched on the sea near the fjord coast. Should they be questioned, Eckhardt asked himself, but did not venture his opinion as the ship swept on.

The fjord was clearly very wide and, to him, seemed to extend far inland, with two possible waterways leading away north. If the plane had come down in one of those, even if it landed safely, it would be impossible to find it without taking the ship into them. He doubted the captain would do that; the plane wasn't that important. When he thought of the crew ashore, somewhere in that bleak landscape, facing cold, perhaps starvation, never mind polar bears, he decided the eskimos were their best hope for salvation. His one-hour stints ashore had shown him that no one could probably survive the cold for any great length of time. The eskimos he and Jahncke had encountered hadn't given them any trouble. Yes, best to be found by eskimos.

He scanned the high cliffs on the fjord's eastern side, wondering if the plane might have crashed into them. If the plane or crew were on top of them, then they were lost.

The next fjord seemed to have more than its fair share of ice floes and rocky islands. Could they have successfully landed in that? Could they be seen in all that? A ribbon of very broken ice stretched across much of the mouth of this fjord and the ship again moved farther out to sea to keep clear of it.

As the ship altered course away, he saw it, a flare, unmistakeably. It arched upwards, perhaps a hundred metres, fiery red against the snow and rocky backdrop. He was not the only look-out to see it and collective voices called out: 'Flare!'

14

The Narrows

It was half an hour after dawn, their twenty-third day since leaving Wilhelmshaven. The heavy cloud that seemed to stretch to the horizon in all directions graciously allowed a faint lightening along the eastern edge. Körner tugged at his coat collar, endeavouring to keep out the wind and rain. He also had to contend with heavy spray from periodic waves sweeping over the fo'c'sle. He wasn't complaining. As always, such conditions suited him fine. Soon after leaving Cape Farewell, some twenty hours ago, they'd run into rough, slate-grey seas, and strong winds with dark, rain-filled skies. The weather had since toned down its anger. The rain inhibited visibility, which varied greatly, but was seldom more than ten or twelve kilometres. The wind, now slightly abated, blew against their starboard side as the ship ploughed a north-easterly course towards the Denmark Strait.

'It would be good if this kept up for another day,' said Körner, a rare smile on his face, 'but all good things must pass.'

'Quite so, Sir,' replied Schellenberg, 'though it could continue. I believe Iceland has a bit of a reputation for wet weather.'

Gärtner, standing to one side of the select Bridge group, said nothing, though a slight nod and a smile suggested his agreement. Their conversation moved onto the waters ahead of them and they entered the Chart Room to study the plot. The navigator did some calculations and announced: 'Keeping to this course, at our current eighteen knots, we should enter the narrowest part of the Strait in nineteen hours.'

'Nineteen hours,' mused Körner. 'Any darkness?' he asked.

Gärtner looked again at the map, spoke to one of his *leutnants*, then answered: 'No, Sir. At this time of year, there will be no real period of darkness at these high latitudes.'

Körner expected as much. He'd asked before, when deciding on the course home, but felt obliged to ask again. There would be no way to avoid the near-total daylight that would prevail in the Narrows.

The 'narrowest part' or 'the Narrows' were the loose, unofficial terms he and his officers had adopted for the 100 kilometres or so of the Strait waters flanking Iceland's protruding north-west peninsula, which reached out towards Greenland some 300 kilometres away. What occupied their minds was not so much the length of this stretch of water, but how wide it was. They all knew that the ice from Greenland would reduce that 300 kilometres and probably by a considerable amount. They'd come through it easily enough on the voyage south, but the extensive and unexpected ice they'd met off Greenland's west coast raised questions about ice conditions elsewhere. Körner accepted that the Strait ice could extend all the way from Greenland to Iceland, as Kehlmann had said it could, but after further deliberations he reckoned that would be unlikely and, even if ice did prove to be an insurmountable problem, they could yet swing south of Iceland.

It was during the refuelling that Körner had reached a decision on the route home: they would travel via the Denmark Strait. They were no longer seeking a place to refuel, which had influenced their previous discussions on the Strait, just a safe route back to Germany. Although all acknowledged the concerns about the Strait's ice and enemy warships, it was the extra distance it put between them and Scapa Flow which sealed the matter. That consideration had also been the primary reason for its selection in the planning of *Georg*. Körner could have gone east of Iceland, the waters between Iceland and the Faroe Islands. He knew that Nerger had successfully used the Iceland-Faroes gap on his return, though only after ice prevented him taking the *Wolf* through his intended course, the Denmark Strait. However, while that east-of-Iceland route offered greater sea room and was ice-free, Körner deemed the proximity of Scapa Flow to be too great a risk. There were risks with any route; weighing them up was the issue. Körner accepted that the narrow point of the Denmark Strait, between Greenland and Iceland, did offer the enemy an opportunity to find and attack the *Hindenburg*, but, given available Admiralty intelligence, he did not think the enemy would station much force there. So, with any luck they would slip through the Strait unobserved and shape up for the final leg of the journey back through the North Sea.

In determining their course for the Narrows, there had been discussions about the daylight transit. Körner would have loved to have had the cloak of darkness, but Schellenberg and Gärtner were content, especially considering the difficulties of navigating the ice and likelihood of an enemy attack. At least in daylight, these dangers might be kept at arm's length, so to speak. They all thought the enemy would be there, but not in any great strength. If they were found, they could expect action or pursuit. Either event, whatever the outcome, would almost certainly lead to the enemy confirming the *Hindenburg*'s position. With their whereabouts known, Körner judged the English would then be well placed to bring considerable force against the lone German ship on her likely course to the North Sea. He was not done yet. The weather could yet influence matters in their favour, but, as always, he could not plan for it.

Geiger still marvelled about their Cape Farewell rescue. He'd feared it was the end. Before that he'd always thought it was other men around you who died, not you. As a flyer, he'd experienced several scary moments, but, on each occasion, none had caused him to think 'this is it, this is the end!' So, sitting quietly in a cockpit, plane on the water, with the engine off, no enemy around and with time to contemplate one's end, it was surreal and unexpected. If they hadn't been rescued in the next few hours and well before dark, he'd determined to get to the eskimo fjord, one way or another. They couldn't have survived the night.

Falbe had seen the ship first, well her smoke. Geiger, busy considering his escape options, checking nearby ice floes as a possible way to the shore, was caught unawares by his observer's shout. He'd never felt such elation. It had still taken several hours for their rescue and the recovery of the plane. The ship kept a kilometre or so offshore and her boats effected the retrievals.

Eventually they were back on board. Straight away he'd reported to *Fregattenkapitän* Schellenberg, explaining what had happened. During their short discussion the first officer had said the report of the flare sighting had been 'excellent news', but dampened Geiger's pleasure in being rescued by going on to stress the need for the plane in the journey ahead. The first officer did advocate that he and Falbe report to the sick bay. Geiger sent Falbe, but despite feeling cold 'right through to my bones' had first sought out Kühl and Brandt to brief them on what had happened. They were in the hangar, where Brandt and his men were already beginning their repair work on the plane. Outwardly, the plane looked in remarkably good condition. Geiger examined the float damage, confirming he would have got very wet exploring its extent.

Even with the canvas down on all sides, the hangar was too cold for Geiger and reminded him to get to the sick bay, but, conscious of the first officer's comments about the need for the plane, he didn't want to waste time. With the three of them standing in one of the less-draughty corners of the hangar, Geiger gave a quick outline of what had transpired, the outward flight, how the engine had first spluttered and then failed, the forced landing and float damage and what he and Falbe had attempted to do. Such as it was worth, he threw in his ideas on possible fuel pump and carburettor problems, though expected Brandt was already sorting out any problems. Not surprisingly, Brandt's initial observations were about the rescue. Kühl, fully recovered from his plane event, listened impassively.

'We're all pleased that you were found safe and sound, Sir.'

'Well, thank you, Warrant Officer. Exactly our own sentiments,' said Geiger with a broad smile, but quickly got down to business. 'We need the plane ready as soon as possible. What do you think?'

'The float is not too bad. We should be able to repair it, probably using one of the spares,' offered Brandt. 'The engine .... Well, we'll check out the problem quickly. If it is the fuel pump or one of the carburettors, again we can hopefully utilise the other plane's, though we have already cannibalised those for parts before. If things are straightforward, I would expect it could be done by tomorrow. Of course, the float should be tested to ensure it's watertight and the engine should be given a thorough run-up before any flight.'

'A thorough run-up!' interrupted Kühl, his tone undeniably aggressive. 'This engine failure should never have happened in the first place, if you'd done your job right!'

Brandt's mouth moved slightly, though nothing came out, but his body stance changed, as if he'd been ordered to stand to attention. Not knowing where Kühl's animosity might lead to, Geiger stepped in before either man could get in another word.

'Er, thank you, Brandt. Get on with it. Dismiss.'

Brandt's head moved slightly to face Geiger directly; he saluted, stepped back and about-turned. Geiger could feel Kühl's obvious disapproval of this action, though imagined any dissatisfaction was now directed at him, not Brandt. 'I'm going below. I need to change my clothes and get to sick bay,' he said to Kühl. He could see his fellow officer's eyes had clearly narrowed. Kühl was about to say something to him, but he held up his hand to stop him and then waived, indicating he should accompany him.

They said nothing as they descended to the cabin, but hardly had they entered when Kühl asked, 'Karl, am I still responsible for the ground crew?'

'Er, yes, Ernst.'

'Well, may I ask why you stopped me speaking to Brandt?'

'I'm sorry, that wasn't my intention,' lied Geiger. 'I just thought he should get on with it.'

'I'm concerned that your forced landing was due to poor workmanship. If he'd done his work properly, the plane should have caused no trouble,' said Kühl, asserting his right to manage and criticise Brandt. 'Do I take it you think your forced landing was not brought about by Warrant Officer Brandt's failure to check the engine thoroughly in the first place?' Without taking much of a breath, his hands animated, he continued: 'He needs to be told and told forcibly about poor workmanship; that it's unacceptable.'

Geiger felt like citing Brandt's unstinting efforts thus far in the mission, not to mention his record on the *Santa Elena*, but, on the specific issue, he could not be sure that poor workmanship was not a factor. 'Ernst, I've always been confident in Brandt's work,' he stated, as calmly as he thought warranted, thinking the unfolding scenario must be an example of the burden of command. 'It remains to be seen what exactly caused the engine failure, but if there was any failing in how the engine was put together, it was in me insisting that we fly as soon as possible and not permitting a proper test flight as Brandt had sought.' He wanted to inject 'while you were in sick bay', but thought that an unwise addition.

'If we do not make it clear what we expect,' responded Kühl, 'we could rue the consequences.'

'As I said, I've every faith in Brandt. After your crash, Brandt and his men worked like devils to get the plane assembled. I ... we ... rely on them, but they're not magicians. If they make mistakes, they're only human.'

'Precisely! Except if they make mistakes, we die!'

He's right on that score, thought Geiger. 'I'm sure Brandt will readily accept responsibility for any failings; that's his way. What do you want? If it happens again, should he be put up against a wall and shot?' As the words left his mouth, Geiger realised that is was a totally foolish comment, completely unworthy of a commanding officer, but before Kühl could respond, he followed up with, 'Look, I think we should await the outcome of Brandt's work. If that reveals any failure, then we can consider the matter further.'

⚑

Something woke Eckhardt. He opened his eyes. He couldn't see anyone, but, suspecting someone had unwittingly brushed against his hammock, swore at the unidentified offender nonetheless. Despite his now ever-present tiredness, annoyingly he couldn't get back to sleep. Awake, his senses absorbed his surroundings. Normally he tended not to notice the usual mess-deck smells, so he was surprised on this wakening to be able to discern several quite clearly. The aromas of tobacco smoke, dampness and men assaulted not only his nostrils, but also his mouth, he could taste them. The smell of men was a mix of stale sweat and unwashed clothes, supplemented by the occasional whiff of farts, surreptitious or otherwise, but funnily enough not that genital odour commonly encountered in a mess deck full of hammocked-seamen. Perhaps the gravity of their situation had got to them.

As his hammock swung gently from side to side, his unwanted conscious state had his mind switch to a recent discussion he'd had with some of his mess-mates about *Georg*. Most had seemed content with how things were going, but were now largely focused on getting home, wishing that was also their captain's desire. No one had approached Helmers for a prediction—that might be tempting fate. Eckhardt accepted that the operation was obviously unlike anything any of them had experienced before. He also put it down to the long, continuous period at sea. He knew that the Fleet's submariners could expect to be at sea for several weeks, but that was not the case with the big ships. Normally, with North Sea or Baltic operations, they would be in harbour every few days or near to a friendly port or land; *Georg* was very different. There was still a degree of routine and boredom, so often part of naval life, though the current circumstances moderated them, gave them less prominence. On reflection, Eckhardt reckoned the levels of tension were also greater, driven by the far from usual situation and the increasing expectation and no-little accompanying anxiety of encountering enemy ships. Even though the seas had largely been empty throughout the voyage and there was still confidence in their ship, some thought it unlikely they could get back to Germany without a fight at some stage, though most were quiet on the subject. However, other than how he'd felt at the very start of the action with the enemy cruisers, Eckhardt was not at all fearful. Everything still seemed to be going well, the ship was undamaged, they had enough fuel, the plane, feared lost, had been found and, as everyone regularly discussed, they were on their way home. Morale was still good. Anything was possible, including getting back safely.

When they got back to Germany, he imagined—hoped—that, especially after such an operation, leave would be granted. He naturally wanted to see Anna, though he also looked forward to being at home, where he would be warm and dry, could truly relax and have a damned good night's sleep!

The captain's visit to their mess deck after supper had been a welcome surprise. He'd visited each mess deck, primarily to award Iron Crosses for the convoy action, but also said how proud he was of the crew, how well everyone had performed throughout the mission. This went down well. Those rewarded with an Iron Cross had to settle for a handshake and a piece of paper in lieu of the medals themselves, which would be given out when back in Germany. Schwarz was one of the recipients. Some said the normal process would have been a more formal ceremony on the quarter deck, but that there just wasn't the opportunity for such a mass gathering. A shame, thought Eckhardt, as it offered greater, crew-wide recognition of what was an important event in his view.

After breakfast he was once more aloft scouring the misty horizon. Schwarz, alongside him, said nothing about his medal, though he thought the blonde look-out's face beamed and he seemed more alert, more committed, even taller. So, it came as no surprise to Eckhardt when Schwarz shouted 'Ice ahead!'—even his eyesight was probably improved by the medal.

⚐

It was hardly a minute or so before Bridge personnel also saw the ice. Körner had only just gone into his Sea Cabin when the sighting was made and he quickly returned to the Bridge. The ice, barely five kilometres ahead, looked to be an extensive and impassable barrier. Its spread completely blocked their intended path, so he ordered the ship's course altered to starboard to parallel it.

After all the ice they'd encountered since leaving Hornvik, there was an undoubted expectation that ice would be encountered back in the Denmark Strait, but Körner had hoped it would not be so soon. Through his binoculars he could see the ice was more a loose mass, ice floes, rather than solid pack ice, but still dense enough to keep well clear of. Look-outs reported that it stretched away as far as they could see. Körner's immediate worry was that it foretold of extensive, perhaps impassable ice in the Greenland-Iceland Narrows. However, he contented himself that if there was any indication of that, he could still make for the Iceland-Faroes passage, though he hoped it would prove to be no more than a temporary obstruction. Schellenberg, standing nearby, made some comment about the extent of the ice. Körner interpreted it as 'I told you so', but would not be drawn into debating the matter. He was still focused on the passage of the Denmark Strait.

Reminiscent of their trek down Greenland's west coast, this ice continued sea mile upon sea mile, always four or five kilometres to port, undulating slightly with the sea swell and forcing them ever closer towards Iceland. Körner did not reduce speed, even though some pieces of ice crossed their path, as he was keen to judge the extent of the ice quickly and decide whether he would have to swing south of Iceland. After an hour, courtesy of the ice, they were still on an east by north course. He debated the course implications with Gärtner, especially if the ice did not relent soon.

In fact, it was over seven hours before they saw a change in the ice, when, quite suddenly, the ice edge turned almost north, bearing away towards Greenland. Körner, very thankful for this development, turned the ship, this time away from the ice and back towards the Strait Narrows. The ice continued to give way, falling back quickly off their port quarter and it was not long before the look-outs could not see any but the occasional, itinerant piece. If anything the rain was worse, with the solid, featureless grey clouds providing an almost constant drizzle or unleashing the occasional heavier downpour to soak all exposed men. There had been a slight fall in the wind speed and the sea swell, though considerable, had moderated to some extent.

After nine hours on this nor-nor-east course, they were at last approaching the narrowest part of the Strait between Greenland and Iceland. The eastern reaches of Iceland were less than 150 kilometres off their starboard beam. Fortune was with them and no ships or ice were seen. There was some change in the weather, though still misty conditions, especially to port. The sky remained overcast, though the wind had reduced and now blew from Iceland. The sea swell, pushing north through the Narrows, was still with them.

Given the proximity of Iceland and the experience of their previous journey through these waters, everyone was at least expecting to see fishing boats. None had been encountered. Perhaps they were out there, just hidden by the rain and mist. Fishing boats aside, there was an expectation to see ships—the enemy's. If the English were going to challenge them on the route home, these restricted waters must be an ideal place to do so. Körner had long since had Battle Stations sounded; the ship was ready. The forward turrets were pointing ahead, with the aft turrets trained to starboard, the anticipated direction of any enemy. Intent on a fast transit, he'd also steadily increased speed to 22 knots. The ship's copious funnel smoke, often blown almost ahead of them by the prevailing winds, added to their own visibility problems.

'Ice ahead!'

The ship swung to starboard, brushing aside some ice pieces adrift from the main barrier now just a kilometre away to port. Körner disagreed with Schellenberg's suggestion for a reduction in speed. Schellenberg respectfully argued that while visibility had improved, it could change quickly and they might find themselves in amongst the ice. Körner accepted that possibility, but wanted to leave these waters behind as quickly as possible and he also felt higher speed gave them an advantage in any action that might arise. Nevertheless, he was wary of the ice edge, so moved the ship farther away from it. There was little they could do about the direction of travel, however, which once more took them back towards Iceland.

Eckhardt, like everyone in the Spotting Top, was intently staring outwards, trying to penetrate the rain and mist, binoculars tracking back and forth. The ship had moved away from the ice-barrier, now some ten kilometres off the port beam. He was looking to starboard. He was not comforted by the limited visibility, not believing it would make them invisible to an attacker. Was anything out there? What would the English throw against them, he wondered. No one had suggested a likely opponent. Whatever, he expected 'ship sighted' or the like to be called at any second, accompanied almost immediately by the big guns' blinding flash as they threw their large shells at the enemy. While the attacker might be a submarine, already eyeing them from below, or a squadron of dreadnoughts specially detached from the main enemy fleet to confront them, he actually expected some sort of scouting vessel to be the first contact, perhaps a light cruiser or even an auxiliary cruiser. He recalled that the English had established a squadron of armed merchantmen to guard all the routes leading from the Atlantic into the North Sea, mainly to intercept merchant ships trying to break through the blockade of Germany. These ships, apparently a dozen or more, were reported to be scattered right across these northern waters, all the way from Scotland to Greenland. Look-outs had been warned about them on the outward leg of the voyage and Eckhardt had been surprised that not one had been encountered then, but he didn't think such luck could hold again. However, reportedly armed only with 15cm guns, he thought they shouldn't pose any real threat and being merchant ships, mostly old liners like the one in the convoy action, he imagined their high hulls would present a very easy target.

As the minutes went by, the tension couldn't be sustained. Nothing happened! Then a change: the ice abandoned its menacing presence and once again turned away, pointing back towards its home coast, Greenland. The ship followed it, putting some welcome distance between them and Iceland. Eckhardt heard some officer say they were 'through the gap!' As if to mark the event, a single, small shaft of sunlight managed to break through the clouds, angling down and illuminating the surface of the sea far ahead of the ship. Such phenomena always seemed like a heavenly demonstration, but Eckhardt attributed no divine meaning to the beam of sunshine or what it might imply for their good fortune. He was left asking: where are the English?

An alarming message came up from the Bridge: 'Strong wireless signals detected.' The tension was back. Someone *was* out there.

ᛈ

The ship was still at Battle Stations, speeding along at over 20 knots, pitching into the swell, with grey seas occasionally sweeping over the fo'c'sle. Visibility was still poor, with rain and mist, especially to the west, though, alas for Körner, it was clearly improving. The previous day, minimum visibility at times was down to four kilometres. Now, to the east, one could see at least ten kilometres or more. The signals they'd detected had upset his hopes that they would get through the Strait without being seen. Schönert, summoned to the Bridge, was questioned by Körner.

'No, Captain, we've been unable to decipher the signal. It was a short message. As it was in code, it must be from a naval vessel. If it was about sighting us, I would have expected more signals, indeed many more.'

'Perhaps,' replied Körner. 'Has there been anything more from the Admiralty about shipping in this area?'

'No, Sir. None of the signals from Nauen mentions enemy shipping in these specific waters.'

Körner knew that, while Schönert's team may have been unable to read the enemy message, there was a chance that the special decipher station at Neumünster, if it had picked it up, might yet come up with its meaning. However, he also knew that would probably be too late to affect the immediate situation. At least they were through the Narrows; the English had missed a golden opportunity, he thought, but what to make of the enemy signal? What action should he take, if any? Change course? Which course would bypass the enemy ship? Was she near the ice or Iceland? Impossible to tell. Indeed, had they already passed her or was she just ahead? Was she alone?

At least the change in the ice-barrier had allowed more sea room if there was to be action. Just before the ice relented, Gärtner had put the Iceland coast at less than fifty kilometres away, off the starboard bow. With their more northerly course putting Iceland almost astern, Körner was pleased that the distance to that island was steadily and thankfully increasing. Whatever, Körner wanted to get clear of these waters before the improving visibility revealed them. Not for the first time he wished the plane could sweep ahead and show him the way, but, although it was reported to be ready, even if the sea state had been suitable for launching, he could not risk halting the ship with a potential enemy contact in the offing.

He, Gärtner and Schönert discussed the options. He questioned Schönert again, who affirmed that there had only been the one transmission, close by to judge by its strength, but only the one. He noted Schönert's suggestion that if there were more ships, there might have also been other calls, perhaps between them or with their base. He agreed with Schönert's thinking that it was unlikely they'd all be observing a W/T silence regime. Their discussion also considered the possibility that the English had established a patrol line of one, two or three enemy ships. They were all of the same opinion that it could be difficult to get through a three-ship patrol line without contact, but a two-ship patrol or especially a single ship offered a reasonable chance of getting by. Without more to go on it was something of an academic issue; Körner saw no alternative but to press on, which was supported by his two senior officers. However, he called for a map of the waters.

Given the ship was at Battle Stations, Körner didn't want to leave the Bridge, but retired to its covered section to consider the map. After a quick appraisal, he said: 'As we were not challenged at the narrow point,' his hand circling the waters off Iceland's prominent and almost detached north-west peninsula, 'I will go with your suggestion,' nodding to Schönert, 'that our friend is a lone ship.' He smiled, hoping the supposition was indeed correct. 'She is patrolling this northern coast, but particularly this north-east corner,' his fingers lightly brushing the other, right uppermost corner of Iceland where the name *Cape Risfstangi* curved out from the coast. 'She may think we're like any old blockade-runner *en route* to Germany, just seeking the shortest line back to the North Sea. We'll give her a wide berth. If we do run into her, or her compatriots, … well, that'll be bad news *for them*.

'Unless you see any reason against it, I intend to steam further into the Greenland Sea before shaping a course for the North Sea.'

No one challenged the captain's intention.

The original, planned course had indeed been to steam towards Norway after skirting Iceland's northern coasts. This was changed. The *Hindenburg*, still at Battle Stations, turned east-north-east, keeping well away from Iceland's north-east corner.

15

The Erda

As the plane was hoisted off the deck to begin its descent to the sea, Geiger caught the look on Kühl's face, staring up at him. Barely a few minutes before, they had chatted about the plane and the intended flight, with both men being respectful, even friendly to one another. Kühl's face now seemed stern, eyes narrowed, and Geiger wondered if the look was directed more at him personally than at anything to do with the plane. For a moment it unnerved him, but he put it to one side, as he concentrated on the launching process.

The sea still had a bit of a swell on it, but, surprisingly, few breaking waves or deep troughs. The north-easterly wind was light, though sufficient for a successful take-off. Falbe soon had the plane unhooked and Geiger taxied away from the ship. The float showed no indication that it was not watertight. It had been tested on board in a large, water-filled canvas contraption Brandt had knocked up; relying solely on a test at launching could be risky. The engine, tested repeatedly on board, was working well, with no sign of any problems. A thorough check of the fuel system had revealed that some grit had affected the flow of fuel. Its origin was unclear. In the rebuild, the fuel system had been thoroughly cleaned through, which suggested the contaminant had come from one of the *benzin* cans. Kühl wasn't too content with this explanation, again giving his views on Brandt's capabilities and even suggesting the prospect of a deliberate act, though stopped short of actually using the word sabotage. Geiger was shocked by that possibility, mainly because he'd not even thought of it, though considered it very unlikely. He did joke to himself that Kühl was probably the guilty party. Anyway, Kühl had then kept a close eye on the repairs, but reported nothing untoward. All fuel was now put through a filter.

Geiger took the plane up and circled the battle cruiser twice, keen to give the engine a final test before committing to the full flight. Content, he approached the ship from astern, the usual practice, confirming the ship's heading and direction of the flight. It was not long after dawn, such as it was at that latitude, and hardly an hour since the ship had completed her northerly trek beyond the Denmark Strait. Now she was heading south-east, towards warmer climes, the North Sea and Germany. Looking down at her, there were some signs, mostly her hull paintwork, that she had been at sea for many days, but he thought she seemed well capable of getting them back to Wilhelmshaven. She was resuming her cruising speed, with near-transparent smoke issuing from both funnels, but soon she was far behind the small plane.

Geiger continued his assessment of the plane. All seemed well, she was flying as well as ever, despite the ongoing repairs undertaken in such circumstances and including being made up from two planes, one of which had been in a terrible crash. In reality, there was little difference in all that to what might well have occurred on the *Santa Elena*. Whatever, despite Kühl's misgivings, Geiger still had nothing but praise for Brandt and his ground crew.

There was still the usual comment from the first officer that the plane would continue to be used to scout the waters ahead, but Geiger had reasoned, even when the plane was pronounced ready for operations, that circumstances would most probably prevent another flight. He didn't expect these northerly seas, hundreds of kilometres from the nearest land, would ever be calm enough to allow a take-off or, especially as they neared the North Sea, that the captain would permit the ship to stop long enough to launch the plane. So, despite the day's calmer weather, he was surprised that the Bridge had ordered a reconnaissance flight. Recognising the repairs that had been done, it was agreed that the first flight would be no great exploration, just an hour or so to check out the sea ahead of the ship.

Soon, Falbe and Geiger were alone, a vast, flat panorama below them stretching away thirty or forty kilometres. There was some cloud scattered across the pale sky, though the thickest concentrations, possibly with rain, lay far away to the south. Geiger gradually climbed until they were about two thousand metres above the sea and several hundred below the lowest, blue-grey clouds. From that height, the surface of the sea looked deceptively calm. It was also a steely, blue-grey colour, much darker where cloud shadows touched it. Visibility was good. The first officer did not expect there would be any ships to report, so far from land and away from wartime shipping routes, but advanced warning of anything ahead would be a precious advantage.

⚑

Körner and Schellenberg watched the plane disappear.

'Well, for once, I really hope they find nothing in front of us,' said Körner, a serious note to his voice, 'or, I should say, I hope there's nothing out there for them to find.'

'Yes,' confirmed Schellenberg. 'I've told the pilot,' he quickly added, 'that we need his reconnaissance capability as much as ever. I've told him that we aim to fly the plane as much as we can.'

Körner gave a single nod of approval. He and Schellenberg had talked about the need a number of times.

'Naturally,' continued Schellenberg, 'he's keen to do so, but, now we only have one pilot, there may be a limit to how many flights he can undertake in a day. However, it may well be other factors which could limit flying operations, most probably the weather and the state of the sea, not to mention the state of the plane itself.' He then threw in: 'Whatever its limitations, the plane has been a real bonus.'

'Without doubt,' agreed Körner. 'On further flights, I leave it to you to judge how fit the *Leutnant* is to undertake them, but reconnaissance is vital. You know my views on the matter.'

'Yes, Sir.'

'I'm surprised the Fleet didn't employ planes more before,' advanced Körner. 'Perhaps too much faith was put in zeppelins. If we'd had a plane at Skagerrak, perhaps we could have avoided the enemy's battle fleet.'

'Quite so,' said Schellenberg, 'but the whole process of launching and recovery needs further work. We can't always stop to launch or recover planes.'

Körner acknowledged Schellenberg's observation. They had discussed it on several occasions, both before and during the mission. They knew the English and Americans had used flying-off ramps before the war and that the Americans had successfully used ship-board catapults to launch aircraft, so it seemed likely that these offered a way forward on the problem. They also knew that the small cruiser *Stuttgart* was being converted to an airplane ship, one capable of keeping up with the Fleet, though neither knew if it would have any ramps or catapults. Körner affirmed that such matters and what they'd learnt about handling and using their seaplanes, along with his views on the benefits of airplanes, would all be included in his post-mission report.

Schönert arrived on the Bridge. He saluted his captain. Körner immediately wondered 'what now?' Schönert had not been summoned to the Bridge and usually sent less important signals via others. Earlier, Schönert had reported the Admiralty's appreciation that an enemy ship was considered to be located off Iceland, which must have been the one whose wireless signal they'd detected.

'Captain, the *Erda* appears to have been lost.' There was no sense of alarm in Schönert's matter-of-fact delivery.

'What? … How? … When?' It was a bit of a shock, not at all expected and Körner couldn't help himself, couldn't hold back the questions.

'Captain, the signal from the Admiralty gave precious little detail, only that the *Erda* is considered to be lost. We've picked up no signals from her, … though not surprising, given the distances. There's also nothing from the English. From the signal, we only know she's been lost. The message does not say how the Admiralty got the information. I suppose,' Schönert casually ventured, 'there's even the possibility that she may have been sunk by one of *our* U-boats; she was to sail close to the western edge of the War Zone. Perhaps she did get off a signal and it was intercepted and passed on by one of our U-boats.'

Schellenberg started to debate the matter with Schönert, but Körner stood aside, said nothing. He did not want to add any further speculation on how the *Erda* was sunk. Unless an enemy ruse, she was lost and that was that. Admittedly, there was the concern that she might have been boarded before being sunk, but she may equally have taken her secrets with her to the bottom. He interrupted his officers: 'Gentlemen, this news has a bearing on us, but rather than rush to conclusions or change to our plans, please let me know, say, in an hour your observations on the matter and any proposals. I'm going to my Day Cabin.'

Despite his instruction, while looking at the picture of Maria and the children, Körner couldn't stop himself from mulling over the implications of the *Erda*'s loss. Conjured up when they were coaling in Greenland, a plan to utilise the supply ship after the two ships left those cold waters had been developed. The two ships would separate soon after leaving Greenland and, while the battle cruiser followed a northerly course for Iceland and Germany, the *Erda* would swing south into the Atlantic before herself returning home or, as circumstances demanded, seeking internment in some neutral port. Four days after the separation, as the *Hindenburg* approached Norway and the North Sea, the supply ship would transmit a signal informing the Fleet of the warship's intended route and likely timings. Although she'd still be far from Germany, perhaps too far to transmit, she was instructed to send her signal during the night when atmospheric conditions could greatly enhance W/T range. Her signal might have enabled the Fleet to take some action which would facilitate a safe passage for the *Hindenburg*. It was only a small ploy, but it would allow a signal to be sent to the Fleet without compromising the *Hindenburg*'s wireless silence and, if picked up by the English, might even have drawn some forces towards the *Erda*, if her position was located. It was not guaranteed to be a successful ruse, but was worth trying. Whatever, now that plan was undone.

Although Körner was saddened by the loss of the *Erda*, the loss of any ship no longer seemed to have the same impact as it would have done in past times, especially in pre-war days. Even so, he hoped the crew had been saved. Likewise, when the time had come to turn south-east towards Norway, Gärtner had casually reminded him that Jan Mayen then lay some 200-odd kilometres off their port beam. Körner had responded that he hoped the *Torsten Meyer* fared well, but there was no great discussion about their other supply ship, no doubt waiting patiently to help if called upon. He had his own ship's welfare to consider and the *Torsten Meyer* must fend for herself, though prompted by thoughts of the *Erda*, he did wonder about her plight, especially the cold weather at the isolated island. He would liked to have taken her 30.5cm shells and top up with her fuel, but he expected he could get by without those staples.

The hour was soon up. A meeting was held in the stateroom. Körner was not surprised that Gärtner was also present. There were no pleasantries; Schellenberg set out their views.

'Captain, we think the loss of the *Erda* has not fundamentally changed our situation.' He paused for a moment, perhaps to let that sink in or to allow his captain to speak, but Körner said nothing. 'We are still heading for Norway and the North Sea. We would have continued on that course even if the *Erda* had transmitted the intended signal. There is even a chance that the signal might not have been picked up or not have altered the situation. It *may* have drawn away some enemy forces or have generated some supporting action from the Fleet, but, then again, it may not. Overall, the *Erda*'s signal was not guaranteed to change anything. The English may even have been able to discern it was not from us and thereby guessed at our intentions, allowing them to focus their full attention on us as we cross the North Sea.'

Körner still said nothing, so Schellenberg continued: 'We still face the risks of crossing the Norway-Scotland convoy route and any additional measures the enemy may have instituted to try and catch us. There is also the risk of alerting the Fleet too early or too late of our position.

'Anyway, surprise is still with us ... the enemy does not know where we are. Also, there are many sea miles between Scotland and Norway. I think there's a good chance of getting through without making contact.

'As you and I, Sir, have discussed, our return through the North Sea is probably the riskiest part of *Georg*. Using the *Erda* both to draw attention from us and give the Fleet early notice of our return had merit, but could not be a guaranteed success.

'I agree,' said Körner, 'but can we reduce the risk?'

'As I said, Sir, we still have the element of surprise,' responded Schellenberg, '... the enemy does not know where we are ... and the Fleet can yet support our return. Some things we can alter and some things we can't.'

'*What things*?' reacted Körner, his voice calm, but challenging.

'Forgive me, Sir,' responded Schellenberg, 'we *have* considered most things, it's just that we have limited intelligence on them and that puts us at risk.'

'Please explain.'

'Well, for example, we are obliged to cross the Norway-Scotland convoy route. We do not know the sailing times of those convoys and are, therefore, at risk of encountering one ... and its escort.'

Körner did not challenge the point. He and Schellenberg had concluded that the Fleet's unsuccessful attempt to attack one of those convoys as part of the break-out was the result of bad planning, in that no convoy could be found. It seemed highly likely that the actual sailing times were different from that expected or the enemy had deliberately changed them for some reason. It was also likely that, after that sortie by the Fleet, the enemy would have altered any subsequent sailings *and* strengthened the convoy's escort, probably with dreadnoughts.

Schellenberg continued to explain the risks faced. 'The enemy will probably hope to catch us in the North Sea and may have increased their patrols to do so. We have no knowledge of these, so we risk discovery. Nothing so far from the Fleet has reached us about enemy dispositions or the convoys, but that is not to say that we won't get any. We can't ask the Fleet for such information without breaking wireless silence, so we are dependent on the Fleet in that respect.

'This issue also raises the question of when to signal the Fleet that we are coming home,' finished Schellenberg's summary of the main risks they faced.

Körner well understood the risks. There was no sensible alternative way to avoid crossing the convoy routes. As to the enemy's forces, they would have to rely on alerts and direct support from the Fleet. One positive factor, as Schellenberg had mentioned, was the extent of the waters they would be passing through. He knew the distance between Norway and the Shetlands was at least 300 kilometres and much more between Scapa Flow and Norway. To all that Schellenberg had said, the *Erda*, the convoy route, the enemy's ships, he gave a simple, 'Good. I agree. We continue, as planned.' He expected no change to previous ideas of traversing the area, but asked nonetheless: 'We still cross at night?'

'Yes, Sir,' said Schellenberg, 'the course and speed we're on will put us off the Norwegian coast at sunset. Of course, as the hours of darkness will be short at these latitudes and there is quite some distance to get south of Norway, we will still have Norway to port for some hours during the day. I suggest we increase speed during that period; indeed, all the way home.

'I also suggest that we should keep to the Norwegian side and, if possible, get the seaplane to scout ahead for us.' Schellenberg then added, with a smile: 'As we also know from personal experience, the weather around Bergen can be pretty foul at any time of the year, so we may get some help from the elements.'

All smiled at this, relieving a bit of the tension felt.

The issue of when to break wireless silence and send a signal to the Fleet was discussed by the three officers. The adherence to wireless silence appeared to have worked well, but, even though there was some brief dialogue about continuing with it all the way back into German waters, *Georg* required a signal be sent, not only to secure the Fleet's early support, but also to warn their own U-boats of their whereabouts. Especially without the *Erda*'s subterfuge, all accepted that the signal must be sent, but also agreed it would most likely bring the English out. So, the only real issue was when. A decision on that would depend on any developments, but once they had reached a point where the English could no longer catch them, say east of Scapa Flow, would be an appropriate position. They also discussed the option of the Skagerrak-Kattegat route to Kiel, as used by Nerger, if circumstances warranted or demanded it, but Körner was not keen, reminding his officers that planning for *Georg* had concluded on Wilhelmshaven as the best goal.

⚐

Geiger circled the ship, for once doing his best to check for submarines. Neither he nor Falbe could see anything suspicious. He shaped up to come in. There was a little bit more wave action than when they took off, but it didn't worry him and he expected an efficient recovery by him and Falbe and the ship. Over the course of the mission, seaplane handling had greatly improved, especially the launching and recovery procedures. For these the ship still had to come to a halt, but all was now as efficient as it could be. The ship also played its part in recoveries. The ship headed into the wind and, as the seaplane began its descent, she was steered to port. This helped to create both a lee and some smooth water for the plane. So it was this time; Geiger made a good landing, with only one small bounce. He quickly taxied up to the ship, doing his best to avoid the ship's still evident bow and stern waves. Falbe wasted no time in getting up to catch the swaying hook. There was still a slight swell and timing the plane's rise and fall on the water was important. Nonetheless, Falbe missed the hook, uttering a quiet swear word. Geiger, concentrating on holding the plane away from the ship, felt Falbe jump a little to grab the hook, successfully this time, and the cable was swiftly looped over it. A quick signal and the plane began to rise; Geiger cut the engine.

Once on the deck, both men got out of the plane. Falbe descended first. Geiger began to get out of his cockpit when he heard Falbe swear, followed by the sound of him hitting the deck. He thought little of it, but called out, 'You OK, Günther?' intending to comment on his observer's poor acrobatic skills. When he looked over the side, his smile instantly fell away. Falbe was crumpled up alongside the port float, making light of his fall, but gripping his ankle and obviously in some discomfort.

From Falbe's description, despite the scores of times he'd done it, his foot had got caught in the fuselage footstep when his other foot slipped off the lower wing. He'd managed to free it before almost falling upside down, but had still injured his ankle. Walking with evident great difficulty, he was helped off to the sick bay by a member of the ground crew. Geiger went to report to the *Fregattenkapitän*, leaving Kühl to oversee Brandt and his men who were already about the plane, checking it over, replenishing fuel and oil and replacing the ammunition fired in testing the guns. As he made his way for'ard, it suddenly dawned on him that, if Falbe was unfit for duty, then Kühl would be his observer. As usual, he'd just been focused on his pilot role, one where he and Falbe would team up for future flights. He'd never even given a thought to taking Kühl instead, though it was not something he would have relished. Now he might have no option.

His report to the first officer was simple: they had seen nothing. *Fregattenkapitän* Schellenberg was content; it was what he and the captain had hoped for. He voiced no concern about the implication of Falbe's injury. 'Kühl is an observer, it's his job' was how Geiger interpreted his remarks. Another flight was agreed, once Geiger had had a rest and the ship had advanced farther. There was no point in flying immediately, which would just cover most of the same water as the first flight. Geiger didn't expect it, so was not surprised that the first officer said nothing about any promotion, acting or otherwise, but his comments still indicated that he was in charge.

Before returning to the hangar, he stopped off to see Falbe. His ankle was swollen, probably only a sprain, rather than any broken bones, but sick bay advised that it was best to keep the weight off it for now. Falbe naturally made no comment on the news of Kühl replacing him, but Geiger thought the observer's face betrayed his thoughts on the matter. A little over two hours later, the plane waited to be lifted down to the sea. Geiger had had a short snooze, had eaten and felt refreshed—and had made his customary, last minute visit to the heads. He sat in the plane, engine running, with Kühl standing above him controlling the lifting process. The ship slowed and soon they were on the water and taxiing away from her. All was going well; Kühl was fulfilling his observer duties, indeed seemed more animated, more buoyed up by the whole process and was saying nothing that made Geiger feel his authority was being challenged. He was annoyed with himself for allowing these thoughts to affect him, trying to excuse himself because of his *non*-promotion and Kühl's attitude. Anyway, he felt that he was in charge. They took off.

Twenty-four hours later the ship was still on course for Norway, still almost 400 kilometres away. During the time, Körner had met with each of his senior officers. He'd also taken the opportunity to visit various parts of the ship. As the end of the mission was in sight and they faced perhaps the most difficult stretch, he wanted to ensure for himself that the ship and crew were in as good a condition as possible, considering what they'd been through and how long they'd been away from the benefits of a major base like Wilhelmshaven. Overall, he was pleased with what he'd seen and heard and confident that the ship was up for the task ahead.

The big guns, a dreadnought's *raison d'être*, were reportedly functioning well. Kruse had continued to maintain a programme of exercises to ensure his men and equipment were ready. There was the issue of whether they had enough ammunition for any lengthy combat, but action was not what Körner wanted. In sinking a convoy, he considered he had accomplished the primary aim of *Georg*, but getting the ship safely back to Germany was also, from various perspectives, an essential component, a victory in its own right. Therefore, he would now flee from any opposition which could damage the ship and inhibit her safe return to Germany.

The engines and boiler rooms were judged to be sound, all things considered, though Faber, citing the long time at sea and some leaking boiler tubes, put the ship's maximum speed at no more than 25 knots. Fuel and water were ample for the journey ahead, but provisions were poor. The supply ships had restocked the ship's larders, but only just. Thank God they were on the last leg.

Equally to be thankful for, nothing had been seen by either the ship or the seaplane. The plane had undertaken three flights, the last one ending late in the day, but it was more the tired state of the air crew, rather than concerns about the lateness of the hour which had precluded another. He accepted Schellenberg's view on the matter. That was not all he'd discussed with Schellenberg.

He, Schellenberg and Gärtner had gone over the proposed course to Norway and beyond. They confirmed the line which would take them to a point about seventy-five kilometres off the Norwegian coast just at dusk, such as it was. From there they would continue on a course paralleling the coast. At that point speed would be increased and maintained for the rest of the journey back to Germany. Even at the higher speed, it would be many hours and well into full daylight before they reached the area of Stavanger and began to draw away into the main, wider part of the North Sea. Scapa Flow, at the closest, would be at least some 400 kilometres to starboard, making interception difficult for any vessels beginning their chase from there. As with the Denmark Strait passage, the main issue was there would be no real, black night. At least at this lower latitude, there would be a period of darkness. The sun would be below the horizon, but its influence would still be evident. It would be dark, but the horizon would still be visible and any ships on the horizon would be equally able to see the *Hindenburg*. Schellenberg's earlier remark about Bergen's perennial bad weather also gave him hope.

With Norway and the North Sea ahead, the spectre of submarine attack had again begun to crowd in on Körner's already busy thinking. After all that had transpired and travelling thousands of sea miles in the process, for obvious reasons this part of the journey was certainly the most dangerous. He was not worried about engaging any enemy warship, but the underwater, unseen menace concerned him, perhaps more so than before. The fear of submarine attack had been in his mind at many points during the mission, mostly whenever the ship was stopped or slowed, either to launch or recover the seaplane or when limited by a slow supply ship. The measures taken before, including zigzag courses or turning away from a reported periscope, offered some counter to the submarine threat. There had been various sightings of periscopes during the mission. On reflection, he considered most, perhaps all, were false, as they were one-off sightings and had led to no subsequent enemy action. They'd also detected no wireless signals that indicated submarines had reported their whereabouts. However, in the North Sea, an area of major naval activity, such sightings might well be real.

Körner was sufficiently concerned to generate a debate about the submarine threat. He was always keen to hear Schellenberg's views on important matters; he never felt he had all or any of the answers to problems.

'We must expect greater submarine activity as we get closer to Germany. How do you see things?' he asked Schellenberg, in a casual tone, endeavouring not to appear overly concerned about the threat.

In his usual manner, Schellenberg took a moment to respond. Körner admired his first officer's delivery process. His momentary delay was not a sort of pregnant pause, just enough to show that some thinking process was underway, that he was collecting his thoughts on the matter and not in any way unable to marshal any suitable response.

'Captain, the waters ahead undoubtedly pose a new level of danger for us. Compared to our journey across the Atlantic, there could well be more submarines in the North Sea, but I suspect the danger from them may be no greater than that faced when we first sailed on *Georg*.'

'How so?'

'Well,' he responded, '*if* the English can find us, I expect they will throw everything at us.' He paused, before adding: 'However, submarines, by the nature of their capabilities, will be waiting in areas to attack passing ships and, while a possibility, we should count ourselves unlucky to come across one journeying to and from its assignment area. Even if we are discovered, I doubt the English will have the time and information to create, shall we call it, an effective submarine barrier ahead of us.'

'Do you not expect more submarines ahead?'

'Possibly, if they've been able to increase the number of boats in operation, but I would still expect them to be in the waters around the Bight. I would not expect them to be scattered across our course home in the hope that we might pass by one, ... especially,' he smiled, 'if they do not yet know where we are. None of this means we're not open to such an attack, just that the risk may not be much greater than a few weeks ago.'

Körner was annoyed and pleased. Annoyed that he had not thought through the risks himself, pleased to hear Schellenberg's analysis of the situation. Nevertheless, he still asked: 'Do you think we should adopt a zigzag course at any point?'

'In truth, I think we should remain flexible on that option. Let circumstances dictate it,' he said. 'Perhaps, it is warranted once we reach, say, the Bight, where we *do* expect submarines, though, hopefully, by then we'll have some escorts. Until then, I would put our faith in vigilance *and* high speed. In the coming hours I would suggest we keep as much water as possible between ourselves and any pursuing warships. While I have a healthy regard for submarines, I would rather prefer not to encounter a squadron of dreadnoughts. They will be the warships after us, if we are discovered. A zigzag course will only allow any chasing warships to close the distance on us.'

Körner saw no sign of satisfaction on Schellenberg's face or indication that he was suggesting he knew better than his captain. He was glad he'd raised the matter with Schellenberg. He was still concerned about the submarine threat, but the discussion had put the risks in perspective for him. He concluded by reaffirming the 'high speed' run back to Germany, though would adopt a zigzag course if and when circumstances warranted it.

The first flight of the day was seriously delayed. During the previous day's flights, Brandt had commented on the engine's oil-consumption rate. After the last flight, subsequent checks confirmed his concerns. Geiger was alarmed when Brandt announced that the plane shouldn't fly again until the matter was corrected and that the engine had to be removed and virtually dismantled to address the problem. Given the importance of the forthcoming flights, Geiger imagined the first officer wouldn't be at all happy, but there was little more to be said on the subject. With a full array of spares, not to mention a spare engine to hand, it would have been easy to deal with the problem and it had been clear that this particular predicament would take time, effort and possibly some ingenuity to address. They all knew that this was only the latest episode that demonstrated how difficult it was becoming to keep the plane flying. Geiger reported the likely delay to the first officer, received with dismay and reluctant acceptance. He and Kühl let Brandt get on with it.

The repairs indeed took some time. Brandt and his crew worked all through the night and the day was almost half over before the plane took off. Geiger took it as the clearest sign yet that the plane was probably nearing its end. As he flew alongside the ship, he waved to the watching Brandt and the ground crew, intending it as a sign of his thanks.

Before take-off, *Fregattenkapitän* Schellenberg had told him that the day's flights were important as ever, though Geiger thought he usually said something like that. Nonetheless, Geiger was keenly aware that the ship was approaching Norway, getting ever closer to waters where more shipping, enemy and neutral, warships and merchantmen, could be encountered. Thinking this over as he flew, he then realised he had no knowledge of Norwegian warships; he hoped it would not be necessary and did not mention it to Kühl.

The first officer had also inferred that if the *Hindenburg* was sighted now it could well create greater difficulties than at any point so far. Again, Geiger recalled similar comments before other flights, but accepted the point. He knew the waters ahead were closer to the enemy's main naval bases, where scores of warships could be—*would be*—dispatched to confront the *Hindenburg*. Clearly they were coming into dangerous waters and the seaplane would be vital in alerting the ship to any threat that lay ahead.

In view of this, he had agreed with the first officer that, in contrast to the previous day's flights, today's would now be up to four hours' duration. After the long and demanding flight which discovered the convoy off America, he and Brandmann had agreed that there should be no more maximum-duration flights, but things were different now, indeed he'd thrown the idea into their discussion. The first officer agreed and there was no debate about the navigational or distance problems the plane would face. Each successive flight of the previous day had flown farther, so—subject to the plane not having an oil problem or developing any other faults—he imagined it could cope with a slightly longer flight. The favourable wind and weather should also not pose a problem in finding the ship.

Despite the various problems of all the flights to date, he was never as attentive to his instruments or the sounds and feel of the aircraft as he was on this flight.

One outcome of the previous day's flights—or so it seemed to Geiger—was a change in Kühl's attitude. It was difficult to be definitive about it, but Geiger thought his new observer was, well, less hostile, less negative towards him. He could only put it down to him being allowed to fly, functioning as an observer, rather than just being stuck to the deck of the ship. He was still the 'superior than thou' Kühl, but his attitude towards Geiger was decidedly less aggressive and he seemed easier to get on with. Naturally, Geiger didn't mention it to Kühl, he was just pleased with the change. It made him feel better, whatever it had done for Kühl.

As usual, there was little or no conversation between them, though, early in the flight, they shared a thermos of some hot coffee, exchanging the odd, shouted word on the cold and the weather. The wind, a little fresher than the previous day, was still coming down from the north. The clouds were also less, with thin clouds here and there stretching across the sky. Geiger took advantage of the clearer weather, increasing altitude to maximise their view. He flew near the cloud base, at times flitting amongst the clouds, thinking they could offer useful cover if they came across a ship. From their high altitude, they did see one vessel, a sailing ship, a topsail schooner. It was heading towards Norway and deemed not to be a concern.

As observer, Kühl had primary responsibility for surveying the sky and sea, allowing Geiger to concentrate on flying the plane, though naturally the pilot had a view forward. It was Geiger who first saw the plane, though it was little more than a speck in the sky. As soon as he realised it was most likely a plane, he had a sort of frisson, not of excitement, but fear. The plane was about twenty degrees to port and below them. It was flying in what appeared to be a near opposite direction. He guessed it to be six, seven, perhaps eight kilometres away.

Geiger signalled his sighting to Kühl, repeatedly stabbing his left arm down at the intruder. Kühl leaned close to his ear. 'What do you intend?' he shouted. His question seemed tinged with challenge.

To Geiger, it couldn't be a German plane, not that far from Germany. 'It might be Norwegian,' he shouted back, 'but I don't know if they even have any planes. It's probably English!'

'Yes! Agree! We should attack!'

There was no time to debate the matter. The distance between the two planes was coming down quickly, very quickly. There was no time to signal the ship. Kühl was right: Attack! If they took no action, it would soon pass them and they'd never catch it. If the plane kept on this course, it might come across the *Hindenburg*! If Norwegian, … well, they would hold off. If English, they *must* stop it discovering the ship. Attack!

On various occasions Geiger had pondered aerial combat in the FF49, but always concluded that it was best avoided, given the plane's low speed and poor manoeuvrability, its single forward-firing gun and, most importantly, his lack of the necessary experience. For once, these negative factors did not come into his mind. He could feel his heart thumping and adrenalin flowing, coupled with as great a sense of fear as he'd ever had before, but he was committed to offensive action. He'd read the list of tactics for fighter pilots by German air ace Oscar Boelcke, but, as he wasn't a fighter pilot, he hadn't committed them to memory and definitely hadn't had the opportunity to practise them. He did recall the first was about altitude, speed and surprise. He definitely had these!

He opened the throttle and pushed the plane over, heading towards the black shape. The planes' combined speed rapidly—and scarily—narrowed the gap between them. Soon Geiger was able to confirm that it was a large, brownish-coloured, twin-engined plane and, by its shape, a seaplane. It was also clearly English, to judge by the large red, white and blue roundels visible on its upper wing—or were they Norway's colours? He was unsure of its type, so knew nothing of its capabilities. It had a large, single-hull, flying-boat fuselage, from which sprang its lower wing, with a much larger wing above. It looked like the two engines, separate from but just above the hull, nestled between the two wings. As the distance reduced quickly, he noted what appeared to be a circular position at the nose, possibly for a machine gun, with a large cockpit just behind it. If he could, he would aim for the enemy's nose, to try and hit the pilot. At their high closing speed, he decided there was no time for any manoeuvring to try and get onto its tail, nor any certainty that he could achieve that. It seemed better to use his altitude and speed to hit first and fast. He would attack head-on!

For what seemed like a long time, but was probably only ten or so seconds, the big plane, perhaps twice the FF49's size, showed no reaction, but then suddenly began to slip to port. Geiger took the movement as showing they had seen him and that the pilot meant to force him to overshoot. Geiger pushed forward, further increasing the angle of the dive, trying to keep the enemy in his sights. He wanted to get much closer, but feared losing the opportunity; he opened fire. The Spandau spat a line of tracer at the increasingly larger target.

卐

Robert Walton, a captain in the newly constituted Royal Air Force, was sitting in the left seat of the cockpit of the Felixstowe F.2A flying boat. Captain Edward 'Ted' York occupied the right seat, though, on a six hour flight, at that point he was taking a break for a piss. York was in charge of the plane; Walton, the second pilot, was taking his turn at flying her. A few minutes before, he'd been in the nose, machine-gun cockpit, just ahead of the pilots' seats, searching the sea. York had waved him in, when he wanted to relieve himself. Walton took his seat and York went forward, though only to do his business, not to man the gun or scour the sea.

They were on a reconnaissance flight, searching for the German battle cruiser *Hindenburg*. This was their third such flight in the last six days. They were one of three of the large, twin-engined Felixstowes that had been sent to the very north of Scotland to search for the German warship. Before that their job had been mainly anti-submarine flights across the North Sea from their Norfolk coast base. Everyone knew of the German battle cruiser and was keenly aware of her Atlantic voyage, especially her devastating attack on a convoy—it had been the talk of the mess. Walton heard no dissenting comments about their change in orders, just a few concerns about their, reportedly, unfinished northern base and jokes about sheep-shagging and likely brass-monkey weather.

Their journey north had been something of a leisurely affair, done in a couple of steps to Scapa Flow, largely following the coast, before the 100 mile short flight beyond to the Shetland Islands. Their new base, Catfirth, was located on the eastern shore of Cat Firth, a very small, almost land-locked bay, about seven or eight miles beyond Lerwick. It was a bleak location, but, in stark contrast to giant Scapa, the bay was hardly more than half a mile long. Catfirth was the most northerly RAF base in the British Isles; 'next stop North Pole' usually greeting a newcomer.

Work was still going on at the base, but was sufficiently advanced to cope with the three planes. The Navy had been working on it for quite some months, with completion—now a RAF responsibility—expected in a month or so, but events had changed priorities. The *Hindenburg*'s convoy achievement had galvanized matters. No battle squadrons were scouring the ocean for her. They knew she must come back through the North Sea; they would catch her there. The planes' job was as a first line of reconnaissance; find her, direct the big ships onto her. Despite the arrangements, it had taken several days before the first reconnaissance flight, the weather didn't always help. There was some concern that the enemy ship would slip past before they got into the air.

Intelligence expected the *Hindenburg* to attempt a return to Germany through the Shetland-Norway waters. Other passages would be covered, but this most northerly route was considered the most likely option. The only problem was they did not know where she was. The Germans had been very canny in keeping their whereabouts a secret.

The crews thought the Felixstowes to be excellent planes, well capable of undertaking long-range reconnaissance missions. They could carry bombs, but not on these flights; it was believed—not by the crew—they'd achieve little against a dreadnought's armour and the weight saved allowed more range. York, Walton and their crewmen, Owen Jackson and Ken Lambert, had been together for several months and flown many missions, though mostly without seeing much of anything, in fact only one enemy submarine. There were a couple of occasions when enemy fighters were encountered, though without much damage or loss on either side. All the members of the crew were very confident about their plane and keen to get on with their new assignment.

Walton was pleased to do some flying and to come in from the for'ard, very cold and open cockpit. With York away from his seat and the other two crew at their posts behind him, Walton got on with his flying. Their flight plan took them on a near-500-mile course almost to Norway and back. There were some variations to the missions they'd flown, excepting that this was by far the longest. On the two previous flights, both straight runs to within sight of Norway and back, they'd seen nothing apart from what was taken to be some Norwegian fishing boats. This flight's much longer and triangular course had produced no sightings thus far. Walton checked the chart on his lap. They would soon reach the end of the second leg and turn towards the Shetlands.

The pilots' cockpit was a semi-enclosed structure, with a good windscreen in front, but open above. Glancing up from the chart and through the cockpit's open roof section, he was shocked to see the unmistakeable shape of a plane diving towards him. Experience showed that any plane coming straight at you was bad news. Whatever or whoever it was, he wasn't waiting around to find out. He immediately banked the plane to port and screamed, 'Enemy plane!' He shouted the alarm with all his might, hoping that it would be heard above the noise of the powerful Rolls-Royce engines. Tracers streaked all around him.

York was then on his way back to his seat, coping well with the plane's movement. Looking up, he shouted 'Where?' but then suddenly spun round and bounced off one side of the fuselage and slumped against the other.

'Ted! Ted!'

There was a slight moan from York, his crumpled body moved slightly. Walton could do nothing for his commander, he had to fly the plane. 'Owen! Ted's been hit!' he shouted, endeavouring to summon help for the wounded pilot. Jackson, the wireless operator, was also responsible for first aid.

The enemy plane, now clearly seen by its floats to be a seaplane, flashed by to starboard, a winking flash coming from an aft cockpit, with hits clearly registering. Walton continued to slip to port, gaining speed, heading down towards the grey sea. Behind him he heard Lewis guns firing. He wanted to shout encouragement to Jackson and Lambert, but just felt his teeth clenched shut as he gripped his control wheel.

⚐

Geiger recovered from the dive and pulled the plane to starboard in a tight turn, hoping that would put him in a favourable position, but really he was completely unaware of the enemy plane's location. It was all happening very fast. He had little time to think about tactics, other than to avoid being on the receiving end of the enemy's guns. As he completed the turn, he breathed a sigh of relief when he saw the enemy plane was flying away ahead of him. It was descending, a thin line of exhaust fumes coming from each engine. No, the starboard trail was thicker.

Had it been hit, damaged? He recalled some tracer passing his own plane as he dived past, but felt no hits. Kühl shouted something; he didn't catch it all, but it could've been: 'I hit him!'

He was going as fast as possible, but not really gaining on the enemy. The FF49 was no racehorse, no fighter plane. When they attacked, he'd been in an excellent position, above his opponent, accelerating towards him. He was surprised the enemy pilot hadn't reacted more quickly, with no change in direction until he was about three or four hundred metres away. Then the big plane began to slip to port, moving away from Geiger's line of attack. He'd increased the angle of his dive so as not to lose his quarry, but opened fire as soon as the enemy pilot began his escape manoeuvre. He thought the single line of tracer, scores and scores of bullets, seemed to touch the nose area before tracking off across the upper wing and then harmlessly into space. As he dived past the plane, he'd heard Kühl open fire.

The two planes were both descending, still a thousand or more metres from the surface of the sea. He was directly astern of the large plane. There was clearly a line of smoke issuing from the enemy's starboard engine. He felt elation; still terrified, but elated.

'Get closer!' was Kühl's shouted *command* in his ear.

He didn't respond. What did Kühl think he was trying to do? The Benz engine was going flat out and he was no longer worrying about oil pressure. The two planes were obviously similar in speed, as he didn't seem to be able to get closer, though neither did the English plane seem to be able to get away from them. He was several hundred metres astern. He could open fire, but to what effect at this range? Wasting ammunition? He was no fighter pilot, with virtually no experience of aerial combat; he was learning as he went. Flashing lights at the rear of the enemy showed gunners were firing at them; tracers whipped by. Completely ignoring his concerns about firing at long range, his angry response was to return fire; the Spandau coughed its retaliation, spewing tracers towards the enemy plane, though without seeming to hit.

The wounded engine produced even more smoke. Geiger stopped firing. Kühl shouted in his ear: 'Keep firing!' The enemy plane began to dive more steeply, turning to starboard, and he altered his heading to keep it in his sights. Geiger opened fire again, his tracers now appearing to hit the enemy plane. He could see more smoke. Was the engine on fire? The plane's starboard turn put it almost side on to him, it looked a perfect target, but his gun stopped firing; it must've jammed. Thick smoke was clearly coming from the enemy's starboard engine. Did that mean the enemy plane was already doomed, he wondered? He was about to attend to his gun-jam, when he saw a square-shaped opening on the enemy's starboard side near the tail show some movement; a gun fired at them. He was close, too close, and instinctively pushed forward to dive below the smoking plane. Tracers flashed in front of him; he could not avoid flying into them. There was series of rapid, thudding noises, with bullets striking the engine, then hitting his cockpit.

⚐

Walton grasped the large control wheel, fighting to keep the plane from spiralling down to a watery grave. Despite his attention to the plane's controls, fear kept him turning his head towards the starboard engine, terrified it would or already had burst into flames. However, it was all a bit pointless, as from his port-side seat, he couldn't see it without lifting himself up from his seat and he wasn't about to do that! He knew that the engine had been hit and had stopped and, if not for the fire potential, he would have tried to fly back to the Shetlands or at least some way towards those windswept isles on the remaining engine.

He couldn't see the other plane. Noise from the port engine inhibited hearing it or just about anything. He drew some reassurance from the absence of tracer patterns, hoping that meant the enemy was at least not in a firing position. Nonetheless, he considered they were still in danger. As well as the engine being hit, which happened on the enemy plane's first pass, there were numerous holes in the plane's canvas sides and the invasive smell of petrol gave a terrifying indication that the fuel tanks located not many feet behind him had been punctured. The fear of an imminent petrol fire or explosion was a good enough reason to get the plane safely and quickly onto the water.

He was soon only a few hundred feet or so above the sea and shaping up to come down smoothly. If the enemy plane attacked now, he'd have no room for any evasive manoeuvring. He gave that prospect precious little thought, focusing on the landing. The sea waves looked daunting, but he had no option. It was no text-book landing. The plane struck the sea level, but hard and, in spite of its near five-ton weight, bounced up and thumped into the next wave crest, a great spray of white water enveloping the whole plane and fogging Walton's goggles. The plane did not stop there, but continued on smacking into another crest and producing more spray before eventually coming to a halt.

The satisfaction of getting the plane down without crashing or sinking her was momentary at best. He switched the engines off and swung his attention to the starboard engine, but still unsure what to do about it. He stood up. He saw smoke still rising from the engine, but no flames. He didn't know how it had not caught fire and didn't care. Jackson squeezed awkwardly between the pilots' seats and went to York, who hadn't moved or been helped since the attack.

Walton looked up, scanning the sky, expecting to see the other plane circling and shaping up to attack them. The sky was empty. He turned back to Jackson.

'How is he?' he asked hopefully.

'Dead,' was Jackson's mournful reply.

'Oh no,' was his muted response. He started to wonder how Ted had died and whether earlier assistance could have helped, but realised that such questions didn't matter. He turned around and looked aft through the plane's crowded interior to see Lambert, their engineer, attending to the three large fuel tanks. Straight away he could see some holes in them and see, as well as smell, petrol.

'How goes it?' he shouted.

'Well, as long as no one wants a smoke, we should be OK,' replied Lambert. His comic delivery fell flat with Walton. Lambert continued: 'I've drained down the gravity tank and shut off the others. I will see if the holes in these can be bunged up.'

Walton let Lambert get on with his work. Jackson had laid out York, as well as the space allowed, and then, crawling back through the plane, checked it out with Walton. Water was getting into the plane, but only, it seemed, through holes in the canvas sides and that only because of waves striking the plane. The hull proper, made of thick wood, didn't seem to have been breached. This all suggested, with a little bailing and pumping, they could keep afloat, at least for some time. The flying boat's tail plane served to bring the bow into the wind and waves. To aid that, they threw out the sea anchor. Other than water periodically coming into the bow cockpit, keeping the bow into the wind reduced the flow of water coming in through the bullet holes down their flanks.

Huddled together, the three damp and cold men discussed the situation and reviewed their options. No one had seen what had happened to the enemy plane, though both Jackson and Lambert reckoned to have put good bursts into it. After it was last seen, the plight of their own plane had become the focus of their attention. Had it been brought down was the unanswered question.

Lambert attempted to repair the wounded engine, but numerous hits and now obvious fire damage had done irreparable harm and, despite his best efforts, he reported he could not fix it at sea. While he was attempting to repair the engine, Jackson tried all means to get a message back to Catfirth. The wireless aerial, a three-hundred-foot metal wire, hanging beneath the plane was useless, but he rigged a short-range alternative. A wooden post, with wires stretched across the top wing and bow to tail, provided the chance to send a message, but it could only reach about thirty miles. Hopefully some wireless-equipped vessel was that close. He tapped out a message giving their approximate position. After an hour, despite many sendings, there had been no response. While Jackson continued to send his wireless message, Walton turned to their carrier pigeons. The plane had two birds. He prepared the small strips of paper to be put into the little capsules attached to the birds' legs. Jackson, who was responsible for the birds, of course agreed they should be released, but pointed out that it was known the pigeons were affected by petrol fumes and that theirs had had a thorough dose. He examined the birds; they seemed OK, but would be sent whether or not affected. He released the message-laden birds, one after the other. The men willed the birds to fly home. The first bird circled once and landed back on the plane. The other flew off energetically enough, though west, not south-west to the Shetlands. After a while, the first bird could not be seen anywhere on the plane. No one knew if it had flown off or fallen into the sea.

With their chance of recovery looking slim, the three men debated using the port engine to taxi towards the nearest land, Norway, only about fifty miles due east, compared to the one hundred and fifty back to the Shetlands. Walton thought it an unlikely solution, but agreed to try it.

16

Returning To Port

One day from Wilhelmshaven. After all that'd happened, just one day's steaming and we'll be home, thought Eckhardt. He imagined everyone was thinking the same as him, but few spoke of it. For one thing, they were all at Battle Stations, the night run was almost over and the daylight would soon be upon them. One day from Wilhelmshaven. One way or another it would probably be one of the most memorable days of the whole, long voyage. He just hoped it would be an *uneventful* day.

The night, such as it was, had been full of tension. Battle Stations was called as soon as they turned onto a southerly course. They were told little, but all knew that Norway lay away to port and that they would soon be entering the North Sea. He wondered if he'd recognise it. After all those Atlantic sea miles, would the North Sea show a different, but familiar face? The weather continued with north winds, a bit stronger than those during the run towards Norway, and a cloudy sky. Mist and periodic rain reduced visibility.

With the change of course and, particularly as it got darker, Eckhardt realized that the instruction to watch for the seaplane could no longer be fulfilled. As the day had rolled on it soon reached everyone that first the plane was overdue and then that it must be out of fuel. Some half-joked, as with the Greenland incident, that the plane would be found, that a flare would signal its position. Eckhardt certainly wanted that outcome, not just for the airmen, but so the plane would be able to continue its role of searching the waters ahead, required more so than ever as they got ever nearer to home. It had been suggested that the plane may have had to make for Norway, especially as engine problems were rumoured. Eckhardt wondered if this was the end of their little aerial friend. He hoped the plane had indeed made it to Norway or, if not, would be found afloat by someone.

Look-outs were told to be especially alert as enemy convoys crossed between Norway and Scotland and that, after the Fleet's attacks on them, they probably now had powerful escorts. After having searched untold thousands of hectares and only finding one convoy, Eckhardt did not hold out any hopes of coming across another, well, not without the plane to help. He'd revisited that thought when a sharp-eyed look-out reported a sighting, something on the horizon.

At that time of year, the night at those high latitudes was not a pitch-black darkness. For a few hours it was dark, but the horizon could still be discerned. It was a very risky period. The sighting to the west was judged to be a ship's smoke. The ship itself was below the horizon. Much to Eckhardt's relief, the *Hindenburg* turned away east. Very soon the smoke could not be seen. Unlike their encounter with the American convoy, everyone knew they would be avoiding contacts on the run home. Fortunately, if the ship was part of a convoy, they did not chance upon the convoy's escort force, whatever that might be.

Eventually they had returned to the southerly course, keeping up a high speed, over 20 knots. Now, very early at this time of year, dawn was creeping on. It was still misty with occasional rain, but the increasing brightness started to illuminate everything, though only colouring the waves a very cold-looking grey. A hot drink was brought to everyone. Eckhardt kept watching the waters, as he enjoyed the liquid's warmth, but, thankfully, saw nothing. He was tired, as tired as he could remember, but kept alert, kept awake, feeling he had a part to play in this drama, which all knew was so near its end. Iron Cross-Schwarz was to his left, moving his binoculars slowly across the sea. Eckhardt hoped his colleague's sharp eyes would, for once, not prove to be better than his and only confirm there was nothing out there.

The coming daylight would soon leave them with no hiding place, thought Körner, but he knew with every sea mile, every hour of sailing towards Germany, that it would be much more difficult for the English to catch them. Soon they would be passed the turning point.

The night, the dark period itself being a very short affair, had been busy for everyone on the Bridge, reacting to sightings, imaginary and real. They never did see an actual enemy ship, but, perhaps unlike at any time in the mission so far, Körner did feel that there'd be real contact at some point. So, turning away from the reported funnel smoke was something of a welcome relief. There had been no confirmation that it was even a convoy; it might have been only a single ship. It was only a brief sighting, one difficult to confirm, but it was enough for Körner. While the sighting added to the level of tension, it served to give a tangible location to the enemy, one by which to aid his decisions on course changes.

With the ever-increasing light, naturally they could see more, but after an hour visibility was seldom more than seven or eight kilometres. The sky was largely cloudy, especially ahead of them. The wind was still from the north; there was occasional rain. Not for the first time, Körner was pleased with the prevailing weather situation. The short period of near-darkness had cloaked them, but, in a way, so did these daylight conditions. Even so, the reconnaissance capability of the seaplane came to mind. It had offered them advantages, whether in attack or retreat, but he still felt confident they could get home without it.

Schellenberg had put its loss down to recent engine trouble or, more probably, to the pilot's failure to locate the *Hindenburg* on the return leg. He had reckoned they'd been fortunate on that score before and that there was always the potential for the pilot to fail to locate the battle cruiser, especially on longer flights, as the last one had been. Schellenberg had also thrown in that in either event there was a chance that the pilot could have safely landed on the water, but offered nothing about what that meant for the two airmen's prospects. Körner considered they'd been lucky in Greenland and privately doubted if they could rely on such good fortune this time.

After a few hours, the sun had begun to burn back some of the mist, raising Körner's apprehension levels, though he said nothing about it. That was not the only thing on his mind: occasionally he did look over at the navigator, waiting for him to announce on the distance to the enemy bases.

Before long, Gärtner came forward. 'Captain, we have reached the point,' he said, a slight smile evident. 'We are over two hundred sea miles due east of Scapa Flow and two hundred and seventy from the Firth of Forth. If, as we discussed, we now turn to south-south-east ... actually, now one-five-two degrees ... then ships starting from either base could never catch us.'

There were matching smiles on all those within hearing distance. They had done it. The enemy had been caught napping. Everyone knew that nothing could be taken for granted, there was still a sea to cross, but they'd given themselves a good chance, perhaps a very good chance, of getting home.

'Thank you, *Herr* Gärtner,' said Körner. He tried to be professional about his response, but could not resist a smile. They could've set the 'point' some distance back, but he wanted to give them a greater safety margin. 'Make to Admiralty: SMS *Hindenburg* is returning to port. Request cover at Horns Reef Light ... and add our position and estimated time of arrival at Horns Reef. Course: one-five-two.'

♭

Framlington awoke. He saw it was still, annoyingly, about twenty minutes before he had to get up for his next watch. He tried to get back to sleep, but without success, then thought he would soon have to get up anyway. Nevertheless, he could spare a few minutes, so did not immediately leap out of his not-so-warm bed or even contemplate the operation they were on, but only thought of returning to Perth. The ship needed some work on her, scheduled for when they returned to Rosyth, so probably meant some leave might be in the offing. If so, but if the admiral didn't transfer to the *Glorious* or if another sweep wasn't required—alas, too many *ifs*, he feared—he would arrange a trip to Perth. It wasn't very far to the 'Fair City', as Perth was known, and he was sure his aunt would welcome him back. A month before, he'd been to see her, something he now regretted he hadn't done more often before. His widowed aunt, Lady Margaret, was his father's elder sister and he'd been under a bit of pressure from his parents to visit her ever since he was posted to Rosyth, hardly twenty miles away. They'd had little contact over the years, with her in Scotland and him a naval cadet. Even when he was with the Grand Fleet at Scapa Flow, there was no real opportunity to go and see her, except on one of the times when his ship went to Rosyth for a refit. On that occasion they'd met at some sad tea shop, but he'd made some lame, war-blaming excuse not to take up her invite to her home. Once based at Rosyth, he took up the offer. The visit had proved to be quite wonderful, though mainly because he'd met Jane. The War, Scapa Flow and his injury had all militated against meeting women and sexual encounters had become distant memories. Jane seemed to offer an opportunity.

He'd gone to Perth with Archie Wainright, a lieutenant he shared a very small cabin with on the *Courageous*. Archie was not aristocracy, but came from a well-off family and knew how to behave. They stayed a couple of nights with his aunt in her grand house outside Perth. His aunt had arranged a small tea party, inviting two well-bred girls from Perth to meet the young officers. Over tea and sandwiches, though later ending up with a glass of stronger stuff, he'd got on well with Jane, Archie with Penelope. Both girls were slim, elegant and good-looking, Jane the more so. A portable gramophone provided music for an impromptu bit of dancing—well, slow dancing for Framlington's leg. One of his abiding memories of the tea party was how Jane allowed him to hold her so tight when dancing, she must have felt him. He was very keen to resume where he'd left off. His thoughts of her were pressing on the bed clothes, but were deflected when he realised the ship was turning hard to port and then Action Stations sounded.

Getting to his station, Commander Cox spoke to him: 'We have the *Hindenburg*'s position. She's only ninety miles north of us!'

For a moment, Framlington was taken aback by the news, even though this was exactly why they were steaming across the North Sea. He said nothing, though realised his mouth had opened, catching flies. The commander showed him a signal. It was a position of the *Hindenburg*, based on the direction finding of a wireless signal she'd made. It was her position about an hour and a half ago. Not always, but it could take a few hours for such news to be relayed to the Fleet or ships at sea.

'We are the closest ships to her. We have no indication yet of what's in her signal, but, as it's the first she's made … well, the first picked up … it's likely she's announcing her presence in the North Sea and intended action, probably her route home. The sudden increase in German signals suggests as much. She's probably heading to Wilhelmshaven and we can expect they're putting forces together to escort her in. The admiral intends to upset their party!'

Cox briefed him further, adding to his own knowledge, the main element being that the First Cruiser Squadron, with the Second Battle Cruiser Squadron, some way astern of them, would steer to intercept the German. The First Battle Cruiser Squadron, now returning to the Firth after its own sweep, would put about—depending on its fuel situation. The Grand Fleet would also put to sea, but it would be some time before these other forces could get to their side of the North Sea. They also knew that another battle squadron was already at sea, providing escort to Scandinavian convoys and had now been directed towards them. Framlington absorbed the various details and the implications for his signals role. There would be many wireless and flag signals between the squadrons and, no doubt, a steady stream of messages to and from the Fleet and the Admiralty. Their speedy and effective execution was the commander's unspoken requirement.

Dealing with the signals, delivering them to the commander and the admiral and transmitting new ones, Framlington felt he had a good grasp of the likely state of affairs. The *Hindenburg* was back in the North Sea. Her course was as yet unknown, but had been projected as heading for the Horns Reef Light, the route the German fleet had used to escape from further action at Jutland. If she was on the suspected course, she would be brought to action, quite probably in the next few hours.

Things seemed to have gone as planned. Being a member of a flag-officer's staff, Framlington had sufficient information on the *Hindenburg*'s exploits over the past weeks and the thinking on her likely intentions. She'd successfully eluded the various searches of the waters round Newfoundland and Iceland, even Greenland, but it was always expected that she would seek to return to Germany through the North Sea and that would be the most likely place to bring her to action. All they had to do was find her! Increased air and sea patrols across the North Sea's northern entrance had been established, but, just in case she got by them, regular sweeps across the North Sea by the Fleet's big ships were instituted. Given the failure to intercept the *three* enemy sorties into those northern waters and, especially after the *Hindenburg*'s demoralising convoy attack, there was a steely determination throughout the Fleet for revenge and not to let this one get away. The sweeps were necessary because ships starting out from British ports would be hard pressed to cut off any fleeing German, as she would probably just have too much of a lead. Such sweeps imposed their own pressures on ships and men, but having ships at sea gave more chance of an interception.

However, to catch and sink a ship like the *Hindenburg* would require fast *and* powerful ships, which meant the burden of the sweeps falling on the Battle Cruiser Force. The First Battle Cruiser Squadron, with its 13.5in-armed 'Splendid Cats', as the Lion-class battle cruisers were called, and since supplemented with the 15in-gunned *Repulse* and *Renown*, seemed amply equipped for the task. The ships of the Second Battle Cruiser Squadron, comprising the navy's oldest battle cruisers, all 12in-gunned, were less powerful than their larger and younger sisters, but could still deliver a respectable punch. Oddly, to Framlington, they were assigned to Admiral Smitty's First Cruiser Squadron, though that added the light

214

battle cruisers' 15in guns to the force's firepower. The *Furious*, a curious sister-ship of the *Courageous* and *Glorious*, now fully converted to an aircraft carrier, was the focus of a third group undertaking the sweeps.

The *Courageous* and her consorts had left the Firth the previous evening, just after the *Furious* and her group were returning from a sweep. They were to steam across the North Sea, heading for the Naze, Norway's southernmost point. From there they would swing north or south, up the Norwegian coast or into the Skagerrak, before returning to the Firth.

While Framlington was as keen as any to see the *Hindenburg* stopped from getting back to Germany, he was quietly impressed by her achievements and sadly unimpressed by the navy's failure to put an end to her shenanigans before now. She had crossed the Atlantic, devastated a convoy and was now within a few hundred miles of getting back to Germany. Survivors from the convoy had also attested to what seemed to be her excellent gunnery. Clearly, she was an ably-run ship and probably a formidable opponent. Accepting the *Hindenburg*'s undoubted capabilities, Framlington nevertheless had no concerns about confronting her. He accepted that, individually, any of the force's big ships might find it a challenge to deal with the *Hindenburg*, but collectively they must surely defeat her. The *Courageous* and *Glorious* between them fielded eight 15in guns against the German's eight 12in. Add in the eight 12in mounted on each of the four battle cruisers of the Second Battle Cruiser Squadron and they had overwhelming firepower. There was also the better part of a score of destroyers and a squadron of light cruisers to throw into the mix. Given the force confronting the German ship, Framlington thought any battle would be *very* one-sided. Again, the only concern was finding her.

As he gleaned more from the commander, other officers and signals processed, the picture improved. The 'ninety miles north of us' was actually ninety-one nautical miles north-west at the time of the *Hindenburg*'s signal, assuming that was an accurate bit of direction-finding. Of course, in the time before the information was relayed to the *Courageous*, she could be thirty or forty miles further on and that might also be anywhere farther to the east or west. Therefore, at that point she might be closing on the Norwegian coast or on a heading taking her astern of the British ships. So, if he were honest, despite the sizeable force moving against her, there was still a chance that she could escape them.

The First Cruiser Squadron was now heading north-east, aiming to cross the enemy ship's likely course, now put at barely twenty or so miles away. When he went on deck, Framlington could just see, a few miles ahead of the two light battle cruisers, the Third Light Cruiser squadron, its four cruisers and attendant destroyers spread out in a wide, line-abreast formation. On both flanks of the *Courageous* and *Glorious* were a couple of destroyers. Three miles astern was the Second Battle Cruiser Squadron. The force's speed was now 21 knots and all ships were putting up variable clouds of funnel smoke, which were being blown to starboard by the north winds. Dark clouds were above, producing periodic curtains of rain. However, the rain, mist and funnel smoke all combined to reduce visibility. It wasn't his job to worry about such matters, but he began to wonder if the *Hindenburg* would continue to enjoy the luck which had undoubtedly been with her so far. He hoped she'd used up her quotient of good fortune.

卐

Luck was not something Körner set much store by. He had previously accepted that there were times in his life when it must have played its part, but he did not count on it in any real sense. There were many, many factors which turned out a good ship or influenced a battle, but trusting to luck was not one on his list. If a shell hit you, well, you were unlucky, but he had endeavoured to make sure his ship was sound and crew well trained and capable of dealing with the effects of that shell. On enemy gunfire, his preferred approach was to hit the enemy first, make him worry about shell hits, stop him shooting at your ship. Accurate gunnery had always been his objective.

After breaking wireless silence, Körner then put a halt to further signals, fearing any more wireless traffic would almost certainly strengthen the enemy's knowledge of the *Hindenburg*'s whereabouts. There was a regular flow of signals from the Admiralty, including some muted congratulations on their achievements. Most of the signals were about the support they could expect to help them get home: U-boats had been alerted, zeppelins were already out scouting and others would be dispatched and the Fleet would sortie to challenge any enemy ships which may seek to interfere. The previously agreed plan for the *Hindenburg*'s return had envisaged zeppelin and aircraft reconnaissance flights over the North Sea to alert Körner of any enemy ships, giving him the chance to avoid them. As yet they'd seen no aerial machines, but had picked up one zeppelin report about enemy ships off Scotland and another, albeit incomplete message, from a zeppelin about visibility limitations. Providing no real insights on concerns, these signals nevertheless suggested the reconnaissance arrangements were in place, which pleased Körner and gave him some small comfort that the *Hindenburg* was not totally alone on her high speed run in towards Wilhelmshaven.

The weather was proving to be typical North Sea, with limited visibility, sometimes quite good, other times very poor. There was a very occasional chink of blue sky, but it was mostly very cloudy, with some rain thrown in. The sea state was conducive to a high speed passage.

The run home was not proving to be a straightforward affair, but Körner never expected it would be. There had been three, separate sightings of periscopes. Whether real or not, each was taken seriously. The *Hindenburg*'s high speed would be no guarantee of avoiding torpedoes. Körner turned the ship away from the sightings; a safe move, perhaps, but inevitably delaying their journey home. He had relaxed the ship, standing down from full Battle Stations. There was no need to keep everyone keyed up unnecessarily. He was even tempted to lie down in his Sea Cabin, but had decided against it.

'Aircraft!'

Amidst the clamour of Battle Stations' bugles, drums and shouted calls, Körner looked up, scanning ahead. After a few seconds, he saw it, a small shape coming towards the ship. He confirmed it was a plane, but quickly noted it was a wheeled affair, not a seaplane. Against the lighter southern sky it appeared black, little more than a silhouette. It was rapidly approaching the ship's starboard bow. Was it one of ours, the expected scouts—unlikely, given the distance to Germany—or was it one of theirs, he said to himself. Was it possibly a Norwegian plane? 'Any idea what type it is?' he calmly asked Gärtner, standing nearby.

'I can't see, Sir. Until he gets closer or turns, we won't know if he's English or German, but, ...' he paused. 'Suggest we open fire, Sir!'

Körner thought no more on the matter, being always likely to support his senior officers' opinions. He rapidly reasoned it was unlikely to be a German plane and too bad if it was Norwegian—the pilot should know better—so, he agreed, it must be English. The order was given and in just a few seconds the starboard 8.8s were banging away at the speck in the sky. He was not, however, surprised to see the fire was ineffective; ineffective in that, despite the 8.8s' rapid rate of fire, it did not result in the plane's immediate destruction. Even so, he concluded that the multiple, dark bursts in the sky may well have altered the pilot's intentions, as the little plane turned quickly to its right and then continued round and flew directly away from the battle cruiser. The little black clouds pursued the tiny craft until it was lost in the mist.

Everyone on the Bridge kept watching the sky, binoculars tracking back and forth, but the plane failed to reappear.

'How did you know it was an enemy plane?' asked Körner.

'I wasn't sure,' replied Gärtner, 'but thought the round engine shape more common to them than us. I certainly wouldn't claim any great knowledge on the matter,' he smiled, 'but think there are few such round-engined biplanes being flown by our navy.'

'Well done, anyway,' offered Körner, as a sort of reward, genuinely surprised and impressed at his navigator's knowledge. 'We didn't appear to damage it, but our fire seems to have scared it off.' Before there was any thought or discussion with Kruse about the effectiveness of the ship's anti-aircraft gunnery, Körner considered why the plane was there in the first place. 'I suppose the real issue is what is such a small land plane doing in this part of the North Sea?'

'Yes, you are right, Captain. A small plane like that couldn't fly too far, ... certainly not from Scotland.' Gärtner paused, a revelation lighting up his face. 'It must have been launched from a ship *and* not too far away.'

'Yes, quite so,' replied Körner, remembering the various discussions he'd had with Schellenberg on the flying-off ramps carried by British ships. The plane raised various thoughts, not least that his hope of a clear run home now seemed less likely. 'We'd better work on the basis that there are enemy ships in the vicinity.'

⚑

The Sopwith Camel was flying well enough, with no obvious problems, but Second Lieutenant 'Jack' Pennywell was still concerned. He lifted his oil-smeared goggles and began to check the plane, looking for any damage to the fabric, struts or wires. As well as he could, he looked over the whole plane. On those parts he could see, he didn't see any evident damage and was relieved to conclude that everything really was OK. The anti-aircraft fire had been a bit of a shock. Most of the explosions were well away from him, but he felt a few buffet the plane. It was the first time he'd been shot at and was naturally concerned that it might have damaged the plane. He didn't want to end up in the drink.

He pushed forward and dropped down through the clouds. Under the cloud base it was misty, but, with the sea about four thousand feet below him, he had a good view of the way ahead. He kept to a southerly heading. He wanted to get back, had to get back. Although he had quite a few flying hours under his belt, this was his first real action. He'd taken off in earnest from a ship before, to attack a zeppelin, but it must have seen him and escaped by rising to a much higher altitude or, much to his chagrin, he'd just lost it in the mist and clouds. This mission was completely different and unexpected.

Pennywell had only been with the *Glorious* ten days. In size and guns, she was quite a different experience to his previous ship, the light cruiser *Galatea*. Both ships employed 'Ships Camels'—Sopwith's shipboard version of their successful single-seat biplane fighter—but the *Galatea*'s take-off platform was fixed, not a rotational affair like the *Glorious*' turret-top platforms.

He knew that the Squadron was shaping up to engage the German battle cruiser *Hindenburg*, which had destroyed an Atlantic convoy and was now homeward-bound. The crew was keyed up, ready for action. He was kitted up ready to fly, to attack zeppelins that might try to interfere or perhaps just to fly off to clear the gun turrets for action. When called to get his orders, he didn't realise he was in for a bit of a surprise.

'The *Hindenburg* is out there, but, in truth, she could be anywhere along a line stretching to the east or west of us. Your job is to find her!'

At that, Pennywell had looked with slightly raised eyebrows at the Lieutenant-Commander and then tentatively glanced at Alasdair Reid, the ship's other pilot. He'd wondered if Reid had the same thing on his mind: is this a job for the Camels?

The commander answered their unasked question. 'I know this … reconnaissance mission isn't what you're aboard for, but circumstances are such that we need you aloft to make sure the blighter doesn't slip by us.'

No more to be said. The need was obvious. The method may be risky, but what wasn't in this man's war? Primarily being single-seat fighters, the Camels had no wireless-telegraphy set, no way of sending a message other than by returning.

His launch from the fore-turret had been easy, textbook, he was airborne within a few feet. As he circled the ship, waiting for Reid to join him, he'd seen that the three groups of warships, though some distance apart, were on a north-east course, intending to cut off the *Hindenburg*'s expected line of advance. Each squadron would fly some of their planes: the *Glorious*' two planes would fly due north; four planes from the Second Battle Cruiser Squadron would search out the north-west quadrant; and a couple of the light cruisers' planes would cover the north-east all the way to the Norwegian coast. This effort would expand the search front by more than one hundred miles. The Battle Cruiser Squadron had some Ship Strutters, quite a recent addition. With their two-man crews and wireless and extra range, they were well up for reconnaissance work, so were an obvious choice. However, there were only two of them, so the Camels had to fill in the gaps.

All the Camels flew as pairs, seen as giving more chance of spotting something and keeping a watch on the enemy ship, if found. He and Reid had been told the *Hindenburg* could be close, but the flight would be an hour out, then back. Alas, after only ten minutes, Reid signalled that something was amiss with his plane and turned back, leaving Pennywell to continue alone. He flew on, the thick cloud, mist and rain not filling him with much confidence about his reconnaissance role, especially recalling his missed zeppelin. If he couldn't locate a 600-foot-long zeppelin, was there a chance he might miss a dreadnought?

Pennywell had expected a long and lonely flight, but it wasn't to be. Only ten minutes after Reid had left him, he'd reduced his altitude to clear some low clouds, when, out of the mist and slightly to starboard, he saw a ship—a big ship! She was only a few miles ahead, steaming almost straight towards him. He could not say immediately if it was the *Hindenburg*. He and Reid had been shown a page from *Jane's*, but there were no photographs, just plan and elevation line drawings. He tried to remember their salient features, as he took in the ship's appearance from his near-head-on position. She was obviously a big bastard. She appeared to have a couple of big-gun turrets up front—like most dreadnoughts—but he had been especially struck by her high, black-painted tripod mast and control top. He didn't recall that feature on the drawings. Despite such doubts, he'd figured she just had to be the *Hindenburg*, but thought he should get closer, to get confirmation of whether she was indeed the elusive enemy ship, and also to try to assess her course and speed. It would only take a couple of minutes to pass her. He reckoned she was steaming fast, to judge by her large, white bow wave and plentiful funnel smoke. Suddenly, flashes sparkled on her and a small black cloud, then several, began to appear ahead and to the left of him, each one making a small crump-like noise. One detonation was uncomfortably close. For a moment he was annoyed at his naivety about seeking to get closer, but didn't have to think twice about what to do next. The Camel was seen by many pilots as a difficult plane to fly, but he used its excellent agility to slip easily away to starboard. Another blast had rocked him, so he threw the plane around, until he was swallowed up by a low cloud.

If he'd had any doubt about the ship's identity, it had quickly been dispelled by the anti-aircraft fire. He could only conclude it was the *Hindenburg*.

His return flight was a mixture of relief and concern. Relief at not being shot down and having something very important to report; concern that his jinking around the sky may have altered his position relative to the British ships and that he might miss them. Given an expected two hour flight and the *Glorious*' north-east heading, he and Reid had been instructed to return on a south-by-east course to effect a rendezvous. However, he'd only been flying for a fraction of that time, so thought the ships would not be greatly advanced on their own course to intercept the *Hindenburg*'s estimated line of advance. He had no facility to carry out the necessary calculations, so simply made an educated guess that south-south-east would be adequate. However, as the minutes went by, he began to fear that he had indeed missed them and wondered if he should alter course. There were always cases of returning planes failing to make a rendezvous. Would he be one? He tried not to think on it, but concentrated on his flying, even readying the Very pistol, already loaded with a white flare, the pre-arranged signal that he had found the German ship. Alarmingly, he then had the disturbing thought that the ship might not actually be the *Hindenburg*, that it might have been a British ship, opening fire because of her uncertainty about his plane. He worried that he should have pressed on with the reconnaissance, done more to confirm the blasted ship's identity.

As he wrestled with this discomforting consideration, his heart leapt and he swore out loud, when he saw a ship's wake below him. He quickly turned and in less than ten seconds was flying above a Royal Navy destroyer; then on her starboard side, he saw a line of large warships. Familiar with their profiles, he knew immediately that they were the Second Battle Cruiser Squadron. Elated, he pressed on and within a few minutes was upon the First Cruiser Squadron. As he flew by the *Glorious* and then the *Courageous*, he excitedly fired his Very pistol.

౨

The enemy might well be in the vicinity, but where? Körner looked forward, his eyes travelling quickly across the misty southern horizon; ships could possibly emerge at any moment, at any point. He was pleased, concern reduced, when the Spotting Top reported no sightings. Despite having had her own planes, he reprimanded himself for not expecting to see an enemy plane. Anyway, however alarming, he had to use the opportunity it provided. He wanted to discuss it with Schellenberg, but he was at his Battle Station aft. 'What's your estimate of the enemy's position?' he threw unceremoniously at a clearly surprised Gärtner.

'Well,' started the navigator and, after a noticeable pause, continued, 'I did notice that the plane was flying north ... yes, north, ... when first sighted ... and when we last saw it, it was flying away ... south ... or thereabouts. That could suggest the plane's, ... er, mothership could be south of us. Of course,' he paused again, 'there's no guarantee of that. The plane's heading could have been due to other factors. It might have altered course towards the *Hindenburg* when the pilot first sighted us; and his course away, to the south, could have been due to the ship's gunfire.'

Körner thought for a few seconds about his navigator's assessment. He agreed that the plane's direction could only be taken as an indicator, but, based on that evidence, a southern location for the enemy seemed logical. His own reasoning, based on what he would do in the enemy's shoes, also suggested the enemy would be to the south, perhaps south-west. That thought left him with the prospect of running headlong into a strong enemy force. The Skagerrak memory of the horizon-filled-arc of English dreadnoughts belching fire at the approaching German Fleet suddenly came to mind. 'Yes, I agree.' Then, 'Change course,' he called, 'nor'-nor'-east!'

The ship came round to port and settled onto the new course. Körner kept the ship at Battle Stations, though summoned Schellenberg to the Bridge. He and Gärtner, joined shortly by Schellenberg, went into the Chart Room to continue the debate on the implications of the aerial interloper. Schellenberg agreed with the assessment that enemy ships could well be close at hand and also with Körner's decision to change course away from the likely threat. Amidst uncertainty about the plane's radius of action—estimated to be at least one hour—enemy vessels were placed on the chart as being not more than 100 sea miles to the south, though could be anywhere. No strong W/T signals had been intercepted and none that was thought to emanate from the plane. There'd also been no signals from the Fleet on enemy movements in the area. The Fleet was still reported to be putting out to shepherd them into Wilhelmshaven.

'I intend,' stated Körner, 'to keep on this course ... towards the Norwegian coast,' his fingers lightly traced a line towards Norway, which Gärtner had previously confirmed was at its closest about two hours steaming away, 'before altering course back towards the Skagerrak.'

Gärtner said nothing, though Schellenberg, that pensive look on his face, asked: 'How close will you take the ship to Norway, Sir? We might find our sea-room restricted.'

'I agree,' replied Körner. 'There are risks in moving towards the Norwegian coast, but if the enemy *is* south or south-west of us, I fear we cannot steer to west and hope to get round them.'

Schellenberg agreed, but Körner could see that was not the answer he sought. 'We'll keep well to seaward of the coast,' continued Körner. 'We'll certainly keep well away from their territorial waters,' though in saying that he knew he would be highly unlikely to venture close to the three-mile line, but, then again, he would go wherever seemed most likely to offer them the best advantage. At this stage of *Georg*, he was not worried about violating Norwegian neutrality, he just wanted to get the ship home. 'For now, we'll keep on this course for an hour or so. If there are no more enemy sightings, we'll turn for home.'

⚑

Even though it seemed the whole world was at war, Eckhardt's naval life had often been stress-free, at times even boring. Of course, he had been in periods of absolutely intense activity, most notably the Skagerrak battle. As he'd pondered before, *Georg* had been different for various reasons. Now, this leg of the mission, this final, home stretch, seemed to raise anxieties to a new level; at least that was how Eckhardt felt, he couldn't speak for others. With the plane encounter and a major course alteration away from Germany, he felt a certain degree of apprehension was being added. Eckhardt had half-expected as much; he'd tried not to think about the dangers ahead, but had feared that the fates would not allow them an easy passage home.

He'd watched the enemy plane neatly side-step the numerous dark puffs that chased it across the sky. He'd hoped with every crack of the eight-eights that the next aerial explosion would be its undoing, that it would be blown to bits or at least spiral into the sea. Frustratingly, no such luck. One or two had looked close, but the little mite seemed undamaged by them. The plane had been absent from sight for some time, though everyone continued to scan the sky. At last, the general conclusion by all in the Spotting Top was that it was truly gone, but where to was the new question on everyone's lips and were there any more of them flying around out there? A new responsibility for the look-outs. Eckhardt had never thought such a tiny enemy could pose such a threat to a giant ship like the *Hindenburg*. Everyone knew that planes could not damage a dreadnought, whether battleship or battle cruiser, but they might bring the enemy's big ships down onto them.

Listening to officers talking and, when he could, exchanging the odd word with sailors, he gleaned that the English may well have been waiting some way ahead of them and he silently agreed with the captain's decision to turn away. Especially at this stage, Eckhardt thought it was obviously best not to confront any enemy ships, whatever type or number they might be, but the question of what might be barring their way home or what was the best way to proceed was obviously on everyone's mind. If only they'd still had their own plane.

It was still morning, many hours till dark. He wondered, but doubted that they could steam around in circles waiting for the night to aid a break-through. With the last change in course they were obviously heading towards the Norwegian coast. They couldn't keep to that course; he expected another change, but would it be north or south? He glanced at the sky to the south; it had more cloud than overhead of them and looked to be raining, which further reduced visibility—all the better in his view.

⚐

Action was expected, quite probably in a matter of minutes. Battle ensigns, outsized affairs, adorned all the ships. Framlington had always wondered how he would face up to battle again after his experiences on the *Calliope*; now would be the test. He actually felt quite calm, with no evident feeling of fear, just what he imagined was a normal level of apprehension. Anyway, concentrating on his job gave him little time to bother about such issues.

When the first Camel returned so soon after its launch, the arrival of the other not that long afterwards was seen by many as another case of engine failure or the like. So, the white flare caught quite a few off guard, including him.

Nevertheless and frustratingly, it still took some time for the details to be passed to the flagship. The plane had to ditch near a destroyer, the pilot rescued, his report made and passed up the line. In his signals role, Framlington heard as early as anyone the news that the pilot had located the *Hindenburg*, reckoned to be only about twenty-five miles almost due north of the British ships. There was much discussion when it was determined that this confirmed the original estimate of the German's course to have been just about spot on and—damn it—even without the successful reconnaissance, the British ships would have run right into her. Well, no one knew that at the time; to use the planes had been judged as the right thing to do. However, all that debate was a bit academic, as they'd already reached the projected 'interception point' before the pilot's findings were known.

The ships continued beyond the intercept point. They were fully alert, closed up, though with guns still trained fore and aft, but ready to engage the expected enemy. After some thirty minutes, the whole force reversed course, the Second Battle Cruiser Squadron leading. There was still no sighting of the German battle cruiser. Tension levels began to subside, replaced with a degree of disappointment that they may have missed their chance to bring her to action. Framlington knew that there had already been some discussion that, in doing its job, had the plane unwittingly alerted the *Hindenburg* that ships were in the area? With no sign of the enemy ship, it seemed likely that, now forewarned, she had changed course. Commander Cox told Framlington that the admiral had said: 'Well, that's what I'd do!'

Signals were sent to all ships and the Admiralty and the Fleet that the intended interception had not occurred. During all this activity, the other search planes started to return from their reconnaissance flights, but there were no white flares. While the Camels were obliged to ditch because of their fuel situation, someone had the bright idea to get the Strutters, with their greater endurance, to continue the search. Signal lights were directed at them, telling them not to come in, but to keep aloft and await further instruction. While they circled, new courses were quickly calculated about where the *Hindenburg* could be. Framlington saw them fly off, northwards, diverging slightly from each other.

†

Standing on the *Nereus*' bridge, Pennywell also saw the two Strutters fly off to the north. He was not absolutely sure of what they were doing, but guessed they were again off to find the *Hindenburg*. With their extra endurance, he reckoned they might be able to search for another hour or so.

After firing his Very pistol signal, he'd selected one of the four destroyers in the First Cruiser Squadron's screen to pick him up and it proved to be the *Nereus*. The destroyer was on the port side of the *Courageous* and *Glorious* and he'd come in and ditched about two hundred yards ahead of her. His water landing, a nerve-wracking experience, thankfully went well. Such landings were, in effect, controlled crash landings, albeit at sea, and could be just as dangerous as crashing on terra firma, flipping over being an especially dangerous outcome to avoid. He'd managed a very slow, almost stalling, descent onto the water, with no major structural damage to the plane *or* himself. Initially, the plane's floatation bags seemed to work well, but when the nose and wings began to sink, he'd scrambled out onto the tail section. While he sat on the fuselage, clinging onto the tail, a boat from the *Nereus* was quickly alongside to rescue him. Normally the plane would have been winched aboard, to try and salvage some or all of it, but not on this occasion: he was told to get into the boat and the plane was abandoned, its engine and wings already largely underwater. Only his legs got wet in the whole ditching and rescue process.

Once he and the boat were on board, the destroyer took off smartly, chasing its two big ships. He'd declined the offer of dry clothes, until he'd spoken to the *Nereus*'s commanding officer. Wrapped in a blanket, he'd hurriedly declared to her young, but war-aged and weathered captain, Lieutenant-Commander Beaumont: 'I found her!'

After making his report, Beaumont had sent Pennywell below to get warmed up and into some dry clothes. Pennywell did go below, but was soon keen to return to the bridge. He'd ended up at the back of the bridge, tolerated, but unable to contribute in any way. Keeping to the back of the bridge, sporadic spray on his face, Pennywell had watched some other destroyers stationary, engaged in the rescue of some of the ditched Camel pilots. By the sight of the Strutters heading northwards, the orders coming into the *Nereus* and her men at Action Stations, with most attention focused to the north, as well as the activities of the ships around him, it was clear that the *Hindenburg* had been expected, but had disappointingly declined the invitation to join them and that they now had to

THE BATTLE CRUISER HINDENBURG

re-find her. He thought nothing of why she may have changed course, nothing about his possible role in all that. He'd done his job, carried out his assigned task.

Framlington watched the light cruisers react to the latest flag signal. It was soon evident that they were picking up speed and the distance between them and the flagship was slowly increasing. In ordering the new signals, Cox had revealed that the admiral was not completely sold on the air search and had decided to search with the ships as well, rather than hang around in one place waiting in hope that the Strutters would find anything. Even if they did relocate the *Hindenburg*, she may still be too far away to catch.

The signals also reversed the force's course again and sent the cruisers off towards the Norwegian coast, over a hundred miles away. The First Cruiser Squadron and Second Battle Cruiser Squadron would follow, though at a slightly slower speed. Cox said little about the thinking behind the new search plan, though Framlington had his own opinions. The *Hindenburg*'s options seemed predictable: steaming to the east, nearer to Norway, was most likely to him; if she broke west, there was a good chance that she must be trapped between their forces and the Fleet coming across the North Sea; continuing on her previous southerly course would seem to be least likely and must be picked up by the Strutters. On one aspect, he was surprised that the big ships were not to keep up with the light cruisers, as they would all have no difficulty in doing that. He said nothing to Commander Cox. Perhaps the admiral was extending the search line or still wanted to be able to head west.

After an hour, no signals had been received from the planes and, as the ships had moved further east, Framlington wondered if the pilots would be able to find them on their return. It was only a passing thought, there were many other signals to deal with. One W/T transmission from the *Offa*, one of the Third Light Cruiser Squadron's destroyers, was electrifying: *Enemy in sight*.

17

Death Of A Ship

Eckhardt was first to see the intruder.

At some 24 knots, he thought the *Hindenburg* was almost flying, easily ploughing her way through the sea. No doubt like everyone, he was pleased when the ship had turned south, well south-east, back towards home. They had come close to Norway, reportedly only about two hours steaming away, before turning to a course roughly parallel to the far-off shore.

Despite his earlier assessment of the weather situation, he was not surprised that the visibility had improved steadily as the day wore on. The north wind had been relentlessly pushing the clouds south, opening up the odd blue crack astern. Ahead and to the flanks it remained misty, hazy; visibility was variable, but seemed worse ahead than astern. His view for'ard was also inhibited by the ship's considerable funnel smoke that was being blown almost ahead of them, though, fortunately, not interfering much with the Spotting Top itself. He swung his binoculars across the starboard horizon, round to the starboard quarter. He abruptly stopped his lateral movement. While seeing an enemy ship had been an extremely rare occurrence during his whole war service, something was out there! He fairly bellowed: 'Ship! Bearing, green one-three-oh!'

Others soon confirmed his sighting. The enemy—it seemed highly unlikely it could be anyone else—was far off, ranged at about 14,000 metres, probably at the visibility limit. Keeping his binoculars on the ship, he doubted he would have seen her earlier in the morning, the visibility had just been so much less. Even now, this was something of an extreme sighting, given the weather conditions. Indeed, if the billowing funnel smoke had been blowing towards the enemy ship, he might not have seen her. When an officer quietly and unexpectedly said 'Well done', he felt especially good about himself; such small praise was a rare occurrence.

Eckhardt could see the distant ship was small, probably a torpedo-boat. He counted three-funnels; must be English, he reckoned. He reported that she was initially on a north-east heading, but had quickly changed her heading and now looked to be matching the *Hindenburg*'s course. With her change of course and the movement of the *Hindenburg*, her bearing had altered, now more astern, to green 150 degrees. To judge by her funnel smoke, she didn't seem to be steaming hard, but occasionally he saw white, which he took to be water cascading over her bow.

At that distance, she was no threat at all, far too far away to use her torpedoes. He wondered if the guns would soon dissuade her from closing on them. He noted the big aft turrets already swinging round to her direction, but, somewhat to his surprise, it was the ship's secondary armament which opened up.

Pennywell was still at the very back of the *Nereus'* small bridge. The destroyer's increased speed, with her bow digging more into the grey sea, often had water sweeping over the fo'c'sle and just as often coming up over the bridge. In his location, he was not fully protected by the bridge awning and at least some of the spray caught him. He wanted to step forward, to get under the awning, which stretched back from the bridge windows and covered about half the bridge, but was concerned that he would inhibit the work of the others on the bridge. Instead, he repositioned himself, seeking to put the thick and tall, column-like base of the for'ard searchlight, which stood in the centre of the bridge's u-shaped rear section, between him and the spray. His change of clothes, including a duffel coat and oilskins, some rum and a mug of kye had all contributed to ridding him of the chill of the flight and his partial immersion, though the warmth he'd gained from all those was now fast disappearing.

Commander Beaumont, a soft-spoken Scot, had warmly welcomed Pennywell to the ship's small bridge and been very keen to hear about his encounter with the *Hindenburg*. However, developments soon inhibited their dialogue, as the captain increasingly concentrated on the handling of his ship. Beaumont hadn't banished him from the bridge, but Pennywell thought it best to stay at the rear and keep out of everyone's way. After his report about finding the *Hindenburg* had been made, he really had no job, no function on this ship. He was a flyer, it was his only skill; anything else he knew about shipboard life really played second fiddle to it. Yes, he'd joined the navy, but early on opted for the air branch—the Royal Naval Air Service—and now, in circumstances beyond his control, found himself in the new Royal Air Force. So far, that had brought about no real change; the Navy still gave the orders.

From his more exposed and frequently damp position, Pennywell, now little more than an unplanned look-out, could see and hear much of what was going on around him and was able to gain an understanding of what was happening. One thing was certain: more than at any point in his short naval career, he now realised he could soon be in the thick of a big-gun naval battle. Funnily enough, such a prospect was not something he'd given much thought to, always seeing his war as one of aerial actions, like dogfighting or bombing. He'd only been in the navy for little over a year and had missed the Heligoland action at the back end of 1917, so had no real expectation of what lay ahead. If it had not been for his personal confrontation with the *Hindenburg*, his usual enthusiasm at the likelihood of battle would have displaced any concerns he might have of the coming encounter. However, those shell bursts that had chased him across the sky had had a sobering effect and with no job to occupy his mind, his thinking did stray onto what might await him. He'd seen and heard dreadnoughts practising their big guns before, but, of course, had never been on the receiving end. He could only guess, but knew it must dwarf the explosives the *Hindenburg* had flung at him. Nevertheless, even though that may well have been small-fry weaponry, it had been a heart-pounding experience.

After the expected meeting with the German ship did not occur, a sweep towards Norway had resulted in the 'enemy in sight' signal which energised everyone on the bridge. The sighting had led to an increase in speed and a change in course. He heard that this was an intercept course, not a rush to support the light cruisers.

The *Nereus*, stationed off the *Glorious*' port beam, was now powering along with the light battle cruisers and their other three escorting destroyers. Pennywell gazed in muted admiration at the *Glorious*, only about two hundred yards away. In comparison to the destroyer, she was massive. She towered over the *Nereus*, her control top easily twice as high as the destroyer's foremast. At high speed, she looked spectacular, moving quite easily through the water, and, while she had no great funnel smoke, her speed was evident by the foaming, white water at her bow and stern.

Looking back along the track of the *Glorious*' wake, the Second Battle Cruiser Squadron was not far behind. Their ships didn't seem to be directly astern, but off the *Nereus*' starboard quarter. He estimated they were at least three thousand yards away. He wasn't sure, but, compared to when he last looked at them, the distance between the two squadrons seemed to have increased. Unlikely, he thought, but then pondered whether they could match the 30 knots he'd heard Commander Beaumont call for. Surely the admiral would keep his force together. He wanted to quiz one of those on the bridge, but thought better of it. Anyway, by their funnel smoke, it seemed like the Battle Cruiser Squadron was at full speed.

He swung right round to check on the other ships of the force, the Third Light Cruiser Squadron. They were off the *Nereus*' port bow, but even further away than the Second Battle Cruiser Squadron. He reckoned they were five or six thousand yards away, perhaps more. They were a hazy sight, somewhat indistinct against the pale, grey background, but he was able to make out all four of the light cruisers, as well as some destroyers, all apparently in line ahead, on what seemed like a similar course to the *Nereus*. He searched the whole horizon on either side of them; no sign of the *Hindenburg*. Suddenly, his eyes were drawn back to the cruiser squadron, to what seemed like white water spouts—shell splashes—near the leading ship, one of the destroyers.

From the Bridge's aftmost, starboard corner, Körner watched the distant ship, waiting to gauge the effectiveness of the first 15cm salvo. It had been some minutes since she was seen before he gave the order to open fire. He had been discussing the appearance of the English ship with Schellenberg, when Kruse interrupted them, seeking approval to engage the target. This led to a short voice pipe exchange between Körner and Kruse on the target's range and reaffirming his preference not to use the main armament on such a ship. He and Kruse had previously debated the use of the 30.5cm guns, especially the targets that merited the use of the remaining, precious, main armament shells. Actual circumstances would determine use of the big guns, but Körner had detected no disapproval by Kruse of his view that if they yet met the enemy's heavy ships, every shell for them would be more useful than firing them at distant, smaller ships. With the enemy destroyer, Kruse did not challenge Körner, he confirmed the target's range, as Körner well knew, to be within the maximum range of the secondary armament (which had fortunately been increased after Skagerrak). Körner's decision: 'Open fire!'

With an enemy in sight, it was right to engage her. Even so, while Körner earnestly hoped Kruse would again demonstrate his gunnery skills, he feared the 15cm guns might not be successful, given the range and small target. Körner held his binoculars on the enemy destroyer, still partially below the horizon from his Bridge position. The 15cm gunfire sounded much less impressive than the big guns, but what it lacked in volume, it enthusiastically tried to make up for in rate of fire. Alas, as he thought likely, all the shells flung at the destroyer during the first minutes seemed to cause her no problems. There were numerous splashes in her direction, but he was unable to judge if they were straddling or hitting her.

Körner was disappointed to be discovered; he hoped he had out-foxed the enemy. His ploy, after the plane encounter, of turning away north-east, away from a possible confrontation with enemy ships, seemed right at the time, but did not mean the ships were no longer out there. He'd gone over the options with Schellenberg and Gärtner and had decided to turn south-east, rather than continue north or swing west. The south-east option would, of course, mean the more direct route to Germany and earlier support from the Fleet. Its possible downside was the proximity of Norway, but they had seventy kilometres of sea room to play with. As it had been well over an hour since the turn, he dared to think that they had outflanked any enemy force; so the sighting was a disappointment.

He still could see no effect of their gunfire on the lone destroyer. Schellenberg was at his shoulder. Slightly lowering his binoculars, Körner leaned a bit closer and shouted to be heard above their own gunfire, 'One destroyer. No real concern, … but clearly she's not alone. No destroyer would be out here sight-seeing on her own!'

'I agree, Sir. She'll almost certainly be one of several destroyers, possibly with the Grand Fleet, though perhaps with the Harwich force.'

'Quite so,' responded Körner. The cruiser-destroyer force out of Harwich could well be encountered, but the more northerly position suggested *Grand Fleet* to him. 'Well, whatever she's screening, it must be lurking in the mist … but why isn't it showing itself?'

Schellenberg said nothing for a second or so, then, 'Either it's not capable of taking fire from us, perhaps a cruiser, and just letting the destroyer do the shadowing. *Or* our speed is too great for it and it's unable to close the range.'

'Yes, you're right,' replied Körner, then added: 'We could increase speed,' while recalling the engineer's view that the ship may be limited to 25 knots, 'but we can't outrun a destroyer, … unless the weather deteriorates. Let's hope our guns dissuade her!'

As he lowered his binoculars, he could not fail to notice the muzzle of Bertha's right-hand gun only a few metres away. Despite not firing, they were still trained on the enemy. To bear on the enemy, the forward turrets were pointing quite a way aft, in fact they looked to be at maximum aft bearing, allowing him a perilously close and unwanted view of this gun's rifling. Neither man said anything about it, but they both well knew that the blast from the guns was incredible and, at this proximity, dangerous, at the very least able to dislodge caps, if not heads. The two men moved away.

⚑

A shout! Another ship! Eckhardt hardly had to move his binoculars. To the right of the first ship another appeared, of similar appearance. This addition was to be expected. It only confirmed what was being discussed: there must be more than one enemy ship, probably several more.

Eckhardt kept his glasses as steady as possible, hoping it would help reveal more about this new ship. He quickly decided it *was* of the same type—a three-funnel torpedo-boat, or as others were labelling it, a *destroyer*. He thought it looked enough alike to be of the same class, which would be logical, given normal practice to make up flotillas from the same class of vessel.

Now there was another target, he wondered if the guns would resume their firing. After only ten minutes or so, the 15cm guns had fallen silent, no longer hurling shells at the first ship. There had been no indications of any hits. From what he could see, all that had been achieved was to make the destroyer take evasive action, snaking its course to make things difficult for the *Hindenburg*'s gunners. Well, whatever, the little opponent had seemingly managed to dodge the scores of shells sent at her. At times, Eckhardt had lost sight of her when shell splashes blocked his view, but she always emerged, outwardly undamaged. Was it her luck or our bad shooting, he pondered. When the guns had stopped firing, he'd heard officers behind him having a short chat on the difficulties of such long-range shooting and that the target was beyond the guns' 'effective range'. Was that any reason to stop firing, he would have put to them, if he was brave enough to break in on their discussion.

Anyway, the guns did not renew their firing. Eckhardt did not appreciate the subtleties of *effective range*. He just continued watching the waters on the *Hindenburg*'s starboard quarter. He relentlessly covered his whole allotted sector, moving his binoculars to and fro in a measured and controlled manner, watching for anything, be it on or below the surface, though, after the day's events, not forgetting threats from the sky. Nevertheless, his eyes were easily drawn back to the two enemy destroyers and the misty horizon just beyond them. If there was anything else out there, he thought it would appear behind those two.

The *Hindenburg* continued on her course, with the two English destroyers continuing to follow. Eckhardt knew they could close, they had the speed, perhaps as much as 35 knots, but they kept their distance, just shadowing the big ship. It was beyond doubt that they must be part of some larger force.

It was only four, perhaps five, minutes after the sighting of the second destroyer that another ship emerged from the misty horizon. Eckhardt shouted out the new sighting. With others' binoculars focusing on the enemy, his shout was one of several calls. He didn't care if he was first to make the sighting, his eyes were on this new ship. Another destroyer? No, something larger.

A voice called out: 'Cruiser!' Another added, 'Liverpool-class!' Eckhardt silently agreed it was a cruiser, being much larger than the destroyers. He could see it had four-funnels. He knew from his studies of *Weyer's* that the English had many four-funnel cruisers, both armoured and protected. However, he straight away dismissed the thought that it was an armoured cruiser, as it didn't seem to have the bulk of such ships, nor the usual tall and generally upright funnels, but most especially because he knew the English armoured cruisers couldn't churn out the 24 knots the *Hindenburg* was now doing. He had his doubts that the ship was a Liverpool-class protected cruiser, but at 14,000 metres accepted that the differences between similar classes could be difficult to discern. He certainly didn't feel he had the evidence to start challenging the caller's opinion. One thing was certain: like the destroyers, the cruiser also posed no great threat to them. Nevertheless, he wondered if she would be a big enough target to tempt the main armament.

᚛

Körner had expected more ships to appear, but was relieved that the new arrivals did yet not include any dreadnoughts. Surely they would make their entrance sooner or later. He hoped *later*, though also hoped *never*.

He had called a halt to the firing at the first destroyer, but Kruse again sought permission to open fire when the cruiser appeared. After the lack of results with the 15cm against the destroyer, Körner was sceptical about their likely effectiveness against the new target. He accepted he would have readily agreed to use the main armament, if not for the shell situation, so there was no reason to hold back with the 15cm. Would the cruiser open fire, he thought, she probably has 6in guns and has the range. If she did open fire, he'd have no option but to engage her. Schellenberg said nothing, though his look suggested 'open fire!'

Körner returned to Kruse, though again sanctioning only the 15cm, gave the order to open fire.

The six starboard 15cm guns—the forward gun would not bear—renewed their fire. Soon, shell spouts were visible around the enemy ships. Alas, as before, while shell spouts reared up near the enemy cruiser, no hits were reported. There was one effect: the destroyers began to lay smokescreens, largely obscuring the cruiser. After fifteen minutes, Körner gave the order to cease fire.

During this time, like the destroyers, the cruiser gave no indication that she was intent on closing the range. Why should she, thought Körner. It would be her end to do so and, no doubt, she was content just to do her job: keep an eye on the *Hindenburg*, wirelessing her position, course and speed to other, as yet unseen, ships. Schönert had confirmed that there was a fair bit of W/T traffic, though could not be more specific. So, as the enemy now knew exactly where they were, Körner sent signals to the Fleet, reporting the enemy ships and giving data on position and progress towards the Horns Reef Light. He also sought information on support from the Fleet. Precious little came back, though the Fleet was reportedly 'out'. There were no Fleet messages suggesting or ordering him to change course, so this only added to his intention to keep on for Horns Reef; to him, there lay salvation.

'Captain, I'm still curious about the cruiser's late entrance,' observed Schellenberg, 'and, indeed, why no more ships are showing up. Of course, she could just be the destroyers' flotilla leader ... or, if not, she may be the lead ship of a cruiser squadron, in which case there must be others behind her. Whatever, looking at her smoke and the time she's taken to come on the scene, I can only think she is just about at maximum speed. I suspect, especially if it is a *Liverpool*, she can probably not do much better than twenty-five or six knots. You mentioned before that we could increase speed. May I suggest that that would now be an appropriate step?'

'Well, yes, we could,' replied Körner, 'though, as you know, the Engineer has suggested we may not be able to do more than twenty-five knots, ... and, as we discussed, even if we do, we won't rid ourselves of the destroyers. Whoever's out there would still have their wireless reports to guide them.'

'Well, on the wireless reports, we could attempt to block their signals,' suggested Schellenberg. 'On the ship's speed, I would like to test the Engineer's hypothesis. We'll at least know what we're capable of. Admittedly, a few extra knots possibly won't allow us to escape any interception farther along the course we're on, but increasing speed will not only put pressure on the cruiser, but may well put more distance between us and any chasing warships.'

232

Körner said nothing, though gave a slight nod.

'Whether their plan,' continued the first officer, 'is one of interception or just to try and catch us, if we can throw off our pursuers,' his head turning momentarily towards the three enemy ships on the misty horizon, 'with any luck, we'll yet have an opportunity to avoid contact with any big ships.'

Körner acknowledged the possibility, but his focus was on getting home, meeting the Fleet. Any deviation from their present course would only delay that desire. He was gambling that he had the march on the English. Nevertheless, throwing off the ships astern was a prudent move. 'Yes, you're right,' he heard himself saying again. 'Increase speed, twenty-six knots.'

Word of the speed increase fairly quickly reached Eckhardt. He didn't think of the stokers' plight, but did think a couple of extra knots wouldn't make much difference, though believed it was always good to be at full speed whenever the enemy was around.

The minutes passed; five, ten, twenty, with no obvious change. The enemy ships maintained their position, though he reported the cruiser as still making considerable smoke. If the expectation of putting more distance between them and the enemy ships was the intention, Eckhardt didn't think it was working, so far. One of his fellow look-outs quietly told him of what he'd heard some officers discussing: the captain was waiting for the visibility to reduce, then, accompanied by broadsides to distract the enemy ships, he'd quickly turn the *Hindenburg* away. Before the enemy ships knew what had happened, 'we'd be out of sight and they wouldn't have noted the change of course.'

Eckhardt thought it seemed a feasible plan of action, though he wondered whether any plan should rely on mist. Anyway, no specific orders had come to report such mist conditions or if the enemy ships were lost from view. Of course, he'd report such matters without any orders. Orders or not, he monitored the visibility situation closely, but it never altered, they were always there. In fact, he personally reckoned the visibility had increased since they first saw the first English ship. Astern there was still the odd blue crack to be seen and he surmised, as day wore on, the effects of sun and wind might well improve visibility, perhaps markedly. He began to think they would never throw off their pursuers.

It was almost an hour since they had seen that first enemy destroyer. He was scouring the horizon, but gave the little enemy flotilla its fair share of attention, ready to sing out any apparent change in their position, course or the visibility, though there was little to report. It seemed odd to be running from such a small force, something they could probably easily swat aside, but he knew they almost certainly signified other enemy vessels nearby and, more importantly, it was no time to get caught up in a battle, with Germany closer all the time.

As his binoculars fell yet again on the three ships, the clearer, sharper image of them confirmed to him that the visibility had indeed improved. He was going to report the situation, when another ship, astern of the three, came into sight. He called out immediately: 'Four ships, bearing green one-five-five!' A second later, he called: 'Five ships, ... er, seven, ... ten ships, bearing green one-five-five!'

His sighting generated much interest, though no officer praised him on this occasion. The ten ships, now described as a cruiser squadron, were soon assessed as four cruisers and six destroyers. The range finder confirmed that the visibility had indeed improved, with the aftmost ship at almost 15,000 metres. For the most part, what was probably the whole enemy squadron was visible, though occasionally the mist faded out the rearmost ships.

The cruiser squadron attracted much attention, especially as it confirmed what they'd expected to be out there. While the officers were debating the implications, passing messages to the Bridge, Eckhardt, feeling good about his 'morning's work', kept to his look-out duties. Sweeping his binoculars from aft, he had only just gone a bit for'ard of the enemy squadron, when he saw something else in the mist, a faint, but all too recognisable and familiar shape. It was something he definitely didn't want to see: it looked like the Spotting Top of a dreadnought. For a fraction of a second he realised that no one else was declaring the sighting. Were they asleep? He shouted, louder than any of his previous calls: 'Ship! Bearing green one-five-oh!'

⚑

Körner had returned to the covered section of the Bridge and once again was discussing their situation, especially in light of the enemy cruiser squadron, with Schellenberg and Gärtner. The dreadnought sighting report quickly reached them. Anticipating action, Schellenberg went to his station aft; Körner went to the starboard side of the Bridge and brought his binoculars onto the new challenger. Like the enemy ships astern, she was at the limits of visibility, now nearer 15,000 metres. She was still somewhat in the mist, though clear enough. From the sighting report, she was obviously closing on the *Hindenburg*, a gradual approach, but still almost head on. His immediate impression of her was that she was definitely a dreadnought. He could see she had a high and large Spotting Top, common in English dreadnoughts. Aft of the Spotting Top, there appeared to be one, big, single funnel, from which smoke was pouring out, emphasising her high speed. At this distance, from his Bridge height, he was unable to make out her gun turrets or any other lower details. Annoyingly, he wasn't sure of the class, but, with her single funnel, thought her to be a Royal Sovereign-class battleship. He sought confirmation, calling out: 'What ship is that?' If he was correct, then she was amongst the most powerful English dreadnoughts, armed with eight 15in guns, but, he recalled, of no great speed. Lowering his binoculars for a second, he saw that Kruse already had the guns onto this new target. He was just about to order open fire, when he saw a flash from the distant enemy. He felt some anger at his failure to get in the first shot and quickly shouted, 'Open fire!' Almost immediately there was a tremendous roar from the *Hindenburg*'s main armament, the blast wave hitting his face.

The *Hindenburg* was doing nearly 26 knots. This was no time to debate the engineer's concerns about limitations on speed. Faced with this new and altogether different threat, he needed all she could do. He shouted, 'Utmost speed!' Then, almost as loud, 'So, what ship is that?' he asked again, a trace of annoyance in his voice.

'Sorry, Sir,' shouted a gunnery *leutnant* stepping closer to his back. 'Not absolutely clear at this stage, but it could be a Courageous-class battle cruiser.'

Körner raised an eyebrow at this. He was familiar with the name—he quickly remembered that he could have come to blows with two of the class last November—but, for once, he was unsure of the type's full details, failing to recall the ship's profile in *Weyer's*, though recollecting they too had 15in guns. He half-turned to the *leutnant*, but before either he or the young officer could speak again on the matter, the enemy's first shells arrived. One, then another, struck the sea, but thankfully quite some way off the *Hindenburg*'s starboard quarter, throwing up huge, white splashes. They were well off target and had quite a spread, but clearly displayed they came from large-calibre weapons.

He was prepared to tolerate the presence of the smaller ships chasing them, but he had no wish to trade punches with even a single dreadnought. At this stage in the mission, getting home safely was all he wanted. Even if he could damage or sink this enemy ship, she might still land a telling blow, one which might threaten that safe return. Furthermore, it also seemed unlikely such a ship would be operating alone; he reckoned there must be others in the mist. Schellenberg's opinion, given only a short while before, that the enemy might seek to intercept them somewhere along the course they were on, had proved right. His plan to break away from the shadowers had been frustrated; the hoped-for conditions of worsening visibility had not come to pass.

He had also hoped to meet the Fleet and be escorted safely into Wilhelmshaven before any action came about, but now that was just wishful thinking. He should have been better prepared for this possibility. He didn't have time to berate himself further; more shell splashes appeared astern of the *Hindenburg*. An officer relayed information to him: 'Another battleship, astern of the first! Destroyers off their starboard bow!'

Körner swept his binoculars to left and right of the enemy ship, endeavouring to take in this new information. He saw masts, another ship; to be expected, he thought. Temporarily lowering his binoculars, he half-turned his head to the young gunnery officer. 'Remind me again of the Courageous-class.'

The *leutnant* stepped closer, referring to a small book in his hand. Körner knew it was *Weyer's*, though turned back to the enemy, again looking through his binoculars. Over the roar of the big guns, the *leutnant* loudly read out: 'The class is shown as approximately thirty to thirty-five thousand tons, … approximately thirty-five knots, … guns: probably only four thirty-eight-point-one.'

Yes, mouthed Körner silently, the officer's words refreshing his memory. He did not dwell on the incredible size and speed of the ships, only their *four* 15in guns. Seeing splashes from the *Hindenburg* in the direction of the enemy ship, he lowered his binoculars for a few moments, but continued to look at the enemy. Enemy shells continued to strike the water, still some way off. The *Hindenburg* again replied, with gun smoke temporarily obscuring his view of the enemy. His mind was considering all the possibilities, weighing up all the options, especially in light of the new sightings and data about the *Courageous* and her sisters. The enemy's course offered a desirable opportunity. If only he was leading a division of dreadnoughts, he would immediately turn to starboard, sail across their on-coming course, cross their 'T', and subject them to his broadsides, while they could only reply with *two* big guns. It was tempting, but not with his lone ship. He might well score some blows, but the enemy would undoubtedly turn to parallel his course and, with the two sides closer, send in destroyers. He had to keep his distance. The safety of the ship and her return to Germany were overriding considerations. For a few more seconds he stood looking at the enemy ships, then announced: 'Come to course east-south-east!'

꒐

The course change was two points, south-east to east-south-east, putting the enemy almost directly astern. Eckhardt didn't question the possible rationale behind this manoeuvre, but accepted it kept the enemy at bay. Even if they were faster than the *Hindenburg*, he thought it would take them some time to overhaul her. Naturally, this change of course did restrict the *Hindenburg*'s fire to her two rear turrets.

Eckhardt could see the two main enemy ships, reported to be battle cruisers, were now indeed almost directly astern. Slightly to port were the cruisers and destroyers which had tracked the *Hindenburg* for over an hour and were most probably responsible for calling in their big ships. He could see the destroyers had increased speed and were pushing ahead of the line of cruisers. Just to starboard of the enemy battle cruisers, he could see more destroyers—four, he counted. The destroyers would endeavour to get into torpedo range, he thought. Well, even if they were 10 knots faster, they would still have their work cut out and could expect to get a hot reception from the *Hindenburg*'s 15cm guns.

For now, the main issue was the enemy battle cruisers' big guns, said to be 38cm. He knew these were the biggest guns in the English fleet, though he did not contemplate what damage their size might do only whether any hits would interfere with their escape.

He considered the enemy's gunfire poor, no great spectacle; their shell splashes were few, often just one at a time. He reckoned they must be firing very deliberately to get the range. Also, with the two battle cruisers in line and, obliged to chase, he wondered if the rear ship could even get a clear view of the *Hindenburg*. As with the convoy battle, he could actually see the enemy shells in flight, as they came closer and flew in towards the ship. The shells—just black shapes—coming straight at them often appeared to be on a collision course, looking for all the world as if they must strike the ship, but then would quickly fall away and splash astern or, with a rumbling sound, go right over. Most were well off target—thank God!

In comparison, the *Hindenburg*'s gunfire seemed excellent, almost a training shoot. Within five minutes, shells were splashing all round the leading battle cruiser, clearly straddling her, though he couldn't see any indications of hits.

Watching from the bridge of the *Nereus*, Pennywell was rather alarmed when shells began to fall about the *Courageous*. It was all new to him. The first splashes he'd seen had landed some distance ahead of her, but he watched with some unease as each set of new splashes showed an almost inexorable march across the sea towards her and it was hardly any time at all before she was steaming through the sky-high, mostly white, eruptions. Indeed, when the shell splashes first surrounded her, the sight almost made him call out, but he managed to hold his tongue. Very soon, in between the enemy's shell splashes, he realised that the *Courageous* had been hit. Smoke, with a lick of fire, could be seen amidships, aft of her big funnel. The accuracy of the German's gunnery was unnerving.

Before any shooting had started, the *Nereus* had been ordered, along with the other destroyers, to the battle cruisers' starboard side. He didn't ask, but imagined it was to put them on the disengaged side and to get out of the way of the big ships' guns, but also perhaps to be ready to deliver a torpedo attack. With the *Nereus* at the rear of the line, the four destroyers stormed ahead, 34 knots he gleaned, and slowly, but clearly, overtaking the swift battle cruisers, accompanied by more and more white water crashing over the destroyer. He ventured a quick look aft. The Second Battle Cruiser Squadron was far away. If they couldn't see the enemy, then he doubted they could play any part. It would be up to the First Cruiser Squadron to deal with the enemy warship.

When the sighting cry had gone up; he'd strained to see the enemy. Through the mist and increased spray and pitching, he'd seen her, a dark and distant, menacing shape. The *Courageous*' guns let fly, drawing his attention back to the flagship, hardly two hundred and fifty yards away. Her forward turret settled into a regular rhythm, at first firing a few single shots, then salvoes. He saw no fire from her aft turret, though it was evidently trained well round to port. He'd looked at the *Glorious*; he reckoned she was manoeuvring, moving to port of the *Courageous*, no doubt to unmask her guns. He turned back to the enemy, hoping to see the *Courageous*' shells strike home. All he'd seen were bright flashes, not hits—the *Hindenburg* had responded in kind.

⚑

Framlington seemed to have spent most of the last hour rushing to and from the compass platform, where the admiral was directing operations, ensuring the admiral's signals, be they flag, signal projector or W/T, were correctly actioned and also processing messages from other ships and the Admiralty. Like everyone else, he went about his job efficiently, though still mindful about the upcoming situation. Earlier he'd overheard Admiral 'Smitty' and his flag-captain, Nicholls, discussing the interception and likely action. He had wondered, but thought it unlikely, if they'd debate the fact that the *Courageous* and *Glorious* would be the only big guns on the scene, the other battle cruisers being unable to keep up with the faster pair, or of the pair's thin armour in a clash with other big-gun ships. Since he'd joined the ship, the armour topic had been touched on by some officers, but, given her opponents were more likely to be the enemy's light forces, it was not viewed as a concern. Some joked that they were just too fast to be hit and the only big guns they had to fear were their own—a reference to the fact that the blast from their big guns could damage the ship's decks, as had happened in the Heligoland action.

He had just returned to the compass platform, delivering an Admiralty signal to Commander Cox, when the enemy was sighted. Through his telescope he could only see a dark, but obviously dreadnought shape. The first blast from the *Courageous*' fore turret caught him somewhat unawares, he didn't hear the 'open fire'. He wasn't allowed any time to take in the battle. Signals of *enemy in sight* and *am engaging enemy* were sent. Hardly had that been done when he saw large shell splashes ahead of the ship. The *Courageous* advanced towards them, or, he thought, they seemed to be coming towards the ship. Within a very few minutes, through the regular gun smoke rolling back over the superstructure, a few splashes rose up not far off the ship's starboard bow. Suddenly, some were on both sides of the ship and he felt a tremendous shudder; the whole ship seemed to shake. He steadied himself and glanced aft. Smoke was rising from a hit. Reports came in about the hit, but whatever they said, he didn't hear any details, as more shells rained down on the ship. Some hit the sea, but others may have hit the ship.

In the next few seconds, everything seemed to happen both quickly and slowly. He was aware of a curious rushing, background noise, but before he could take that in, he felt himself being pushed over to one side and crashed into something, though was aware of a large object flying past him. Something made him look up; the tripod mast, whose legs came up through the platform, seemed like it was leaning at an odd angle. Then he saw that the whole front of the ship, bows, guns, everything seemed to be rising up. He couldn't keep his balance, he fell and tumbled over to the port side of the platform, where he saw the sea rising up faster and faster. He was quickly swallowed by the cold water as it flowed onto the platform and very soon he was underwater, arms flailing, trying to swim upwards. Relief, he was obviously getting closer to the surface, as it was getting lighter above, but he was absolutely desperate to take a breath. Something hit his leg, causing pain and fear as he felt himself being dragged down. Frantic, he reached down, feeling something wrapped around his foot. He struggled to free himself, his shoe came off, but he was still trapped; then, unexpectedly, he was free and rising, but the water was dark, he had obviously been drawn much deeper. His lungs were bursting. He could hold out no longer, he felt water enter his mouth, then into his throat, but it seemed to close shut.

The destruction of the *Courageous* was hard to take in. When it happened, the *Nereus* was abreast of her forward turret and Pennywell was looking directly at her. She had just been straddled again, with shell splashes on either flank, but everything seemed fine. Then, hardly a second or two later, as the splashes began to collapse, the aft end of the ship erupted. To a great roar, smoke, flame and debris ballooned out and up from the ship, expanding faster and faster, threatening, in his opinion, to reach across the gap between the two ships. He instinctively brought an arm up across his head. When he next looked, debris of all sizes was falling into the sea, but the sight he would never forget was of the battle cruiser torn asunder. Covered by an enormous, rising and expanding cloud of black and brown explosions, he saw her bows raised up, the stem clearly free of the water. The long fo'c'sle and tripod mast then fell away to port, with her red-coated hull showing as she twisted onto her beam ends. Amidst the smoke, he could see the up-turned, wet hull lingering on the surface for a few moments, before quite rapidly sinking completely out of sight. He would have doubted anyone's description, if he had not seen it for himself. It was all over so quickly: in only a few minutes a very large warship, charging into battle, her battle ensigns flying, her big guns firing, had been utterly destroyed. Seeking some sort of solace, he looked at the others on the bridge. Their faces showed they too were in disbelief.

The captain said something to one and they all seemed to snap out of it and got on with their jobs. At 34 knots, very quickly the sky-high pall of smoke was left behind, as the *Nereus* and her sisters chased after the *Hindenburg*. Still drawn to the scene, Pennywell saw the *Glorious*, emerging from behind the smoke, steaming to port of her sister-ship's last position, her forward turret firing at the culprit. His thoughts went to the *Courageous'* crew: who would rescue the survivors? He was aware of the battle cruiser losses the navy had sustained at Jutland. He recalled there hadn't been many survivors when those ships blew up.

As the *Glorious* dashed on, forward turret firing again, he saw a big splash rise up, perhaps only a couple of hundred yards off her port bow. A few seconds later, there was another, then another. The Germans had rapidly turned their attention from the *Courageous* to the *Glorious*. His mind raced: would there be a terrible repeat of what he'd just witnessed?

⚐

The sight of the explosion pleased Körner—one less opponent—but he did not join in the cheer that erupted from the *Hindenburg*'s Bridge. To him, the death of a ship, any ship, was a sad event. With that tremendous explosion, he realised a thousand men had just met their Maker. The men on the Bridge probably also realised that, but, given the situation, he could understand their elation. He knew word of the success would be sweeping into all corners of the ship. If any men were apprehensive, even fearful about the many ships that were trying to sink them, he expected their morale and their courage and their belief in their ship must have been uplifted by what had just been achieved. The battle was not over, but they would have reforged their mettle and be even more ready to deal with all comers.

Körner would have liked to congratulate Kruse, but did not want to distract him for even a minute. He had a job to do. His expert shooting had, at a stroke, reduced by half the big guns the enemy had at his disposal. Could he do the same again?

The *Hindenburg*'s aft turrets let fly, once more. As the guns' smoke blew away to starboard, Körner looked for the second English battle cruiser. He soon located her. He saw shell splashes strike near her, as far as he could judge. He lowered his binoculars for a second, in time to see two splashes from the enemy's guns rise up abeam. They were closer than their compatriot's shooting had been, but they didn't appear to be as close to their target as his ship's.

For ten or twelve minutes, the contest between the two great ships continued. The enemy's one or two shell splashes marked her efforts, coming ever closer, though without result, whereas the *Hindenburg*'s aft turrets appeared to be well on target, straddling and, hopefully, hitting. Körner was tempted to turn the ship and bring his whole broadside into play, but, as before, he was fearful of the reduced range that would result and the threat posed by the destroyers.

Notwithstanding any such tactical considerations, the enemy destroyers were a growing threat. They were now on both flanks and closing, their range now reported as twelve or thirteen thousand metres. Körner gave the order for the secondary batteries to engage them. The enemy destroyers were obviously steaming hard to get into torpedo range; it was right to deal with them. At that range, he expected the guns to fare much better than before, when they were shooting at almost maximum range. He was right. His binoculars showed the leading destroyer was being deluged with white splashes.

Word came down of possible hits on the second enemy battle cruiser. Excellent; he gave more unspoken praise to Kruse. Körner could see little from the Bridge, other than that their shells appeared regularly to be on target, with splashes surrounding the enemy ship.

Within the next five or six minutes, reports came down of more hits on the enemy's ships. He could see that the leading destroyer was being overtaken by the rest of her flotilla; she must have been hit, seriously reducing her speed. The other three destroyers were taken under fire. Reports came to him of hits on the other, port-side enemy destroyers. Such shooting was good, very good, but what of the main threat, the battle cruiser? The aft guns had slowed their rate of fire, but why? For a second, he feared they were out of ammunition, but quickly discounted that; they had not been firing long enough. He swept the horizon, but could see no sight of the battle cruiser. In response to his enquiry, came: 'Sir, target reported to be no longer visible!'

In another minute, with more reports, it was clear that the enemy battle cruiser was indeed no longer to be seen. The most likely reason being that she too had been hit. Perhaps she hadn't blown up like her sister-ship, no-one had reported that, but she may well have suffered damage that had reduced her speed, allowing the *Hindenburg* to pull away from her and putting her beyond the visibility limits. The lack of large splashes in their vicinity also suggested the enemy ship could not see them, could no longer direct her 15in guns at them and had been forced to cease fire.

They would never catch us now, was Körner's first thought.

18

Wilhelmshaven

When Körner's 'returning to port' signal was reported to Hipper and Bünzlin, they were on the *Niobe* in Wilhelmshaven. It generated wide smiles, with Hipper adding a simple 'Splendid', but any celebration was quickly muted, as they both knew the *Hindenburg*'s long journey was still some way off completion. The signal placed the ship some 700 kilometres away. That was many hours steaming—some 20 hours at 20 knots—and bringing her safely into Wilhelmshaven could not be left to chance. However, plans were already laid. As he began the process of contacting people and instigating actions, Bünzlin felt eagerness and apprehension in equal measure. He had not been out there with the *Hindenburg*, but it felt like it; he'd been with them from the start, now for the end game.

One aspect Bünzlin did not mention to his admiral was the latest on the North Sea reconnaissance flights—there was nothing to report—and he knew Hipper was not enamoured by the zeppelins' reconnaissance performance to date. Of course, no reports of any sightings certainly did not mean there were no enemy ships in the vicinity. Furthermore, he knew the reconnaissance was not comprehensive.

Four zeppelins were deemed necessary to provide a line from Norway to Scotland, with a fifth watching the Firth of Forth. These dispositions were considered the minimum to be able to alert Körner of any enemy forces seeking to inhibit his passage. Such reconnaissance could also safeguard the Fleet, as it sought to rendezvous with the *Hindenburg*. Of course, to be effective this aerial coverage had to be almost continuous and, before the *Hindenburg*'s course and position could be confirmed, a regular shuttle of airships was necessary. Much work had been done on the likely timing of the *Hindenburg*'s North Sea return journey, but, as it was all based on a variety of information about the *Hindenburg*'s attack on the convoy, there was considerable scope for error in determining when to begin the reconnaissance effort. After the flights were instigated, all seemed to go well, but, as had happened before, adverse winds, mechanical problems and the enemy started to impact on airship availability. When the *Hindenburg* at last broke W/T silence, Bünzlin was aware that only two zeppelins were on station, with a third heading towards its assigned position. None of their reports that day had included sightings of enemy ships near the *Hindenburg*'s position. Seaplanes were to supplement the zeppelins, but they had nothing like the range and so were limited to a few hundred kilometres from their bases. Now that Körner's signal had been received, Bünzlin would order their flights to begin.

While there might well be concerns about the effectiveness of the aerial reconnaissance, at least the Fleet's ships were ready to assist Körner's return. Things began to happen quickly, though they were not the measures Bünzlin had originally argued for.

In Schillig Roads, Wilhelmshaven's anchorage nearest to the open sea, the battle cruisers *von der Tann* and *Derfflinger*, along with support ships, were at very short notice. It was not unknown for ships in Schillig Roads to put out ahead of the Fleet, but usually only to assist on matters in the immediate Bight. However, Bünzlin's proposal that these two battle cruisers be immediately dispatched to go to the *Hindenburg* had been rejected. Instead, the full Scouting Force of four battle cruisers, supported by the battle fleet, would proceed to her aid. The long-standing desire to cut off and destroy a portion of the English Grand Fleet worked just as well in reverse. Allowing a small number of the Fleet's capital ships to be destroyed in detail would achieve nothing and further damage morale and the navy's standing. Not even the *Hindenburg*'s safe return was worth that.

Bünzlin accepted there was a risk in sending the two battle cruisers far ahead of the Fleet, but was keen to bring support to the *Hindenburg* as soon as possible. Any other arrangement would just further delay that support. His arguments, endorsed by Hipper, did manage to get approval for the early sailing of the two battle cruisers, but they were instructed not to proceed beyond Horns Reef until reinforced by the other battle cruisers, *Seydlitz* and *Moltke*, plus the Scouting Force would then still be tied to the battle fleet no more than 100 kilometres astern. W/T silence would be maintained until the *Hindenburg*—or an enemy ship—was sighted.

It was almost two hours after receipt of the *Hindenburg*'s signal that Bünzlin received confirmation from Schillig lighthouse that the *von der Tann* and *Derfflinger* were underway. That was good news, but Bünzlin knew it would still be quite some time before the Scouting Force sighted the *Hindenburg*. He had one other, small card to play.

With Hipper's responsibilties including the security of the Bight, Bünzlin knew of other forces at sea in that area. Near the northern edge of the defensive minefields were minesweepers keeping the swept channels open. These vessels were protected by some cruisers and destroyers. Sending any small group of warships beyond Horns Reef involved risk, but he obtained permission to recall the minesweepers and send the cruisers and destroyers on to the *Hindenburg*. Importantly, they were only some 400 kilometres away from her. Although few in number, they could provide essential screening before the Scouting Force made contact with the *Hindenburg*.

Bünzlin was not wholly resigned to the situation. His original proposals had been rejected, but he knew that events in the North Sea might yet lead to plans being altered and see the two battle cruisers or the whole Scouting Force pushing on beyond Horns Reef to bring earlier support to Körner.

卍

Information about the zeppelin patrol was supposed to be passed regularly to Bünzlin, but, despite his requests for more frequent reports, he was not always notified immediately of changes. For example, he did not know that the navy zeppelin *L14* had had to cut short its mission and was then on its way back to Germany.

The *L14* maintained a steady 50kph, with the wind blowing from astern. Her commander, *Kapitänleutnant* Otto Bergmann, stood in the forward control gondola looking out at a sunlit, white carpet of ruffled cloud tops below them. As usual, his multiple layers of clothing were not really keeping out the cold at their altitude of over two thousand metres. Repeating what he had done innumerable times during the flight, he tugged the fur-lined lapels of his leather coat up around his face. He could handle the cold; his focus was getting the *L14* back to Nordholz, her airship station near Cuxhaven. The *L14* had been assigned a patrol off the south-west coast of Norway, first in the chain of airships stretching from Norway to Scotland, all aiming to assist the *Hindenburg*'s safe return to Germany. When the *L14* first took up her position, droning back and forth along her portion of the scout line, visibility had not been too restricted, but cloud cover had gradually increased, seriously reducing her reconnaissance capability. Bergmann had reduced height, periodically dropping through the clouds, but there the visibility, with occasional rain and mist, was less and he feared they would miss anything not close, so just as often he rose above the clouds, using gaps in their cover to monitor the waters below. Hardly five hours after reaching their patrol area, problems with an engine had led to difficulty in holding their position and, when the engine completely failed, brought about Bergmann's decision to turn back for Germany. He had intended to take a south-easterly course skirting the Norwegian coast, before turning south for Nordholz. However, it had subsequently proved evident that they'd overestimated the wind speed and ended up flying over Norway. Travelling above thick clouds, it was some time before their flight error was identified and course altered. He wasn't particularly concerned about any transgression of Norwegian territory, imagining the *L14* had probably not been seen above the clouds.

Through the gondola's glass and celluloid windows, occasional gaps in the clouds allowed Bergmann to see a cold, grey and uninviting sea. When he looked aft, he could see the outboard engine propellers. These, two of the three powered by engines in the aft gondola, were held just beyond the zeppelin's side on brackets. As expected, the port propeller was still stationary. The forward gondola had its own noisy engine, though he knew the noise levels were nothing compared to that in the aft gondola. The mechanics had worked without success trying to get the engine to work. The airship was slower, but would still get home. Although his mission had been to scan the Norway-Scotland waters for the *Hindenburg*'s return, he concluded that his somewhat disabled craft was now released from that task; nevertheless he would do what he could from that height as they headed back to their base across the Skagerrak.

19

Torpedo!

Quite suddenly, the battle seemed over; well, almost over. The port 15cm guns continued to fire, but at a much slower rate. Körner was informed that the enemy destroyers were falling back, range was increasing. After checking for himself, he was satisfied that the enemy ships were, for now, no longer gaining on the *Hindenburg*. From the port wing of the Bridge, he watched some shells falling amongst the destroyers on that flank. The small ships were producing much smoke and seemed to be taking evasive action, which he thought was good, as it would frustrate their attempts to get into torpedo range. As he watched them, Gärtner approached, swinging his binoculars onto the destroyers.

'Congratulations, Captain,' he said, lowering his binoculars. 'You have won *another* great victory.'

For a moment, Körner said nothing. He didn't see this particular encounter as completely over, the enemy might reform and attack again, but Gärtner's congratulations seemed heartfelt, real enough. Quickly running his mind over the events, he realised it had been less than forty-five minutes since they'd opened fire on the enemy battle cruisers; after twenty, one had spectacularly blown up and, within another twenty or so, the other had been forced out of the action. He marvelled at the result, not least because, yet again, the enemy had failed to land a single hit on the *Hindenburg*. Considering all that, he could accept the action would probably be hailed as a great victory, *if* they got home. 'Thank you, *Herr* Gärtner, … though I'll be more pleased to celebrate any victory when we're alongside in Wilhelmshaven.'

'Er, yes, Sir. Quite so.'

Körner judged that his response had not been what Gärtner expected, but he could not bother about such niceties. 'If our friends,' looking out towards the distant enemy destroyers, 'have decided not to press matters, let's resume our course for the Fleet and Wilhelmshaven.'

'I have it, Sir,' responded Gärtner. 'South-east by south, a quarter south,' he said, with authority.

Körner, pleased by such navigation precision, ordered the change, though dismissed a question from Gärtner about whether to include a zigzag pattern. The zigzag course alterations, while slight, would have affected their rate of advance and Körner, recalling Schellenberg's comment about maximising the distance to any chasing warships, wanted first to get clear of the pesky destroyers. Once the new course had been implemented, he asked Gärtner: 'How long till we meet the Fleet?' He expected an equally confident assessment. He'd asked this before, when they'd first sent the 'returning to port' signal, but at that stage only a broad estimate could be given. Now Körner expected a more definitive answer and hoped for a small number.

'Sir, I can still only estimate a range of times. We still have no clear indication of the Fleet's actual position or even when they left Wilhelmshaven. We only know they are reportedly *en route*.'

With that, Gärtner went quiet, presumably to allow a question or comment, but Körner just said, 'Yes, yes, but what's your best estimate of … earliest contact?'

Instantly, Gärtner replied: 'Sir, if the Fleet dispatched the ships on picket duty, say, within an hour of our original message, it will be at least five hours, somewhere north of Horns Reef, before we would rendezvous with them. Every hour's delay on their part puts the meeting later and farther south.'

Körner said nothing; he was disappointed, though not at the navigator's estimates. He knew that the Horns Reef Light was over 250 kilometres from Wilhelmshaven. At 20 knots, it would take the Fleet over six hours to get there, but sustaining 20 knots would be unlikely, he thought, given the various minefields to be negotiated and possibly while also zigzagging. In any event, it would probably be the faster Scouting Groups that would be their first contact. Of course, he would be well satisfied by the sight of Hipper's battle cruisers. 'Contact the Fleet. Seek confirmation of their time at Horns Reef.'

'Yes, Sir,' replied Gärtner.

Körner turned back to the battle, such as it was. After a quick assessment, he ordered cease fire. There was no evidence that their gunfire was actually hurting the enemy ships and, with the range increasing, one could expect even fewer hits and more wasted ammunition. Until he saw the Fleet—whenever that would be—Körner thought it best to conserve his remaining shells. On that, he spoke to Kruse about the ammunition situation, but also took the opportunity to pat him on the back for his excellent shooting. Kruse's voice pipe response betrayed his pleasure in being praised, but also, Körner wondered, a touch of embarrassment.

It seemed like some time before Kruse was back with the ammunition statistics: 'Sir, main armament shells fired were approximately one hundred and seventy, almost all from the rear turrets. We are still compiling the secondaries' figure, but it is probably quite significant. Initial estimates indicate over seven hundred, perhaps as many as eight hundred shells fired.'

Körner had been principally wondering about the 30.5s. As Kruse gave him the big shell figure, he did his own quick mental calculation suggesting about 270 or 280 left—a number to draw some comfort about. However, Kruse's report of the large number of 15cm fired, added to over 1,000 used in the convoy action, meant perhaps fewer than 400 remained—not many per gun and quickly used at their rate of fire. He was going to ask about the distribution of the 30.5s, though thought better of it and sought no more from his gunnery officer, giving him a plain 'Thank you.'

As he talked through the implications of the shell situation with Schellenberg and was well pleased with the relatively few big shells used to see off the English battle cruisers, their discussion was brought to an abrupt halt.

'Torpedo! Starboard bow!'

Lieutenant-Commander Kenneth Smith had his face pressed to the periscope's eye-piece. Other than being blocked by the occasional large wave, he had a good view of the target: a German dreadnought. His voice louder than normal, he called out: 'Fire Starboard!'

The order was immediately repeated back to Smith, commander of HM submarine *E28*, quickly followed by the satisfying 'Starboard tube fired!'

The sub shuddered, as the 18in torpedo, weighing over half a ton, was discharged. At 40 knots, the torpedo raced after its port tube neighbour; it had hardly been fifteen seconds between the two firings. Smith kept his face to the periscope; he especially wanted to watch the effects of the torpedoes. Normally, he was very wary of keeping the periscope up for long periods, having developed a healthy respect for enemy retaliation, whether by the threat of ramming, gunfire or depth charges. However, on this attack, his various periscope surveys beforehand and listening for the sound of propellers had all suggested the target had no escort ships. The decision was taken for him: clang! The noise of one, then another metallic-like bang sounded throughout the sub; it was the noise of shells striking the sea near the sub, the pressure waves of their explosions crashing against the sub's hull. 'Down periscope!' he shouted. 'Take her down to sixty feet!' He couldn't risk damage, so would have to forego the hoped-for pleasure of watching the torpedoes strike. Anyway, he would not have to wait long. The sound of a successful attack would be heard in the sub. His only other regret was that in his view such a target demanded a whole barrage of torpedoes, but the *E28* only had two bow tubes. The sub's three other tubes, one pointing astern and one on each beam, might be employed as the situation developed. He had had the torpedoes set deep to cause the most damage to such a ship and, given the target's high speed, set the torpedoes at high speed. A high speed setting could cause problems for the torpedoes, but he thought the target's high speed and range deserved high speed torpedoes.

This attack was rather unexpected and not *E28*'s specific task when she left port almost a week ago. It had started just over half an hour earlier, when a curious noise was picked up by the sub's hydrophones. Telegraphist Donald Cooper, *E28*'s hydrophone listener, had reported the unusual sound. He didn't know for sure what it was or in what direction it had come from, but he'd not heard anything like it before. Cooper, sitting awkwardly on a wooden box, wearing his headphones, had been putting all his efforts into picking up the sounds of a U-boat travelling on the surface, so was surprised by the noise. His job was difficult enough, because he really required almost absolute silence. It didn't take much to interfere with his listening, be it the boat's speed or even noises generated by the crew. The noise he'd detected was not a submarine, he was pretty certain of that, nor any of the things he was usually alive to, so he quickly reported it. He described it as a single rumble. His best guess: an explosion, a large one. Smith had quickly decided on 'Up periscope!'

It was *E28*'s third North Sea assignment specifically aimed at sinking U-boats as they sought to pass north of Scotland to get to the waters west of Britain. On this patrol, *E28* had been allocated a new 'billet', an area of sea which it had to keep to, otherwise other subs on similar missions might sink her. After a night charging batteries, Smith kept the sub underwater during the day, there to await the sounds of a passing U-boat, then come to periscope depth and torpedo her. A simple enough process that was generating results, though Smith and *E28* were yet to enjoy any success.

On their first patrol, a U-boat was detected. Smith adroitly manoeuvred the boat to deliver a perfect attack. A torpedo was fired. It appeared to be on target, but there was no explosion. Smith, sure his attack was sound, concluded that the weapon had either failed to explode or perhaps passed under the U-boat. Moreover, their attack must have alerted the enemy sub, as it changed course and was able to elude Smith's further attempts to get it into his sights. A U-boat was also detected during their second patrol, but it had not been possible to get into a firing position.

Attempting to resolve Cooper's noise, Smith had swung the raised periscope through 360 degrees quite quickly. Searching the horizon was always limited by the sea state, visibility and the low height of the periscope itself. None of these issues seemed to be a factor, though visibility was not great. However, he saw nothing that might indicate the source of such a sound. He listened to the headphones, though could discern nothing and, quite rightly, left that task to Cooper. Joined by the sub's two other officers, lieutenants David Rowland, Smith's Number One, and Edward Mackay, the origins of the sound were debated at length. Their best guess: a mine exploding, perhaps several mines, not an unusual event. Cooper stopped the officers' discussion with: 'Sir, propeller noise!'

The periscope was raised. Smith started his usual quick walk-around, but stopped half-way. 'Ship,' immediately corrected to 'Large ship, bearing port one-seven-oh!' He stared intently, trying to gauge whether she was German or British. It would not do to torpedo one of your own warships. From the funnels and superstructure, he quickly concluded it was a German dreadnought. He also noted that she was firing, he could see what looked like gun smoke, possibly from her smaller guns. What was she shooting at?

'Down periscope!

'It's a German battleship,' he said confidently. To those surrounding him in the sub's small Control Room, he rattled off: 'Two funnels; high speed, heading south-east, … range three to four thousand yards. … I reckon she's firing her guns, but I can't see what at.'

This last bit of information produced an exchange of glances between everyone, but without much to add, though it probably confirmed the presence of other ships.

'Port, come to course oh-five-oh!' ordered Smith, followed by, 'Up periscope!' all the while trying to remain calm, but conscious of possible excitement in his voice—he had never fired a torpedo at a battleship before. He put his eye to the eyepiece and hardly had to rotate the periscope to locate the big ship, but he then quickly swung right round, checking for other ships, then back to the would-be target, all thoughts of their U-boat mission gone. 'No other ships visible … prepare to fire bow tubes.' He was determined not to let this one get by … and not to give away his position. 'Down 'scope!'

He had not long let go of the 'scope, when came the response: 'Bow tubes ready, Sir.'

Rowland, unshaven and dirty, like all of the crew, had put new thoughts to his captain: 'Two funnels, high speed? Do you think it's the *Hindenburg*?'

Smith offered no answer to Rowland's question, just 'Up periscope.' He knew all about the *Hindenburg*, she was a regular discussion topic, though he had not been briefed specifically about her on this mission, never mind that she might appear in his cross-hairs. He was focused on the enemy vessel, but responded to Rowland: 'I see no other ships, no destroyers. Unusual. … Perhaps it is the *Hindenburg*.'

Smith studied the enemy vessel again, getting confirmation from Rowland that her configuration, turrets, funnels and superstructure all pointed to it being the *Hindenburg*. She was a quite a way off, at the limits of their torpedoes' range. He began to calculate the variables which would allow him to get a torpedo into her. As he'd watched, she changed course, turning more towards the submarine, presenting an easier target.

⚑

An emergency turn to port had been instantly ordered, though the *Hindenburg* was initially slow to turn, but soon the bow began noticeably to swing to port. Without much thought on the matter, Körner had elected to turn away from the torpedo, rather than towards it. His anxious wait to see if they would avoid the torpedo was disturbed by the firing of the 8.8s and especially by the shout that another torpedo had been sighted. He did not see the new torpedo track, he was focused on the first and the ship's turn, but was momentarily distracted by some 8.8 shell spouts hitting the sea some distance away to starboard. An officer called out: 'It's missed!' Then Körner saw it, just to port, the torpedo track. Had it passed under the ship? Anyway, it had indeed missed, thank God!

The great spout of dirty water which rose up from the starboard bow came as something of a surprise. '*Verdammt!*' Körner muttered under his breath, not just for being hit, but also for not concentrating on *both* torpedoes. Whether he could have done anything more to avoid the second torpedo hardly occurred to him. He was especially angry that his previous concerns about the submarine threat, expressed throughout the voyage, seemed at this crucial stage to have completely vanished from his mind. He was equally annoyed that he'd turned down Gärtner's earlier zigzag suggestion. Once the submarine was judged to be astern—he did not wish to offer it another shot—he maintained a course away from it, roughly north-east by east. As soon as they were judged to be clear of the submarine, he determined to institute a zigzag course; they were now undoubtedly in a submarine zone.

The torpedo hit seemed to Körner and those on the Bridge to have done nothing material to the ship. Outside of the column of water it caused, which crashed down onto the fo'c'sle and sprayed all those on the Bridge, there was no particular sense of damage to the ship. To Körner, the hit generated only a slight tremor, there was no great explosion and the ship's motion did not seem to be affected. Damage reports soon came in. The torpedo had struck about ten metres abaft the bow and damage was judged to be confined to that area; the engines and armament were unaffected. Several compartments in that forward part of the ship were flooded, including the forward torpedo room. Flooding, which was estimated at 3-400 tons, was largely contained, but the ship's high speed was a concern and it was recommended that speed be reduced to reduce pressure on bulkheads. It was still to be confirmed, but twenty or so men in those areas were feared lost. Körner was also concerned that one of the ship's own torpedoes may have been touched off, but this too could not be confirmed. Anyway, there was no time to worry about that possibility or indeed to consider reducing speed or even adopting a zigzag course.

'Destroyers!'

Without alarm, Schellenberg said, 'Destroyers closing, Sir.'

Körner went to the port-side. He could see the enemy destroyers, looking closer than they had before. He saw that they were in two distinct groups, one almost astern and one off the port quarter. He couldn't judge with certainty how many of the small ships were now seeking to close, but both groups seemed small, each about a half-flotilla. He thought they were, quite rightly, taking the chance offered by the *Hindenburg*'s plight. No doubt, seeing the torpedo strike and with the change of course bringing their quarry closer, they had been ordered to attack. They might not get a better opportunity. His short discussion with the navigator, not long before the torpedo hit, came to mind. He gave the order to open fire with the 15cm guns.

⚑

Like everyone in the Spotting Top, Eckhardt had reacted less than calmly to the torpedo call, turning immediately to that bearing. He'd quickly picked up the torpedo's track and, with the ship's turning motion, just as quickly judged it would miss. He'd then looked back along its track to see if he could locate the submarine. He was aware that someone must have already discovered the submarine, as the 8.8s were banging away at something. He had barely begun his own search, when he saw the second track, its tell-tale bubble trail clearly evident. Along with others, he shouted out a warning, not that anything could be done about it. He lost sight of the first torpedo, but unlike that one, he immediately concluded this second underwater threat *would* hit the ship. The ship was still turning, leaning over, but her motion and the weapon's direction and speed seemed to put them on a definite collision course. Despite his look-out responsibilities, he was completely fixated on the torpedo track, hardly breathing, heart pounding, convinced that the torpedo would hit the *Hindenburg*, but hoping against hope that it would, at the last minute, miss, fail to explode or even pass under the ship. It didn't! The water column that rose up thirty or forty metres and spray which hit the fore part of the ship, even reaching the Spotting Top, announced its impact, though the explosion was not particularly noticeable. He felt a slight movement, but it didn't appear to affect the ship, almost as if she had shrugged off the impact, not deigning to be affected by such a cowardly, underhand weapon.

Looking around, Eckhardt could see that the torpedo hit had affected everyone, he could see it on their faces. Fortunately, not everyone had been drawn to look at the torpedoes and wager with themselves on the prospect of them hitting or missing. Some look-outs had kept to their job and were watching elsewhere. Schwarz's voice announced: 'Enemy destroyers closing! Port side!'

Eckhardt, with everyone else, forgot the torpedo hit and swung round and levelled his binoculars away to port. Schwarz was right. The enemy destroyers had clearly put on speed, no doubt shaping to get closer and launch a torpedo attack. An officer relayed the sighting to the Bridge, putting the destroyers' range at 12,000 metres.

Eckhardt agreed with the range. He was sure that was still way too far for a torpedo attack, but it was plain they were closing all the while. The port 15cm guns greeted these upstarts, who were trying their luck again; white splashes erupted around both groups.

He turned away, scanning the complete horizon. Others could watch the destroyers, he was looking for the submarine *or* other submarines. He was concerned and annoyed, annoyed at himself. The torpedoes had come from the starboard side, his side! The look-outs had sectors to watch, though that didn't strictly preclude them from looking elsewhere. Should he have seen the enemy's periscope, should he have seen the torpedo tracks earlier? If he had, would things be different? The sight of the second torpedo boring in to hit the ship was burnt into his mind.

He looked out across the grey, undulating and shiny surface, searching for the plume of water from a submarine's periscope cutting through the water. There was no longer any 8.8 fire to guide him. He saw nothing, but continued his search, determined. He felt the ship change course.

⚐

Without the support of the *Courageous* and then the *Glorious*, even Pennywell could see that the destroyers would have a hard job of tackling the enemy ship alone. No sooner had they surged ahead of their battle cruisers, when water spouts had risen up beside them, with the lead ship—the *Nepean*—attracting most of the enemy's fire. Quite soon, she'd pulled out of the line. As they went by, Pennywell could see she was damaged, with thick, black smoke emerging from her innards. She still appeared able to steam, not dead in the water, but it was obvious that she was out of the fight. It didn't matter, the chase ended.

Hardly five minutes after the *Glorious* had been hit and started to fall back, a signal had come through cancelling their attack. Who from, Pennywell couldn't say and didn't care. He thought it was an entirely sound move. He didn't think the remaining three destroyers, in broad daylight, could safely get into torpedo range of their large, fire-spitting adversary, without the help of their battle cruisers' 15in guns. With the new order, the little line of three destroyers, the *Nereus* still at the tail end, first circled off to port, but then, unwinding from that manoeuvre, had continued after the enemy, but now in a shadowing role. The *Hindenburg* was still in sight, but at the edge of visibility. She had continued to lob a few shells in their direction, forcing the destroyers to snake the line, but then ceased firing.

Wondering how things might progress, Pennywell looked around. Away to port, he saw the light cruisers' destroyers; they seemed to have adopted the same shadowing role. The cruisers, some distance behind their destroyers, didn't seem to be catching up. Off the *Nereus*' port quarter, he saw the *Glorious*, now some distance away. She was still largely bow-on, but, from what he could discern, the smoke coming from her looked like it wasn't just from her funnel, so he figured she was indeed damaged and would play no further part. Beyond her, there was a lingering smoky mist where the *Courageous* had met her end. Almost dead astern he could see the still distant shapes of the Second Battle Cruiser Squadron. Their funnel smoke showed they were powering on, but looked no further forward.

He'd only just turned back, facing for'ard, intent on the distant *Hindenburg*, to see alongside her a grey-white shape rise up. This time, he couldn't keep quiet and exclaimed: 'What the ....' He wasn't alone, others on the destroyer's small bridge were raising questions about what they had just seen. The ensuing debate quickly decided that the *Hindenburg* had either struck a mine or been torpedoed.

The *Hindenburg* was then seen to change course, more to the north, well away from her previous south-east course. Listening to the talk on the bridge, but not daring to add in his own, probably worthless, opinions, Pennywell heard Beaumont speculate that the *Hindenburg* was avoiding whatever—mines or submarines—had damaged her. The destroyers altered course to follow her. A yeoman brought Beaumont a signal. It was from the *Pigeon*, now the leading destroyer of the little flotilla, alerting all ships of what they'd witnessed and that they were still in pursuit.

It was not long, perhaps ten or fifteen minutes later, a yeoman approached the captain with another signal. Beaumont looked at it and then read it aloud: 'It's from the *Australia. To First Cruiser Squadron and Third Light Cruiser Squadron. Destroyers attack enemy with torpedoes.*'

So, what Pennywell had only just been thinking was a very unwise action was now going to happen. As the three destroyers began to put on speed, to do battle with the distant enemy battle cruiser, Pennywell at last thought he must do something, he couldn't just continue to be a spectator. He was an officer, albeit a very junior one, but the *Nereus* only had a few; he felt a fraud, he must do something. Not sure what to expect, he moved forward. Commander Beaumont was looking ahead, whether at the next ship, the *Vanquisher*, or the *Hindenburg* wasn't clear to Pennywell. 'Captain, I wonder if there's some job I might do.'

Beaumont half-turned his head, but then resumed his forward gaze. 'Well, thank you, Mr Pennywell. Let's see. Apart from flying, what was your action station on the *Glorious*?'

'My action station was on one of the four-inch mounts, Sir.'

'Did you say you'd only been on her for a week or so?'

'er, ... yes.'

Beaumont went silent for a couple of seconds, which Pennywell took to mean *this officer would be no great help on any of the Nereus' guns.*

The captain continued: 'Perhaps you'd be so good as to go below and assist the Doctor. I'm sure he'd value your help, but hopefully there will be little for you to do.'

Pennywell did not challenge the request. As he made his way down the starboard-side companionway, with the captain's comments still in his mind, a shell splash rose up not more than fifty yards away from him.

Körner watched the enemy destroyers, now confirmed as two separate groups, the closest having five ships, the other three. They were steaming directly for the *Hindenburg*, both in line ahead. They had been able to close the distance, but at present were still no nearer than some 8,000 metres. Not long after the *Hindenburg*'s 15cm shells began to rain down on them, they had begun to make smoke that he thought quite effective, in that it blew south and largely obscured his view of all but the lead destroyer in each line. Gunfire was now being wholly directed at the larger group. To judge by the shell splashes, particularly around the lead ship, the guns were apparently on target, but with no reports of hits. He was disappointed. Kruse's gun crews, especially the main armament, had always delivered excellent performance, but today's shooting by the 15cm guns was not living up to expectations. Of course, the situation could change rapidly; one 15cm hit could cause any one of the small ships serious problems. Anyway, he felt obliged to take steps. In normal circumstances, he would have had his own cruisers and torpedo boats to deflect such an attack, but this was far from a normal situation. He had to use all means at his disposal. Although silent, the main guns were constantly tracking the enemy ships, ready for the order to fire. Körner spoke to Kruse: 'Open fire with main armament.' Körner's earlier reluctance to bring the main guns into the action against such targets could not stand. It might prove difficult for them to hit such small, nimble craft, but a hit or even near miss from a 30.5 would indeed cause them much distress.

Kruse was obviously very ready for such an order. The big guns let fly almost instantly. As previously, the 30.5s were soon on target, straddling the nearer and larger of the two groups. It was not long before a report came to Körner that its leading destroyer had either been hit or was snaking the line. The destroyers continued on towards the *Hindenburg*, full speed ahead. Körner could see they were under tremendous fire, storming through shell splashes. They were brave men, he considered, but what else would you expect? It was still difficult to see all the attackers, except for the lead ship, because of their smokescreen. Suddenly the lead ship was totally engulfed in water spouts and then, emerging from them, appeared to alter course away and be overtaken by the others. She had obviously been hit hard. Well done, Kruse!

Körner could easily see that the successful shooting had not stopped the destroyers' charge, though the speed of advance of the group to his right seemed less, reportedly because they were taking evasive action to put off the *Hindenburg*'s gunners. In contrast, the left hand group, which had not been under as much fire, kept on and the two groups had drawn closer to one another.

Körner spoke to Schellenberg, who was just on the point of leaving the Bridge for the aft control station. 'They may be prepared to sacrifice themselves … and we don't seem able to deter them. Soon they may be in a position to launch torpedoes.' As he spoke, the 8.8s joined in, flinging their smaller, but more frequent shells at the enemy destroyers.

'Yes, Sir,' replied the first officer, calmly as ever. 'I suggest we turn away. Make their task harder. Our course is also favouring their smokescreen.'

'Agree,' said Körner, but, before he could pronounce on a new course, he saw flashes from the enemy destroyers; they had opened fire with their own small guns, probably 4in affairs. 'New course: due east!'

Moving to the starboard wing of the Bridge, he saw the change of course had only partially eased the smokescreen problem, but had brought the destroyers astern of them, the right hand group almost dead astern and the other off the starboard quarter, both now only some 6,000 or so metres away. This new course also altered the ship's gunnery, reducing the main armament fire to the four aft guns, which was now targeted on the group astern. The starboard 15cm guns tackled the other group, with straddles quickly reported.

Körner would have liked to swing a couple of points to starboard, not only allowing the for'ard turrets to rejoin the action, but also, if the destroyers matched the turn, then their smokescreen would be less effective, especially for the port-side group. However, such a change in direction would again offer them a chance to reduce the distance, which he feared must encourage them to launch torpedoes. Even now, they could still risk a torpedo attack, but with the *Hindenburg* stern-on, the chances of a hit must, he earnestly hoped, be low. Ideally, they would probably prefer to get ahead of the *Hindenburg* before launching their weapons, or, worse, attack from both flanks. He quickly discounted any turn, determined to keep them astern, hoping the guns would have more time to stop them.

The guns did in fact do their utmost. The group off the starboard quarter was clearly straddled and he thought he saw the red flash of hits on the lead destroyer. While he stared at that destroyer, trying to gauge the effects of any hits, his attention was brought to the other group of attackers: Kruse's big guns had struck again, their lead destroyer had clearly taken hits. Excellent!

᛫

Concentrating on the small enemy group off the ship's starboard quarter, Eckhardt instantly called out any change of course they made. With each crash, blast and boom from the *Hindenburg*'s guns, he watched intently to see the result, willing every shell to hit the little ships, to hit them hard, drive them off, sink them! When straddled and especially when hits were apparent, he shouted out, though trying as calmly as possible to give an accurate report.

Despite the *Hindenburg*'s high speed and formidable gunfire, the small flotilla's three ships were closing with each minute, still some kilometres off, deluged by shell splashes and occasional waves sweeping over their bows, but closing nonetheless. In every respect, they were small fry, perhaps only 1,000 tons, hardly a hundred metres in length, minimal superstructure, with only a few, very exposed guns. He could see the little, but rapidly repeating winks from their puny guns. He told himself that even if they managed to get a shell on the battle cruiser, they could do no real harm, but it was their torpedo tubes—of which he knew they only had a small number—that caused him the greatest apprehension. The *Hindenburg* might have weathered one hit from a submarine, but Eckhardt didn't think she could so easily brush off further hits from the dastardly and destructive weapons. He wanted to see the little ships stopped before they got into a position to launch their torpedoes.

The lead ship had occasionally twisted her flotilla's course to throw off the gunners' aim, but eventually the shells fell all about her and he saw the unmistakeable flash of a hit, then another. He sang out, 'Lead destroyer hit!' He couldn't see exactly where the shells had struck, just that they were aft of her three funnels and it was not long before he could make out flame and smoke in that area. Others had obviously seen what happened and a spontaneous, but somewhat muted cheer erupted. Even so, the destroyer still came on. She appeared to be changing course with each salvo, no doubt trying to avoid the next one being on target. He marvelled at her twinkling guns, especially the one on the bow, which, at her high speed, was being regularly covered with white spray. The smoke from each destroyer was black and thick, streaming off to their starboard sides. It provided them with some cover, but less so on their changed course. They were more visible; surely the guns could get them now!

He watched the little ships intently, noting any change of course. Most of the water spouts suggested the gunners were focused on the lead, already damaged, ship, but he wanted to see shells striking each of them. He did think the 15cm's rate of fire less, but gave it little consideration. Just then he noted a small water spout appear off the *Hindenburg*'s starboard quarter, no more than twenty metres away. He felt indignation at this attempt by the small ships to strike *his* ship. As he watched for the retaliation he considered warranted by this insult, he saw the lead ship, still streaming smoke from her wounds and funnels, turn to starboard. She'd jinked to starboard and port several times in the last five or ten minutes, but this time the change seemed greater. Astern of her, he saw the other two swing round to starboard. He had his own views on what this change of course meant, but simply called, 'Enemy turning to starboard!'

He searched the water around them, then shouted: 'Torpedoes!'

He hadn't actually seen the launch of the torpedoes, but, he could be wrong, he thought he saw marks on the sea that he reckoned were torpedoes. He didn't dare wait to be certain, it would be too late by then. He would not fail this time to alert the ship.

He continued to watch the enemy destroyers and the sea. The little ships had indeed turned to starboard and were not turning back; they must have launched their deadly weapons and, content, were breaking off their attack. Their turn had made their smoke less effective, indeed, if anything, they were well silhouetted by their black clouds. He reckoned they were now less than 5,000 metres away, point-blank range for the guns, but they really seemed to enjoy a charmed life. Several shell splashes rose up around all three ships, but he saw no evidence of any hits.

⚑

Pennywell had quickly located the ship's *doc* in the seamen's mess deck, under the fo'c'sle. A tall, youthful-looking, clean-shaven and smiling RNVR sub-lieutenant had introduced himself as Charles Pike, Surgeon Probationer. To Pennywell, Pike seemed to be about the same age as him, so too young to be a *proper* doctor.

Pike had welcomed Pennywell, though when he was asked about the flyer's medical experience, he saw his answer 'none' led to a momentary raising of the surgeon's eyebrows, but, no doubt reflecting on the action they now found themselves in, Pike still thanked him for his help. Pennywell had countered, asking about the whereabouts of the sick berth attendant, but got the response: 'There's none on small ships … just me … and you.' Pike explained further that there was no sick bay, even joking that he himself didn't rate a cabin and slept on a wardroom sofa, and that it seemed appropriate on this occasion to 'set up shop' in the crew mess, which offered plenty of space.

As the minutes passed, the ship's frequent alterations of course and the pitching and crashing into the waves obliged the two men to keep tight hold of something, with Pike also endeavouring to keep his medical odds and ends from flying onto the deck. Pennywell could hear the 4in gun just above them repeatedly banging away, but he was unable to conjure up an image of what might be going on topside and instead began to wonder how he'd fare when confronted with the first casualty. His war so far had not exposed him to any real blood and gore. He had seen injury, even death, though all caused by the many plane crashes in training, not from actual fighting, and it had always been at a bit of a distance, not close up as he now anticipated.

The two men spoke intermittently about the day's events, with Pennywell outlining his encounter with the German ship, but neither saying anything about the difficulties facing the destroyers in attacking the *Hindenburg*. Suddenly, there was an almighty bang and Pennywell found himself over to one side of the mess. For a second or two, he was disorientated and tried to make sense of what had happened. There was some smoke and a terrible smell of cordite. His back felt sore, but he was able to prop himself up on his left elbow. The mess deck was in a shambles, smashed tables and debris everywhere; clearly, it had taken a hit. He could see several holes of varying sizes in the ship's starboard side, some occasionally letting water in as the ship continued to rise and fall. Other than his back, he couldn't see or feel any other sign of injury. He couldn't see Pike, so called out to him. No reply. He flipped himself over to find Pike was lying a only few feet behind him. The young doctor, amid a smashed mess table, was on his left side, with his back to Pennywell, his right arm hanging oddly across his back. Fearful, Pennywell scrambled over to him, pulling away bits of wood, to be confronted by his first casualty. As he rolled Pike over, he was not prepared for the ghastly sight he beheld. Whatever had hit them had resulted in Pike's head and some of his chest being ripped from him. Blood and guts were mixed in with the debris. Pennywell vomited.

⚑

Körner reacted quickly to the torpedo alarm. He didn't ask for confirmation, just their likely direction. He swung the *Hindenburg* away from this latest threat. It was a small turn; conscious of the other enemy group to port, he could not present them with a beam-on, inviting target.

No one on the Bridge saw the torpedoes, so when the hit occurred, some were almost knocked over. The shock was much greater than the submarine torpedo and consequently Körner immediately expected it to be more damaging. He could only judge that the torpedo had struck aft, possibly on the starboard side. However, until damage reports came in, he would not speculate, but ordered a turn away from the port-side group of attackers, especially when he heard that the starboard group appeared to have broken off their attack. Concerned that the remaining enemy group would take this new opportunity to launch an attack, he went to the Bridge's port-side wing. Through gunfire smoke, he could make out that the enemy ships were close, even closer than the others had been when they launched their torpedoes. He could only see two ships. There had been five; had the other three been disposed of, he wondered. No matter, it only took one, he reminded himself, and they were clearly determined to continue their attack. The ship's course kept the remaining assailants dead astern. Shell splashes surrounded these two remaining destroyers and, at these ranges, he hoped some shells would be hitting them. He saw them turning; he instinctively knew they too were going to launch their torpedoes.

⚑

The torpedo hit had shook the Spotting Top, making Eckhardt hold on tight. There was no time for analysis, the destroyer attack was still underway. He saw that the enemy group on the ship's starboard side, those who had scored the torpedo hit, had done a full turn away from the *Hindenburg*, though it was difficult to follow their manoeuvres, given the smoke and mist that abounded. The smoke sweeping over the seascape from both destroyer groups was added to by that from the *Hindenburg*'s own funnels and gunfire. Anyway, he judged that group to have pulled back, but calls by other look-outs had him turning to the port-side attackers. No sooner had he focused on them, but he saw them, now just two ships, make a turn away, offering their broadsides to his gaze. He had no doubt: they were not withdrawing, they too were launching their torpedoes.

A torpedo alert was shouted. Even as the guns continued to fire at the would-be giant killers, everyone in the Spotting Top searched for the torpedo tracks. Soon they were seen, a spread of faint lines stretching out, inexorably powering their way towards the wounded *Hindenburg*. She kept her course; the faint white lines kept on, approaching directly from astern. Eckhardt couldn't say how many were loosed against the *Hindenburg*, but three were sighted. One torpedo was spotted paralleling the ship's port side, then another to starboard. The other appeared to be coming straight at the stern, but amid the ship's great wash was lost from sight. After a few minutes, the general agreement was that it had either gone under the ship or been deflected by the turbulent water.

Relieved, Eckhardt swung back to his main task. He could see no more destroyers shaping up to attack the *Hindenburg*. One of the last attackers had obviously taken one or more hits and appeared dead in the water with black smoke issuing from her, though a few shells continued to fall around her.

Sinking several enemy destroyers and surviving that latest attack was marginal comfort to Eckhardt. He knew the *Hindenburg* was obviously damaged and more so than from the submarine torpedo. He could feel the ship listing and also thought her speed was falling. She could probably have withstood many hits from big shells, but this single, bloody torpedo now threatened everything.

Once more that day, the distressing sight of a torpedo hitting his ship was added to his memories. It had taken some minutes before the torpedoes had been sighted. Two, as in the final attack, coming at them from dead astern, had swept down either side of the ship, missing. Alas and surprisingly, another had struck on the starboard quarter, throwing up a great column of white water, liberally shot through with grey and black, and, unlike the submarine torpedo, had sent a shockwave through the ship which he imagined everyone must have felt.

It did not displace his thoughts about the torpedo hit, but he was pleased to see that the enemy destroyers, the few as had survived, appeared to be falling back. Then, a couple of destroyers were reported to be following, but, thankfully, seemed content to watch from a distance. Hopefully they had shot their bolts and had no more with which to threaten the *Hindenburg*. However, there was no denying the impact this torpedo hit had on the ship *and* his thinking of the day thus far. Expecting—or hoping—to be back in port that day and without a shot being fired, they had now been in a running fight for almost two hours. They had more than held their own, sinking or damaging several enemy ships, but now the blasted torpedo had totally altered the situation. Even as he concentrated on his job, he found it difficult to ignore the possible implications of the torpedo strike. His first thoughts were that, as well as flooding and listing, it might have damaged the engines or propellers, affecting their speed. The consequence of losing their great speed—undeniably one of a battle cruiser's main assets—was really not something he wanted to consider. He concentrated on searching his sector for the enemy. He tried not to be despondent and still thought the *Hindenburg* could ... no, *would* get them home. Surprisingly, he realised that up to that point he'd thought little of any meeting with the Fleet, but now it seemed he longed for that rendezvous. He found himself not just looking for enemy ships, but hoping the next ship he did see would be German.

20

Dissuasion

This war cruise had regularly tested Körner's abilities, but the day's actions and especially the torpedo hits had raised matters to a completely new level. He tried not to contemplate what the latest torpedo damage meant for a successful conclusion of *Georg*, just the safety of his ship, but he did feel some apprehension while waiting for more detailed damage reports to come through and there was still the possibility of further attacks from the pursuing enemy ships. With all that was happening, he still couldn't fail to recall something Bünzlin had said to him, from what now seemed a long time ago:

'I'll be honest, Rupprecht, I fully expect you can get your ship out into the Atlantic and, most probably, attack and destroy some convoys, but I am genuinely concerned about how we get you home.' Bünzlin had continued: 'Of all the issues we've planned for ... and all the likely solutions, it's the return journey through the North Sea that bothers me the most. And, of course, I accept many things could have happened by then, so your plans and options could well have changed ... for good or bad. A passage back through the North Sea is the only logical option ... as it will be to the English. But, *with assistance from the Fleet*, it should be quite possible to get you into Wilhelmshaven. The proposal not to break wireless silence until you're on your final leg is understandable, but I do worry about how quickly the Fleet can come to your aid ... if need be.'

Prophetic words.

Like all the other elements of *Georg*, much work had gone into this final phase of the mission, but ensuring a safe return through the North Sea to Germany seemed to rely on luck as much as anything else—not something that figured in German planning. The two attacks on the Norway-Scotland convoys, with the successful return of the attackers, had been taken as tangible proof that it was possible to get back safely to Germany. Wireless silence was judged to be a good measure, but, if Körner held off notifying the Fleet of his position till the *Hindenburg* was on the very last part of the transit across the North Sea, then the delay in big-ship support would leave a lot of sea to traverse alone.

Ideas to assist the transit always seemed to clash with the breaking of W/T silence. Körner's new-found belief in keeping quiet would not only inhibit the enemy's direction-finding, but also interfere with the measures most likely to offer the *Hindenburg* real assistance in that final part of the run home. Other suggestions had focused on the Fleet and submarines. Lines of submarines positioned to disrupt enemy patrols were rejected, because it would, as always, divert them from their ongoing assault on British merchantmen, plus such deployments had not been wholly successful in the past. More tangible support could come from the Fleet putting to sea either to distract the enemy or, if already at sea, shortening any time it took to effect a rendezvous with the *Hindenburg*. However, both of these relied on an early enough W/T signal and, disappointingly, were judged to be a risk to the Fleet.

The solution selected was the easiest, but limited in that it could not of itself deflect any enemy ships. Rather, it centred on regular and plentiful reconnaissance flights by zeppelins and, nearer Germany, supplemented by aircraft, which could all help the battle cruiser to avoid enemy ships. It should have been relatively easy to implement and did not rely on the *Hindenburg* breaking W/T silence. Based on an assessment of when the *Hindenburg*'s North Sea return journey would begin, reconnaissance flights were supposed to be mounted continuously to provide the necessary warning signals about enemy ships. However, as with other aspects of *Georg*, planning was not a guarantee of outcome. Anyway, Körner had given up on scanning the sky for a German airship or plane and couldn't waste time considering the reasons why they'd seen none and had only picked up two W/T signals from zeppelins—he had other things to worry about.

The first damage reports about the torpedo hit were worrying enough. The torpedo had, as he'd first thought, struck the starboard quarter, reported to be at about frame 100. There was considerable flooding, estimated at some one and a half thousand tons, creating a starboard list, which had been reduced by counter-flooding. The worst aspect was that water had got into the starboard low pressure turbine room, which soon had to be abandoned and led to the shut down of the starboard inner propeller. Maximum speed with the loss of the propeller and damage and flooding from the two torpedo hits, plus counter-flooding, was now judged to be no more than 21, perhaps 22 knots. Fortunately, at least for now, bulkheads seemed under no immediate threat and, despite earlier concerns, there seemed no reason to reduce speed to lower water pressure. Damage control teams were working to stem the flooding, though the loss of speed was not the only concern. The torpedo damage had also affected the ship's guns: turret Caesar had been affected by the blast and was untrainable, but frantic work was now underway to bring it back into working order.

Since the first contact with the enemy, Körner had sent regular signals on events as they happened. There was no need to keep W/T silence once the enemy was in visual contact. 'Second torpedo hit. Maximum speed 21 knots. Enemy ships shadowing', along with the *Hindenburg*'s grid reference, was dispatched. Gärtner reported that, frustratingly, there was still no indication of the Fleet's likely appearance.

With the engagement over, Schellenberg had returned to the Bridge and set to assessing damage and directing resources as required. 'Sir, flooding is contained,' adding, '... for now. On the turbine, it's doubtful whether there'll be any way it can be brought back into operation.'

'Yes, yes,' replied Körner, disappointed, but expecting such news. He had already resolved that they would probably have to make the run to Wilhelmshaven on three shafts. Naturally, the flooding would be monitored.

Amid the changed atmosphere that was now evident on the Bridge, if not throughout the ship, thought Körner, Kruse reported via voice pipe: 'Captain, the destroyer attack has used virtually all our fifteen-centimetre shells. We have only about twenty shells left.'

As Körner feared, the 15cm guns had made short work of the 400 shells they had less than hour or so ago. He said nothing about that, but asked: 'What of the main armament? What's the situation with the main guns?'

'A quick assessment shows we have about one hundred and sixty, though, other than two dozen or so, they are mostly in the for'ard magazines.' Before Körner could debate that with himself, Kruse then added more to the news on Caesar: 'The latest evaluation on Caesar suggests the training fault cannot be corrected without shipyard assistance.'

Körner sought no more on it. With the rear turrets' ammunition situation, he knew that whether or not Caesar could be repaired was no longer an issue to worry about.

With this news about the ammunition, Körner didn't want to admit circumstances had changed, but there was no denying the odds against them had worsened. Körner glanced at Schellenberg, who had heard most of the voice pipe exchange with Kruse, but he could gauge no great concern on his first officer's face on the shell situation. They always knew any prolonged action could leave them exposed. The need to get home without any further action seemed obvious, but whether that would be possible was in the hands of the gods. At least with the enemy ships well astern, there seemed no immediate threat of action, which was a little comfort, given there was little or no ammunition for the aft-facing guns.

'We should resume our course for Horns Reef,' he threw at Schellenberg and Gärtner, intending it more as expecting agreement from his first officer and asking for the course from his navigator.

'I agree, Sir,' was Schellenberg's unusually speedy reply. 'The quicker we get there, the quicker we'll meet the Fleet.'

Gärtner went to the Chart Room, but returned quickly with 'South-three-quarters-east, Sir,' adding: 'One hundred and thirty-seven sea miles.'

Another seven hours, if we can maintain 20 knots, reasoned Körner, though could not help thinking that, but for the day's actions and various course changes, they could have just about been there by now. Those *what if* thoughts were quickly dismissed from Körner's mind, as he just as swiftly contemplated the implications of the necessary course change. With the enemy off their starboard quarter, turning ninety degrees to starboard could see the enemy ships off their starboard beam. It would also give them the opportunity to close, but it would mean they would face the *Hindenburg*'s broadside, albeit reduced. He was about to order the turn, when Schellengberg spoke.

'Sir, we do have the option of heading for Kiel.'

'I do not consider that is our best option,' was Körner's instant response, a touch of authority in his voice. 'We've agreed before it was an option, but only if circumstances warranted it. I'm not sure that is the case.'

'Sir, if enemy dreadnoughts are ahead of us and contest our passage' replied Schellenberg, no hint of subservience, 'without the Fleet, we may be ... hard-pressed.'

Körner had always tended to dismiss the Kiel possibility, even in the discussions with Bünzlin, never accepting that they would not get through to Wilhelmshaven, with or without the Fleet's assistance. During *Georg*'s planning, no less than with other issues, the route home had been much debated. He had always accepted the alternatives for the return to Germany included sailing to Kiel—by way of the Skagerrak, Kattegat and Danish Little Belt—but that route was seen as the most unlikely option, largely because the expected Fleet support made Wilhelmshaven by far the natural choice. Kiel offered no benefit, as he saw it. It was farther, affording the enemy more opportunities for attack, and, compared to Wilhelmshaven, had less facilities for dealing with a damaged dreadnought of the *Hindenburg*'s size. Sailing for Wilhelmshaven was always Körner's preference and he felt the delayed appearance of the Fleet, for example, was still no reason to give up on it. 'Yes, we could,' said Körner, 'but you know it was always my intention to head for Wilhelmshaven and ... unless you have reasons against it, I see no need to alter that now.'

'Just a thought, Sir, but with all that's happened today, I think the odds on avoiding any heavy ships are better with Kiel than Wilhelmshaven.'

Körner normally took notice of his first officer's observations, generally finding him wise counsel, but his own instincts still said 'Wilhelmshaven'. Enemy dreadnoughts could just as easily be following behind the cruisers. With the *Hindenburg*'s reduced speed, if he continued on their east course, those dreadnoughts might catch them up. Without the Fleet, that would indeed be a dangerous situation. He did not feel he needed to argue the matter.

'Thank you, but we are going to Wilhelmshaven. Course: South-three-quarters-east.'

Schellenberg made no reply, nor did his face give any indication of how he judged his captain's decision.

As the *Hindenburg* came onto her new course, many eyes, binoculars and telescopes focused on the pursuing English warships. Gärtner had done some calculations, suggesting the enemy ships could in 10 minutes or so close to well under 10,000 metres, if they so chose. Would they be so brave, would they take this opportunity to gain on the *Hindenburg* and launch a new torpedo attack? Turrets Anton, Bertha and Dora tracked round and pointed at the challengers, ready to engage at the captain's order.

Körner kept his binoculars on the lead cruiser, watching for any alteration in her profile which might indicate a change in her course. He had already spoken to Kruse about firing on the enemy ships; he would hold fire until their intentions were clear. He judged it wiser to hold onto his remaining ammunition until there was a real threat of attack by them or other ships. It all seemed counter-intuitive to that expected. Under normal circumstances, at such a range, he would engage them without fail. What did the enemy intend to do?

'Sir, from Spotting Top,' reported Schellenberg. 'Enemy ships have changed course ... south ... and closed slightly. Range now thirteen thousand metres.' Then, repeating himself, 'Thirteen thousand. ... Perhaps unwise, ... even foolish, ... unless they are considering torpedoes.'

Turning his head to Schellenberg, Körner acknowledged the concern: 'Yes, quite right. They do not need to get much closer. ... They could well try their torpedoes. Alert look-outs.'

Körner claimed no great torpedo expertise, but was well aware that the range of German torpedoes had improved significantly during the war. The *Hindenburg*'s own massive, 60cm torpedoes were set to engage targets at 12,000 metres, indeed could reach farther at a slower speed setting. Before the war, English torpedoes were judged to have a maximum range of some 9,000 metres, but wasn't it reasonable to expect they too had increased the range of their own torpedoes? The possibility had been discussed in the Fleet. Schellenberg was right. All of a sudden, 13,000 metres seemed *too* close. The enemy ships were abeam of the *Hindenburg*, paralleling her course and speed—an excellent opportunity for a torpedo attack. He could not allow them to have such an easy chance, whatever the cost in ammunition. He spoke to Kruse: 'Guns, please dissuade them. Open fire!'

The great guns spoke. The first three shells, each weighing over 400kg, arced their way towards the enemy ships.

⚑

Eckhardt had kept the whole enemy formation under scrutiny since it coalesced shortly after the last destroyer attack. He put it at the same four cruisers, but now with no more than three destroyers. He could only conclude (or hope) that the other destroyers had either been sunk or damaged and forced out of the fight. He thought it odd that two of the three remaining destroyers were ahead of the line of cruisers, with the other astern of them.

Intent on the enemy ships, he clearly saw the *Hindenburg*'s first three shell splashes, startlingly white against the grey, misty background. They all struck the water a couple of ship lengths to port of the leading cruiser, but, as much as he could judge at 13,000 metres, were also short of her distance. Not long after, the next white trio rose up and looked in both respects closer to their target. Those first shots were obviously too intimidating; he judged the enemy ships were altering course. Eckhardt announced smartly: 'Enemy turning away!' The next salvo had yet to arrive, when he saw sparkles from the enemy ships—they were returning fire. With contempt, he asked himself what did they expect to achieve with their 15cm guns and at this range? 'Enemy has opened fire!' he called out, with equal commitment. As he studied the scene, reporting 'Enemy making smoke,' Eckhardt noted that only two, the second and last, of the four enemy cruisers were firing.

Although he was surprised at the enemy's gunfire, wondering how they would fare, he kept his binoculars on the ships. He was very soon rewarded by the sight of shell splashes around the leading cruiser, with a couple of splashes on the nearest side and, though not seeing it, had to conclude the other shell had landed beyond the ship—a straddle! He couldn't say if the straddle had actually hit the ship, but could not restrain a 'yes!' escaping from his lips and calling out 'Straddle!' Others around him reacted similarly. Whether by chance or the gunnery officer's expertise, the enemy's turn away had connected with the salvo. Excellent shooting, whatever!

The next salvo had hardly left the barrels, when the *Hindenburg* began turning to port. The look-outs had been warned about torpedoes, so he presumed that was why the ship was being turned away from the enemy. He methodically swept the waters between them and the *Hindenburg*, looking for signs of torpedoes. Satisfied he could see none, Eckhardt refocused on the enemy ships. The next salvo missed, but the following one was again right on target and he thought he saw hits, red flashes, on the leading ship. He loudly proclaimed: 'Hit on leading cruiser!'

There was a similar call from Schwarz and exclamations of delight and achievement by others in the Spotting Top.

The *Hindenburg* continued her turn, loosing off more shells at the enemy, and it was not long before only turret Dora was able to bear on the cruisers; she continued the fight, but Eckhardt noted that she ceased firing after sending only one salvo at them.

He continued to check the enemy ships. The picture was made very difficult by the smoke the cruisers were putting out, but he felt sure the leading cruiser had been hit. He thought her smoke was not only coming from her funnels, but, seeing she was becoming detached from the others, also pondered whether she may have lost speed. The other cruisers were soon difficult to make out, being beyond her, with the increased smoke and near the limits of visibility. The two lead destroyers had reversed course, coming back towards the wounded cruiser. Both they and the other destroyer were also laying smoke, further obscuring the scene, trying to protect her.

Körner was quick to order cease fire. Very pleased with the undoubted success, he was equally pleased to stop the gunfire as soon as it was no longer required. There were no enemy torpedoes, well none had been seen, so not only had they achieved the aim of interfering with the shadowers' torpedo ambitions, but reportedly had also hit one of them into the bargain. Furthermore, the enemy cruisers had turned away and were now described as being at the very limits of visibility—and probably beyond a long-range torpedo.

Only three cruisers were now reported, further indicating that one had in all likelihood been hit. Nothing more could be seen of that cruiser, her plight hidden behind much smoke and mist. Körner expected that even a single 30.5 hit might well have done her serious damage, quite possibly enough to force her out of the chase. He clearly recalled how the *Potsdam* had been brought to a standstill by such shells. When he gave the order to fire, he wanted to disrupt any plans the cruisers had to launch torpedoes. While he naturally hoped to hit them, he would have been satisfied just to force them away. Both had been achieved. Perhaps it was a lucky hit, but the 13,000 metre range was a comfortable distance for the *Hindenburg*'s big guns. They had paid the price of venturing too close. All in all, a very pleasing result and, in the circumstances, a useful morale boost for the ship's company.

Of course, as he anticipated, this small success had come at a further reduction in available shells. Kruse, duly congratulated by Körner, soon reported that over 50 shells had been fired. That left about 100-110, Kruse calculated. Perhaps worse, Kruse told him these shells were all in the for'ard magazines, the aft magazines were, apart from one shell, now empty.

Körner said nothing in response to the ammunition statistics, but he was depressed by the 100 shell figure—hardly ten or fifteen minutes' fire for the two for'ard turrets—and feeling somewhat naked. He tried to put it in context: the torpedo threat had been all but eliminated and, with any luck, they might not need those shells. He turned the *Hindenburg* back towards Horns Reef. The surviving English cruisers would be wary of coming closer, but they were still out there, watching and reporting her course.

'Captain, Damage Control reports increased flooding. Request that speed be reduced.'

Körner, thinking of the ship's safety, did not question the accuracy or implications of Damage Control's request; however reluctantly, he immediately called for speed to be reduced to 17 knots. Schellenberg set about checking the situation.

After obtaining further information, Schellenberg confirmed that seawater from the submarine torpedo damage was no longer being contained; more water than could be dealt with by the pumps was entering the ship. The manoeuvring during the cruiser action may have exacerbated the situation. Anyway, whatever the cause, he supported the need for a reduction in speed to reduce water pressure. Whether 17 knots would be too much remained to be seen.

⚑

High above the Command-Bridge, Eckhardt laid his lips to the mug and drained the last of its contents. The lukewarm liquid did little for him. As he rubbed his hands around the mug, seeking to draw its residual heat into them, he tried to concentrate on his job. Ten or so minutes before, he had felt pretty good. Like everyone in the Spotting Top, the successful action against the enemy cruisers had been good for morale. There had been smiles all round and, after the disappointment of the torpedo hits, he'd discerned an air of uplifted spirits and a general, though unspoken, reaffirmation that they would indeed get back safely to Wilhelmshaven. Now all that seemed some time ago, replaced by a new reality, one no one wanted to debate.

Everyone in the Spotting Top had registered the ship's latest reduction in speed. Eckhardt thought it was only a few knots, but there was a noticeable reduction in the disturbance of the waves created by the ship. Obviously, something was wrong. 'Why?' was on everyone's lips. Was it a deliberate act for some, as yet, unknown reason or could the ship's engines no longer deliver the required speed? Amid exchanged glances and some comment from officers, one thing was obvious to all: a reduction in speed at this point was unexpected and an unsound tactical move. Soon the message, official or rumour, filtered to them that the flooding was worse and their high speed was a contributing factor.

Eckhardt put the empty mug down and brought the binoculars up to his eyes, focusing once more on the enemy cruiser force. Whatever happened, the ship's speed was not his responsibility, he had his own job to do. He quickly confirmed that the cruisers, ghostly images on the indeterminate horizon, periodically disappearing, were keeping their distance. He expected that they would now be very wary of reducing the range; if they did, he would immediately declare it.

'Watch for submarines,' an officer called out. 'As we get closer to the Bight, we can expect to encounter them.'

Eckhardt acknowledged the instruction, but straight away it brought back the visions of the submarine attack only a few hours ago and that he felt personally responsible for not spotting it. Look-outs, it had been drummed into him, may not be operating guns or any of the other parts of a great warship like the *Hindenburg*, but they play a very important role in spotting threats to the ship, indeed would probably be the first to do so, essential to enable early decisions on guns, speed and course to be made. He redoubled his efforts, determined not to fail the ship again, even though he had, like everyone, been at Battle Stations for many hours and was very tired. His sector on this never-ending watch was the usual starboard quarter, everything from ship to horizon, from abeam to right aft, though his sector overlapped slightly with look-outs covering the starboard bow and port quarter sectors. The faint enemy cruisers were in his forward overlap section, sharing it with Schwarz. He and Schwarz would periodically join in studying the enemy cruisers, quietly exchanging the odd word, but smartly reporting any changes. Despite the ship's damage and reduced speed, he was relaxed about the situation: the *Hindenburg* continuing south toward Germany, the chastised enemy cruisers on the horizon and the Fleet, reportedly, on their way to assist.

Twenty minutes later, Eckhardt was probably not the only person taken aback by medal-winning Schwarz's calmly delivered: 'Ship! Green, oh-four-oh!'

Eckhardt's first thought: *The Fleet ... at last*!

21

Zeppelin

Although it was outside his designated search zone, Eckhardt, like everyone else around him, could not resist swinging his binoculars onto Schwarz's sighting. With his training in ship recognition, in a few seconds he realised he was not looking at a hoped-for German warship. Once more during that long, long day, he was confronted with the undoubted profile of an enemy dreadnought. Schwarz beat him to it, calling out: 'English dreadnought!'

Eckhardt reckoned her long, low profile, with multiple funnels, suggested her type, even her identity. So, not intending to correct his fellow-look-out, he daringly added: 'Battle cruiser! Australia-class!' Then, almost immediately, he amended his call: '*Four* battle cruisers!'

Sweeping ahead and astern of the first battle cruiser, he'd quickly seen she was not alone. Ahead of her were two or three destroyers; astern of her, emerging from the veils of haze and mist, was another big ship, then, as he moved his binoculars only slightly to the right, another and yet another.

His correction had hardly left his mouth when he saw them all fire. The gun flashes, starting with the lead ship, then on down the line, did not unduly concern him, he was not especially frightened at the sight, but suddenly he was conscious of his heart beating ferociously. 'Enemy firing!' he shouted—an unnecessary call.

They all fired again, without reply from the *Hindenburg*.

⚐

John Goodyear, the *Inflexible*'s captain, had the *Hindenburg* in sight, at long last! The flagship, HMAS *Australia*, gave the signal and the ships of the Second Battle Cruiser Squadron—the *Australia*, *New Zealand*, *Indomitable* and *Inflexible*—opened fire at her, almost simultaneously.

For Goodyear, so far the day had been one of frustration. The Squadron had sailed back and forth, but had never sighted the enemy and been well astern when the action started. Now events had worked to their advantage. The enemy, damaged and slowed, had fallen under their guns.

Since the chase began, things had not started well. Firstly, the age of the Squadron's four battle cruisers was sadly revealed; they'd been much too slow to keep up with the swifter *Courageous* and *Glorious* and, alas, unable to help them when they engaged the *Hindenburg*. Indeed, the only indication to Goodyear of the *Hindenburg*'s presence had been the distant sight of large shell spouts erupting around the *Courageous* and *Glorious*. Then the *Courageous*' explosion had shocked all on the *Inflexible*'s bridge, especially those who had been on her at Jutland, reminding them of the *Invincible*'s destruction. The straddling of the *Glorious* had also been watched with alarm, with some apprehension that she would suffer her sister's fate. The fact that she avoided that outcome was an undoubted relief, but there was still disappointment that she had ended up being forced out of the chase.

With the outcome of the First Cruiser Squadron's action with the *Hindenburg* and the loss of Vice-Admiral Backhouse-Smith, their own admiral—Rear Admiral Albert Cook—was now the commanding officer of the whole British force. The admiral had no other thought than to keep after the *Hindenburg*. Goodyear could see that the day was young and anything might lead to another chance to engage her.

When the Squadron had swept by the scene of the *Courageous*' destruction, Goodyear was not alone in being unable to avoid scanning the patches of oil and debris. No survivors were seen, but, even though an engagement might yet come about, Admiral Cook had detached one of their destroyers to undertake rescue work.

A few thousand yards further on and the *Glorious* had been overtaken. Signal lamp messages from the injured vessel told of her damage and her much reduced speed. Admiral Cook had ordered her to return to Rosyth. Later, another casualty, the damaged destroyer *Nepean*, was detailed to join the *Glorious*. These were not the only damaged ships encountered. To the north, Goodyear had seen various smoking destroyers.

Given the *Hindenburg*'s greater speed, Goodyear and his executive officer had discussed the possibility that she might escape. However, after the reports that the she'd struck a mine *and* turned north, spirits were raised. Admiral Cook had quickly ordered the destroyers to close and torpedo her. Goodyear and his officers had deduced that the admiral's intention was to slow the *Hindenburg* or perhaps delay her from her course back to Wilhelmshaven, enough to allow the Squadron to overtake and engage her—Goodyear thought it was a reasonable proposition. They all waited for the results of the destroyer attack, fearing it must take a heavy toll of the destroyers, but accepting it was probably the only way to stop the enemy getting clean away. Subsequent signals that one or two torpedo hits had been made by the destroyers spurred everyone on.

After the destroyer attack, the Third Light Cruiser Squadron, then periodically visible about 11,000 yards away to the nor-nor-east, had become the Squadron's link with the *Hindenburg*. Their signals showed they were in touch with the enemy, put at some 15,000 yards ahead of them on an easterly course. The enemy battle cruiser was at that point plotted to be some 30,000 yards away to the north-east of the flagship, enticingly close. For a time it had looked to Goodyear like the courses of the two forces were diverging too much and the enemy might yet elude them, but when a signal from the cruisers announced that 'the enemy has turned south', he realised that the admiral's plan to intercept the *Hindenburg* looked like it might well come to fruition.

Not long before the expected interception point, ships were sighted to the nor'-nor'-east. Moving in and out of the murky horizon, the Light Cruiser Squadron's ships were glimpsed, along with the occasional high and white shell splash. It seemed that they had come under fire from the *Hindenburg*, then somewhere to the east of them. Signals from the cruisers had confirmed they were indeed in action and included the disquieting news that the cruiser *Chester* had suffered damage, enough to be in a perilous condition. Given the threat to the cruisers, Goodyear was surprised that the admiral did not immediately turn towards them to bring big-gun support, but just as soon that need seemed to disappear as the *Hindenburg* ceased her assault. The cruisers were then able to return to their role of shadowing the enemy. The regular information flowing from them had continued to signal the enemy course and speed and affirmed that action was imminent, as the tracks of the Squadron and the *Hindenburg* were converging and put the German ship at just over twenty thousand yards to the north-east. The main turrets were already trained round to that bearing, with everyone expecting the order to open fire to be given in a very short time. The destroyers were directed to the Squadron's disengaged side. Even the mist, which all day long had affected visibility, had thinned somewhat, adding to Goodyear's expectation of early visual contact *and* battle. The cruisers' signals had also indicated a reduction in the *Hindenburg*'s speed, which posed many questions.

Quite suddenly, the *Hindenburg* ploughed out of the mist, almost 17,000 yards away. In the few seconds before firing, Goodyear could see she had her starboard bow towards the Squadron, noting her twin funnels and large and dark tripod mast. No one around him could confirm it, but he also thought she may have had her guns trained fore-and-aft, suggesting she had been caught unawares. The whole mile-long Squadron was engaging the *Hindenburg*, before she had fired a shot. He silently took his hat off to the admiral: his plan to catch a faster enemy had worked a treat.

⚐

Körner, Schellenberg and Gärtner were discussing the possible position of the Fleet, how long to a meeting, when the enemy sighting was received on the Command-Bridge. By the time he'd raised his binoculars, the initial report of an enemy dreadnought had been quickly amended to 'four enemy battle cruisers'. His attempt to gauge them for himself was interrupted by them firing. His response: 'Open fire!' He had been beaten to the punch again, but *firing* was not *hitting*.

With the first report of a single ship, his fleeting thought was, even in the *Hindenburg*'s condition, if Kruse could work his magic, one enemy dreadnought would not prevent them getting through to the Fleet and Wilhelmshaven. Now that preference was forgotten.

With one quick look at the horizon all round, Körner calmly ordered, 'Hard-a-port. Make smoke.' Just as calmly, he followed that with: 'Signal Admiralty. Am in action with enemy battle cruisers.'

Despite their clearly precarious situation, everyone on the Bridge showed nothing but expected professionalism. Even so, Körner detected more than the usual glances in his direction. All were waiting on him, his directions, his orders, but were obviously also scrutinising his bearing, his attitude, his steadfastness. As captain, he set the prime example, one which, in the circumstances, must exhibit a new level of confidence, certainty and fearlessness.

As Schellenberg headed off for his station aft, he and Körner exchanged glances, Körner giving a slight nod, but neither spoke. As Schellenberg left the Bridge, Körner could not help wondering if his second-in-command was thinking: *I told you so.* Körner himself retreated to the armoured conning tower; he felt this could be an engagement where its superior armour might be especially important in running the ship.

Before he stepped into the cramped structure, the enemy's opening shots arrived, just as the *Hindenburg*'s guns blazed their defiance. He saw several great columns of white water, fortunately some distance away from the *Hindenburg*, though noted a few that were much closer. Inside, Körner peered through the conning tower's view slits, intending to make his own assessment of the enemy. He caught sight of them, but often as not they were obscured by the *Hindenburg*'s gunfire or enemy shell spouts. To his demand, he was quickly told that the four ships were identified as being two Australia-class and two Indomitable-class battle cruisers. At least four destroyers were also in attendance. He well knew, if they had been correctly identified, that they were the enemy's oldest and nominally their weakest battle cruisers, but there was absolutely no comfort in those facts, with each armed with eight 12in guns.

Körner needed no debate on the *Hindenburg*'s own situation: the ship was damaged, outnumbered, outgunned and slower, with enemy ships ahead and to the flank; the enemy also enjoyed the advantage of the north wind blowing their funnel smoke away, giving them a good view of their target, though he hoped it also blew spray onto their range finders. Despite all these negative factors, something inside him wanted to trade punches, see if Kruse could indeed work wonders and force their way through the enemy line, but he knew that would be impossible, even madness.

To beat a path from the enemy was his only move, even knowing that his aft turrets were useless and the ship's speed insufficient to escape. He would periodically have to yaw from side to side to allow Kruse to throw some shells at their pursuers. Putting up a smoke screen would inhibit his attackers. He could see no way out, but time would tell, an opportunity might well arise. His only other thought was *where is the Fleet?*

The Spotting Top was far from quiet, as look-outs called out their observations and officers gave orders and made voice pipe reports. Eckhardt counted at least ten shell splashes to his front from the enemy's opening salvo. These were regularly replaced by new eruptions. As earlier that day, the enemy's shells could actually be seen as they neared the ship, great black shapes, unnerving, with some coming straight at her, but then dipping abruptly and landing short or, sometimes very audibly, going right over her. From what he could see and hear from others in the Spotting Top, shells landed all around the *Hindenburg*, with only a few coming close to the ship. In fact, these were considered to have straddled her, but no one felt any tremor or other indication that the ship had been hit.

In contrast, the *Hindenburg*'s first shots were well on target and very soon bracketed the leading battle cruiser and produced the characteristic red or yellow flash of a hit. Those who saw that could not hold back and shouts of approval rang through the Spotting Top.

Uplifted by this great gunnery, Eckhardt dragged himself away from the conflict with the enemy's battle line, turning his binoculars onto the enemy's cruiser force away to starboard. They were in his quadrant, his focus of responsibility, he had to report their activity, their course and speed, their gunfire. Immediately, he could see they were turning towards the *Hindenburg*, but could see no gunfire. He reported all this.

The *Hindenburg* began to turn to port, shifting Eckhardt's sector onto the enemy battle cruisers. He immediately saw splashes around the lead battle cruiser. *Great*, he mouthed, even though he saw no indications of hits. To him, straddling at fourteen or fifteen kilometres was all that could be asked of a gunner. In reply, the enemy's fire was considerable, but wayward, putting no shells near the *Hindenburg*. So let it continue, he said to himself.

As he watched the gunnery exchange, reporting the *Hindenburg*'s gunfire, the ship's funnels began to pump out thick, black smoke that was carried away south. As a smokescreen, Eckhardt judged it to be only partially effective. The ship's heading and wind direction left the aft part of the ship visible to the enemy. Soon the ship's turn put the enemy big ships almost astern, but Eckhardt still thought the smokescreen failed to hide the *Hindenburg* completely. Nevertheless, he hoped it would yet interfere with their gunnery.

Eckhardt couldn't gauge whether the enemy gunnery was affected by the smokescreen, though their shooting continued to be poor. There was a seemingly continuous eruption of white, sky-high water spouts all around the *Hindenburg*, but no shells were reported to have hit the ship or come close enough to do any damage. As he expected, in endeavouring to escape, the ship's for'ard turrets could no longer bear on the enemy battle cruisers and fell silent. He'd heard that Dora had no shells. It was frustrating to be shot at and unable to reply.

Largely above the smoke, he could still see the enemy battle cruisers. They were changing course. 'Enemy turning to port!' he shouted. They were all turning towards the *Hindenburg*, no doubt intent on chasing her. However, he quickly noticed that it only appeared to be three ships. After further, careful scrutiny, unable to see the fourth ship, he called: '*Three* enemy battle cruisers astern!'

This led to officers checking and confirming Eckhardt's observation. They could only conclude that one had been forced out of the line. This was reported to the Command-Bridge.

꒰꒱

Goodyear, all his attention on the *Hindenburg*, was taken aback by signals of serious damage to the *Australia*. He had been informed that the enemy was shooting at her—it was to be expected that the leading ship of an attacking force would attract fire—but it was wholly unexpected that the flagship would be damaged so early in the exchange and forced out of the line. He knew that the *Lion*, leading at Dogger Bank, had been knocked about and similarly forced out of the line, but, heavens above, that was after two hours' fighting! There had been discussion about the *Hindenburg*'s gunnery prowess, now it was being powerfully demonstrated.

The news about the *Australia*'s plight was quickly overtaken by a turn together signal, as all ships pursued the escaping *Hindenburg*. Other signals showed the destroyers were ordered to attack the *Hindenburg*, though the disruption to the line caused by the flagship's problems seemed also to have interfered with the smooth execution of that intent. Instead of keeping together to deliver an attack *en masse*, the Squadron's seven destroyers, previously all to starboard of the battle line, had become separated. Three were reported ahead of the *New Zealand*, as two came round astern of the *Inflexible*. The other two went to the flagship's aid. Goodyear could only figure that the admiral intended to transfer to one of the other battle cruisers.

First blood to the enemy, thought Goodyear.

His concerns at the way the battle seemed to be going were exacerbated when his own ship ceased firing; the gunnery officer had lost sight of the enemy—too much smoke and mist.

꒰꒱

Körner was well pleased with the news of likely damage to the enemy flagship, though restrained his feelings. With the change of course and the enemy now astern, he could still see no satisfactory resolution. The for'ard guns could not fire at the enemy battle cruisers and the *Hindenburg*'s slower speed meant they must eventually overhaul her. Kruse sought permission to engage the enemy cruisers, now off the ship's port quarter, but Körner refused, still intent on directing his few 30.5 shells at the enemy's big ships.

'Starboard thirty!' he ordered, seeking to allow the for'ard turrets to rejoin the action.

The guns thundered again and again. Soon reports came in that the lead ship had been straddled. Körner even allowed himself to think that they could yet defeat this enemy force. The sight of several shell spouts to port of the *Hindenburg* brought him back to earth. The enemy gunners were not proficient, but how long could they go on missing?

The range was closing, now put at only 11,500 metres. 'Port ten!'

Again, straddling of the enemy was reported, but they kept on coming. Enemy destroyers were now reported coming up on both flanks, with one from the cruiser squadron, reportedly out on its own, well ahead. The spectre of torpedo attack loomed. The 15cm guns had remained silent, the few shells available distributed amongst all the guns. They might yet prove important, but had to be held back until sure of striking home. Of all the ship's guns, only the 8.8s had plenty of ammunition and had been engaging the enemy destroyers for some time. The ship still had its own formidable, 60cm torpedo armament, but he agreed with those who'd voiced concerns that her single torpedo tubes, one at the bow, one on each beam and one at the stern, could not deliver the multiple torpedoes likely to generate a hit. Anyway, the broadside torpedo room, affected by the for'ard flooding had been abandoned. This left just three of the 2,000kg torpedoes in the stern torpedo room; nevertheless, he authorised their use. A hit would be tremendous and even the sighting of a torpedo wake could force a ship to change course.

Goodyear's disappointment at the *Inflexible*'s inability to engage the target was removed when the *New Zealand* led them on a new course, chasing the enemy, though by keeping the three British battle cruisers slightly to starboard of the *Hindenburg*, allowed all to get some guns on target. For the *Inflexible*, this meant that only the for'ard 'A' turret and the port-wing 'P' turret could bear. From his position, Goodyear was not always able to see the enemy ship, which was periodically hidden by his ship's gun smoke and the *Hindenburg*'s smokescreen. When he could see her, she was invariably surrounded by white shell splashes. This boded well, but he knew that correcting shot with three ships all firing at the same target was sure to complicate the firing solutions. In contrast, the enemy was still evidencing good shooting, as he saw shells landing all about the *New Zealand*.

This state of play continued for some fifteen minutes, when the Chief Yeoman, his telescope permanently on the *New Zealand*, reported: '*New Zealand*, Sir. She's signalling: *Am damaged. Speed reduced. Continue chase.*'

'What? Damaged? Not again!' exclaimed Goodyear to his bridge officers. None offered an opinion, though his comments were little more than his own thoughts and there was no time to debate such matters. Ahead and to port, Goodyear could see the *New Zealand*; she was clearly leaving the line. He saw no sign of major damage, though one of his officers thought she was listing slightly to port. He could only think that hits had led to serious flooding or damage to her engines. Was that what had happened to the *Australia*, he wondered. He couldn't help but think that whatever the cause, clearly these battle cruisers—first the *Courageous* and *Glorious* and now the *Australia* and *New Zealand*—were just not capable of taking hits from big guns. What did that say for the *Indomitable* and *Inflexible*, he asked himself. Could they avoid the same? Could they finish the *Hindenburg*?

These were all academic issues. The battle continued. The *Indomitable* led the *Inflexible*, as they steamed past the *New Zealand*. Even in her damaged state, she continued to fling salvoes at the enemy. Goodyear had thought her turn to port was a bad move, temporarily inhibiting the other ships' line of sight, but now he was prepared to accept it as a wise manoeuvre, as it still allowed her to contribute to the battle; a starboard turn away could have taken her right out of the action.

The enemy ship had altered course, keeping her stern towards the British battle cruisers. The *Indomitable* and *Inflexible* turned to follow. One of Goodyear's officers quizzically remarked: 'She's not firing!'

Very odd, thought Goodyear. Certainly, he could see no gunfire emanating from her and no shells were landing about the British battle cruisers. Whatever the reason, he was not concerned; his job was to hit her! 'Port ten!' he ordered. He wanted to clear his line of sight, get out from under the *Indomitable*'s wake. Soon, with the *Indomitable* off the starboard bow, the *Inflexible* had a clear view of the *Hindenburg*, though the chase still limited fire to A and P turrets. The range was closing, now about 12,000 yards. Both battle cruisers kept up their barrage and, as much as he could judge, Goodyear could see shells were falling around the *Hindenburg*, some seemed very close.

'Destroyers closing on *Hindenburg*, Sir!'

This call had Goodyear dragging his view away from the quarry and quickly scanning the seascape around them. Ahead of the two battle cruisers, he could see some destroyers. They were indeed closing on the *Hindenburg*. Off the *Inflexible*'s port beam were two more destroyers and beyond them were the cruisers.

Pᴅ

The *Hindenburg* had been straddled several times and reports reached Körner that there had been some hits, but any damage done had not affected the ship. Amidst

278

the noise of the ship's own guns, he hadn't felt their impact. Kruse reported by voice pipe: 'Captain. All thirty-point-five shells have been fired, ... including practice rounds.'

For a moment, Körner said nothing. The news, fully expected, but nonetheless very depressing, signalled more than anything that the battle was nearing its end. 'Thank you, Commander.' Intending to convey a final appreciation of all Kruse had accomplished, Körner added a simple, 'Well done.' His final order to Kruse was 'Get your men up top.' There was no point in keeping men in the magazines and shell rooms.

A few more shells and a few more knots and even this action could have been very different, thought Körner. That was a fleeting thought, displaced by another report on the ships closing on the *Hindenburg*. Destroyers were off both the starboard and port quarters, each less than 5,000 metres away. They'd faced the same threat earlier in the day and escaped with only one torpedo hitting the ship. Of course, the ship's full armament—30.5s, 15s and 8.8s—had been used then to great effect, sinking some of the attackers, damaging others. Now, the situation was dire. He gave the order for the 15cm guns to open fire. There was little to be gained in holding them back any longer. The enemy destroyers were well within torpedo range, but had not yet launched their killing weapons, no doubt wanting to be sure. All he could do was to manoeuvre the ship to avoid any torpedoes. With destroyers on either side that was going to be difficult. Whichever way the ship turned, her flank would be exposed.

⚑

Without any formal announcement, Eckhardt knew the 30.5 ammunition was all gone. The ship's big guns had fallen silent. They still pointed at enemy ships, there were plenty of targets, but said nothing. The secondary 15cm guns blazed away, but within a minute or so, they too were silent. The 8.8s defiantly continued to spit their tiny shells at the closing destroyers. Eckhardt continued to report what he saw. Shells churned up the water around the destroyers, but none that he could judge hit the little ships; they came on, pushing through the *Hindenburg*'s smokescreen which had drifted across their path.

Up to then, the shooting by the enemy battle cruisers, now just two in pursuit, with a third some way farther astern, had been nothing short of appalling, but they were now finally getting their guns on target. Huge, ship-high towers of white water were regularly erupting all around the ship, straddling her and, at last, hitting her. He didn't see where shells struck, but voices around him told of hits to main turrets, deck or hull. When he glanced below, some smoke and fire was evident.

The three destroyers on the starboard beam which had come through the ship's smokescreen turned to starboard, their flanks facing the *Hindenburg*, then continued to turn away. This is it, thought Eckhardt. 'Torpedoes! Starboard beam!'

With the ship turning slowly to port, no doubt intending to avoid the enemy's torpedo attack, he saw them: more than half-a-dozen, thin, white-grey lines etched on the sea were streaking towards the *Hindenburg*. Some would indeed miss the ship, but equally he could see that some would not.

Intently, he watched one, the closest. It struck aft of his position, producing a ship-shuddering, white and grey-black massive upsurge of water. Others struck; he felt their impacts, saw some of their water spouts and vaguely concluded there had been two, perhaps three more torpedo hits along the starboard side—the same side where the two other torpedoes had earlier struck. He knew she could not take such damage.

There was little to time to consider the situation, though Eckhardt's fear level was now very high and he was once again conscious of his fast-beating heart. In less than a couple of minutes there was a sudden and noticeable list to starboard, with everyone in the Spotting Top adjusting their footing or holding onto something. The movement stopped, as if the ship could cope with it, would right herself, but that respite was very short-lived. After less than twenty seconds, the list continued, unabated, indeed the rate increased. Everyone was eventually flung to the starboard side of the Spotting Top compartment, no longer able to hang on against the forces acting on them. Very soon, Eckhardt, someone almost lying on top of him, was staring at the upcoming surface of the sea.

If there was any call to abandon ship, he did not hear it. Being in the Spotting Top, there was little he could have done anyway to get down quickly to the *Batterie* deck. Now the ship was on her beam-ends and the Spotting Top hit the water with some speed. Water flooded in, immediately and completely filling Eckhardt's compartment. With one lung-full of air, he made to get out. Men around him were pushing and shoving their way through some of the observation ports to the front and starboard. Almost resigning to his fate, he changed direction and went upwards, pushing against some inert bodies and exiting through a port-side opening, though did not know how he'd managed it.

He shot upwards, bursting through the surface, coughing and spluttering, feeling half-full of water. He was hardly twenty or so metres from the ship. He was looking at her deck, which towered above him like a grotesque wall. He was away from the ship, aft of the funnels, now both more than half-submerged. Even in her death throes, she was still moving forward. She rolled further towards him; he didn't need any instruction, able to swim from an early age, he pushed hard to get away from the toppling ship. He didn't slow till he was exhausted. As he took an enforced breather, he glanced back for a few seconds. The ship was almost completely turned over and sinking by the stern. He thought he saw some figures on her upturned hull. He continued to swim away. When he looked back again, her bow was sticking up in the air. After several more strokes, when he looked again, she was gone.

With reports of the torpedo attack, Körner had ordered hard-a-port. He was aware that enemy destroyers were also off the port side, but had no option. In her wounded state, the ship seemed slower than usual to turn. Each torpedo hit shook the ship, some around him almost losing their balance. There were no reports on the damage before the ship started to list. He had been faced with trying to save the ship or abandoning her. No one around him had sought escape, but he'd seen some look at him, their faces questioning. He had to make an immediate decision. In as calm but sufficiently loud voice as he thought warranted, he said, 'Abandon ship!' To those in the conning tower, he added, 'Well done. You have fought well, very well indeed. Now go, save yourselves.'

With some difficulty, the armoured, heavy door of the conning tower had been opened and an orderly exit made. Körner was the last to leave. The list had increased, more degrees every second. The ship was obviously going to sink. Abandon ship was being called by various officers, as Körner made his way to the front of the Command-Bridge. Unlike the *Potsdam*, the *Hindenburg* was still underway. He saw many sailors at her starboard rail, waiting for that right moment to jump into the sea.

The list continued and his intention to check through the Bridge and below had been overtaken by gravity. He could no longer keep his balance and grabbed a hold of the Bridge rail. A large water spout shot up just off the starboard bow, greatly annoying him that the English were still firing, even though the ship was clearly sinking.

Körner had no intention of going down with his ship—keeping his promise to Maria—but he could also see that the situation threatened just that. The *Batterie* deck edge touched the sea and he saw scores of men going into the water, joining the many heads already trying to get clear. Initially, he made no move to join them, fearing injury if he lost his footing and tumbled across the Bridge, but that was a foolish thought. He had gingerly walked his way to the starboard side of the Bridge, clinging onto anything that would stop him falling, but that was more and more difficult as the ship's list increased. Before the ship was on her beam ends, the surface of the sea was up to the Bridge. At that point, with difficulty, he'd removed his coat and got into the water, aiming to swim away. He was hardly two or three metres out when the ship began to roll over on top of him.

He was back on the Bridge; the ship's movement had brought the Bridge down onto him. Realising what was happening, he took a big breath and, pushed under the water, began grasping objects that came to hand, pulling himself along, hand over hand. He hadn't known what he was doing, letting a survival instinct take over. Above him was an unnatural darkness, blotting out all above, seemingly intent on falling onto him, crushing him, pushing him down.

Still holding onto something, it was not as dark; he was rising, though not swimming or floating upwards, but being pulled up. It didn't matter, he could not last another few seconds. His lungs were absolutely bursting, he would have to take a breath, even if water, not air.

Unexpectedly, his head was in the air, but still rising. As he coughed the North Sea out of him, he saw that the ship's bow was rising. As her stern sank, she was raising her bow to the sky, pulling him free, saving him! He let go and fell back into the sea. He didn't look round at the pointed, steel mountain behind him, but began to swim as he had never ever done before, hardly breathing, just plunging his hands and arms into the water ahead, pulling himself away from her. He expected that it would be a forlorn race and that she might not want to give up her captain so easily; the *Potsdam* had let him go, did the *Hindenburg* want him? As she went down, he felt the suction; the sea was pulling at him, rushing back to her, sucking all the flotsam and jetsam *and* Körner to her. After a few desperate, tired strokes, he gave up, went under, reconciling himself to this end.

⚑

Eckhart could see heads scattered around, but was too exhausted and cold to think about getting close to any. For a while he employed sidestroke, periodically staring up at the cloudy sky. If not for the cold water, it would have been quite restful. Then the clouds took on an odd appearance, but his trained eye did not need a second to realise that the cigar-shaped cloud above was in fact a zeppelin. Difficult to judge, but he reckoned it was perhaps five or more kilometres away. He wanted to shout out, alerting anyone who could hear of his sighting, but no one could have heard his feeble cry. Despite the distance, he did wave several times, thinking the zeppelin's crew must see him, forgetting his own experience of how difficult it was to see a man's head on the surface of the sea. The sight did give him hope that all was not lost, that rescue was at hand. He wished otherwise, but knew that it was impossible for the zeppelin to swoop down and pluck him from the sea, though surely it was summoning help.

With his attention on the zeppelin, he was surprised to hear a noise, feel a slight tremor in the water. Turning himself round, he saw a ship, a destroyer, obviously English, only about thirty metres away. She was moving very slowly, he could see no bow wave. Was she rescuing the *Hindenburg*'s survivors?

With a new determination, he tried to swim towards her, but either she wasn't coming in his direction or he wasn't swimming well enough ever to able to reduce the distance. He stopped swimming, tried to wave, but could only manage a few pathetic arm movements. He could discern no response. He was cold, almost too cold to worry.

'Come on, sailor!' said a croaky, weak voice, nearby. 'Let's try together ... get their attention.'

He looked up. It was the captain, hardly two or three metres away.

'*Herr Kapitän*!' he said, his voice uplifted, slightly the louder of the two men. 'Aye, Sir!'

He wondered if he looked as bad as the captain. They began waving and shouting, but it was mostly all from Eckhardt. The captain was clearly in a bad way, having some difficulty in keeping afloat, his head occasionally slipping beneath the surface. Eckhardt broke off and endeavoured to help him, holding him with one arm while swimming with the other.

The enemy destroyer was quite suddenly only about five metres away, beginning to tower over them. This gave Eckhardt new energy. Pulling the captain, he swam towards the ship. The ship must have been moving towards them or the current must have been favourable, he thought, as they were soon near the ship's side. He could see sailors throwing lines, reaching down, shouting encouragement, saving souls. Eckhardt would have done no less; a sailor, even a defeated enemy sailor, was worthy of rescue.

As he got closer, a line splashed near him. He wasn't ready and didn't catch it. The sailor above pulled it back and threw again, this time within reach. He got hold of it, but his grip was feeble, barely able to keep his fingers around it. It was enough. The sailor pulled them in, with Eckhardt tugging the captain behind him. At the side of the ship, all he had to do was climb up the three or four metres to safety.

'Come on, Captain, get hold of this,' pushing the rope towards the captain. 'Soon be aboard,' he spluttered.

The captain put a hand on the rope, but said, 'You ... you go first.' After the captain repeated this and refusing any other course of action, Eckhardt, content that the captain was able to keep afloat for a few minutes, began to pull himself up. It was extremely hard going; his hands and arms were frozen, lead weights, he feared he could not make it, but clung on to a knot in the rope. Fortunately, the sailor above was also pulling and he soon felt a strong hand grasp his shoulder. The hand's owner said something he didn't understand, while continuing to pull the rope and him up and over onto the little ship's deck, where he collapsed in a heap. His immense relief at being aboard was disturbed by a noise, a loud noise— an explosion. He looked round, so did everyone on the deck. Almost a thousand metres away the remains of a water column were collapsing into the sea. An English sailor said what sounded like 'Bloody zep!'

Eckhardt looked up to see the zeppelin, almost above them. What was it doing? Bombing them? Didn't the stupid crew understand what was going on? He swore at them: '*dumme Bastarde!*' Another bomb hit the sea, still nowhere near the destroyer. There was feverish activity. The deck vibrated, he could feel her engines; the ship was getting underway. He immediately knew that the ship could not allow herself to be bombed; she must move, put on speed. Suddenly he remembered: '*Kapitän*! *Kapitän*!' His protestations were for naught, strong arms were lifting him, directing him below. Resisting his helpers, all he could do was twist his head round, look over the side. Struggling seamen were still alongside. The captain was one of them. They waved feebly, called plaintively, pathetically, fear on their faces; they too knew what was happening.

The ship began to move, slowly at first, then faster. The men were quickly swept down the ship's side. He knew they would be swept astern, if not caught up in the propellers.

Appendix

Körner's Combat Report

Combat Report
Draft 1

Convoy Action, 5 May 1918, 41.41N, 57.42W, south-east of Sable
Island, Nova Scotia, Canada.

1. On 4 May, as we approached the Canadian coast, we sent out
   our seaplane twice. The first flight reported a single freighter
   steaming towards Halifax, Nova Scotia, and later a possible
   convoy, approximately 100 km away, bearing south-west from the
   Hindenburg. The second flight confirmed the convoy and that it
   comprised at least 20 ships, heading south-east, speed 12 knots.
   Only one escort was reported, a four-funnel ship, considered most
   probably to be an armoured cruiser.
2. We could have readily overtaken the convoy, but not before nightfall,
   so I elected to wait until dawn, if necessary relying on the seaplane
   to relocate it again. Based on the convoy's estimated course and
   speed, we would close with the convoy during the night, so as to be
   ready to attack at dawn.
3. The seaplane took off at dawn (0830 CET) and very soon reported
   the convoy's whereabouts. It was further south than anticipated,
   but still as close, approximately 30 kilometres distant. The plane
   identified two four-funnelled escorts. The convoy was sailing in a
   formation of seven columns.
4. Based on the plane's report we turned towards the convoy and soon
   sighted it at 0852. We approached from the convoy's port quarter at
   22 knots, increasing to 25 knots.
5. The convoy escorts were identified as armoured cruisers, one
   English - Drake class - and one American - Washington class. It
   was soon clear that the cruisers were moving to position themselves
   between the convoy and the Hindenburg.

6. While sinking the convoy's merchant ships was our main focus, I first sought to drive off or destroy the two cruisers. While I considered they posed little real threat, they might have damaged us or otherwise have prevented us from attacking the merchantmen. I brought the ship onto 130 degrees to open up our firing arcs, increasing to utmost speed.

7. The cruisers sailed across the head of the convoy to its port side. They were in line ahead, the English cruiser leading. Merchant ships had masked our firing line, but at 0924 we opened fire at the leading cruiser, as the enemy ship cleared the convoy's port column. The range was 19,000 metres. At that point the cruisers were steaming directly towards us. This was the most direct route to us, but enabled us to cross their 'T'.

8. Throughout the action, our gunnery was excellent. With each target, we quickly obtained the range and began to straddle and hit.

9. At 0936 we scored our first hit on the English cruiser. Much damage to her upper works was evident, though her engines were apparently undamaged, as she continued towards us at high speed.

10. We continued to fire on the leading cruiser, scoring several hits. These produced much smoke and fire and also reduced her speed. She had not yet opened fire on us.

11. Up to then, the American cruiser had been largely hidden from our view, sailing in the English ship's wake. It was then seen that she was manoeuvring to starboard, presumably to clear her line of fire. Indeed, she soon opened fire.

12. Given the damage we had inflicted on the English ship and considering the American's 10inch guns, I made a slight change of course, to 140 degrees, and took her under fire at 0942. The English cruiser had by then opened fire, so I directed the secondary armament at her and the main guns at the American. The range to both cruisers had reduced to 11,400-12,600 metres.

13. We soon straddled the American ship and scored the first of many hits. She continued her turn to starboard to bring her full broadside to bear. During the whole action we were not hit. At one point we were straddled, probably by the American, but sustained no damage. Soon after that the American's shooting became noticeably less effective, presumably due to the effects of our hits.

14. At 0955 a torpedo track passing us about 50 metres astern was reported. I took no avoiding action. Given the enemy's range, I considered it to have been a false sighting. Only one look-out reported it.

15. We continued to engage both enemy ships. By 1000 the American cruiser was clearly damaged, with much smoke and fire evident.

Her firing was also much reduced and she was seen to be listing to port. This continued until at 1008 she suddenly rolled over on her port side and sank.

16. I then directed all guns onto the English cruiser; altered course to 170, range 12,800 metres. Our first main armament salvoes immediately had an effect and, added to previous hits, she sank at 1020.

17. Both cruisers took considerable punishment and, despite repeated hits and being on fire, they did not explode and must have sunk due to extensive flooding. They fought gallantly to the end.

18. With both warships sunk, I turned to the merchantmen. While the convoy had remained as a compact unit for much of the action, about the time the American cruiser sank we saw that the convoy had begun to disperse, with each ship breaking formation and sailing away independently. By 1030 merchant ships were spread over a wide arc at least 13,700 metres away. Despite this, we had a considerable speed advantage and, as the weather and visibility were still good, gave chase. Our pursuit was facilitated because the convoy did not scatter to all points of the compass, but rather dispersed towards the Canadian coast.

19. Initially an auxiliary cruiser attempted to inhibit our progress. She had taken up a position at the rear of the convoy and, as we approached, opened fire with several guns, probably 6in. She was soon hit and on fire. By 1100, her gunfire had all but stopped and she had been brought to a halt, sinking.

20. With the convoy's merchant ships, we began at the port wing of the arc and attacked each one in turn. Mainly, at close range, I used only the 15cm guns, to save 30.5cm ammunition. A few fired their stern guns at us and some dropped smoke boxes, all without effect.

21. By this approach we attacked 14 merchant ships. These were sunk or left in a burning or sinking condition. As we closed and began to sink them, we observed that one may have been carrying troops, some of whom attempted to abandon ship. Overall, only a few lifeboats were seen to be launched. We did not stop to pick up any survivors.

22. The remaining, faster ships succeeded in putting some distance between us and I allowed them to escape. It would have taken some time to catch all of them and I did not consider it warranted. The action had already taken nearly four hours and it would have taken more time to dispatch these last few ships. Throughout the action all enemy ships continued to transmit W/T alarm signals, many in clear. We endeavoured to jam their signals, but other messages we picked up indicated that their signals had been received by other

ships or shore stations. Given the distance to the Canadian shore, it was highly likely that warships would most probably soon be sailing to the position. I therefore broke off the action and sought to get clear of the area. Above all, I did not want anyone to follow us. Surprisingly, we saw no enemy airplanes, which presumably could have easily reached the area and reported our position and course.

23. It would have been possible to capture some ships as prizes. However, I elected to continue our assault on the convoy, as the time to stop and send over prize crews could not have been done without seriously inhibiting our attack on the other ships.

24. After recovering our seaplane, I turned south-east and held that course until out of sight of all the surviving ships. This was done to cover our true course intention.

25. Throughout the action, visibility was very good and allowed us to maintain fire on the various targets. Consequently, 311 30.5cm and 1,071 15cm shells were fired. In both cases this amounts to about 45 percent of our total complement of shells. I hope to replace some main armament shells from the supply ships.

26. Overall, we sank the convoy's escorts (two armoured cruisers and an auxiliary cruiser) and sank or damaged 14 merchant ships (estimated at 75,000 GRT). In addition to striking at the enemy's convoy system, we brought the war to the very shores of America and also may well have killed or at least delayed some enemy troops destined for the Western Front. Furthermore, the action did not affect the ship's capabilities, beyond the resulting ammunition depletion, and thankfully we also suffered no damage or casualties. Throughout the action the crew's performance was excellent.

RK
Kapitän zur See
SMS Hindenburg

Author's Note

This story is fiction, though draws on various First World War ships and events. The core element of the plot, that of a German battle cruiser venturing into the Atlantic to attack merchant shipping, was expected both before and during the war. In pre-war debates, the concept had been discounted, even ridiculed, by some as impracticable. During the war, the British drew up various studies and plans to cope with a battle cruiser loose in the Atlantic. Admiral William S Sims, who was Commander of US Naval Forces operating in European waters during the war, subsequently wrote that attacks on troop convoys would do no major damage, expecting only a few transports to be lost. However, he thought the only way the Germans might undertake such attacks was by battle cruiser raids. The Germans never gave it much thought, though there was a proposal for such action by a German battle cruiser captain early on in the war.

The battle cruiser *Hindenburg* was a real warship.

She was the last battle cruiser completed by Germany during the war. Although she sailed out with the High Seas Fleet on a number of occasions, she came late to the naval war in the North Sea and never fired her big guns in action. In a final act of defiance, she was scuttled by her crew, along with many of the German fleet's surface ships, in Scapa Flow in 1919. Like many of those ships, she was eventually raised and scrapped.

She was the third and last of the Derfflinger-class of battle cruisers, though had various differences from her two sister-ships. Wikipedia sets out her history and vital statistics. See: https://en.wikipedia.org/wiki/SMS_Hindenburg

The German *Potsdam*, a light cruiser, and the *Hindenburg*'s three supply ships are fictitious. The other named warships were all drawn from their real life counterparts. Likewise, the story's flying machines were real aircraft used in the First World War.

Sources
As noted, the story is fiction, but draws on some actual events. This is particularly the case with the German fleet's attempt to attack the Scotland-Norway convoy route in April 1918, sometimes referred to as the 'Last Sortie of the High Seas Fleet'. On pages 51 and 52, I have drawn on works by other authors as to the actual signals made by the *Moltke*, the *von der Tann* and Admiral Scheer:

1, 2, 3   Hugo von Waldeyer-Hartz *Admiral Von Hipper* (1933), p242.
4, 5, 6   Arthur J. Marder *From Dreadnought to Scapa Flow Vol V Victory and Aftermath* (1970), p151.

Battle Cruiser
In this book I used the two-word description 'battle cruiser'. The reader may see it written elsewhere more often as the single word 'battlecruiser' or, less frequently, as 'battle-cruiser'. I decided to go with the two-word version because that is how the British Admiralty officially described the ships in 1911 when they sought to differentiate the type from the older armoured cruiser.

Wikipedia provides a comprehensive explanation of the battle cruiser type and history, though I offer this summary:

The battle cruiser was an upward development of the armoured cruiser. The latter was, before the introduction of dreadnoughts, the largest type of warship after the battleship. Those armoured cruisers were often armed with guns of 8in to 10in calibre, though in 1905 Japan had begun to build armoured cruisers mounting 12in guns. Following the design of the first all-big-gun battleship, HMS *Dreadnought*, Britain created a new type of armoured cruiser featuring an all-big-gun armament and turbine-powered high speed. The three Invincible-class ships (all laid down 1906) were the first battle cruisers, armed with eight 12in guns and capable of 25 knots, though with traditional armoured cruiser levels of armour. As the *Dreadnought* had rendered all existing battleships obsolete, so the *Invincible*s outclassed all existing armoured cruisers.

In line with battleship developments, each new class of battle cruisers continued to be larger than the previous class, indeed they were often larger than contemporary battleships. They also continued to be both armed with battleship-sized guns and faster than battleships. With high speed and large guns, the battle cruiser's role evolved into that of a fast and powerful reconnaissance force, but also one of supporting the battle fleet in gun actions. However, undertaking such tasks inevitably pitched them against other all-big-gun battle cruisers and battleships. As armoured warship design is generally a compromise between the weight allocated to guns, armour and speed, the battle cruisers sacrificed armour (and some guns) to gain their higher speed. The loss of some British battle cruisers during WWI from only a few large calibre shells raised questions about the concept of such ships. After WWI, a few battle cruisers were built, but the difference between them and battleships was blurred as improved engine technology eventually produced the 'fast battleship'.

WWI-era British and German battle cruiser design differed. The British produced faster, more heavily armed, though lighter armoured ships than the German battle cruisers. In many ways, the British ships were indeed up-gunned armoured cruisers, whereas the German ships were more akin to being fast battleships.

Acknowledgements

I am very grateful to various people and organisations for their support in writing this book, not least the many friends and colleagues whose encouragement helped to keep me motivated. Of course, any errors are my responsibility.

My special thanks go to: Doris and Paul for help with German language issues; Dennis, Tim and other former seamen who advised on naval and merchant ship practice; the National Maritime Museum, Greenwich, for access to their plans of the *Hindenburg* and the *Courageous*; and the RAF Museum, Hendon, and the Shuttleworth Collection, Old Warden, Bedfordshire, for answering various questions about piloting WWI aircraft and starting engines such as the FF49's. I'm particularly grateful to the Danish Museum of Science and Technology, Elsinore, Denmark, for their help in explaining some operational and technical aspects of the FF49c and wish them every success with their project to build a FF49c. I also give a special thank you to Alan for his wonderful painting of the *Hindenburg*, which has been used for the cover illustration and, hanging in front of me while I worked, was a further factor in keeping me focused. I am especially grateful to Helen for scrutinising the final drafts and making many helpful and important observations and suggestions. Above all, my love and thanks to my wife, Brenda, who not only commented on the ongoing drafts, but has been a constant support throughout. I doubt it would ever have been completed, but for her encouragement.

MK
May 2021

Printed and bound by CPI Group (UK) Ltd, Croydon, CR0 4YY